Star Crossed

Orca Cove Series Book Three

Jen Flanagan

Serenity Endeavors Press

Star Crossed

Copyright © 2025 by Jen Flanagan

All mistakes are my own.

First Edition: May 2025

This edition was first published in 2025.

Cover design: Crodogial: Sydney Wendler

Editor: Monica Bogza

ISBN: 978-1-961501-07-2 (eBook)

ISBN: 978-1-961501-06-5 (Paperback)

Published by: Serenity Endeavors Press

jenflanaganbooks.com

CONTENTS

ACKNOWLEDGEMENTS

I have to start with my husband and my sister again. You two are still my biggest supporters. I love you both.

Special thanks to my friend Gina, who let me use her name in this book. I had no idea this character would become as key as she was to the book. Her and her lovely husband lended their names.

To my Harbinger Gal's. You ladies are an absolute joy. It's such a blessing to be surrounded by strong, supportive females. Thanks to Stacey and Ellen for always supporting me.

Thanks to all of you on Flanagan Fanatics! I love chatting with you all about my books! I hope to see you all there.

This has meant more to me than I could have ever imagined!

CHAPTER 1

Fury descended upon Keane Lennox like a hurricane. The onslaught of words directed his way whipped around him, filling his entire being with awe as would a raging storm or being thrown by thunderous waves. Shelby stood in front of him, her chest rising and falling with rage. But he knew her. He saw the pain in the pinpoints of her eyes. Those beautiful green eyes. It broke his heart.

But he'd broken hers first.

He was powerless to do anything but revel in her presence. After all this time.

He hadn't seen her, really seen her, for years. He hadn't seen her face, hadn't smelled her spicy citrus scent, hadn't felt her toned muscles gliding under her soft skin. He'd gone away to chase a dream, and after being away too long, he hadn't had the courage to come home to those he had abandoned.

Fifteen years was a long time.

Her face had thinned out from her youth, but the freckle just outside her eyebrow was still there. Her hair was still a dark, rich chestnut, and he wondered if she'd cut it recently. The ends hovered over her shoulders, thick, shiny, and straight. An object of perfection and poise.

All except those eyes. There was nothing proper about her eyes. Green as the grass, her slanted eyes sparked with electricity as though competing with the stars in the night sky above them. Even when they weren't lit with anger, they sparkled with humor, sass, and the promise of mischief. She was as he remembered her, and yet different. Pain and pleasure flooded his heart.

Her fists clenched as another shower of words flowed from her perfectly formed lips, her cheeks burning with a rosy hue. She was power defined.

It was glorious.

A smile twitched at his mouth. He struggled to contain his reaction. She stopped mid-sentence, her eyes narrowing.

"Well?" she demanded.

"It's good to see you, Greene." He released the smile he'd been holding back, knowing he looked like a schoolboy enamored by his crush. Crush? Hell, she was the love of his life.

Shelby's face dropped for a second, a wave of emotion passing over it. Her foot slid back several inches. Then her chin set, and she let out a guttural, frustrated cry.

This time, color rose to ring those beautiful eyes, pinched in pain. Damn, he hated that he had hurt her. If he could change anything, it would be that. But before he could say anything, she wheeled on the ball of her foot and stamped off, her shoulders tight and her back rigid.

Keane lurched forward, taking a few steps across the pebble beach to follow her retreat into the darkness. He froze. No, not yet. She was too angry. There was no talking to Shelby when she was like that. He'd wait until she had gotten used to the fact that he was back before attempting to talk to her. Tonight, it would be raw. She'd probably drown herself in ice cream and fall asleep in a sugar coma.

Keane watched her full retreat, unable to break his gaze from her after so long only holding her in his memory. His eyes followed her figure, illuminated by the parking lot light between the Wild Café and Gil's Market and Marina, to a car in the lot. Headlights passed him as she headed east of town, where he knew her cabins sat on a four-acre lot.

She'd only continued to thrive after he left, not that it surprised him.

Duke's ship sat out at the end of the marina from where she'd come. He knew from his parents that his old friend was still single. Duke was too wild to settle down, at least the Duke he remembered was. But that didn't mean Shelby hadn't found someone to fill the hole he'd left.

She had every right to be pissed at him. He shouldn't have left as he had. He didn't regret his decision, sadly enough, only how he'd done it. He should have talked to her first, explained why he had to go. He'd been so young and had made so many mistakes.

Keane wondered if Nell was on board the ship. Tension laced his heart again. He owed her an apology as well. He hadn't been here for her or for her late husband, his other best friend, when he passed the year before. He'd only found out about it after he returned from a six-month-long art exhibit tour in Europe. He'd been too late.

He didn't deserve to grieve with his old crew if he couldn't even be here to say goodbye to his friend.

Tearing his eyes off the gleaming hull bobbing in the dark waves, he saw an orca fin cut through the water.

Man, he missed the cove. He itched to find a surfboard and get back into the sea, even if it was just to use it as a paddleboard. He'd have to drive it up to the Strait of Juan de Fuca or to the Pacific coast if he wanted to do real surfing.

Or do what he used to in high school and head to Puget Sound for some tug surfing. The thought of it lifted his spirits.

The lights were still on in Shelby's apartment, the one she owned that he was now renting. He trudged through the loose rocks to the back deck and reentered. He'd run into Emiliano a couple of days ago when he arrived in town with no place to stay. The fit, younger man recently moved out and offered to lease it to him, assuming he was doing Shelby a favor by finding a new renter.

The shop owner's kid had grown up and filled out. And from the sound of it, Nell had somehow found love again with him. It was a bit of a shock, thinking Nell and Gary could be anything but Nell and Gary, but then again, Keane and Shelby had once been the same. It was hard to imagine anything different. Back then.

He had something to offer her now. He'd never had the courage to ask his parents if Shelby found someone, but if she had, he wouldn't pursue her. He wouldn't take that away from her. Wouldn't ask her to.

As hard as it would be, he wouldn't be able to stay and watch her with another man. Logically, he knew she'd had to have dated since him. Hell, he'd dated over the years, in between thinking he'd never make it or while convinced she'd moved on. If she'd found love, he'd make things right with Nell, catch up with Duke, and find another place to call home. Maybe closer to New York or Los Angeles. Europe or Belize didn't sound bad either. Anything but seeing Shelby smile into some other man's eyes.

And if she hadn't found someone... Well, he'd move hell or high water to get her back.

Shelby Greene slammed through her front door, finally allowing the sob to escape her throat. Tears flowed freely down her face. She locked the door and leaned against it, as if the wood barrier would keep her safe from all the memories pouring out of her heart. As if it would keep her from running back to him, only to be hurt again.

She pressed her forehead against the thick cedar. The solid wood would never betray her. It would never abandon her. She had worked hard for her little cabin, the last in a row of ten that she owned and operated as Siren's Song Cabins at the edge of town. She'd done it by herself. She'd needed his support to build up her business when she was a teenager, barely an adult, but no longer. She gathered her own strength from no one but herself now.

Sniffing, she pushed away from the door, her hand wiping her cheeks dry. Her spine straightened, and she raised her chin. Nope. Not her. She didn't need anyone anymore.

Opening her freezer, she got out a half-full container of Mint Moose Tracks ice cream. She grabbed her largest spoon, plunked down on her soft leather couch, and toed off her Chelsea boots. Settling into the fluffy pillows, she stuffed her face with the minty, chocolatey goodness.

Ice cream made everything better.

A buzzing in her pocket indicated one of her friends was trying to check in on her. It would be Willa. Nope. She didn't want to talk. Not now.

Tomorrow, she'd put on a brave face and leave it behind her. Today, she was going to nurse her wounds.

How was she going to do that with Keane Lennox in Orca Cove? Keane *freaking* Lennox! Another loaded spoonful popped into her mouth. Mmm. Sugar was good.

Was he here to stay? She shoveled another mouthful in to tamp down the seed of hope threatening to sprout. If she'd mattered to him, he wouldn't have left in the first place. Another mouthful. Not going there.

Her phone chirped. A message this time. She debated ignoring it, but knowing Willa, she would just stop by unannounced. That would be okay if she wanted to shovel ice cream into her face as well—the two had done that when Willa hit a rough patch—but she'd want to talk.

Checking her phone, she found two texts. One from Willa, as expected. *"Are you okay? I can come over."*

"I'm fine. Just need space," Shelby replied.

"I can bring ice cream."

That earned her a snort. The wild child was learning. *"Got some. All good."*

There was no way the herbalist wouldn't want to talk about it. She didn't know when to let a person work through their emotions. Not everything needed to be talked through.

"Talk tomorrow?" Willa texted.

She sent a thumbs-up emoji. Not likely.

The other message was from Emiliano. It simply said. *"Sorry. I didn't know."*

"I figured," she texted back.

A few seconds later, another line appeared. *"I can tell him to find another place."*

She considered it, but decided it wasn't worth losing the money. Cash was king, after all. And the now-famous painter could afford it.

"Nah, New York money is as good as Washington money."

She was definitely increasing the rent.

Emiliano had leased his place, having rented it from her before officially moving in with Nell. Correction, it was *her* place. The shop owner couldn't have realized what that would mean to her. She had bought it for her and Keane to start their adult life together after selling the record collection she'd driven to Spokane to pick up. With that and the entirety of what she'd put into her Roth IRA, against her advisor's urging.

She wasn't able to stay in the cute waterfront apartment after he'd left. Too many memories. It had prompted her purchase of the dilapidated cabin at the edge of town, though. And the submission of her business proposal to the bank. Back when they did that sort of thing. She'd pulled every string, gotten every reference letter she could possibly get, even joined the city council as the youngest member in history, but she'd done it. And they'd granted her the money to build Siren's Song Cabins.

A smile at the memory slid across her milky, icy lips. She'd paid it off in ten years. It was only four cabins back then. She'd stayed in the rundown cabin until the first one was up. She'd fixed up the original one and converted it into a registration office. The rent from the perfect little waterfront apartment paid for her mortgage payments and what conservative amount she allowed herself to live on.

It had taken her three more years to build the remaining units. Yep, she'd done fine without him. She didn't need him, after all. Scraping the bottom of the container, she slurped up the sweet, mint milk cream.

Exhaustion pulled at her. Either that or the amount of sugar she had consumed. Either way, she pushed the now-empty container onto her live-edge coffee table and settled into the corner of the couch. Keane's face floated into her mind, his eyes crinkled in the corners while he laughed. His wind-swept, nearly black hair tucked behind his ears like the surfer boy he was. Washington surfer boys looked different from California ones. Instead of sun-tanned skin and bleach-blonde hair, it was all about staying warm and having the courage to jump into icy water. Teenager Keane had practically lived in his wetsuit.

His hair was longer now; she remembered the man she had verbally assaulted on the beach. He'd worn it pulled back into a bun. Freaking man-bun. She rolled her eyes, even though she couldn't say it didn't flatter him.

He felt different now. More mature. Less devil-may-care.

Shelby squeezed her eyes shut to kill the images of him, but it didn't help. She tried to get angry again, but she couldn't. Sleep tugged, and even though she was fighting it, all she could do was think about Keane.

CHAPTER 2

S helby watched her cute boyfriend exit Spanish class down the hallway. His worn jeans hung low on his narrow hips as he walked with a relaxed, swinging gait. He reached a hand up to run his fingers through his hair. Spying her, he winked, causing a smile to blossom across her face. She leaned back against her locker, pulling her perfectly lined up and color-coded notebooks closer to her chest.

"Get a room." Nell nudged her in the ribs. But she was smiling.

"Like you're any better." Her eyes broke from Keane in time to catch Nell run over to Gary and throw her arms around his neck.

Nell grinned up at him. "Hey, Hon. I can make a bunch of sandwiches if you guys want to meet up on the beach later tonight. Shelby, Willa, and I are going to be there."

"That sounds good." Gary laid a quick kiss on her lips before checking the hallway for teachers. "It is Friday night, after all. Where else would we be?"

"Where are we going?" Willa joined them. She had sheets of paper sticking out from her history book. Their edges were curled, and several were torn. Shelby's hands itched to reach out and fix them. Willa dropped to her heels and shoved the book into her mushroom-shaped backpack.

Shelby bit back a wince. "Friday night. Bonfire on the beach," she said instead.

"Cool, but it has to be after six." Willa slung her pack over one shoulder and lifted her mass of strawberry-blonde hair out of the way of the straps, letting her mane lay even fluffier over the bag. "I'm releasing the frogs from Mr. Denton's lab tonight after the office staff leaves. Wanna join?"

"God, no." Shelby widened her eyes.

Willa raised her eyebrows in question to Nell, who dropped her head and shook it, before mouthing, "Sorry."

Willa lifted one shoulder.

"What are we doing?" Keane finally joined them, slipping his hand into Shelby's and dropping a kiss on her forehead.

"Willa's trying to get detention," Shelby said.

Nell came to her friend's aid. "She is not."

"It's my duty to help them if I can. Why not?" Willa said.

"Because it's a harebrained idea." Shelby sighed.

"Help who?" Keane asked.

"What's a harebrained idea?" Duke shuffled up, shoving his hands deep into his baggy jean pockets, his eyes gleaming with excitement.

"Willa thinks it's a good idea to break into the high school after hours to release the frogs from Mr. Denton's room."

The science teacher had oodles of snakes and spiders in his room, but apparently, Willa was focused on the frogs today. She probably thought they would end up the object of a dissection lesson.

"Cool." Duke rocked back on his torn Converse high-tops. "I'm in. Save the frogs."

He pumped a fist in the air.

"I don't think this is a good idea, guys." Nell's eyebrows were furrowed with worry.

"Of course it's not," Shelby said. "It's an awful plan. You don't even know how to break into the school."

"Sure, I do. I'll kick the door in." Willa extended her leg out in front of her, her face pinched with an attempt at ferociousness.

"They chain them at night."

Her friend bit her lip.

"I have bolt cutters," Duke offered.

"Well, how would you do it?" Willa asked Shelby.

"Not by getting caught." Shelby raised an eyebrow.

"At least she knows where the school is," Duke teased.

Shelby grimaced. She'd gotten lost—yet again—on her way to school after dropping off the water bill as her parents had asked her to when they were on vacation. It wouldn't be so embarrassing if Orca Cove wasn't so incredibly small.

"Those side streets are twisty. It's easy to get turned around."

"It wouldn't be right if Greene didn't have some faults." Keane pulled her close. "She had to have at least one."

It was the only day she'd been tardy that school year.

She sighed. Duke was right. None of them were perfect, and her friend was going to do it anyway. "Science is your last class of the day, right?"

Willa nodded.

"When Mr. Denton releases the class, he heads straight to the parking lot for car duty. It's a warm day. He'll have the windows open. After everyone leaves the classroom, dump the frogs out the window and leave the aquarium lid ajar so he'll think they escaped. Even if he doesn't leave the windows open, he'll assume he did."

"That's pretty smart." Duke nodded.

Keane gave her hand a squeeze and bumped her shoulder with his. "No one is smarter than Miss Greene."

She leaned into him, and he wrapped an arm around her shoulders. He made her feel smart and appreciated. And she had plans, plans that did not involve getting into trouble.

"But it's also way less fun," Duke continued.

Nell looked relieved they weren't breaking and entering that night.

"Ooh, I've got an idea." Duke's eyes rounded. "Miss Parks just got new paddleboards. We could try them out. We'll get them back before morning, not a scratch on 'em."

"Paddleboarding at night is dangerous." Nell tilted her head up to Gary.

The bell rang, and kids started piling into the classrooms.

"It'll be fun. Come on." Duke hop-walked backward a few steps, wagging his eyebrows up and down. "Who's coming?"

"Are you going?" Shelby asked Keane.

"I need to make sure Duke doesn't drown. He's better on a boat than on a board." He dropped a kiss on her cheek. "But don't worry. We'll be back before full dark. I wouldn't miss bonfire night."

Shelby loved that they were different but could still count on each other. Like two halves of a whole.

"I'll meet you after class, Flower Child. Mine is next to yours." Duke raised his hand in the air and pointed to Willa, then turned and jogged the length of the hall to disappear into a classroom.

"I'd better go too." Gary gave Nell a quick hug. "But don't worry. I already talked to Kristen about their new paddleboards. I saw Duke eyeing them. Her mom said it was okay if we borrow them sometime."

Nell sagged in relief as the two girls watched their guys head down the hall. Keane taller and Gary shorter. She and Keane were going to grow up, get married, and have the best life. She'd make sure they always had money, and he'd keep her grounded so she didn't get stuck in the future and forget to have any fun.

Shelby guided Nell into their next class. "What are you going to do before we meet up on the beach?"

"Making sandwiches and a tomato-basil-caprese salad. I have a new recipe I want to try. Wanna join?"

"Nah, I have a student body meeting after school." She was trying to get approval to renovate the park in town. That would get some of the city council on her good side for when she wanted to start whatever business she figured out starting in town. Better to grease the wheels early.

And then she could relax. Work hard, play hard.

Bonfire night was going to be awesome.

Shelby woke with a jolt to find the early morning sun peeking out from the row of trees outside her large, vaulted living room windows. She stifled a yawn and grimaced at the sour-sweet taste still in her mouth and the high school memories still lingering in her mind.

Huffing, she hauled herself up and made her way to the bathroom. She had taken the evening to feel sorry for herself and drown her feelings in ice cream. She was ready to shake it off and move forward, like she always did. Not feeling up to a morning jog, in case she ran into Keane, she jumped into the shower and washed off the night along with the memories.

While getting ready for the day, she pulled a smart camel-colored lady blazer on over her black skinny jeans and ran her hand over her perfectly smooth dark-brown hair, checking her appearance in the mirror before stepping into camel booties. It was Saturday, but she was a business owner, and that didn't mean it was a day off. Besides, she wasn't going to chance running into him without her full armor on.

Clean, polished, put together. She slapped on some lipstick to show everyone she was feeling on top of the world. No high school-sweetheart punk was going to rock her perfectly sound foundation.

And to prove it to herself, she dialed a number on her way out her front door.

"You're up early." The man's voice sounded glad to hear her.

"The early bird gets the worm, Charles." Shelby slid sunglasses onto her pert nose and crossed the gravel lot to the large cabin housing her office. The familiar tickle pulsed gently at her from the cove. The call of the water. It was her gift, not as cool as the ones her friends had, but a lightning strike in the cove had transferred some kind of magical seawater energy to her and her friends several months back. Still. It was magic, and she would take it.

A chuckle drifted through the line. "I'm guessing you're calling about the land. Have you decided to take this little slice outta my hands?"

"I'm considering it. If it's as great a deal as you say." The offer was too good to be true, but he claimed he'd picked up the plot of land wrapped up in a larger purchase and didn't have any use for it. "I'll need to get a perc test and get a wetland eval."

"You're a smart businesswoman, Shelby. I wouldn't have expected anything less."

That made her feel good.

"Is your deal in Port Noble going well?"

"Yes." She could hear his excitement through the phone. "We're closing at the end of the month. I told them about the new building permit regulations coming next year, like you said. You were right. It sealed the deal. They didn't want to risk getting caught up in them."

"They're not that strict, but people tend to steer clear of red tape if they can." Shelby waved a hand at Cleo, who was sitting at the front desk. "And if they're unfamiliar with them, it's a hassle to figure it all out."

It was fun talking about work with someone else. She'd helped Nell out with marketing, but the restaurant owner now had extra business coming in and was building an addition to her apartment above the café. Her and Emiliano.

Shelby felt the familiar sting of a heartache. They had lost Gary, the one who kept an eye on the rest of them, early last year. Nell had had the hardest time of all, of course, having lost her husband. But Shelby had lost her business friend. Gary and her had traded ideas and plans over lunch once or twice a week. He had kept her grounded after Keane left. All her time and energy was focused on jumping into the business world.

She wasn't upset at Nell for moving on. On the contrary, she was happy for the unlikely couple, Emiliano being seven years Nell's junior. They'd watched the kid grow up to be the stocky man he was today. And they made a great couple. It was the fact that Nell and she had both lost the love of their lives and Nell got a chance at moving on that stung the most. Another chance at happiness.

Screw that, Keane wasn't the love of her life. She only thought he was.

All this was after her other friend, Willa, found the solid ex-cop-turned-woodworker Nick. She was happy for them, but it made it more obvious that no one wanted her. And screw it, but she was the full package. She had everything going for her. Except someone to share it with.

"Tell you what. I'll call my guy for the wetland eval," Charles said. "Small price to pay for the advice. The perc test is easy enough to get."

"Really?" She frowned. Wetland evaluations weren't cheap.

"My guy gives me a great price. I've sent him a lot of business over the years. Besides, you saved me another month of negotiations and schmoozing over drinks. Don't worry. He's accredited. I'll get a copy of his certifications."

It generally wasn't a smart idea to let the seller use their own inspectors, in case they were hiding something. Shelby's red-flag alert went up.

"I have someone I typically use."

"Of course. Sorry." He chuckled. "I was just hoping it would be a good excuse to meet up for drinks to review his findings."

Shelby sat down at her desk. Was he flirting with her?

The man wasn't a troll. Far from it. He was poised and fit, with well-maintained sandy-blonde hair. He was night-and-day different from Keane's easygoing personality, lean muscles, and much-too-long mane.

"We need to meet up for dinner and drinks to review the contract you're going to draw up for me, leaving me thirty days for feasibility and a five-percent discount."

A low chuckle rolled through the phone. "Miss Greene. You drive a hard bargain."

"That's not the half of it." She tucked one end of her perfectly smooth hair behind an ear. "We're going out for seafood. Tonight, at Tusks, at seven. Bring your wallet. We can discuss your inspector's merits then."

It wasn't like she couldn't double-check if there were hidden wetlands on the property. It wouldn't be hard to tell with her special ability.

"I like a woman who knows what she wants. But Tusks can be hard to get into. Seven might be difficult."

"You seem like a man who knows how to get what he wants." She grinned, enjoying flirting for what felt like the first time in a long time.

"Consider it done."

She hung up the phone and powered her computer on. If the land worked out, she'd have a big new investment to hold her focus. Right on time, as clockwork. If her calculations were right, she'd be doubling her money yet again, all in about five years this time. She'd have to cash in her tidy nest egg, but risk big, win big, right?

See? She wasn't going to let Keane ruin the life she was building in Orca Cove. She knew what she was doing, and she wasn't going to let him screw that up.

Chapter 3

It might have been a bad idea to rent Shelby's apartment on the beach. Keane woke up on the couch overlooking the cove. Fifteen years ago, he'd woken from this very same position on a makeshift bed of blankets on the floor. It had been graduation night. Shelby had waited until they were done with school to close, wanting their first night of their future to be in this place.

She hadn't asked him. She'd simply told him they were moving in, and that was that. It hadn't bothered him. He loved how decisive she was. He wasn't like that. She grounded him. He was afraid he'd slip off the side of the earth some days.

He closed his eyes tight. Fifteen years was a long time. *Please don't let it be too long.*

Sending that silent plea into the morning, he pushed to his feet and looked around the bare apartment. He had almost nothing with him, having left everything in his New York studio apartment for Gina to pack up.

He didn't have a lot of furniture there, either. Should he have her sell it all and buy new here? Except for the small hand-carved table he'd picked up in Morocco. He wanted to keep that.

Wandering into the master bedroom, he studied the morning light. It was fantastic, better than he remembered. Of course, he hadn't learned to appreciate the nuances of the light back then. A summer in Morocco and another in Budapest had helped with that. Cocking his head, he propped his hands on his hips and strode around the empty room. It would make a great art studio.

He stuck his head in the second, smaller bedroom. It was fine, decent sized, and had two big windows. Even though they had a view of the parking lot, they also included the majestic mountains hovering over the scene like watchful sentinels in the background.

Keane walked back out into the open living space. He much preferred this area. He could put a bed in the center to see the cove when he woke up in the morning. The extra room would be used for storage. He didn't need anything else, except maybe a sitting place for guests?

Mind settled, he got ready for the day and headed into town. If he focused on putting the place together, he wouldn't think on how much it hurt to be back home without Gary alive and Shelby in his arms.

But first, he had some stops to make.

Walking through the door at the Wild Café, he marveled at the handiwork of the wood-planked walls and wooden support beams throughout the front dining area. He could see a second dining area in the back leading out to the back deck he'd spotted the day before.

He'd been nervous about seeing everyone, but after yesterday's encounter, he figured the rest of them were due a visit.

"Hi, there!" A cute little blonde popped up in front of him. Her pixie cut was feathered and sticking up in places, making her appear a bit haphazard, but also like she was loving life. "Table for one?"

"Yes, please." He nodded, taking a few more steps inside. "Is Nell here?"

"Course she is." The perky waitress beamed, and happy creases appeared at the corners of her eyes. "She's busy in the kitchen, but I can let her know you'd like to see her when she has a moment."

"That'd be great. I appreciate it." He dipped his head, feeling out of place in his own town with his own friends. Old friends.

"Inside or out?"

"Inside today, if that's alright." He wanted to approach everyone individually if possible. He had a lot to atone for.

"Of course." The woman led him to a spot under a sunny window. A black-and-white photograph of Orca Cove hung between it and the next window over. It was from the section of beach where they used to sit around a bonfire late into the night, listening to the waves. She saw him appreciating the photo. "It's a beautiful spot. If you have time while you're here, you really should experience the cove at night."

He smiled politely in reply.

"Who can I tell Nell is waiting?" she asked.

"Keane."

Her perpetual smile slipped, and her mouth dropped open half an inch.

"Oh, geez. I'm so sorry. I didn't recognize you from…" Her voice fell away.

"I guess you wouldn't, would you?" He'd been away for so long.

She shook her head. "I mean, I've seen photos of you. Nell has a picture of you all in her kitchen. Your face is angled, and you were much younger."

"No need to apologize." His heart squeezed, and he wondered if Nell would let him have a copy of it. He hadn't saved any pictures of the old crew, only a handful of photos of Shelby and a few keepsakes in an old Vans shoebox. Back then, he hadn't realized how important it would be to have images of the five to look back at. "It's been a while."

She obviously knew about him and looked like she wanted to ask questions, but was too polite to do so. He chuckled. "What do you want to know?"

Checking the tables in a quick scan, she leaned in. "Are you staying?"

He nodded.

"Are you single?"

The corner of his mouth kicked up. He nodded again. She had to know his history with Shelby. No doubt that was why she was inquiring. He burned to ask her if Shelby was.

"Why'd you lease Shelby's apartment from Emiliano instead of going to her directly?"

"She wouldn't have rented it to me." At least, he didn't think she would have.

"Doesn't that put Emiliano in a bad position?" Her eyes narrowed.

"I didn't mean to do that." He shook his head. "I'm sorry. That wasn't my intention."

She pursed her lips. "And doesn't that take the choice from Shelby to rent it herself?"

He drew a deep breath, expanding his lungs. "Yes, but if she asks me to move out, I will."

"She won't."

He shook his head again. "No, I don't think so, either."

At her silence, he continued. "I pushed her, you're right. But I need her to talk to me. To apologize. This was a good way to do that. I promise I won't push any further than to get enough space to properly tell her I'm sorry. I wouldn't do that to her."

She measured him, weighed him, and nodded curtly. "You'd better follow me."

"Excuse me?"

"Nell's going to be emotional when she sees you. It's safer to do that in her kitchen."

"Are you sure?" He hesitated, not wanting to invade her workspace.

"Yep, come on." She stuck her hand out. "I'm Maggie, by the way."

He shook her hand and followed her to the hallway separating the dining areas. The bathrooms were on the right, along with a doorway over stairs marked PRIVATE. On the left was a swing door to the kitchen. The blonde pushed through, announcing her entrance.

"You have a visitor!"

Nell stood, facing a wide cooktop. Her hair was pulled back in a ponytail, and she had a chef's apron tied around her waist.

Emotion hit him like a fist to the nose. Nell was living her dream. This was what she'd talked about when they sat out late at night. Gary had helped her get here. Hell, Keane was sure they all had. And he'd missed out on it. Had missed out on helping.

At least, Gary had been able to see her make it. He'd always been so insanely proud of his chef.

Nell spun around, and her eyes went soft. "Keane?" She rushed to pull him into a hug. "I'm so glad to see you."

"You are?" He stumbled back in shock as soon as she released him. "I thought you'd be upset with me for leaving."

"You're my friend. We all have to make hard decisions in life. I don't know why you left, but I'm glad you're home."

"But I wasn't here for—" He bit off the word. He couldn't continue the sentence. He hadn't been there for her when it counted.

Tears welled in her eyes. "No, you weren't."

"I'm so sorry." He took her up in another hug, this time crushing her to him. They both had hot tears streaking their cheeks when they separated. "I was out of the country. By the time I found out, it was too late."

"It all happened so fast." She patted him on the arm. "He knew how you felt about him."

He hoped that was a good thing.

Nell handed him a tissue, and they both blew their noses.

"I'll take over for a few minutes." Maggie moved to check the dishes on the stove.

Nell eyed her but sat down at the table in her kitchen, then jumped right in. "What are you doing here? And staying in Shelby's place?"

"I'm back." He shrugged, then glanced over at the waitress cooking on Nell's stove. "I needed Shelby to acknowledge me."

"That's one way to do it."

"I know."

"She would have anyway. She's pretty bitter where you're concerned."

"She has every right to be."

"You're back, back?"

He nodded.

"Okay, then." Nell got up from the table and took the tongs from Maggie. "I can take it from here."

Maggie spun out and headed back to the floor.

"She's great." Keane inclined his head toward the short blonde.

"You have no idea." Nell plated two dishes, garnishing them expertly. "She's been here since I opened this place. Came along at the right time. Her and her sister. She helped Gary and me staff it from part time to full time. She's a staple at Wild's."

"I've missed so much. I'm hoping it's not too much."

"That's up to you." Nell regarded him.

"I know what my priorities are now." Keane leaned against the wall near Nell. "I'll still have to travel for gallery showings, but I'm back. I'll be here when it matters."

"Keane?" Nell asked quietly. He raised his eyebrows. "I know you said you're back, back, but don't tell us all that if you don't mean it."

It stung, knowing how much he'd hurt them. Keane studied his shoes for a long moment, then finally met her gaze. "I shouldn't have left the way I did. I'll make it up to you, I promise. And when I say I'm back. I'm back."

Nell nodded.

The kitchen door swung open again, and Emiliano rolled in a crate of fresh fish. "It's not too late for these, is it, Hon?" He stopped, seeing Keane.

His disappointment caused Keane to slump. *Crap*, another in the long line of apologies he owed.

Maggie wheeled into the kitchen, sliding one more order up onto the bar above Nell's face, and disappeared back out the door with the two ready plates.

Keane held out his hand. "Sorry, man. I didn't mean to put you in a bad position."

Emiliano considered his peace offering, then took it. "I'm guessing you did it for a good reason."

"I sure hope so," Keane said. He noticed Nell watching him warily, her eyes hopping back to the muscly, young man.

"So, um." Nell tugged on her apron.

He picked up on her uneasiness. "I heard around town. Loris mentioned it."

"And?"

"And I couldn't be happier for you both." He meant it. "Gary would never have wanted you to pass on a chance at happiness."

"I know." Her eyes grew full of more tears. "Thanks."

Emiliano appeared at her side with a tissue.

"I hope we get a chance to get to know each other as adults," Keane said to the young shop owner. "I always did like you."

"Yeah? Well, if you're going to be around, it's unavoidable," Emiliano said in a friendly way as he wrapped his arm around Nell. "Small town."

"I'd say so." It was one of the smaller towns Keane had seen in his life and was still the most magical to him. It felt amazing to be back home after the busyness of New York City.

Taking his leave and a breakfast sandwich to go, he worked his way into town to see if Willa was at her yoga studio.

CHAPTER 4

S helby rose from her desk and ran a hand down her front to smooth it even though she knew nothing was out of place. It was time.

She'd skipped her normal stop at the café for breakfast or even a coffee after her morning run, not quite ready to bump into Keane again, but it was lunch, and she was hungry. She could handle this.

"Need anything from the café?" she asked Cleo on her way out.

"Nope." Cleo blinked up at her from the computer screen. "Brought my lunch today."

"I might be gone a while. I have a few stops to do."

"It's Saturday, Shelby. You should take the afternoon off."

"I'll think about it." Shelby slid her sunglasses on. "Laters."

It wasn't as sunny as she'd expected. Summer in the Pacific Northwest was a funny thing. Some days were still chilly, and sunshine was a rarity, but they weren't used to it. She left the glasses on and got into her dark-red Chevy Trailblazer. It was getting older, but she loved the zippy thing.

She paused while getting in, spying the kayak rack on top. She hadn't gotten out on the water once last summer. It'd be a shame if she let another year go by without a good paddle. But there was always so much to do, and she had this big business deal coming up. If it worked out—when it worked out, she reminded herself—she'd be back in another season or two of being head down, focused on keeping everything afloat. She should get out there before that. A few times.

Kayaking was one of the few real joys she let herself take the time for. It was completely for her, with no financial gain.

She decided to figure it out later, swung into the SUV, and headed to the café.

Shelby stuck her head in Nell's kitchen. "Hey, whatcha got for me in here?"

"What?" Nell whirled. "Oh, hey, Shelby."

"I missed breakfast. I'm starving." She leaned against the open door, fake fainting from hunger.

"Go sit at a table like a normal patron." Nell waved her hands at her friend. "Maggie will bring you food."

"What's the special? And when have I ever been a normal patron?"

"Fine." Nell fit her fist against her waist. "Clam chowder."

"Perfect." Shelby plopped down at the table in her kitchen. "And bread. All the bread."

"Are we eating our feelings today?" Nell raised an eyebrow. "And are we hiding in here?"

That made her shoot to her feet. She wasn't hiding. This was her town.

"Not at all. I just wanted to say hi to my friend." Shelby made a dramatic half exit, stopping at the door for the retort she knew Nell would make.

"You can say hi to me whenever you want."

Shelby grinned. "You're right, though. Sun would be good for me. It's been so long since we had it. Or heat, for that matter. It's gorgeous out."

"It is. Go find a seat, and I'll join you as soon as I catch up on a few orders. The lunch rush is calming down."

"And coffee. I am so low on coffee my skin is shriveling up."

Shelby pushed back through the door and headed out to the back deck, glancing at the cove. The sun was glittering on the water, and two orcas were playing farther out, where it was deeper. One leaped into the air and splashed down in the water below. The other rolled and disappeared, then popped back up, its dorsal fin cutting through to the other whale. A couple of kayakers and paddleboarders were near the jetty to the left. The narrow row of land and boulders created the almost perfect "U" of the cove.

Even with it being the weekend, only two other families sat at the tables. Shelby found a spot close to the railing so she could watch the peaceful view.

"Clam chowder?" Maggie set a bowl in front of her, along with a plate piled high with slices of sourdough baguette.

"You're fast."

"It's not that busy," the blonde waitress said with a friendly smile, then delivered the bowl of fries she was carrying to another table.

"Still, thanks." Shelby raised her spoon in salute and dug in.

She was halfway through her bowl when Nell slid in across her. "You doing okay?"

"Of course." She straightened. Maggie was wiping off two tables down from her, watching closely. She liked the little waitress, but they'd never been particularly close. "Why wouldn't I be?"

"You know why." Nell sat her elbows on the wooden slat table between them.

"I had my pity party. I'm fine now."

Nell raised her eyebrow. "He was here this morning."

"Oh?" Shelby calmly took a sip of her chowder. It was delicious. "Did he actually say anything to you? All I got was, 'It's good to see you.'"

"We talked. He met Emiliano."

"He knows Emiliano."

"Not as an adult. Not as my boyfriend." Nell's mouth pressed into a thin line.

She didn't like that Nell wanted approval from the unreliable bastard. He'd better have given her what she needed.

"What did he say?" Shelby's eyes narrowed. If he gave her even one iota of guilt over moving on, she'd nail his ass to a tree.

"He was supportive. He reminded me that Gary would want me to be happy."

"Is that still bothering you?"

"Not with the memory of Gary. But I was still worried how you all would take it, last night, telling you he was officially moving in. This was our place. We built it together."

"We don't respect you or his memory any less." Shelby touched her arm. "And he's lucky he didn't give you any crap. He hasn't been around. He doesn't get a say."

"He was one of us."

"Was." Shelby used her spoon to make the point.

"I think he's back, like, for good, back."

"Is that what he said?" Shelby let out a snort. "That's what he says now. We all know how good he is at sticking around."

With food in her belly and a coffee to-go in hand, she took a left on the sidewalk to her old apartment. She might as well get it over with.

Hand raised to knock, she hesitated, seeing a new potted plant by the front door. It looked like something from Gil's Market and Marina. Willa had probably planted it. Poor little ivy. It'd be abandoned by fall...if it lasted that l ong.

After rapping her knuckles against the mossy-green door, she took a step back. She hadn't spent any real time here since Willa rented it from her. She'd been a regular tenant until she and Nick got engaged and moved to the outskirts of town in the house he'd built for her.

The door swung open, and she braced for the impact of seeing him again. In daylight.

"Greene." Her old nickname rolled off his tongue softly. His eyes were lit with humor or pleasure or something she couldn't name.

She narrowed hers. "New York."

He only smirked at the intended insult.

"I know you heard about the place from Emiliano." She jumped into business. "But I'd prefer to rent it outright instead of leasing it through him. He has no intention of coming back."

"Okay."

"So, I need paperwork." She produced the document she'd prepared from the bag hanging from her shoulder. "Also, we are announcing a raise in rent. Cost of living, you understand."

Keane took the papers from her and flipped through them. His eyes found the new number on the final page, and the corner of his mouth kicked up again. He glanced up at her. "Cost of living."

"You understand," she repeated. "Unless it's too much. I'd guess it's a lot less than you were paying in New York. With better views."

"Definitely better views." His eyes never left hers. "Do you have a pen?"

"Of course." She pulled one from her purse and handed it over.

Keane backed into the apartment and walked to the kitchen. She could see past the entryway into the living room. He had a couch front and center in the open space. From her position, she could see a pillow and a blanket peeking over the edge. "You know there are two bedrooms, right?"

"I know." He handed the papers back to her. "This room has a better view of the cove. And the master bedroom has better lighting. It's going to be my art studio."

Her phone buzzed in her pocket. She slid it out to see a text from Charles.

Pulled a few strings. Table for two at seven. Looking forward to it.

A smile tugged at her lips.

"Good news?"

"Dinner plans." She slid her phone back in her pocket, relishing and disliking the pain that flickered over Keane's eyes. "You'd better not get any paint on the hardwood floors."

"I won't ruin anything. I promise."

"That'd be a first," she flung back at him, stuffing the papers in her bag. No, she coached herself. Be cool. He's not going to see her get unnerved. She was in complete contr ol.

"Can I get a copy?" He stopped her from leaving. "For my records."

"Sure. I'll send a signed one over."

He nodded, leaning against his doorway. "Want to come in for a drink? I can make more coffee."

It sounded delicious, but she hoisted her half-empty cup. "Got one, thanks."

"Shelby," he said quietly.

Nope, that's not why she was here. "Gotta run. Work to do."

She spun and left, heading back to get her car at the café and get back to work, where she could drown the rest of her day in spreadsheets and financial documents.

Shelby released a small amount of the tight leash she'd kept on her emotions, letting the ice melt into the anger burning beneath but not far enough to get to the pain. She'd done it. Cool, calm, and collected. He wasn't going to shake the comfortable life she'd created.

Sliding her feet into black heels, Shelby checked her clock on the wall. She was close to an hour's drive from Port Noble and had plenty of time, but she wasn't missing out on an opportunity to eat at Tusks. She knew the real estate owner would be able to afford and gain entry at the coveted restaurant. Smoothing her hair, she swiped some deep-red lipstick on and headed out the door.

She drove through town, keeping her eyes on the road, oblivious to the beach apartment or who was at the café. She had approached him and tolerated the experience. No tears, no losing control. She'd get better at it.

As she drove away from Orca Cove, the tug of the ocean increased. She took Highway 101 North to Port Noble. In the past, she'd have had her GPS on, even though the highway went all the way around Mt. Olympus to her destination. The port town was easy to navigate, but she still often got turned around in the older, windy downtown streets.

But now, the tug of the cove told her right where she was. She'd know where to turn and hadn't gotten lost since she got her water-locator ability.

The constant pull when she was away from home wasn't uncomfortable. She'd grown used to the continuous tickle of energy, the call of saltwater. As Highway 101 edged closer to the Hood Canal, the familiar energy picked back up in places and finally settled in when she crossed into town. Here, she could feel the waters of the Strait of Juan de Fuca. The buzz felt different yet similar. The way maple leaves looked alike enough to tell what species they were, but were varied.

Keeping track of the direction through the Strait's signature buzzing pattern, she located Tusks without any trouble. She pulled into the parking lot outside the tall stone building. The architecture alone was enough to bring people to the restaurant. Hopefully, the food was as good as the hype. Grabbing her portfolio, she made her way into the lobby.

"I'm meeting Charles Timms," Shelby told the young waitress.

"He's at the bar," the young woman replied, pointing through the doorway where carved woodwork stretched from the ceiling to the floor, surrounding the thick wooden slab making up the bar. Eclectic paint swirled around the ceiling, and gold art deco pieces hung from the rafters. It was grand.

Charles sat on a barstool, a glass of whiskey in his hand.

"Good to see you." Shelby slid onto the empty seat next to him.

The smile he offered warmed her to her core and washed away some of the pain she'd been riding on most of the day.

"Aren't you a vision?" His eyes lit on her hair, then traveled down to her jacket. She knew the tawny color of her blazer played well with her dark-brown hair and red lipstick.

"Thanks."

"The table wasn't quite ready, so I grabbed a drink. Hope you don't mind that I started without you."

"Not at all."

"What would you like?" He raised a finger to flag down the bartender.

"A Cabernet Sauvignon would be good." The whiskey sounded better, but not with the trip back home.

"How was your drive?" Charles gave her his full attention.

"Fine." She accepted the glass from the bartender. "Yours?"

"It's not that far for me. I'm used to it. You could have let me meet you in Orca Cove. It's on the way."

She wasn't ready for people in town to see her with Charles. Particularly with Keane's reappearance. Then again, it might be good for him to see she'd moved on. More proof that she didn't need him, after all.

"Next time." She flashed him a friendly smile.

"Your table is ready for you, Mr. Timms." The slim waitress appeared at his elbow to guide them to seats overlooking downtown Port Noble and the bay beyond, which led to Point Peril and the Strait of Juan de Fuca.

Shelby had so many good memories of sea kayaking out here. Most were of her and Keane, some with the whole crew. Recently, she'd helped a researcher in this area connect with Solomon and Percy, their local orca shifter. None of them had known that Solomon's family had a long history with Point Peril's lighthouse and had provided a safe harbor for the orca shifters in the Strait and the Hood Canal. It was time to add to those non-Keane memories.

She made a promise to herself to get back out here soon.

"I got the wetlands evaluation scheduled on the land. My guy should be able to get there in a couple of days."

"That's quick."

"That's why he's my guy. I'm impatient when it comes to things like that." He winked at her. "Can't sit on a good deal."

"I hear ya." She raised her glass to clink with his.

When their waitress arrived, Shelby ordered mussel linguine with a garlic white wine sauce and chili oil.

"Speaking of a good deal." Charles flipped his own beautifully stitched black leather portfolio open and handed it over to her. "Unless you want to wait until after dinner."

"Not at all. I enjoy talking business."

"It's one of the things I like most about you, Shelby Greene."

She glanced over the paperwork, her eyes examining the acreage and price. The offer was almost too good to be true. Almost. But it hovered close enough near that line to make her a little uncomfortable. The price made sense since he had other ongoing business deals larger than this and just wanted to get rid of it. That didn't seem like a red flag...so long as the tests came back clean.

"You're not financing, correct?" Charles went on. "We could close early once you get your feasibility tests done. If you get all the workers lined up, you could bypass the building permit changes and start taking reservations for the holidays."

Her chest constricted. She wasn't financing, but she would have to liquidate a few things. And there was no way she'd be able to pay for a crew to build her new rental units that quickly. It sounded exciting to be working on something new rather than the broken pipes she'd been fixing at Siren's Song Cabins, though. "I'm not financing, but it'll take a few days to get everything in order. If I can get things lined up before that, I'll let you know."

"Perfect!"

"I'd like to stop by the place and check it out to make sure it works for my expansion." She needed boots on the ground to see if she could envision her new development there. Plus, she needed to let out her Spidey senses.

"Of course. I'd be happy to meet you out there some-time." He leaned closer to her. "You've built quite a nice business. I'd love to hear more about your plans."

"Sounds good." Shelby settled back in her chair to enjoy her wine and dinner with the handsome man. Between the business and the gentleman, things were looking up.

Chapter 5

Keane sat on the outdoor deck at the Wild Café that night, sipping on a beer. Nell had brought him one of the best oyster po' boys he'd had in his life. It was the high point in his troubling day. He hadn't encountered Willa at her yoga studio. By the time he found it, she'd already left after her morning classes and was probably back at her and Nick's place.

Not knowing Nick and not yet having a vehicle, he figured he'd wait until the following day to find her. At least, he'd made a mental note of her schedule posted on the door. Maybe it was best to wait on visiting Duke, too. So much had changed.

Then, *she'd* visited.

Initially, it encouraged him, but she'd come armored up emotionally and physically in her polished, professional clothes while brandishing a contract from a portfolio. She'd refused to take even a step inside.

And then, the text. He hadn't meant to pry, but his eyes had found the name Charles on her phone's screen. Dinner. She was joining him for dinner that night.

Right now, they were probably laughing over wine and a beautifully curated meal. The kind he'd love to be treating her with.

He felt resentful, even though he was eating his own just rewards. He lifted a finger to Nell's bartender, Barnaby. They all had a full life out here without him.

He had a life in New York, too. But he'd always known it was temporary. Hell, his small group of friends in the city had teased him when he repeated that he wouldn't be there long. When he finally gave his moving date, he was surprised at their shock. As though they'd thought he'd never leave.

At times, he'd thought he wouldn't, either. Not because of any desire to stay, but because he wasn't sure he'd ever hit his goal or if he had any right returning.

Maybe he'd been gone too long, after all. He shook his head, accepting his fresh beer with a nod.

"That is the face of a troubled man, my friend." Barnaby scrutinized him. "Your head's hanging so low. I thought you were taking a nap."

"No nap." Keane exhaled sharply at the humor. "Just not enjoying the bitter taste of some of my life's choices."

The bartender nodded thoughtfully. "Is it not fixable?"

Keane lifted his shoulder in reply. "I had thought so, but maybe not."

"I think everything's fixable, but not always in the manner you expect."

"That's possible, but right now, any other option doesn't seem acceptable."

"Give it time." Barnaby tapped two fingers on the heavy, wooden outdoor bar encased in resin. "Things have a way of working themselves out."

"I sure hope so." Keane lifted his beer in thanks to the sage bartender, who was moving on to another couple to take their order.

Out of the corner of his eye, he saw a figure with a familiar gait. It was Duke. Hope washed over him. He could use someone to talk to right now. He shot out of his chair at the sight of his old friend. Beer in hand, he slipped through the crowd.

"Hey!"

Duke's eyebrows pinched together when he recognized him, then he dropped a curt nod. "Hey."

Of all the people he'd expected to change, Duke was the last on the list.

"It's good to see you."

"Is it?"

"Of course it is." He seemed hurt. "I've missed you. You're my oldest friend."

"I am now."

The words sat between them with the weight of a heavy tidal swell. The patio seemed silent for a moment, even though the band in the corner was still playing a 90's music cover.

He'd meant since Gary's passing.

"I'm sorry I wasn't here," was all he could muster.

Duke's jaw set. "So am I."

"Would you like to grab a drink?"

"Suddenly, I'm not in the mood. The place is busy. Guess it's a little late." Sliding back a step on his Converse sneakers, he pivoted, pushed through the back gate, and disappeared down the stairs.

"Damn." Keane tipped back his beer, paid his tab, and took off onto the beach.

He removed his Reef flip-flops and walked closer to the edge, where the rocks were smaller, more like charcoal gravel. The moon hung large and low over the water at the end of the cove, casting a pathway through the waves at the opening.

The following morning, Keane's outlook was better. Whether it was because of the good night's sleep or due to the crisp air, he had a spring in his step.

The glowing lights from Willa's studio created a halo in the coastal fog that hovered in the valley.

Bracing himself, he pushed through the glass door thirty minutes before her first class of the day. The tinkling bell signaled his arrival, and the wild mane of riotous strawberry-blonde curls flipped right side up from where Willa was leaning over to light incense sticks at the front of her space.

Her hair settled around her, and her eyes opened wide at the sight of him.

"Keane!" She danced barefoot around the yoga mats to wrap her arms around him.

Spiral curls filled his face. "Hey, Willa."

Joy spread through him. Was it wrong that this was how he'd expected Duke to have reacted when he saw him? Well, maybe not the run and bear hug, but close.

Even so, he hugged her back hard. All his tension poured out as he settled into his childhood friend for a moment. They hadn't been super tight back in the day. He'd been with Shelby, and Willa had been a free spirit, flittering between her friends and other interests, but she'd always been there.

"Oh, what is it?" She pulled back a few inches to peer at him, not fully disengaging from the friendly hug.

He leaned away, breaking free, and ran a hand over his hair. It hung loose today and settled nearly to his shoulders. He tucked one side behind his ear. "It's just been a difficult few days."

"Shelby." She said the word as though it explained it all.

"And Duke." He winced at his own words. "I should have come back earlier. I should have been here for them."

"It's been a rough couple of years." Willa's lips pressed. "But give them time. Have you talked to Nell?"

"Yes. And I got to congratulate her and Emiliano. They seem to be a good fit."

"They are. I'm so happy for them."

"And you!" He lifted a hand, palm up between them. "I heard from Loris at Gil's that you found a lucky guy."

Willa's face lit up.

"His name is Nick Ryan." She raised her left hand. "Did you ever think I'd settle down?"

"Not back then." He glanced over the modest but sparkling ring. "It's beautiful. Congratulations. What's he like?"

"He's great." Her eyes went dreamy. "He's a woodworker. Used to be a Seattle cop. Left that life. It wasn't for him. Now, he's making stuff and selling it at Gil's and online." Willa clapped her hands together and bounced her knees. "He built our house. He builds the most beautiful pieces. Boxes, cutting boards, charcuterie boards. Those are what he sells the most of. But he's started making larger pieces, like tables and furniture, but even these gorgeous wall art pieces. Like burnt wood with copper inlays, some with resin, and local things like rocks or fir boughs inlaid within."

It was obvious she was crazy about the guy. "And he makes you happy?"

"So happy."

"Then, *I'm* so happy." He impulsively gave her another hug.

"You'll get along great. He and Emiliano fit into our crew like they've always been there. Maggie too. But you've met her, right?"

"Just yesterday."

They were six yet again. Or seven, with Maggie. He ignored the ache of Nick and Emiliano filling his and Gary's place. He wondered if he would ever be allowed to join the crew again. Bonfires on the beach felt far, far away.

"You guys can talk about art!" She rocked up onto the balls of her feet. "Although he doesn't see himself as an artist. Go gently on him."

Keane understood the lack of confidence over the term. It wasn't until the last few years that he could securely call himself one.

"I can't wait to meet him."

"Meet who?" The jingle of the bell sounded nearly in time with Loris's words. "Oh, of course you haven't met Nick yet. He's a keeper!" The older woman wagged her eyebrows up and down.

"It sounds like it. Good to see you this morning, Miss Franklin."

"Oh, Lordy, it's just Loris now, young man! You're not a kid anymore."

"No, not exactly, Miss Franklin." He scrunched up his face. "Sorry. Loris."

She batted her hand at him. "You'll catch on. It's been a while since you've been in town. Seen your parents yet?"

She gave him a stern eye.

"Of course, Miss—er, Loris." He caught himself that time. "I stayed with them a few days until I leased Emiliano's place, Shelby's place on the beach."

"Ah, makes sense." She nodded with interest. "You lot seem to be rotating through that apartment."

"We do?"

"I was there since I came back from Seattle." Willa filled him in. "Then, Emiliano stayed there after he moved out from his dad's, Hugo. Now, you're staying there."

"All of you, old crew and new," Loris said.

He hoped that was true.

"How are Kalani and Elias?" Loris went on, asking about his parents. "They hadn't told me you were coming back for a visit."

"Not a visit." He shook his head. "I moved back."

"From New York?" Her eyes went wide. "But your career just took off. I've been hearing all about your paintings selling all over the world. The newspaper prints a story, now and then, but the New York Times has featured you twice this past year."

"Thank you for noticing." It still felt strange that people praised him for his ability to put paint on canvas. He'd wanted a career, not notoriety; however, the two were intertwined in his business.

"Hard not to notice. Besides, Kalani is a proud mom."

"She is." Keane smiled warmly at the memory of his mother and father showing up at his first gallery opening. They'd made almost every stateside show over the years, and a couple of international ones. With them visiting the city so often, it was an easy excuse to not return home. "I lucked out in the parent department."

"You certainly did."

"I bet Shelby's glad to see you back."

"I'm not sure she'd agree with that."

"Ah, she's feeling jilted since you ran out." Loris called it as she saw it, laying it out there.

"It would seem so, ma'am. And fairly so."

She nodded, then clapped him on the shoulder. "You can fix that.""I appreciate the confidence. We'll see."

They had drawn an audience with the other yoga students filing in over the conversation.

"Would you like to join us?" Willa asked.

"Not today, but soon. I need to get back in shape for a surfboard." It had been a while since he was able to get out. The waves on the East Coast were better in winter, but wicked cold. Even with a Washington surfer's tolerance.

"Hey, we still have an old paddleboard sitting in my garage," Loris piped up. "Haven't used it for years. It's not a surfboard, but it's a nice, solid one, narrow and long. Feel free to use it. You'll have to get it down from the rack. It's above a table, and I'm not sure I could reach it. Just let yourself in. You should remember how to do that."

Loris stuck a pointy elbow into his ribs.

Keane's eyes widened. It took him a few moments to get that she was teasing him for his youth. "I couldn't."

"You can," she pressed. "It should get some use. I'm certainly not getting it out."

"I appreciate it." He would buy a new board, but getting back onto the water would do a lot to settle him back into who he'd been here.

Excusing himself, he stepped back into the street and decided to get reacquainted with the town.

It should have occurred to him, but it hadn't. He hadn't only abandoned Shelby when he'd moved. He'd also left his other friends. Somehow, he'd never expected them to be as hurt by it. But Duke had been left alone to deal with the loss of their friend, the one who'd kept them all grounded. He'd messed up more than he'd even realized, and that was saying something.

His feet took him closer and closer to the cove, unaware where he was headed until he was shin deep, wading through the saltwater. The waves splashed up to his knees, soaking the bottom half of his jeans, the water-logged fabric tugging at his waist when the tide pulled away.

The trees were different along the coastline, taller than he remembered, and more houses dotted the hill line. The city of Orca Cove rose from the center of downtown, denoted by the Wild Café and Gil's Market & Marina.

Main Street traveled straight up the hill from there, with only a few branching paths of downtown shops before housing sprawled around the remaining streets above it. Mt. Olympus stood watching over it all to the west. No matter where you lived in town, you had a great view.

Six dorsal fins trailed through the calmer water farther out. Even that looked different. It was orca season, but six of them in the cove at one time? That was more than he'd ever seen.

He'd dreamed of coming home to Orca Cove, but it didn't exactly feel like home anymore.

Chapter 6

The light from the shed illuminated a dust-covered kayak. Lifting the cover, Shelby peered in, checking for spiders. Not seeing any, she hauled it off the rack and set it down on the foam she'd spread out for protection. It was a Current Design, seaworthy, but with the lighter, fiberglass hull and its thirteen-foot length, she was able to load it herself. It was worth the extra care the fragile material called for.

After snagging her paddle, life jacket, and a bucket of straps, she ran a cloth around the inside, just in case. It only took a couple of minutes to hoist her kayak onto the waiting rack on her Trailblazer. She dumped out her bucket, then flipped it upside down and used it as a stool to reach the mounting point for the straps. Once she slid the webbing into their cam buckles and tightened them, she was ready to go.

Standing with her hands on her hips, she smiled. She hadn't done this in ages. She slapped her sun hat on her head, jumped in, and wheeled to the marina.

Typically, she pulled in near her beach condo and stored her things on the back deck when Willa lived there, but now that it wasn't being rented by someone she wanted to stop in and see, she parked next to the café. The waves were a little heavier there, but it would be equally easy.

The beach was quiet this morning, even with the good weather. Several boats were farther out, but they didn't seem to be in her path. She would skirt near the shoreline and then consider going out into the rest of the Hood if the waves stayed as calm as they currently were. Good thing she'd gotten out so early. The surface of the cove was like glass.

After unloading and setting her beautiful blue-and-green kayak on a patch of soft grass and moss, she locked her bucket and straps in the vehicle and secured her phone and ID in a dry bag with a lanyard around her neck. She clipped her keys to that. It was highly unlikely she'd go over.

The moment she entered the coastline, the internal draw of the saltwater eased. In its place was a sense of deep peace.

Wading into the water was the tricky part; the pebbles and rocks could scuff her hull. She didn't set it down until the tide was knee-deep. Balancing herself on one leg, she leveraged herself into the boat, bracing her arms on either side of the opening. She lowered her butt down into the seat and finally pulled in her second leg.

Having successfully boarded, she dipped her paddle in the water and dug in, executing quick strokes to glide through the glass-like surface, deeper into the cove. The ground quickly dropped away. Silver fish darted underneath her, and nearly translucent jellyfish floated along next to her.

Shelby wiggled in her seat, getting settled. Her feet were firm on the foot pegs, which tucked her knees against the sides of the interior hull. The boat sat deep in the water, the surface close to waist-height. It allowed her to be mobile. She was one with the kayak as if it was an extension of her body.

Taking longer strokes, she angled the paddles deeper to move faster. Light danced on the surface as each paddle rose. The redirected droplets shimmered like crystals falling into the reflective pool.

It was the perfect day.

She had actually taken the morning off, even from her run. She'd get a good exercise out on the water while enjoying the relaxing morning.

That afternoon, she would make a list of the accounts she needed to liquidate and any additional items to validate for the land feasibility. It would be a good idea to double-check with the county on permits for yurts. The last she'd checked, the canvas-covered structures were still allowed. Charles was right; it was better to get in while the regulations still held.

But she could worry about that later when she had her notebook in front of her and was able to make adequate lists. Right now, she'd focus on the water.

A couple of tourists walked on the beach near her apartment. Shelby pointedly didn't give it her full attention, not wanting to see Keane lounging on the back deck—*her* back deck.

She thought she saw movement but stubbornly directed the nose toward the east side of the cove, where it was sheltered by large trees. Tiny, dark, bobbing heads in the water started moving toward her. The otters came from one of the nearby rivers that fed the Hood, but this particular family was often found on this part of the coastline. She loved watching them. There were six in all, moving around each other as though executing a water ballet.

Movement on the shore caught her eye, and curiosity got the better of her, making her glance over to see what was going on.

A paddleboarder was in the water, gliding out near her. Shelby noted the grace of the shirtless man standing casually on the board. He paddled in sure strokes, his long, lean muscles visible from the distance.

His dark hair danced in the breeze. Keane.

She hadn't picked up on the familiarity of his form. It had been too long, and he'd changed too much. But it was hard to forget the way he moved.

"This is my cove," she said to herself through gritted teeth. She'd been out there, trying to take a few minutes for herself, which she *never* did. And he was stealing that, invading her peace.

Angling her kayak, she returned to her normal cruise around the cove, straight into his path. Keane glanced back, seeing her track him. The jerk paddled right and then executed a sweeping stroke to zigzag hard across her heading.

Even with her faster kayak, the length of the paddleboard and the strength of his strokes awarded him some maneuverability. Instinctively, Shelby pitted to the right, then paddled hard and banked a sharp left, completing a zigzag against his trajectory. Together, they formed a figure eight in the water. She found herself enjoying the sport. The familiarity of it felt comfortable.

He was showing off, but more than that, he was playing an old game. He was playing with her, like he had when they were kids.

A furry, dark-brown head popped up next to her kayak, only a few feet from where she sat half submerged in the water. It chirped at her, startling her. She hadn't realized she'd gotten into their raft. Moving away from them, she saw Keane had stopped.

"You okay?" His voice carried across the waves.

Of course she was okay. The furry little dude was simply telling her she was getting too close to his family. It had only surprised her.

And with that, she drove straight through the ripples of his last zag and toward the mouth of the cove.

The water was deeper here. She was in the orcas' playground, and kept an eye on them, not wanting to intrude. She knew at least one of them was a shifter and likely wouldn't hurt her, but there was a lot they still didn't understand. On top of that, she wasn't sure how the whole shifter form worked with logic and reason.

In her peripheral, she saw Keane following at a distance.

One of the orcas was heading her way. Its blunt nose rose from the water, and the white lower part of its mouth bobbed above the surface. She lifted a hand. Was she waving? She didn't even know. She dropped her hand. What was proper shifter etiquette?

Probably not kayaking into their pod was a better choice. Even if they were shifters, at twenty-plus feet in length, they could easily capsize her, even by accident. Four orcas. Five years ago. Hell, two years ago, she'd be freaking out right now.

She banked to the right, toward another of the black-and-white whales, but angled closer to the shore and around it. The orcas traced a lazy path back to the center of the cove.

There was a large rock just past them. Beyond that, the waves kicked up. Even at this time of the morning, there were a few white crests. She took the path.

Out in the wider, rougher waters of the Hood Canal, Shelby settled into a heavier stroke pattern, heading straight for the rising sun.

She would like to say she didn't notice Keane had rounded the orcas as well and made it out to the Hood but didn't follow. But she was done lying to herself. She'd paid attention and was proud of the fact that she'd outmaneuvered him. He could suck it.

"Laters," she whispered under her breath before picking up steam and disappearing around the bend to the right.

"How many?" Nick asked Shelby from his seat across his and Willa's octagonal dining room table.

"I was thinking ten." She worried her bottom lip between her teeth. Ten would be expensive. She wasn't sure she could afford ten.

"You're doubling your business?" Willa asked from the kitchen, where she was pouring tea into mugs for the two of them.

Shelby had called Nick after loading up her kayak. He was available to meet, and she'd driven straight over to talk shop.

"More than that," she explained to Willa. "The yurts will each have two bedrooms plus a fold-out couch. It won't be just for single couples or couples with small kids. I can rent them out to groups wanting to hike, fish, hunt, or experience the great outdoors."

"It's a great idea. Lots of guys come out here to fish in groups of three or four," Nick said.

"Either one sleeps on the couch, or they can get two yurts back-to-back." Shelby nodded. "Still cheaper than getting three single cabins. And they'll have space for their equipment and their own fire pits instead of sharing the ones at Siren's Song Cabins."

"And girlfriends visiting the local wineries," Willa said. "Like Mt. Olympus Winery."

She'd already thought of sharing advertising with the winery. Nell knew the owner. Fran had recently partnered with her on wine-and-dinner pairings and seemed open to business ideas.

"Are you planning on spacing them out?" Nick asked. "They might need separate septics if so. Otherwise, you can share septics for some of them."

"I need to see the land first, but I was thinking of grouping them in sets of two for sharing utilities and to reduce the cost of running water and electricity," Shelby answered.

"Smart." Nick nodded.

"Besides, that way, I could always expand into the property later down the road."

Or a place only for her farther off on the property. She liked her cozy cabin, but she could use the second bedroom. One room was tight.

"And you want to do kits, right?"

"Yes, because of the canvas and setup. I think they'll make more sense." The price was reasonable. Shelby was only worried about the rest of it. "I'll need to finish the inside. That's the tricky part. I need to add a kitchen and bathroom. They can share a wall. Then add a couple of partitions for the bedrooms. That still leaves a large section for a living room across from the kitchen."

"Okay." Nick nodded, making marks in a spiral-topped notebook that always seemed to travel with him wherever he went.

"That's why I'm here," Shelby finally spat out. She was nervous he would say no.

Nick blinked up from his notebook. "Oh. I'm not sure I can do all of that. Ten yurts is a big commitment. I'm not staffed for it. It would take a crew."

He glanced uncomfortably at Willa.

"No." Shelby shook her head. "I wasn't expecting you to build it all. I'd like to ask for your help with the design. I have started some rough blueprints, but I need advice on what would cut costs. I've talked to some crews and think I have one that will do good work, but I need someone who knows what they're doing to keep an eye on them."

"Like a contractor?"

"More like a foreman, if you can spare some time here and there. I can handle the calls and organize the crews, but I want someone to make sure they're not cutting corners. I'm pretty familiar with general electricity and construction, but not what choices may lead to additional cost and risk."

Nick drifted off in thought. He jotted down a few more notes. When he finally spoke again, he still wasn't focusing on her; he was fully absorbed in the planning stage. "If I bring a few things on-site, I could set up a canvas shelter and work there for part of my day, taking breaks to help out or check in on things while they're developing."

"I'm adding a gazebo in the center for larger groups to use. If I have them put that up first, you can use that space. It'll be covered."

"Can I build it?" Nick's eyes lit up. He leaned forward in his chair. "I could add some gingerbread without it being too Victorian."

"Dude, if you want to build me a gazebo, I'm not saying no." Shelby laughed. "Get me a quote for your time and the construction, and you've got a deal."

The woodworker tended to underbid jobs. She wasn't too worried about being able to afford it, but she still wanted it to be fair.

"Hang on, and let me grab the plans." She shot from the table to get them from her car. She'd been traveling around with them in case she wanted to make tweaks.

Spreading them out on the wood table, she pointed out her thoughts on the gazebo and the walls for the yurts. The dimensions were noted on the sketch.

"I'm putting up privacy walls here and here," she went on, showing him a rough site plan. She needed to get on the land and adjust drawings based on the terrain and old-growth trees. "Each yurt will have its own outdoor deck and grill with dedicated fire pits. The walls will actually be gates. If the renters know each other, they can open them up and share one of the fire pits."

"Did you take drafting classes?" Nick's finger lingered over the blueprint of the yurt.

"I took a class in college. Added it to my business degree. It was helpful to investigate structural integrity, but for this, I used the blueprint for my original cabins. I just made adjustments to them."

"I'll say. It's completely different, structurally speaking, but the required elements of the blueprint are still there. Nicely done."

Shelby preened inside. She had scraped to pay for the architect to draw up her original four cabins. They'd been used again when she added the last six, but yurts were a whole different ball game. Luckily, the kit plans gave her a starting point. She painstakingly attempted to add electric wiring and plumbing.

It wasn't easy, but when was anything worthwhile?

"You'll do it?" she asked. She wasn't sure she could afford it without some knowledgeable help.

"Yeah. Sounds like fun."

Shelby stood and shook his hand to make it official.

One step down, several more to go.

CHAPTER 7

"That's plenty." Keane grinned up at his mom, who hovered over him.

"Are you sure?" Kalani frowned, then added one more large fried butter clam to the already heaping baguette on his plate. If he knew his mom, she'd picked the bread up that morning from the Wild Café. It looked like Nell's handiwork, perfectly risen, with a blistered, crunchy surface. The shades of golden drifted to brown over the edges, reminding him of the sun-drenched beaches of Morocco. "But it's your favorite."

"It is, but this is a huge dinner, and it's only the beginning of the season. I'm sure I'll get more. Besides"—he winked at his mom—"I live here again, remember? I'll get them every time they open harvest days."

"Really?" Her mink-brown eyes went glassy with moisture.

"I told you I was moving back, Mom." He stood and wrapped his arms around the short, slender woman. "And I'm unpacking over at Willa's old place."

"I know, but it still seems too good to be true." She sniffed and wiped at the tear forming in her eye. "You've been running all over the world for the past fifteen years. I can hardly believe you're settling down."

"Well, you better believe it." He squeezed her gently before letting her go and sitting back down to the beautiful po' boy in front of him. He would have settled down earlier if it had been up to him. But he'd had work to do.

"And you'll be here for the festival!" She clapped her hands together. "That's always the best day of the summer, possibly of the whole year."

"Better than your birthday?" He teased her. Birthdays were big in their house. Not because of the presents, but because they always did something together and the person they were celebrating got to pick the activities. It was always special, except on those few years when all he'd wanted to do was spend time with Shelby and the gang.

His parents eventually gave in and let Shelby join them on birthday celebrations. She'd been part of the family.

"Hmm." His mom tapped a finger on her nose. "No. Not better than my birthday."

"Speaking of birthdays." His dad came into the dining room, carrying a beer. He raised his eyebrows.

"What?" Keane frowned.

"Well, mine is coming up." Kalani sat in her seat and picked at her smaller half sandwich. "I was thinking we could drive up to the strait and spend the day on the beach, like we did back in the day. New York is fun, but you haven't been home for it in years."

It was Keane's most common choice of a birthday, wanting to spend the day surfing. His mom and dad always had about as much fun as he did. They brought food for a picnic on the beach, and it was some of his fondest memories, especially after Shelby joined them.

"I'd love to join you guys." Keane took a large bite of his sandwich, the crunch of the cornmeal accentuating the tender clams inside. It was perfectly seasoned, and his eyes rolled up. "This is delicious."

"Don't talk with your mouth full," his mom scolded him, but her eyes sparkled with pleasure. "I was thinking we could invite Shelby."

Keane paused mid-chew. He swallowed the large bite too early and coughed. "Shelby?"

"You've barely hung out, that I can tell." She toyed with her napkin.

"Mom." He set his sandwich down. "It's going to take more time than that."

"Especially when you're not hanging out at the café or with your friends."

"She's still pissed, and rightly so. I've got to be patient."

Kalani blew out a heavy breath. "Did you apologize?"

Keane frowned. "I didn't quite get the chance."

She swatted him with her brightly colored napkin. "Good grief, boy. What are you doing? You've got to take care of that. Let her know you came back for her. That you left for her."

"I don't think it'll be that easy, but you're right. We need to talk."

"Sooner rather than later," his dad added.

Keane frowned. He'd made a point to tell his parents he didn't want to hear about any relationship she had or didn't have. And not to push updates on her about him unless she asked. They would catch up on life when the time was right. Was his dad saying that to indicate he was running out of time?

"I was giving her a little space to get used to the idea of me being back. I'll talk to her soon."

"How's the unpacking going?" His dad thankfully switched subjects.

"Nothing to unpack. I didn't bring much."

"But what about your things from New York?" his mom asked.

"They don't mean much to me. I might have Gina sell them."

"Even that carved table from Morocco?" She placed a hand over her heart. "And that box from Romania? I absolutely adore that box."

She loved special objects as much as he did. "No. I'm keeping those."

"Oh, good." She went back to her sandwich.

"You should see what they have at Gil's," his dad suggested.

Keane nodded. "I should be able to get most of my kitchen stuff there, but I need some furniture."

"You're still living on that couch we gave you from the basement?" Kalani tsked. "Elias! He doesn't even have a bed. You can take the one from our extra room, your old room."

"No, it's fine, Mom. I'll get some furniture. I just have to find it."

"There's that antique place in Liberty," his dad suggested. "Or you could ask Nick Ryan to build you something. He built his and Willa's new place. You can use my car if you need wheels. You basically bought it anyway."

"I did not," he argued. "Your retirement bought that. I just upgraded it."

"A lot." He grinned at his son. He loved his Land Rover.

He'd need a truck for a bed, but he could use the SUV for smaller things. "Thanks, I appreciate it."

"Anytime, son." Elias clapped him on the shoulder. "I can make some calls. One of my old buddies has a truck."

"I'm good, Dad. Promise. I'll figure it out."

He had thought he could ask Duke, but at the moment, his friend didn't want much to do with him either.

"The Moroccan side table?" Gina asked.

"Yes."

"That's it?" He could hear her frown through the phone.

"Oh, and the espresso machine. I can't leave Nessie behind."

"Perish the thought."

"Did you get furniture, then?" He could hear the judgment in her voice over the line.

"Not yet."

"I'll have movers come and pack up your stuff, Keane. They'll have it out to you in no time. You can sell them later, when you've found something else."

"No." He said it with finality. He didn't want reminders of his half-life out in New York to tarnish the one he was rebuilding. He had been miserable and depressed out there. Traveling with work and painting was different, but the studio apartment? It was a reminder that he was missing out on another life. The life he was meant to live here, in Orca Cove. "I'm going into town now, to pick up some stuff."

"Promise?"

He rolled his eyes, turning the corner onto Main Street. Gil's Market and Marina came into view with the rest of the cove. "I promise."

"Do you need any clothes?" "Pack up some of the casual stuff, if you don't mind. And the stoneware from Budapest. Oh, and that box from Romania."

When he left New York, he'd only brought a backpack with him. It held an overnight kit and a change of clothes. Since then, he'd had to buy a few odds and ends. But he'd been able to make do with that and the leather couch from his parents.

After his success in Europe, it had been easy for his agent to schedule another world tour of gallery events in key locations throughout the year. Apart from that, he'd spent the last year and a half steadily painting to fill those events. They'd had to turn some down, which only increased interest. He had finally reached a point where he could take a step back.

The moment he realized that, without any commitments looming, he'd simply walked out of the studio. The backpack from his last trip had been sitting near the door.

"I'll send a few odds and ends."

"Gina."

"Just your favorites from your travels."

"Okay. I appreciate it."

"You got it."

Disconnecting, he crossed Water Street and headed into Gil's.

The small grocery store wasn't exactly as he remembered it. The large octopus mural sprawling across one wall was the same. The brush strokes were now familiar to him, with their hues of California poppies and henna.

Local crafts donned tables scattered between the produce section and canned goods. Freezer doors lined the other wall. They'd built onto the back of the market to accommodate the marina Hugo Gil had purchased several years ago. His parents had told him about it. The fresh-fish stand was located back there to receive the early morning deliveries from the local fisherfolk.

The registers stood on the other side, and a large glass door between them opened to the marina itself. Keane could see the docks with a few sailboats bobbing alongside their slips. It was a clean, interesting place, full of fresh foods and odds and ends, and its location on the cove made it that much more appealing.

"Keane."

The voice from behind him shook him from his thoughts. He turned to find the young shopkeeper carrying a laptop.

"Good afternoon, Emiliano." He reached out to shake the younger man's hand.

"It's good to see you in the shop. Anything we can help you with today?"

"I need to furnish the apartment. I didn't bring a lot with me."

"What are you looking for?"

"Kitchen stuff mostly." Keane's eyes scanned the cast-iron pans. "I need some furniture, but I'm guessing you don't stock much of that."

"I have a few side tables." Emiliano pointed to a craft one set up nearby. "But nothing large. If you want something custom, you could talk to Nick, Willa's fiancé, for that. He could build you something beautiful with live-edge wood or wood inlays."

"That would take some time, I imagine."

"He might have something ready. He's been selling in the area." Emiliano leaned against a stack of canned goods. "You can order some stuff through me, but it'd be fairly generic."

"I don't need fancy stuff, but I do like things to have meaning."

"There's a resale store in Liberty, Days Gone By. You'll find some cool stuff there."

Exactly the same suggestions his dad had made. Small towns didn't have many options. But how to get things home from Liberty?

"You don't rent out trucks, do you?"

Emiliano frowned. "Not generally, but I'm sure I could ask around. One of our delivery guys could probably bring it back for you, too."

"That would be great."

"If you don't mind me asking, why don't you ask Duke? He has a truck."

Keane's eyes fell to his Vans, and he chose his words carefully. "It's taking a little longer to adjust back to life in the cove."

Emiliano nodded without judgment. "I'll make a few calls."

"Thank you."

It was an understatement. He'd known it would be difficult to adjust to the changes back home, but he hadn't realized it would be this hard.

Determined, Keane wandered through the kitchen items with a cart. He would make this work. He added a cast-iron Dutch oven and skillet, then some heavy saucepans. A few towels and oven mitts went in as well as a colander and an assortment of wooden spoons. He made a mental note to tell Gina he needed his knife set and the wok from Chang Mai, but she'd probably send them anyway.

An electric teakettle. He needed one of those. Searching the aisle behind him, he saw Randall and Mick, two guys he knew from high school. They were grinning at him. He hadn't always gotten along with the two jocks, but that was a long time ago.

"Hey." He lifted his head in greeting. "How's it going?"

"Not bad," Randall, the taller of the two, said. "Haven't seen you in forever."

"Yeah, I've been on the East Coast."

"You've been painting, right?" Mick's lips curled.

He nodded. Maybe they hadn't changed. He could still see them in their football gear. He blinked at the replacement of their adult forms, clad in weekend wear of jeans and T-shirts. Their trim forms had regressed into softened versions of themselves. He tried not to take pleasure in the devolvement. "Yep."

"I remember your painting of that elk in Mr. Landes' class. It was awful." Mick guffawed. "Do you remember it? Its mouth was all swollen-looking."

Randall snorted. "Yeah."

"I had a lot of room to grow," Keane said. He'd had his share of critics. This was nothing new.

"I'd say." Mick punched Randall in the ribs.

"What do you paint now?" Randall asked, ready to pounce on whatever Keane had to say.

"Abstract landscape mostly. I had a lot of inspiration from living in the Pacific Northwest."

"I'd say." Mick leaned in. "But what about nude models? I bet women would strip down to be drawn."

Keane had painted a lot of different styles, including nudes, when he was learning, but it wasn't his genre. "I pretty much stick to landscape. But now that I'm back in Orca Cove, I can focus on PNW artwork."

"Back in Orca Cove?" Randall frowned. "You mean you moved back?""Yeah. I'm staying in Willa's old place."

"Hey." Mick swatted his taller friend. "Do you think he's going to try to get back with Shelby Greene?"

Keane's stomach lurched. He didn't want Shelby's name on either of their lips.

Randall's mouth twisted down.

"No way. There's no way Keane is dumb enough to think he can skip town on someone like Shelby, an A-lister, with those amazing"—he grinned in a leering way—"eyes, and then waltz back in years later to find she hasn't moved on to something better."

They were talking about him, about his biggest fear, like he wasn't even standing there.

"I could never understand why she was with him in the first place. He didn't do anything but mooch off her." Mick moved to stand at Randall's side so the pair could run their eyes over him in judgment.

"Me neither. No matter." Randall smirked. "We dried her eyes for her."

"Yeah, she's moved on."

"And she'll never forgive him."

"Gents." Duke's head appeared between the two post-jocks, and he brought his hands down hard on their shoulders. "I see you're welcoming back one of our own."

"Ye-ah," Mick stuttered. "It's good to see you, Keane."

"We were just on our way." Randall gave him a sneer.

"Some people never change." Keane watched them disappear out the side door.

Duke humphed. "They certainly didn't. It's unfortunate."

"They respect you now."

"I stayed." Duke crossed his arms. "Earned the town's trust. Took me long enough. I had a lot of growing up to do."

"We all did."

Duke nodded, finally shifting his attention from the door and onto Keane. "They're just being jerks."

"I know."

"I'm not saying Shelby will take you back. That's up to her. And it'll be a long, grueling road if you decide to stick with it. But I wouldn't listen to two idiot jocks."

"I won't. Thanks."

Duke inclined his head. "I gotta get back out there. I'm figuring out a sailing route for tomorrow."

"Anything I can help out with?" Keane asked gently.

"No." His friend took a couple of steps backward. "I'll see ya around."

It wasn't exactly friendly, but he wasn't as cold as the last time he'd seen him.

Duke walked out onto the marina, where a large, built black man with a huge scar running down his face was leaning against the railing. They fell into step with each other and went down onto the docks.

It could be worse.

CHAPTER 8

erc test, wetlands, building permits, investment planning. Shelby tucked one of her fuzzy sock-covered feet underneath her. She was curled up on her couch, making a list, with a glass of red wine. Lists were one of her favorite things to do. That and making money.

She eyed the signed contract on her coffee table. She had thirty days. That was if she didn't move the date up, as Charles suggested. Shelby tapped the end of her pencil against the paper. She didn't want to rush things, but he had a point. If she didn't start soon, she might not have the canvas stretched on the yurts before the winter rains.

Being open for the holidays sounded like a dream, but it might be possible if she moved fast. And it would be a quicker return on her investment. She could be bringing in more revenue by the beginning of the year. Seattle businesspeople loved to find a cozy place outside the city to hole up during winter. And then Valentine's Day specials. Her mind was whirring with the possibilities.

The building permit alone could take a couple of months to get signed off, particularly with the yurts. They weren't new to the county, but they might have more questions because they were going to be used as short-term rentals.

Shelby already had some, so she knew what type of occupancy permits and neighborhood notifications would be involved. It wasn't too taxing, but it would take a while to get everything done by the holidays. That was if she could get it going by then.

Charles had mentioned he could help with a few of the permits. He had friends who could speed things up. Once again, she felt the urge to talk to Gary. Her heart sank. She missed him. It wasn't like her parents had ever been any help with business decisions. They were always away on some sort of trip.

She'd had to grow up fast. And so, she had.

Gary had helped. Keane was always supportive and reassuring, but Gary had a keen business sense. Both of them had grown in that regard, until he left them, just as Keane had. Bitter, Shelby walked back to the kitchen. She needed a few bites of sugar in her favorite form: ice cream.

Standing at the island, she scraped shallow tunnels in the fudge-ripple-brownie ice cream as though the answer to her problems would appear in the ridges and valleys of the multiple shades of brown.

It would be so easy to let Charles help.

But it wasn't her style. She and she alone was the reason she had everything surrounding her. The land under her feet, the walls around her, the cabins scattered around the property. The apartment on the beach. Her stomach lurched.

For once, would it be so bad to let someone help? He knew what he was doing. Hell, he had enough money. It wasn't even like it was a big favor to him. She chewed on her lip.

It was nice having the attention of a handsome man again. She had suitors, sure, but no one who stimulated her mentally. There was something different about Charles that she couldn't put her finger on.

Her last boyfriend had been the town's bank manager. He was smart, but he wasn't very interesting. The one before had a charter operation on the Hood, but he was too interested in locking her down in a relationship. She wasn't afraid of commitment, but he'd wanted to move too fast. No man was going to tell her what to do with her business or in her personal life. Keane had never tried to control her. He'd offered his opinion when she asked for it, but otherwise, had just supported her. He'd been thoughtful and fun. And pulled her out of her obsessive focus when she needed it.

When would she stop comparing men to him?

Popping the lid back on the ice cream, she returned it to her freezer and flipped her lights off. She'd finish the list in the morning. That was assuming there were no more issues with the cabins. The pipes had busted twice in the last few months. No, it would be better to be proactive. She would do a thorough inspection of them before she got started on the yurts.

Shelby opened her closet door to get her robe from its hook on the back and found her tool belt on top of the shelf. She'd forgotten to take it off in the shed. She'd need it tomorrow if she was going to do any maintenance. Anything she could take care of herself saved her money.

As she grabbed the belt, the nylon webbing latch snagged on something behind a stack of boxes and a stuffed orca fell to her feet.

She knelt to pick up the black-and-white toy. It was from many summers ago. Keane had won it for her at a festival downtown. She could hear the band playing in the background, people chattering, the bells from the games, and his laughter carrying over it all. Her chest squeezed tight at the memory. It should have gone out with the trash years ago. It must have escaped her mind back there.

Her fingers sunk into the soft fluff.

It held a lot of memories. Memories from a sweeter time. She'd been full of love and hope back then. Not today. She squished the plushie back behind the boxes and shut the door. She could figure out what to do with it another time.

Shelby's fingers scraped against the wires in the electric box in cabin four. It was one of the oldest. The plastic around the wire was worn away, and it appeared there was mouse damage, but they hadn't had any mice in the cabins in years. All the holes were well sealed and maintained. Shelby inspected the area under the box for droppings and found a small scattering of evidence. It was summer. Mice weren't searching for warm places to hide. Still, they didn't need much space to get in.

Pulling out her notebook, she made a note to check the cabin foundations. She'd had some reports of the lights shorting out from the renters who'd checked out that morning. At least, this was a repair she could handle. What was unfortunate was that new renters were expected later that afternoon. She'd have to work fast to get it done before they arrived.

Sighing, she moved on to the next cabin. The pipes under the sink in number six appeared fine. No wear on the P trap. The bathroom ones were okay, too. The wear on the two that had busted previously was isolated to the sink. Odd. She'd have thought the bathroom sinks got more use. Replacing the ones in the other cabins with PVC would be a good investment. The last two repairs required new flooring and a cabinet. It would take her a couple of weeks to retrofit them all, plus the foundation and electrical check. She closed the box. Mouse traps were in the shed.

One would go in each cabin, under the sink and behind the couch near the wall.

Just when she wanted to get started on the new development.

Reeling her brain back in, she dialed Charles' number.

"Well, this is a nice surprise." His voice sounded like velvet.

Shelby instinctively smiled at the calming sound. "Good morning. I've been busy making plans. I'd like to stop by the property today if that's okay."

"Of course. I can meet you over there."

"I'm sure you're busy. You don't have to take time out of your day," she argued, not wanting to put him out. Besides, she planned to poke around on the property and let her creative mind wander.

"Are you kidding me? I could use a break, and besides, it's not every day I get to visit with a beautiful woman."

She couldn't argue with that. It sounded good to see him again, but she didn't need the distraction.

"I'd like to wander a bit, if that's alright. I want to measure some things and do some planning. Don't feel like you have to stay the entire time."

"Ah, you want to disappear into the process, and I'll kill the mood."

"Not at all." She chuckled. "But you're right. I do tend to zone out. I don't want to be rude."

"Don't think twice about it. I'll meet you out there and then get out of your hair. And if you zone out, I won't take it personally."

Shelby blinked at her phone. This guy couldn't be more understanding. It was like they were cut from the same cloth.

"Besides," he went on. "I'm waiting on a few phone calls. I might be a little distracted myself. But I don't want to miss out on seeing you."

That didn't make her feel terrible.

"Sounds good. I need to do a few things. Want to meet right after lunch?"

"Perfect. See you then."

She clicked off and headed to the shed.

Twenty minutes later, she banged through the registration office doors at Siren's Song Cabins.

"What's wrong?" Cleo blinked up from her computer.

"The wires are chewed up."

"In the cabins?" The receptionist frowned. "That would explain the flickering lights. I told them it wasn't haunted."

"I wish." Shelby dropped into a chair in the lobby. "Haunted cabins I can sell. Mouse infestation, not so much. Unless we advertise to the hippies who want to share their space with the wildlife."

She snorted at her own joke.

"Willa might know some people."

"And that's why I like you." Shelby raised a finger. "You think like me. But no, it would just be more work to fix later down the road. Better to get it taken care of now. And it's not only cabin four; it's the spare wire in the shed. I should have put it in a storage container."

"Need me to order a spool?"

"Nah, I'll run by the electrical store and get a few yards. It'll be more expensive, but I need to get it done before the afternoon reservation gets here."

"Are you sure you won't let me call Phil?" Cleo pointed at the phone. "I bet I could talk him into coming this morning."

It was true. The retired construction worker was always happy to come in, but she didn't need anything digging into her investment money. Especially if she was going to do some repairs to the cabins. The list was already piling up.

"I'll get it. But thanks." She stood from her chair. There was no time like the present. The wires weren't going to repair themselves.

The figure on her spreadsheet kept getting larger. Shelby had just gotten off the phone with the yurt manufacturer for a quote on ten yurts to her specifications. The saleswoman would be working on the engineering design for her building permits.

She knew her estimates for the shared septics, electrical, and plumbing were a little conservative, but she had to plan in extra for when the builders ran into trouble. She added in the cost of the gazebo, decks, and privacy walls, plus some landscaping. Depending on how much land clearing needed to be done and how level the land was, she would need to increase the development costs. Hell, they'd already increased from a year ago when she started working on her financials for this project.

She clicked her laptop shut. Ten would be hard to manage. But it would cost more if she added them on later. The additional building permits, the costs of lumber, and the material could increase.

She'd even started expanding her website. Although her site could use a redesign. Emiliano might be willing to help her jazz it up. Stretching, she stood.

"Heading out to look at the land for the yurts," Shelby called out to Cleo.

"You didn't get lunch."

"I'll snag a sandwich at the market before I head out of town."

"Okay, see you later," Cleo called as she swept from the room, already focused on her next goal.

She'd been back and forth in town all morning. The wiring in cabin four was fixed. Luckily, the damaged wire had an outlet nearby, and she'd been able to tie it to the old one and pull it through. Easy enough. But the outlet was also worn, and she ran back to get a box of new ones to have on hand before replacing this one.

"Morning, Shelby," Emiliano said when she entered the market.

"It's afternoon already," Shelby teased as she hopped over to the deli section and rummaged through it for a peanut-butter-and-jelly sandwich. Nuts were her favorite food, after ice cream. Finding one, she stood and cocked her head. "Did you have a late morning?"

"He got in late. Living with Nell is making him lazy." Hugo, walking out from the storeroom in the back, teased his son.

Emiliano blushed.

"Ew." She didn't need to hear about Nell's love life. Then she repeated what Charles had said a few days ago. "'The early bird gets the worm.'"

"See? Shelby understands. She's a businesswoman." Hugo smiled broadly.

"Damn straight." She fished out a few bills from her wallet and paid the clerk at the register. Then, before leaving, she said to Emiliano, "If you've got time, would you help me with my website? I'm working on the expansion and would like a refresh. Something clean and crisp but still highlighting the area."

"I'd be happy to look at it," Emiliano said. "So, is it official? You're doing it?"

"Of course. When I set my mind on something, it's hard to derail me."

"Congrats. Give me a call sometime, and we can meet up to see what you're hoping for."

"That would be great, thanks!"

Waving, she exited through the side door and drove out of town, doubling back past the cabins. The new property was farther out. Close to her apartments, but too far to walk to town as she sometimes did after a late night at the café and a couple of glasses of wine. Maggie's offer of a couch might come in handy in the future.

The land was still on the Hood Canal, but farther away from the cove too. She felt the aching tingle of the water calling to her as she pushed past the outskirts of town.

CHAPTER 9

"*You overnighted my things?*" Keane texted Gina. He'd been cleaning the cabinets for the new kitchen supplies he'd picked up the day before when the doorbell rang and five large boxes were unloaded into his second bedroom.

"*You needed things,*" Gina typed back.

"*Yeah, but this is extravagant.*"

"*Like you can't afford it. Besides, you left with one change of clothes. Seriously, enjoy some of your money.*"

"*I don't need money to enjoy life.*" All he needed was Shelby, his friends, his surfboard, an easel, and some paints.

"*Then, I need a raise.*"

Keane snorted. He already paid his assistant a healthy wage, and she knew it. *"How about I let you work from home from now on?"*

Three dots floated across his screen. *"LOL. I get so much more done now that I don't have you in my ear all day."*

It was the other way around. She'd get frustrated at how quiet the studio was. He wasn't one to chit-chat.

"Haha," he texted, then sat on the floor to slice open the first box. It was Nessie. Gina had wrapped her in bubble wrap and included two large bags of his favorite espresso beans from the shop near his old apartment. *"And thanks for the beans."*

"YW."

He carried the gleaming stainless-steel appliance into the kitchen, plugged it in, and was relieved to see the light flicker on. He filled the water reservoir, then found the burr grinder. Before long, he had a perfectly pulled double espresso.

Taking it out on the back deck, he stood overlooking the cove. Shades of dove gray, cyan, and turquoise brushed each other in the space between the sky and water. The gray shifted to charcoal off to the west. A storm was brewing near the mountain. The bitter taste of the espresso excited his senses, and his fingers itched for his paints.

He glanced back inside. Had she sent them? Of course, she would have. It was the one thing she'd threatened when he called to say he was waiting for a flight to SeaTac. *"Don't you dare stop painting. This is my livelihood, too."*

It was unneeded. He wasn't going to lose everything he'd built up. It had taken too long, and he'd lost too much to make it happen.

Hurrying back inside, Keane set the tiny clay cup he'd picked up at Gil's on a large unopened box and cut into another one. It was full of clothes. His favorite Blundstone boots were at the bottom, and a mustard-colored beanie he loved was tucked inside. Taking them out, he pulled the hat over his head and pushed the clothes box aside.

The next held treasures from his trips. The Moroccan table was packed upside down on a blanket from Peru. Wrapped in the center was a set of wine glasses from Italy, the carved Romanian box, and a Turkish rug wrapped around it all. He'd forgotten he bought it.

It would take a few days for the folds to relax, but with less than twenty-four hours in the box, it would be okay. He pulled it out and unrolled it immediately in the living room, setting the small table in the center, top down, for weight.

Trying the largest box next, he found what he was searching for. His easel was carefully wrapped and packed in the center. A few larger canvases were snug on each side, plus a roll of canvas he'd have to stretch himself. At the bottom was a selection of paints and a beautiful wooden box full of his brushes and knives. The box was new. His brushes had never had a real home, being scattered around the studio after being c leaned.

He'd have to thank Gina for the gift.

One of the smaller boxes held more paints and his plastic pallets. There were fancier versions, but he liked how easy these were to clean. After stripping his flannel off, he set his easel up in his new studio.

He was right; the light was perfect. Washington's Olympic Peninsula would never be considered a sunny place, but the filtered light worked for what he needed. He wasn't painting the sun-bleached structures in Santorini. He was painting home.

Scrolling through his phone, he set a playlist of Bon Iver, Noah Kahan, Forest Blakk, and the ever-inspiring Hozier.

It didn't take long to unbox the paint colors he needed, and soon, images were taking shape on the canvas.

Dark, mysterious forest green struck through with golden shoots of sunlight. Varying shades of chestnut-brown tree trunks. With swirls of colors spread throughout. The forest floor shifted to lighter shades. Peach, blended with ivory, highlighted where the rays of light lit the layers of fallen pine needles. The barest shade of auburn touched here and there.

He didn't paint the sky. Instead, he took the green to the top. There would be no gray in this one. The rich colors of the deep woods overtook the canvas.

Progressively, a picture took shape. Big blocks of color slowly formed into something resembling a copse of trees. Dropping his brush, Keane started in with smaller tools to add details. Paint blended and built, layer upon layer.

He left to warm a bowl of soup he'd picked up from the market. As he stood in front of the painting, the image became clear. It was the Olympic National Park, sure, but it was also Shelby. Her signature hues reflected at him. It might not be noticeable to many, but to him, it was raw and exposed.

He'd painted home, alright. Just not the home he was expecting.

Keane answered his phone. "Hello?"

"Hey, you still need a ride?" Emiliano's voice resounded through his phone.

He'd left his number with the clerk to be notified when the convection toaster oven he'd ordered arrived.

"Yeah." He stared longingly at the canvas in front of him. He'd been adding layers to the paint but could use a bed.

"Tommy has an old truck. It's not that big, but he said Heath could use it for a pickup in Liberty. If now's a good time, he can swing by and pick you up."

"Okay, thanks. Now's good."

The rumble of an old truck announced Heath's arrival a few minutes later. Having cleaned his brushes, he shoved his feet into his Blundstones.

Locking the door behind him, he hurried to the white, rusted pickup.

"Hey." The young man behind the driver's seat grinned crookedly at him.

He nodded in reply, sliding into the passenger seat next to him. "Hi. I'm Keane."

"Oh, I heard," he said, checking the rearview mirror as he reversed and headed out. "I'm Heath."

Keane bit his tongue. He wasn't sure if he meant through Shelby or about the scene with Mick and Randall. He took in the kid. T-shirt, ripped jeans, and Vans. Fifteen years ago, this could have been him.

"You like driving for Gil's?" he said instead.

"Yeah." Joy shone on the younger man's face. "Can you believe it? Getting paid to drive. It's awesome."

"You like driving?""For sure. I have a BMW 328i. It has a 6-cylinder under the hood. It's light, and it drifts like a dream."

The wistful expression on Heath's face made Keane remember his early days painting. He'd been nervous about his enjoyment of art. It was a strange thing to be good at, spreading color over a surface. But much like driving, what we loved somehow found a way into our lives. "How long have you worked for Gil's?"

"I drive for them, but I work for myself," Heath proclaimed proudly. "It was scary at first, but Shelby helped me figure out the taxes thing. She said it was better to work independently than to work for the man. I don't have any issues with Hugo or Emiliano, though."

Keane bit back his smile. "I hope you're investing."

"Oh, Shelby made me." Heath's face tilted down. "It kinda sucks to have ten percent of my pay deducted, but she tells me that future Heath will thank me someday. She's probably right."

"I'd say so. She's pretty good with money."

"Yeah. If this delivery service thing keeps up a few years, I'll be able to compete nationally. Driving, I mean."

"That's cool." Dreams were important. He'd had several. Only a few had materialized, but Keane was holding out on one more.

"So, what are you looking for?" Heath pulled into Days Gone By. The sign was retro, which fit the charming, dated place.

"A bed. Somewhere to put my clothes. Honestly, I'm not sure."

Heath nodded. "You okay if I leave you to it? I have a few places to pick up from."

"No problem."

"I can come back in an hour. Does that work?"

"Yep. Thanks for the ride." Keane shut his door and headed in.

The store was cool, but nothing was sorted. Piles of finds were hidden in each corner. He'd have to hunt long and hard to find what he needed.

A tall wooden wardrobe caught his eye. He walked toward it and opened the door to inspect the workmanship and artwork. It was much wider than he needed. It would take up most of one side of the wall. But it was beautiful. Carved figures danced across the front. They appeared to be Norwegian. If he had to guess, he'd say they might have been Norse Gods. He'd have to research Norse mythology artwork.

"We just got that piece in." An older gentleman appeared on his right. "You have room for it?"

"I have empty space. It's not large, but I don't plan on a lot of furniture. So, I think I could make it work." He loved it enough to try. "But do you have any beds? I need one of those, too."

"Sure, but nothing as nice as this." The man led him to a stack of metal bed frames. "We carry some new mattresses in the back if you find something you want."

Keane knelt to inspect the frames. The simplest one was black wrought iron and sat only three inches from the floor. High enough to get a dust mop under. "I think I'll take this one. Is it queen-size?"

"Yep."

"I need a couple of sitting chairs, too. And some bars stools." He could use the kitchen island as a table, but chairs would be nice for looking out onto the cove. Especially when the weather changed and it was too cold to sit outside.

"Yeah, there are a few over on that wall." He pointed to a row not far away.

One set of four was orange with a fringe. The second was simple and black. He liked the look of them, but the third set was only two chairs. They were wing-backed and covered in a rich, warm brown that reminded him of Shelby's hair. He ran a hand over the leather. A streak of paint he'd missed on the back of his hand matched the color perfectly.

"They're teak and leather. You'd never have to buy another set."

"I'll take them." Keane ached to see Shelby sitting against the natural material. He glanced back at the wardrobe, considering. "I'm not sure I can take both today. I only have a small pickup truck."

"I can hold the rest with some money down. What do you want to take right now?"

"The bed and the chairs," he said decisively. "I don't have that many clothes. I can get that another day."

Five minutes later, Keane stood in front of the store with the chairs, mattress, box spring, and frame. He'd gone ahead and paid for the wardrobe to make it easier. And to ensure the guy wouldn't sell it out from underneath him in case he got another offer.

"Hey! You found something," Heath said, pulling into the space before him.

"I got a wardrobe too, but it won't fit this trip." Keane carried a chair over to the tailgate and lowered it.

The young man hopped up and hoisted the chair to him in the truck bed. "I'll be back this way tomorrow. Want to come with me to get it? I'm sure Tommy will let me use his truck again."

"Sure." Keane turned to see the kid had brought the second chair over. He reached to take it. "We might need one of the store helpers to load it. It's pretty big."

"That's okay. I'm up for it."

Within thirty minutes, they were back at Keane's place and unloading it into his living room. He'd had to move the boxes to one side of the spare room to get the couch in.

"You're putting the bed in the living room?" Heath tilted his head questioningly. Keane stood next to him to study the space. "Wicked cool."

"Yeah." Keane bound his hair up in a tie behind his head. "I think it will be."

It was unconventional, but he'd never been conventional. It was natural to do what felt right. He'd been fortunate to have parents who always encouraged him to think without the confines of a box.

The two men moved the bed into the room facing the cove. He'd found dark-green sheets at Gil's that he'd put on later. The bottom half of the bed covered the hand-knotted rug, whose faded warm greens and golds would contrast amazingly with the cool grays and blues outside. And they'd tie in the surrounding forests. The Peruvian blanket had rich shades of greens, oranges, and browns.

A few minutes later, they had the chairs against one wall near the kitchen. Keane positioned the hand-carved table between them. It was a cozy sitting space. The wardrobe would go on the other wall, in front of the TV stand. He wouldn't need one of those. He could set one up in the spare room, across from the couch, for the rare occasion he wanted to watch a movie.

"This is so awesome," Heath breathed.

He couldn't agree more.

CHAPTER 10

S helby pulled off the road onto worn tire tracks on a rough piece of land. The address marker on the land indicated she was at the right place. When she got out of her Trailblazer, she picked up the tingling sensation of water. It wasn't the same as on the cove. It felt a little more jagged but also...faster. A new feeling.

She stretched her fingers out to shake them and direct them around her. It came from farther ahead, away from the cove. Maybe there was a lake on the property. She took a few steps in that direction when a black Audi pulled in behind her.

Dropping her hands, she firmly plastered a smile on her face. Hopefully, he hadn't seen her zombie walk.

"You beat me here." Charles beamed at her. He picked his way over the ferns and weeds to join her in his clean lace-up boots. Even his hair was neatly trimmed.

Shelby tugged on the lapels of her lady blazer and resisted the urge to check her hair. "I only just arrived."

"What do you think?" He spun around, gesturing to the view of the mountain to one side and the Hood Canal to the other.

Didn't see the zombie walk, then. Phew.

From this distance, she couldn't see downtown, but the cedars and firs framed the sparkling waters of the fjord. It was a beautiful view for vacationers and close enough to get into town for groceries, the café, or for other activities around the cove within a six-minute drive. Best of all, it was close to Siren's Song Cabins.

The familiar tug was even stronger here. It was like an elastic band pulling her to the water. She'd get used to it. It was just tighter than usual.

"I think it's beautiful." She gave her hand a final shake to release some of the tension. The land hadn't been cleared, and there were still some old-growth trees scattered around. Hopefully, she'd be able to keep most of them. "The land's pretty level, right?"

She'd seen the county map of the property with the elevations listed, but sometimes, the lines could be misleading.

"It's level for the first hundred feet here." Charles waved his hands in front of them. "Then it gets a little rocky, and the land steadily rises in longitude from there. You could terrace it between properties."

If she placed her house near the back, she could have a clear view of the water and the rest of the rentals in front of her. "That's a great idea."

"It's roughly eight hundred feet from the road and one thousand feet wide." He pointed to the markers too far for her to see.

Shelby nodded, placing yurts around the property in her mind. Tiering them sounded perfect. The lots on either side were large, with homes tucked back between trees, so she wouldn't be invading their privacy. She could easily get six on the lower portion, then the remaining four on the second tier. Her place would be nestled into whatever opening of flat land and towering trees she uncovered during clearing. She still hadn't decided between another yurt for herself or a larger cabin. Whichever was cheaper, probably. It didn't matter to her as long as she had a good view of the water.

"Will it work for you?" He shifted to face her, moving in close. His eyes held excitement and anticipation.

Shelby blinked, pulling herself out of her planning. "Yes. I think it will."

"Great." He touched her arm gently. "I'm so glad we get to work together."

"Me too." She tried to let herself relax and enjoy the moment of standing with a handsome man, but there was so much to do on the property. And now that she was standing on it, the list took a higher priority.

It was happening.

The new, rougher tickle of energy pulled at her again. It came from the east...and maybe south. It was so different than she'd ever felt before.

"So, it's had wetlands?" She couldn't help herself.

"I don't believe so. But it still needs to be checked."

"If so, it doesn't look like they'd impede my building plans, but they'd need to be surveyed and recorded."

He stepped back a foot. "Shelby, I meant it when I said I'd be happy to take care of that. My guy can get here this week. Then you just have to deal with the perc test.

I imagine you'll want to draw up a site map yourself and select where they dig to test that."

She nodded. "Maybe I will take you up on that."

What would it hurt? It was okay to let someone help once in a while.

And now that she'd seen the land for herself, she was itching to draw it out.

"Done." Charles's fingers flew over his phone for a minute. "My assistant is getting it scheduled as we speak."

"I need one of those."

"A phone?" He frowned.

"An assistant." Shelby winked.

"Don't you have help at the cabins?"

"I do, but they stay busy with customer service, checking in guests, coordinating with the cleaners, and booking stays. Besides, I like to have my hands in it."

"I get that, but you can do so much more if you let others take care of the small details. You should consider it." Charles moved closer again. "With that mind of yours, you could go much bigger. You could expand to a larger development along the Hood, the Olympic Peninsula, or even Walla Walla."

She'd considered it, but anything outside Orca Cove didn't feel right. And a larger development in the cove would change the perfection of the small town. Still, it was nice to be seen. "Thanks."

No, this would be her last short-term rental property. If she did anything else in town, it would be property management for local businesses.

"Could I talk you into grabbing a bite in town?" His hand grazed her elbow.

It would be nice to hash out her plans on-site. Shelby glanced back to the east and the direction of the buzzing. She could always come back another time to investigate. With more appropriate boots.

"What's good here?" Charles asked while perusing the seasonal menu at the Wild Café.

"Pretty much everything." Shelby closed her menu. She'd stashed the sandwich she'd picked up at the market and followed him downtown. "My friend Nell owns the place. She can cook anything. My favorite is the clam chowder."

"That sounds good."

"Afternoon, Shelby." Maggie appeared at the head of their table by the window. "Getting a late lunch?"

Her tiny friend regarded Charles with a lot of interest, and she wasn't the only one. The couple near the door and two men farther back she'd gone to high school with had all been eyeballing them. With good reason. Shelby hadn't been out to lunch with anyone new in a while, especially of the male gender.

"Afternoon, Maggie. And yes, busy morning. This is my friend, Charles." Shelby indicated her business partner and possible date. "Charles, this is Maggie, the best waitress in the Pacific Northwest. Possibly the world."

"Is that so?" He tilted his head up to the young blonde woman's cherubic face. "I have high expectations, then."

"Oh, no. Don't do that." Maggie blushed and laughed. "I just do my best."

"Her best is pretty darn good," Shelby said. "She knows everyone here. And somehow remembers everything."

"I like people."

"Then, you're in a good profession," Charles said.

"I think so. I can't imagine doing anything else." Maggie propped her hands on her hips. "What can I get you two?""Clam chowder for me," Shelby said.

"I'll try the same." Charles handed Maggie the menus. "She said it's good."

Maggie took them. "Oh, it's good, alright. Everything is wonderful here."

"So I've heard," Charles said. "Can you throw in some bread with that?"

"Sure thing. Nell always serves it with some sourdough points, but I'll make sure you get extra. Besides, if I don't, this one will steal yours." Maggie inclined her head to Shelby.

"It's not my fault Nell bakes amazing bread." Shelby raised her eyebrows haughtily in mock blame.

"So." Charles focused his attention back on her as her friend whizzed into the kitchen. "What are your thoughts on the land? I know your brain is still there."

Smirking, she excitedly leaned onto her elbows, aching to dig into her plans. "I'm thinking about grouping them in twos. A lot of my renters are traveling together. Larger parties can share space, but each yurt will still have a tall wooden fence in between them to provide privacy."

"Yurt?"

"Yes, the canvas-covered cabins? They look a little like a mushroom teepee."

"Teepees? I thought they were going to be larger, two-bedroom units?"

"Oh, they are. They're more of a luxury yurt, like glamping, not like you might have seen before."

"Ah, okay." He was still confused.

"They will have a kitchen, a bathroom, and two dedicated bedrooms. The outside fabric is a heavy canvas with windows set into wooden frames. It's somewhat unique to the area and gives the illusion of camping with the amenities and comforts of a house rental."

"That makes more sense. I wasn't sure why you wanted to set up teepees on the property." Charles chuckled.

Shelby made an effort not to frown. It wasn't like she actually planned on putting tents up. There wouldn't be that much of a market for that here. Most vacationers didn't want to stay somewhere that rustic. The weather was too cool.

"Two clam chowders." Nell appeared at their table with a bowl in each hand. Maggie followed behind her, holding a platter with two plates of bread. She was smiling widely.

Apparently, the whole town wanted to see who she was with. It was another reason why she'd waited to bring him into the cove until she knew him better.

"Thanks, Nell," Shelby said. Her friend stood there expectantly. "This is my friend Charles. Charles, this is the nosey woman who owns the place. She also happens to be the cook. Fortunately for us, unfortunately for her growing head, she's the best in the area."

"Oh, good grief." Nell sat the bowls down in front of the two of them. "What's wrong with knowing you're good at what you do?"

"Nothing." Shelby picked up her spoon and held it in front of her to add weight to her words. She didn't apologize for knowing what she wanted. It was a quality she shared with the chef. They knew what they were good at.

Still, she never passed off the opportunity to tease her friends. They might think she didn't like them anymore.

"It's nice to meet you, Charles," Nell said.

"You as well." He tilted his head at the sourdough in front of him. "They're toasted nicely."

"Oh, that one got a little dark, didn't it?" Nell frowned.

"It's fine," Shelby reassured her.

Nell hesitated, but whirled off. "I'll grab another."

Maggie followed her into the kitchen.

Charles scooped a small spoon of chowder and blew on it, then tasted it. "Not bad."

"I'll say," Shelby said, already on to her third bite. She tore a chunk of bread and dunked it in. The warm soup was what she needed to ground her. That and the comforting tug of the cove nearby. The elastic band had relaxed, and the soft buzz spread over her like a hug.

Nell arrived with another plate of bread and slid it onto the table. "Enjoy!"

"Thanks," Shelby said.

Charles regarded her and selected a freshly toasted piece of sliced baguette that was a lighter golden brown. "It's a nice little town you've got here. The people all seem to like you a great deal."

"It's a small town. Everyone knows everyone. They're just trying to figure out who you are."

She was too. The businessman seemed interested enough, but she wasn't sure if she had the time for a romantic interlude, not to mention everything going on with Keane back in town. It had shaken her world. Was now the best time?

"Not sure I could handle everyone being in my business, but the people seem very nice," Charles said politely.

"There've been times it was definitely annoying." Shelby remembered the first year after Keane had left and everyone's questions about her future. "But I wouldn't have it any other way."

"Do they know about your plans?"

"Not all of them. Mostly the basics, that I'm expanding."

"It's nice to have some friends to talk to about business. I could see that."

"I wouldn't say I talk business with them. Not really. My friends, the smaller group, know what I'm working on. They don't get property management or accounting. Well, Emiliano is pretty good at marketing and accounting, but we don't have that relationship."

"Is he part of your friend group?"

"He's with Nell."

"Ah. Good to know he's not competition." Charles winked at her and took another spoonful of soup.

Maybe they were in date territory, after all.

"What about you? Who's in your friend group?"

"I have a few buddies on Bainbridge Island and some in Seattle. We get together every couple of months or so. Lately, we've all been busy, though.""I get that."

"They understand work is important."

"True. Friends are too, though. It's hard to balance it all."

"It is. I'm glad we had time for this, though." He gave her a warm smile.

"Me too."

"What do you have to get back to?"

"The site plan and perc test scheduling, definitely. But first and foremost, I have to do some minor maintenance on the cabins."

"What's going on there?" He tilted his head in concern.

"I had some electric work to do this morning, and I have some preventative plumbing work this afternoon."

"Preventative?"

"A couple of pipes under the sink busted, so I'm replacing all of them just in case."

"That'll take some time."

"It won't be too bad. I'll spread it out."

"Was there a lot of damage?"

"I had to replace one cabinet, but otherwise, it wasn't too bad."

Charles frowned. "It sounds like you need to get these yurts up and running so you can get more income in. That offer of speeding things up still stands."

Shelby nodded. "I only have a couple more things to do, but then I'll be ready to jump into it."

"Don't wait too long." He laid his hand on hers. "Just some friendly advice. I've delayed on deals before. It just adds cost. Inflation keeps rising at the wrong time. Sometimes, the best thing you can do is jump in."

Her stomach flipped. She liked to cross her t's and dot her i's before jumping into a new project, but maybe he was right. "I'll consider it. Thanks."

His phone rang, and he scrambled to get it. "This is the call I was waiting for. I have to take it. Can you give me a minute?"

"Of course," Shelby answered, but he was already halfway out the door.

Maggie stopped back by the table. "Everything good here?"

"Yes, everything is good. Thanks. He stepped out to take a call."

"He seems nice." Maggie cleared their empty plates and laid the bill on the table.

Shelby was itching to get back to the office. The site plans were calling her. "I'll pay this one."

Fishing her wallet out of her back pocket, she handed it to Maggie.

"You're the boss." The waitress disappeared, returning moments later. Charles was still outside.

After signing, she hugged her friend and joined him on the landing out front of the café.

"Everything okay?" she mouthed silently.

He nodded and covered the microphone. "Did you pay?"

She nodded as well.

"Sorry." He frowned, then shook his head with disappointment.

"It's okay," she reassured him.

He held up a finger and shifted farther away. "Yes, sir, I understand. Thank you."

Ending his call, he turned back to her and smiled.

"Good news?" she asked.

"Yes." They headed to the parking lot. "Just one more step, and a business in Olympia might be mine."

"Olympia?"

He nodded. "It's a small business that needs some investors. Should have a good ROI."

"Nice."

"Should be. I'm going to help them with their permit. They're struggling with the red tape."

"That can be the hardest part." She'd called in all her favors around town for help. Luckily, she had a lot.

"I should get back. Thanks again for lunch. I'm sorry you had to pay."

"I didn't have to. I chose to. Besides, you paid last time. It was a much larger bill." She smiled.

"Can you tell your friends it was nice meeting them? I left in such a rush."

"They'll understand."

"Can I see you again soon?" Charles stepped in close.

"I've got a few things going on at the moment, but I'd like that."

"Seriously, you should get some help."

"I have help."

"Then, let them help." He put a hand on her elbow.

"I'll think about it."

Charles leaned in for a hug. He hesitated as he pulled away, his hands trailing on her lower back. The moment was interesting and new. He wanted to kiss her, she could tell, but she wasn't sure she was ready.

Things were complicated at the moment.

Also, she didn't feel like giving the entire town a show. They'd already be talking about her for the next few days.

"I'll give you a call," she said decisively, veering away to her car and unlocking it.

"Please do." Charles raised a hand in farewell, got into his car, and drove off.

CHAPTER 11

"Hi." Keane answered the door to let Heath in. Another young man he'd seen at Gil's followed behind him.

"This is Tommy, my best bud," Heath said. "He's going to help us carry the wardrobe in."

Heath had called early that morning to let him know he was headed back to Liberty and could pick up the wardrobe. Keane was excited to get the last piece of furniture into the beach condo.

"Nice to meet you." Keane shook his hand. "It's nice of you to help out."

"Heath said there's no way you two would get that behemoth out of my truck bed without my help." Tommy grinned widely.

It was probably true.

"We needed two store clerks to help us get it in." Heath slapped Keane on his back. "But no worries, bud. We'll get it in here."

"You want it over there?" Tommy pointed to the empty wall in the living room.

"That's right."

"Sweet."

The three men went out to unload the truck. Heath hopped into the truck bed and pushed the wardrobe out to Keane and Tommy, who were waiting at the end. The two lifted the part hanging off. Then Heath hurried down to center the furniture dolly under it. They lowered it slowly until it was balanced on the wheeled platform.

Once they had it in place in his apartment, they repeated the process to get it off the dolly. The three of them stood back, breathing heavily and admiring the wardrobe in the room.

"That's pretty freaking awesome." Heath stuck his hands in his back pockets.

"Yeah." Keane nodded. "I like it there."

"I think Shelby will like it there too." Heath elbowed him.

They hadn't talked about his history with her, but it wouldn't be hard to learn about their past relationship in the small town.

"If I can get her to forgive me." Keane studied his shoes. "I didn't exactly handle things right with her when I left."

Tommy winced, toeing the ground with his black Converse and rocking back and forth on it.

"What?" Heath asked.

"What?" Tommy said, edging backward.

"You look guilty. What do you know?" Heath pushed.

"It's just that I saw Shelby and some new dude in the parking lot outside the café a couple of days ago." Tommy shuffled his feet. "They looked kinda cozy, and Loris said they had lunch together."

Acid sat in Keane's stomach. "It's okay. Guys, I've been gone a long time. She was bound to meet someone else."

Keane attempted to appear calm, but he was anything but inside. He swallowed thickly. He'd been holding out hope, but it was too late.

"If it helps, he looks like a suit," Tommy said. "He's nowhere as cool as you."

"Thanks, man." Keane gave him a thin smile.

Tommy fist-bumped him.

"You've got this." Heath nodded his head enthusiastically.

A suit was exactly who someone like Shelby deserved. Someone who could provide for her so she didn't always have to work so hard. Someone who had his shit together.

Stepping onto the docks was a blast from the past. The breeze was rich with salt and pine tar. Keane's shoes scuffed along the rough planks as they had when he was young, chasing after Duke on some harebrained scheme. A coastal fog hung low over the water, making it impossible to see the line between the water and the sky. It appeared as though the dock and the boats were suspended inside a soft smoke-gray wall.

Paint—hell, even photography—would never replicate something this ethereal. Even in person, it was hard to visually study. The entire landscape threw off his depth perception.

He went up onto the last section of the docking for taller vessels. Emiliano had told him Duke's metal-sided fishing-boat-turned-cargo-ship sat at the very end. It was just like his old friend to want the last dock slip. It would be the quickest to exit.

At least, he hoped he was still his old friend.

"Keane?"

He squinted through the fog to see Duke sitting on one of the benches on his deck. It looked as though he was repairing a net. He didn't think Duke did any fishing with the ship.

"Hey." He stepped to the edge of the dock, where a rope blocked off the entry. "Do you have a few minutes?"

Duke frowned, then stood and slid his hands into the front pockets of his jeans. "Sure. Come on board."

Keane released the breath he'd been holding. Unlatching the rope, he threw his leg over the metal edge and onto the stairs to the deck, securing it behind him.

It was a large vessel, big enough for two sitting areas with benches, one with a wooden table. The bridge was farther back, with a nice overhang, an outdoor fridge, and another bench under a window. From what Emiliano had said, Duke lived on this ship.

Keane regarded his surroundings. "Nice place."

His friend nodded. "Thanks. This is The Aurelia. She's been my home for something like eleven years now."

"Wow. You must be doing well for yourself to have gotten her that quickly out of high school."

Duke raised his shoulders in a shrug. "I needed a place of my own after Gary and Nell moved in the apartment over their, er, her café. Staying on their couch whenever I was in the cove got old after a while."

"You were gone a lot?" Keane edged closer to the bench across from his friend.

"We gonna do this now?" Duke cocked his head. "Catch up?"

Keane's heart pounded, and he took a chance. "Could we?"

Duke's jaw worked, but he gave a sharp nod after a few long seconds and took a seat. "Yeah, I was gone a lot. After you left, I decided it was time for me to figure out whatever the hell I was going to do, too. I couldn't go collecting small jobs around town."

"Or playing poker with the old fishermen at night, pretending to be a dumb kid." Keane cracked a single-sided smile.

"Or that." Duke's eyebrows rose. "That one got me into a few scrapes."

"I remember."

"You left," Duke said simply.

Keane dropped his gaze onto his shoes. It was his turn.

"I left. I felt"—he sat heavily on the other bench—"like a failure."

"A failure?"

Keane spread his hands wide as he searched for the words. "I had no path, no future. Shelby was doing everything for the both of us. She kept me on track. I didn't have anything of my own. It felt like I was just coasting."

Duke listened in silence.

"I needed to be able to contribute something. Anything."

"You left so you could find a career?"

Keane nodded.

"I couldn't make a living off loving Shelby or hanging out with my friends. As cool as that would have been."

Duke smiled at that.

"And I only had two skills and passions outside of that," Keane went on. "Surfing and art. You know how hard it is to make any money surfing. Especially out here."

"So, art it was. But why didn't you tell anyone, Keane?" A frown appeared above Duke's eyes. In them, he saw how much it had hurt the man.

"I know I should have. I know it." Keane slumped in his seat. "I was so young and dumb. You remember how we were at that age. And you're going to laugh at me, but I honestly thought it wouldn't take long. I don't know if I was being cocky or simply unrealistic."

"In New York?" Duke stifled a laugh. "Seriously?"

"I know!" Keane threw back his head. "It's ridiculous to think, but I thought if I kept my head down, painted every day, and got to know some of the local artists and galleries, I would get good quickly and have my paintings selling by...the end of the month."

Duke let out the laugh he'd been holding. The sound was absorbed by the fog and didn't ring like it should have. "The end of the month?"

"Remember how ambitious you were at that age? You thought you could make enough to pay for rent with a single card game."

"That's true. One more card game, and I'd have enough for *everyone* to be set." Duke's laughter dwindled. "Okay, that's fair. So, how'd it actually play out?"

"I stayed with my cousin in this rathole. It was in the bad part of town. We literally had rats in the hallway. We slept with our shoes on in case someone broke in, but no one ever did, so that was something," Keane reflected. "I tried everything, realism, charcoal, and even photography for a while, but paint was the easy pick. My parents sent enough money for some starter paints and canvases. By the end of the month, I had made some connections with the local artists, mainly up and comers or newbies like myself, no one making any real money. I realized that my painting was only decent. I nearly gave up after that first month, and alm ost came back."

"What made you stay?"

"I called Mom and Dad. They said they'd seen Shelby downtown. Said she was getting better." Keane pressed his lips into a thin line. "I realized how dumb I'd been. I knew I could come back and fix things at that point, but nothing would have changed. It would have been for nothing. I would have hurt her for nothing. And I had finally figured out my voice with the paint. Abstract landscapes came naturally for me. That part felt right. It was the only part that did."

"You always were fast to know what you liked."

"This was no different. I leaned into it. I thought it might take longer, but at least Shelby was okay. She would be fine. It might take six months, maybe a year. I couldn't give up on being the man who deserved her. After a year, it was possible she'd still forgive me."

"Keane." Duke interrupted him. "But who was that for? For her? Because I don't ever remember her being unhappy with you. Before you left, I mean."

He considered his words carefully. "I needed to be more for her. For me. I wasn't happy with myself. If I'd have stayed, it could have taken a lifetime to get anywhere in the art world. It took me fifteen years, but I made it because I could be in New York, paint all night, and travel at the drop of a hat. Hell, I spent almost all the money I was making on flights for something like eight years. Now, I can do a few shows a year and I'm good."

"But at what cost?"

Keane sighed. "I honestly don't know."

The silence stretched between them.

Finally, Duke spoke. "We were dumb kids."

"Yeah, we were." He met Duke's gaze. "Man, I'm so sorry I left you too."

Duke broke away and stared off into the fog where the sky blended into the sea. He nodded. "When Gary got sick, it was hard. Even worse when he degraded so quickly. I didn't think we'd lose him so fast."

"I'm glad he didn't suffer long. I should have made it back sooner." Keane shook his head. "I'm deeply sorry I missed him. It haunts me."

"He was surrounded by love, man." Duke stood, came over to sit next to him, and laid a hand on his shoulder. "His last days were pretty peaceful."

"Was he angry I didn't come?" Keane lifted his gaze.

"I don't think so." Duke shook his head. "He was always so proud of you. He read all the New York Times articles featuring you aloud to all of us, much to Shelby's displeasure, I might add. She fumed, but listened. I could t ell."

"He did?" He wasn't sure which fact surprised him the most.

"Oh, he talked about you. He talked a lot about the old days near the end. And the future too."

"And I missed all of it." A tear slid down Keane's face. He let it.

"If it helps, sometime, I could share the stories he told."

"It would mean the world to me." Keane winced. "Duke, I've been so focused on missing Gary and Shelby, but I forgot about you. You were so headstrong. I guess I figured you'd find your own way. I'm so sorry I wasn't here for you when you needed me."

Duke sat silent for a while, his hands on his knees. "Me too. But if you're really here to stay now. For good. Well, then, I'm damn happy about it."

Keane swallowed hard. "I missed you."

"I missed you too, man." Duke gave him a crooked smile and elbowed him. "Aw, hell."

His friend, being the taller, pulled him into a short hug. He pounded him on the back before releasing him and wiping away a tear of his own.

"Thanks," Keane choked out.

"We need to get the crew together. It's been too long since you've been home."

"Do you think that's okay with Shelby? I don't want to intrude on her inner circle."

"You're part of us. Always have been, always will be. Only." Duke smirked. "We've had a few changes."

"Nick, Emiliano, and Maggie." Keane readily accepted them.

"Not only that."

"Please don't tell me Shelby's new guy is officially in the crew now."

"New guy?" Duke blinked in surprise.

"I heard she was at lunch with some guy at the café."

"Our café?"

Keane nodded.

"That's interesting. I don't know anything about him," Duke said.

"Your new friend, then?" Keane guessed. At Duke's confusion, he added, "The man on the docks. The one who was helping you plan your sailing route."

"Oh." Duke's eyes lit with recognition. "That's Percy. I'm sure you'll meet him eventually. He's a good guy, but no, not officially in our crew. Although we should consider including Solomon."

"Solomon?" He remembered the older fisherman. He had been middle-aged when he was in school.

"It'll all make sense when we meet. I need to talk to everyone else, but they won't object. Except Shelby, but she'll get over it. Trust me."

"Object?"

"You'll see."

Keane didn't push for more. It was obvious Duke wasn't going to say anything more, and he had already gotten everything he needed at that moment. Keane sucked in a deep, cleansing breath and let it out. The two friends sat in silence and stared off into the water.

Maybe things were going to be okay. Maybe a person could come back home.

CHAPTER 12

T he sun was out. Shelby slipped her sunglasses on as she walked across the pristine lawn surrounding the cabins. It had been a busy week. She had already replaced half the sink pipes, even though they were all only gently worn, and found no new issues so far. It would delay future corrosion.

Her site plan was drawn, and she'd already met with the septic guy. He couldn't make it out to dig for the perc tests until early the following week, but at least, it was scheduled. Her financial plan was eighty percent there. A few, final numbers were still coming in, along with the permits from the county.

Unfortunately, with the recent repairs, things were tight. She would have to take the tenth yurt as her own.

But that was okay. She'd lived for nearly fifteen years at the end of Siren's Song Cabins. Why would the yurts be any different?

She'd even had time to meet with Emiliano. The man was going to completely redesign her website. It was being rebranded as Siren's Song Retreats. The yurts and cabins would have different sections with descriptions, photographs, an interactive reservation calendar, and an in-app payment. He was even going to automate the confirmation email. Today, her customers had to call to pay for their down payment, and then her team had to make the official reservation into the system. It was all very manual. This would free up her clerks to handle more of the day-to-day operations, like entering bills into the accounting system and making personal confirmation calls the week before rentals.

Emiliano wouldn't take payment for it, either. He just asked for a week's rental at one of the cabins with Nell after they opened. That, she could do.

Bartering was her favorite method of payment.

Things were looking up for her expansion, even though she hadn't had a chance to get back to the property and check things out for the last couple of days. Next week would be better.

And Duke wanted to talk. They were meeting at the café at two, their normal afternoon meeting time, between rushes, but he'd asked to stop by and pick her up. He must want to talk about Keane.

It was good to want things.

But she was doing things her way. She'd agreed to meet him on his boat half an hour before the crew meeting. Shelby fluffed her hair and slid her lady blazer on, powering up for the visit. Not with Duke, but with Keane. She was going to nip that one in the bud. She was done hiding.

Keane wanted a copy of their contract? She would drop it off personally. She didn't need to hide behind her clerks. That wasn't their job anyway. And she'd find out what was going on well before she saw Duke. He'd probably promised Keane to put in a good word for him. She'd handle that one too. Let the butt-faced miscreant know what she thought of that.

Shelby took her SUV so she could exit cleanly and professionally. She didn't want to chance having him accompany her into town afterward.

A few minutes later, she stood in front of her cute beach condo, her leather-bound portfolio under one linen-covered arm and the other raised to knock on the door. The lavender planter Willa had left on the front porch was blooming, and the dirt was damp from a recent watering.

Keane opened the door, his eyes widening a fraction of a second. His face grew flush, and he opened the door wider. "Greene."

"New York," she said in a clipped tone. Her fingers itched to check her hair, but she fought the reaction. She was sure it was smooth.

"Would you like to come in?" He moved aside to make room.

She hesitated. So many memories were in the place. Sure, she'd been in it loads of times with Willa, but not with him. Not since that night when they'd stayed there. It was right before he'd slipped out of her life without a single word.

It would be worse to let him see her hesitate, though. To think she still had feelings for him. They were a thing of the past, and so were the memories haunting the walls of the small apartment.

Steeling her nerves, she let the comforting call of the ocean, so close now, pulse up her legs and arms and settle in her chest. She strode confidently in, even letting her arm brush the sleeve of his flannel as she passed. She wasn't expecting the familiar scent of saltwater and paint to hit her when she entered his bubble, but it did.

Shelby blinked away the memories and kept her focus on the apartment so he wouldn't see her reaction.

The room in front of her stopped her in her tracks. Gone was the old leather couch from Elias and Kalani's basement. In its place was a large, low bed positioned to face the coast. A wide, intricately carved wardrobe stood where a television would. Although she'd never seen a TV on the wall. Willa hadn't owned one, and Emiliano hadn't been there long enough to put one in. Two elegant but usable chairs stood on the other wall. A small, carved wooden table sat between them. It looked ancient. Nothing in the room appeared to be new. She loved it.

"What is all of this?" Shelby stood, shocked, her armor of determination slipping off her shoulders.

"I got a few things." Keane appeared at her side.

"It looks like a studio apartment." He'd said he planned to put the bed in the living room, but his private space lay before her. It was unnerving. A gorgeous woven blanket lay over the bed in a casual way that made her itch to recline on it.

She lurched back.

They'd lain exactly in that spot on their first and only night here.

"It's quite a view, don't you think?"

It was, but it was unconventional at best.

"What about the other rooms?" Shelby was halfway into the master room before she realized she had barged into his place without an invitation. She froze, glancing back at him. This wasn't how she'd planned this visit.

Keane's eyes were bright. He hurried past her and edged the door open farther.

The lights were on in his studio, and an easel stood in the center, facing the windows. Boxes were flipped over, their taped bottoms covered with paints and supplies. Two canvases were leaning against the wall next to her. She only had to lean in to see what was on them.

Keane's face flushed as he followed her eyes. She didn't want to give him the satisfaction of her curiosity, but she was dying to see them.

Oh, why not? Maybe they'd be terrible. Some of his early work wasn't all that amazing. She'd noticed even though she hadn't wanted to. Exhaling sharply, she took two long strides into the room, her face carefully blank.

"No paint on the floors, I see. You've learned not to make a mess, at least. That's good. Make sure it stays that way."

"You're the boss." He leaned against the wall just inside the room. His arms were crossed loosely across his chest, and his hair was up, messily pulled into a small half bun at the back of his head. He had a green smear under one eye.

"Looks like you need some tables." She angled her body the rest of the way to see the paintings. Greens, golds, and browns swirled in her vision. They were landscape, but they were more than that. They were the woods surrounding the town. And they were breathtaking.

Pulling herself back, she noticed Keane's attention zeroed in on her. He was so still it was as though he wasn't even breathing.

She searched for a witty remark to make, but came up short. "These are... They're stunning."

She heard the breath he'd been holding release, and his shoulders eased back and down.

"Thank you." His voice was barely over a whisper.

Since her moment of strength and resolution was lost, she rounded the easel to see the canvas propped on it. It was obvious she'd disturbed him in the middle of it. Brushes sat in a clay coffee mug on one of the makeshift tables, and multiple colors of paint streaked the edges of the kilned cup.

This one was like the other two, but it had the cove at its center. But instead of the clear, blue water, this one used shades of blue-gray. The water was only a few shades darker than the sky itself.

"Washington weather. A bit dreary, don't you think?" she asked.

"It's moody, alright, but not dreary. I don't mind the rainy weather."

"Ah, it wasn't the rain you were running from, then?" She brushed past him, not wanting to focus on the raw emotion on the canvas.

She stuck her head into the other room. She was being nosey, but so what? She owned the place, and he'd screwed her over. She was allowed to be a little intrusive.

The couch was on the far wall, and a space was cleared around it, but other boxes were scattered in front of it. Otherwise, it was empty.

"I need to get my clothes in the wardrobe." His voice was too close behind her. "But I needed to paint more."

She moved toward him to leave the small room, but he didn't budge. She didn't like being boxed in. "Please move."

"I wasn't running away." He stood his ground.

"You weren't? Coulda fooled me." She raised her eyebrows at his stance. Finally, he moved aside for her to pass. She exited into the living room, and found the bed in front of her. The covers on one side were rumpled from where he had sat earlier, and her heart tightened. She moved past it to the peninsula between the kitchen and the chairs, trying to find something that wasn't oozing Keane's persona.

"Greene." He followed her but kept a distance this time. Smart move. She set her chin.

"I'm sorry you felt like that."

"You're sorry I felt like that?" she repeated, her voice rising in pitch. She was losing control, and she knew it. "How the hell was I supposed to feel?"

"I don't know. Nothing good, I can imagine, but I wasn't leaving to get away from you."

She made a disgusted sound.

Keane took a single, small step toward her. "I'm sorry I hurt you."

She snorted louder this time, pushing away from the counter and heading toward the door. She wasn't hurt. She was over being hurt. Burning anger was more like it, covered up with a thick wall of ice.

"I'm fine, thank you. Can't you tell? I've done great without you." Her words dripped with sarcasm.

"Shelby," he said this time, calling her by her real name.

It stung. The reason she was there finally hit her again, and she paused, opening her folder to give him his paperwork. "You asked for a copy."

"I shouldn't have left like that. I'm so sorry I did."

"Oh, is there a better way than to leave a vague letter at your parents' house for me to find after I couldn't get a hold of you all morning? Panicked and worried? What do you think would have been better?" she snapped. "I'm honestly dying to know."

He gulped. "That letter was crap. I know it. I was being a coward. I should have explained to you why I was leaving."

"And why was that?" It was the question that had lived inside her for fifteen years. She pressed, desperate to shake the answer from him.

"If I had any chance of being a painter, I had to go to New York."

"Don't you think I would have understood that?" Shelby shook her head. "I...I would have supported you. You know that. I had some money saved up. I would have come with you."

"That's just it. I didn't want you to come with me." There. That was it.

"Yeah. That's what I thought." She faced the door.

"If you had left, you wouldn't have what you have now. This is your world."

"*You* were my world, Keane." She could feel tears filling her eyes, damn him. "And you left me."

"I didn't want you to lose everything you had started here. You had just gotten that loan for the cabins and put your savings into the land. I couldn't let you lose all of that."

"How was that your decision to make?" She stared at the door. At least he couldn't see the emotion on her face.

She blinked back the tears threatening to fall. "I make my decisions, dammit, not you."

He was right, though. Some part of the logic worked its way through to her, like a solution to a problem often slowly materialized. She realized she was still holding the stack of papers.

"I know. And I'm so very sorry."

Tears blinked back, she turned to face him and her past. "You should have explained it to me. I would have listened."

"Maybe." He shrugged. His eyes raked over her face. "But you're right. I was a coward."

"Duh. But how so?"

"I was afraid you would have talked me into staying."

She had nothing to say to that. No biting comeback. He was probably right. She'd have cried, and he'd have stayed. He'd always done everything he could to support her and make her happy. Until he didn't.

"I would have been wrong. If you really wanted to go."

"I didn't want to leave you. I just wanted to be a painter. It was the only way."

"Still. We would have come up with a solution. Long distance. Something."

"Maybe, but, Greene, we were both so young. You remember. I had this idea, and I thought it was the only way."

"Well, you were dumb."

"I was."

Flustered, she slammed the papers on the counter since he wouldn't take them from her. "Well, you made it. You're a freaking painter now. Are you happy?"

"No. Not completely."

She rolled her eyes. "Figures."

"Can I ask you a question?"

She was dying to know what he was curious about. "Shoot."

"Am I too late?" he asked gently, softly.

Tears threatened to spill again, and she clenched her teeth to will them to stay. "You were too late the moment you wrote that letter."

With that, she spun and stomped out the door, leaving it open in her wake.

Grateful she'd thought ahead and drove, she slammed the door of her Trailblazer and wheeled out of the lot.

It wasn't until she parked between Gil's Market and the Wild Café that she let the tears fall.

"You requested my presence?" Shelby surprised Duke where he was sitting, typing on his phone. She'd taken a few minutes to compose herself in her vehicle before exiting, ready to hear what the courier had to say.

"Good afternoon to you too, Shelby." Duke punched a few more keys and slid his cell into his chest pocket.

"I'm all ears, but I'll warn you, I just left Keane's. If this is about him, you're wasting your time." She'd worked through her pain and had her ice walls back in p lace.

"It's not, directly, but I was hoping we could talk about that, too."

"I have nothing to say about him. He left. He's back. I've moved on. What more is there about it?"

"He's back, as you said." Duke stood up. "I know you don't like hearing this, but he's still one of us. I'd like to welcome him back to the crew for dinner. That's what I wanted to talk to everyone about at two."

Shelby shook her head sharply. "But..."

The words drifted off. They were her crew. He'd abandoned them too.

But of course, Duke would want to welcome him back into the fold. She wanted to demand that they exclude him, but her mind drifted to the hurt she'd seen in his eyes.

Ever pragmatic, she weighed the pros and cons. Nick and Emiliano didn't know Keane well. Nell would want to have him back, but it would be mainly for Duke. It wasn't fair of her to hold that away from him, especially after the loss of Gary. If Nell and Duke could forgive him and wanted a relationship with him, they should have it.

Besides, there wasn't much Shelby Greene couldn't handle. She'd put on her big-girl panties and armor up. And if she was low, she wouldn't attend. It wasn't as though she shared personal problems with the entire crew. Those were reserved for very rare girl nights and pints of ice cream.

"Fine," she said.

Duke raised his eyebrow. He was probably surprised she'd accepted so quickly. "Fair enough."

"You said there was something else?"

He nodded. "Word around town is you're seeing somebody."

"I can't see how that's any of your business."

"We're friends, Shelby."

"Yes, but—" she started, but he cut her off.

"I'm just asking about you. I'm not judging you, Shel." His voice was softer this time.

Her eyes narrowed at him, but she answered just the same. She had known people would start to talk. "I had lunch with Charles last Monday."

"Is he the guy you had business with?"

"He is."

"Where's he from?"

"Olympia."

"Charles what?"

"You are not looking into him, Duke. I'm a good judge of character."

He frowned, but didn't argue. "Is it getting serious?"

"Not really. Not yet." She wasn't opposed to it, particularly at the moment. It didn't sound bad to focus on someone who made her feel good instead of someone who made her feel bad.

"Are you happy?"

She shrugged. "Enough. I'm buying the land from him. That makes me happy."

She gave him a tight smile. The land was her shining piece of light these days. At least she had something that was going well. She could always rely on her business for that.

CHAPTER 13

K eane brushed his hair one more time, awkwardly shifting this way and that in front of the mirror. He wasn't one to fuss over his appearance, but he was having dinner with the crew tonight.

That meant dinner with Shelby.

Duke had called to invite him shortly after the woman he loved stormed out. After the way things had ended with her surprise visit, he was sure she had nothing to do with him being invited, but Duke assured him she knew and was okay with it.

Being okay with something and being happy about it were two different things, but he'd take the opportunity.

He still didn't know the status of her love life, and the thought unbalanced him. He'd tried apologizing, but she was still so mad. Everything else he thought to say to her only sounded like excuses in his head. Either way, he'd do his best to gain her forgiveness, if nothing else but to be friends. It would be difficult, but now that he was back, he wanted to be in her life in whatever form he could be.

And he was dying to find out what else was going on. Duke had been vague about something else new with the crew.

At least, it wasn't the new guy. There'd been so many changes that he was starting to feel like an outsider.

The summer night was dry, so he laced up his Vans and exited via his deck, taking the pebble beach to the café.

Edison bulbs illuminated the back deck and the marina behind the market, creating bright pinpoints of light against the dark sky. The moon was barely a crescent where it hovered over the cove. Only the tips of the waves carried a reflection of its light as they crashed and pulled back again, over and over, in an endless, calming cycle.

The high tide washed near his feet, soaking through one shoe and a pant leg. He hadn't realized he'd drifted so close to the water. Shaking his leg, he shoved away from the coast and up the stairs. So much for making a good impression.

Raucous laughter drifted down to him from the deck above. His foot hesitated over the bottom stair. Did he belong? Would he be accepted? Fifteen years was a very long time.

Too long.

He hadn't returned only to miss out because he was too afraid to try. Gathering his courage, he took the steps and appeared at the top of the railing.

The conversation on the deck stopped.

Maggie, Willa, Nick, and Emiliano stood near the bar, paused mid-sentence. Keane immediately felt out of place. The back door of the café swung open, and Nell swept through it with a tray full of food.

"Who's hungry?" she exclaimed, carrying it to a table at the center of the deck.

Duke followed her out with another platter of food.

"What're you all standing around for?" Shelby's voice drifted from the café as she skipped out of the doorway, carrying a bottle of wine and a wineglass.

She froze, seeing Keane.

"Let's open that bottle." Duke took it from Shelby after depositing the plates on the table. "Someone get Keane a glass."

Shelby watched him from afar and rolled her eyes before sighing loudly. "Come on, then."

She slogged over to the bar, rounded it, and pulled glasses off the reinforced shelves behind her.

Keane edged forward, still feeling out of place. Shelby immediately returned to her seat next to Nell, ignoring him completely.

"I pulled two tables together." Nell surveyed the spread of food. "I think it fits us perfectly. All eight of us."

It was the inclusion he needed. He approached the table. "Where should I sit?"

"We don't have assigned seats. It's not that type of club." Shelby's words had bite, but a half smirk made it more playful than malicious.

Duke poured wine into his glass. Thankful, he took a long swallow.

"Except for mine." Nell stood at the head of the table, facing the café. "In case I need to get something from the kitchen."

"Sure thing." Keane tipped his head and took a center seat, randomly picking one.

His eyes followed Shelby as she sat down on the other side, one place over.

Emiliano grabbed the chair next to Nell, and the rest took the remaining chairs.

"It's getting cold. Dig in," Nell commanded, picking up a bowl of pasta with mussels and heaping a pile on her plate.

"Gimme." Shelby reached her hands out expectantly. She practically bounced in her seat until the bowl made it to her.

"Did you talk to Solomon?" Willa asked Duke.

"I did," Duke said. "He's more than willing to meet up when we need to talk, but he'd leave dinners to us youngsters. His words."

"Sounds like he doesn't want our drama." Shelby grinned.

"It's probably too late in the day for him anyway," Emiliano added, dishing lemony green beans onto his plate. "He's coming in from fishing when I get to work."

"I saw him clamming the other night," Maggie said, taking a bowl of jeweled rice from Duke.

"Roy was probably telling him where to dig." Shelby stuffed pasta into her mouth.

"Yes, Roy was with him," Maggie said, nodding.

"More like Roy took Solomon clamming." Shelby chuckled at her joke.

Keane accepted the bowl of rice, adding two large spoonfuls to his plate, then took the platter of scallops and added two to it. "Who's Roy?"

They all stopped talking. The rest of the crew turned to Duke, who cleared his throat.

"Roy is Solomon's pelican," Duke said.

"Oh," Keane said. "His pelican."

"Yes."

"Like a pet?"

"Kind of," Duke said.

"Not quite," Shelby said, watching him closely. She had a smirk on her face that was no longer friendly. Keane shifted awkwardly in his seat.

Duke shot her a pointed look, and Keane caught Willa elbowing her.

Keane frowned as well. "What am I not getting?"

"It's a long story." Duke spun his fork in a large bite of pasta and gulped it down. "So, I'd better start at the beginning."

"I'm opening the second bottle of wine." Shelby spun from her seat.

"After we lost Gary, the five of us slowly drifted apart."

"That's partly my fault." Nell's mouth was twisted to one side. "I was having trouble talking about it. I didn't know how to let them help."

"We were all grieving in our own way." Shelby returned to her seat and poured wine for Nell and Maggie, whose glasses were halfway empty.

"When Gary's birthday came around, Willa convinced us all to jump into the cove at night."

"Ever the peacemaker," Shelby murmured to Willa.

Keane's chest tightened at the memory of Gary jumping into the cold water on his birthday when he was younger.

"It seemed like a good idea." Willa shrugged.

"It was," Duke said pointedly to Shelby, who huffed and slumped in her seat. "But then a storm rolled in unexpectedly. Lightning struck the water."

"Crap," Keane said.

"Wait, there's more." Shelby raised a finger. At Nell's warning look, she raised both hands. "What? That wasn't mean."

"We all went back to our places," Duke continued, ignoring Shelby.

"I ran into Nick on the beach." Willa laced her fingers with her fiancé's.

"I thought she was a mermaid coming out of the water." Nick's eyes were trained on Willa. They were full of love and admiration.

"The next morning, I found a body near where I ran into Nick," Willa went on. "Thankfully, it wasn't Nick who did the *unaliving*."

"What?" Keane was having trouble following the story.

"You're confusing him," Duke interrupted. "Long story short, trouble was following Nick. We found out he was a retired Seattle cop. His old buddy was murdered on the cove, where he was exchanging evidence to put a bad guy away. It's all sorted, and the bad guy is in jail. But when we all woke up, we felt weird."

"Tingly." Willa's eyes twinkled, and Nick blushed.

"And Willa brought us all tea," Nell said.

"It was awful, but it worked too well," Shelby said.

"Not too well," Willa said.

"Better than it should have." Shelby shrugged.

"Herbs are very powerful."

"Not that powerful."

"I got magic from the ocean," Willa said directly to Keane, cutting to the chase. She wiggled her fingers in the air. "But only with saltwater or plants from the ocean."

"Magic?" Keane asked, trying to understand.

"Probably just science we don't know about yet," Shelby said, watching Willa.

"Whatever you want to call it," Willa said, shrugging.

"And I can transfer my emotion into seafood," Nell said, smiling.

"Hey, is that why I'm not as irritable as I should be?" Shelby scowled at Nell.

"You're not irritable?" Maggie asked.

"Only moderately." Shelby held her hand out in front of her and tipped it back and forth.

"I only added a little happiness. I didn't make anyone fully blissed out or anything." Nell's gaze slid to Keane, and she winked.

Shelby rolled her eyes and forked up a few strands of pasta.

"I can make it rain," Maggie jumped in.

Everything up to this point seemed innocuous, but rain? That was physical.

"Okay, hang on, everyone." Keane focused on Maggie, trying to get to the heart of what they were saying to him. "You mean to say you can make it rain? Like pull moisture from the air, condense it, and make it rain?"

"That's exactly it, yes." Maggie smiled.

Keane's gaze fell on a glass of water in front of him.

"It works better when it's in the air. Natural moisture has salt in it," Maggie explained.

"And I can move water." Duke raised his head. "It helps during storms or if I need to get to Seattle quickly."

It sounded like his friends had either gone crazy or were all suffering some sort of collective experience. But magic? It seemed unlikely.

"Show him." Nick pushed a glass to Maggie.

"I can try. It's pretty dry out here." She focused on the glass, and Shelby leaned forward and dumped a scoop of flaked sea salt into it. Judging from the waitress's flat-lipped expression, she didn't appreciate the assistance. Still, Maggie mumbled, "Thanks."

Keane found himself desperately hoping it was real. The idea of true magic in the world felt both shocking and right somehow.

When water droplets collected on the sides of the glass, she lifted her hands and held them out to the water like she was calling to it. Keane's face felt sticky, like there was humidity in the air. Mist rose, drops of water collected on the wood slats over the deck where the lights were hung from, and a few dropped onto the table.

Keane's mouth fell open. "You can make it rain."

Maggie said shyly, "This was just a little humidity, but yes. I can."

His eyes flew to Shelby, who was watching him.

"Mine is lame." She shoved a green bean into her mouth.

His eyebrows drew together.

"I can tell where water is." Shelby wrinkled her adorable, pert nose. "But at least I don't ever get lost anymore."

The stress of the moment, combined with the unbelievable surprise and Shelby's exclamation, finally rose to an uncomfortable height in Keane and came crashing down. He let out a loud snort, then a guffaw.

"Are you sure you didn't give him the Giggling Geoduck?" Emiliano asked Nell.

"I haven't made any since last time," Nell said.

"You used to get lost downtown." Keane was still laughing. "Just going to the hardware store."

"Downtown Orca Cove?" Maggie's eyes widened.

Keane nodded. "Even on Highway 101."

"But it goes around the mountain," Nick said, making a circle in the air in front of him.

"Exactly!" Duke lifted his hand.

"Men." Shelby folded her arms and huffed. "Roads should only go in one direction, north and south or east and west. Winding roads throw everyone off."

"Not everyone." Nell grinned.

"But not anymore." Maggie lifted her fork.

"But not anymore." Shelby raised hers in reply, repeating the statement. "You could spin me around, and I'd still feel the pull of Orca Cove's waters. I can even tell how far away I am from them."

"How?" Keane asked. "What does it feel like?"

"It's a tingly sensation, like an electric draw."

"This is incredible." Keane blinked heavily. "Sorry, this is just unexpected."

"You're telling me," Nick said. "I had to feel it to believe it."

"You got it too? From the water?" Keane asked.

"No, I only feel it with Willa." Nick squeezed her hand. "I think it's because I ran into her that night, in the rain, or because she's been healing me ever since. Maybe a little of both."

Willa beamed at her fiancé in a sappy way that made Keane's heart squeeze. He was glad to see the free spirit find someone. The ex-cop turned woodworker seemed like a good match. He was a stable ground to her wild energy.

But Keane had missed so much. Had he been here, with them, as he should have been, he'd have been graced with a gift himself. Magic.

"Don't worry." Nick, sitting next to Keane, nudged him with his elbow. "Except for Duke, all of us guys are outsiders to the magic stuff. We just help them out whenever we can."

"And Solomon," Shelby said. "Solomon was out that night and must have been in contact with the water. He can talk to sea animals."

"He can talk to them? Like Dr. Doolittle?" Keane asked.

"More like Dr. Sealittle." Willa giggled.

"Are you sure you didn't slip in some Giggle Geoduck into this pasta?" Duke lifted a strand of linguini.

"What's Giggle Geoduck?" Keane asked. It felt like all he was doing was asking questions.

"I was pretty happy when I made it." Nell considered, and her eyes lit up. "Emiliano danced around the kitchen with me when I was cooking."

"Oh yeah," Emiliano said. "You did laugh. Oops."

"No apologies for laughter," Duke said. "We all need a little more happiness in our lives."

Keane couldn't argue with that. "So, what caused the magic?"

"The best we can figure out is there's something magical in the water," Duke explained. "The orcas are protecting her."

"Her?" Keane asked.

"We think she's a mermaid." Willa's eyes sparkled.

"*You* think she's a mermaid," Shelby corrected.

"I saw her," Willa argued.

"You saw a mermaid?"

"I saw a tail and iridescent scales."

"Not definitively a mermaid."

"But Percy said she got hurt by the lightning. I'm sure it was her."

"Percy?" Keane asked. What did the newcomer have to do with the magic?

"Percy is an orca shifter," Willa explained. "It makes sense for the other orcas to be as well. We're not sure on which ones, though."

"At least, that's what we think they're called," Emiliano said. "They're not very open about it all."

Keane took a big gulp from his water. He didn't need any wine to cloud his mind. The night kept getting more and more strange.

"We recently found out Solomon's family has been protecting them for generations," Willa said. "His ancestors lived out on Point Peril. They were the lighthouse keepers. They moved down to Orca Cove, and he followed."

"Because of the mermaid?" Keane asked.

"We don't know," Willa said.

"We also don't know it's a mermaid," Shelby added.

"We also don't know it's *not* a mermaid," Willa insisted.

"We do have business to discuss, though," Duke said. "Percy told me they've noticed something with the water. Something's killing fish. He hasn't found the source of it yet, but they're investigating."

"The orcas?" Nick asked.

"I assume so," Duke said. "You know how Percy is. Vague is an understatement. Could be the...magical-fish-slash-mermaid-woman."

"Do you think the seafood is bad?" Nell's eyes widened. "I can't risk making people sick again."

"You didn't make them sick in the first place." Emiliano set a hand on her shoulder.

"It's not all bad," Duke said. "It's in pockets. Percy talked to Solomon about it as well. Roy is helping locate the bad fish. Solomon's catch is clean."

"What about the other fish?" Nick asked.

"What about the clams?" Willa asked. "The clam festival is coming up soon. We're going to get heaps of tourists in town for that. It'd be hard to keep them from the tidelands."

"I think it's localized to the water," Duke said. "At least from what Percy shared. And I don't know if the fish are passing it to people. All I know is Percy said there were some sick fish, and the dolphins complained about bad water. I've cast a few nets and haven't seen anything that appears sick myself."

It explained the net Duke was repairing when Keane stopped by.

"So, we keep a lookout for bad fish and anything causing it." Nick nodded.

"That's right," Duke said.

"I'll keep an eye on the fish and only accept catch from Solomon for the time being," Nell told Emiliano.

"Could it be an algae?" Shelby asked. "We could ask that scientist lady who came into town with Solomon's family letter."

"Meredith," Willa said. "She's staying in Port Noble. I could call her."

"Good idea," Duke said.

"Are the dolphins shifters too?" Keane asked.

"I honestly don't know," Duke said. "Solomon's never said anything about anyone other than the orcas."

"You have to keep this a secret," Maggie warned. "We're keeping it for Solomon. He said you had to promise."

"Why tell it to me at all?" Keane asked. He was still spinning from the news that his world had flipped upside down and into a version out of his dreams. "I'm glad to know, but why?"

"Because you're one of us." Duke said it simply.

Keane glanced over to Shelby, who was watching him over the rim of her wineglass. She raised a shoulder and let it drop, as though saying, "Why not?"

"Welcome to the club." Nick lifted his glass in salute.

Even though Keane had missed out on having magic of his own, things were up in the air with Shelby, and he still only partially understood what was going on, he was finally feeling accepted by his old friends and new ones. Things were looking up.

"Keane?" Shelby asked.

"Yes?" His heart skipped a beat.

"You're hogging the rice. Hand it over." She held out her hand expectantly, wiggling her fingers.

Smiling, Keane lifted the bowl and passed it to the woman who was still the lead in all his dreams.

CHAPTER 14

The next morning, Shelby brushed her hair into a tight, tiny ponytail and went through a few pre-run stretches. She was ready to start the day and hoped she'd hear back from the septic guy at some point. He was supposed to schedule the excavator for the perc tests to ensure the septic systems could go where she wanted them.

Instead, she was met by a herd of elk in her front yard.

They were beautiful creatures, but they were also insanely damaging. Forty large animals roamed between the cabins, grazing on the grass and pawing at the ground. Two of the outdoor firepits had been demolished. The rock around the pit itself was fixable, but several of the Adirondack chairs had been trampled on. The lawn was damaged as well. She'd have to get a rake to smooth the ground and then reseed.

Raising her arms, she whooped loudly and clapped her hands together. A smaller one bolted a few feet and a couple of other elk wandered away, but they didn't leave the property.

"Dammit, go on." Shelby waved her arms at them.

Deer were common, but they didn't get a lot of elk in this area. There wasn't much she could do but wait them out.

Frustrated, she slammed back into her cabin to change out of her running clothes and into her work ones and stomped to the office. If she was going to get everything on her list done today, she couldn't afford the time to fit a run in.

"Terri," Shelby called out when she burst into the building.

The receptionist pried her eyes from her magazine. "Morning, Shelby."

"Did you see the elk?"

"Yeah, aren't they pretty?"

"They are, but they're also ruining the grounds. Some of the Adirondack chairs are smashed."

"Oh." Terri crinkled her nose. "The deer never do that."

"Deer aren't elk."

The younger receptionist had moved up from California with her parents a few years ago. Apparently, they didn't have a lot of elk in Cali.

"Huh. How do we get rid of them?"

"I could scare them off with some pots and pans, but our renters probably wouldn't like that. It's early. Waking up to banging metal might be bad for reviews. Besides, they would probably ruin more grass on their exit." Shelby helped herself to a cup of coffee at the coffee station. "It's best to wait them out."

"Will they just come back?"

"Who knows? I don't know why they showed up, in the first place. This herd never comes this far. If this is a new route for them, I'll have to put up some fencing. Let's hope it's a one-time thing."

"For sure."

Shelby headed into her office and took a sip from the coffee. She grimaced at her swallow.

"And, Terri?"

"Yes, boss?"

"Make some fresh coffee. This is burnt."

"Sure thing."

Secure in her office, Shelby sunk into her desk chair. Elk damage was the last thing she needed.

She powered up her laptop and scrolled through her Excel sheet for the yurt's financial plans. She'd reviewed them a million times already. Things were tight. Tighter than she'd like. She could probably take out a small loan to get things going, but she was already liquidating everything she had outside of the cabins. It felt wrong to get even deeper into the red.

Her phone rang.

"Morning," she answered.

"Hi, Shelby. It's Trace," the postmaster said. "I'm on donations this year for the Clam Festival. Everyone loves a weekend away. Are you able to donate again this year?"

"Sure thing, Tracy. I'll do a free two-day stay in one of our cabins." Shelby scribbled a note on the spiral-bound book in front of her to create a couple of vouchers for the festival raffle.

The holiday was one of her favorite things about Orca Cove. She had a lot of good memories connected to it. Of course, the oldest ones included Keane. The crew would all enjoy the games and live music at the festival, then end up at the tidelands, clamming late into the night. Someone would light a small fire on the beach, and they'd all hang out until nearly sunrise. Which came early this time of year.

Her parents weren't around that late in the summer to object.

Since then, things hadn't been the same, but she still enjoyed the festivities.

Last night brought up a lot of memories. Mostly good. But that was never the issue, was it? They'd gotten along great, never had any problems. Except the leaving part.

That'll put a damper on a relationship.

Not that she'd admit it, but it was fun having the whole crew back together, minus Gary of course. Nick, Emiliano, and Maggie all fit in too. She'd been nice, just as she promised Duke. Mostly.

Keane had seemed so out of place, standing outside the group all by himself. She'd nearly felt sorry for him. But it hadn't taken him long to get into the groove. He and Duke picked up where they'd left off, like two peas in a pod. That part was nice, even if it was hard to get over being tossed aside so easily.

She'd just keep her heart in check. That should do it. She wouldn't risk feeling like that ever again.

"Thanks, Shelby. We appreciate it."

"No problem. I can drop the vouchers off next week."

"That'd be great."

She had barely hung up when her phone rang again.

"Hello," she answered.

"Hey, Shelby. We can get out to do the perc test today if that works for you," the septic designer said.

"Yes." She sat up excitedly. "That'd be great. I'll call the seller so he's aware, but it should be fine. He knows I'm scheduling it."

"Sounds good. Are you going to be there?"

"Ye—" Her words trailed off. "I'm not sure."

She would need to fix the lawn and assess the repairs. No one was checking out today, so she wouldn't be able to get in and update any of the other plumbing, but she would have to order more chairs and grass seed.

Terri could do it, but she wasn't nearly as reliable as Cleo. Who knew what she would end up with. Money was too tight to risk it.

"No problem. Your site plan is clear. I think it'll be okay either way."

"I'll make it if I can."

"We'll be heading that way around three o'clock."

"Perfect, thanks."

Hanging up, she frowned at her list. Another week had passed since she was out on the water. She'd try to squeeze some time in today or tomorrow at the very least. The land was a priority, but even that seemed difficult to achieve now.

Shelby took another sip of her coffee. Its bitter taste hit her tongue, reminding her it was burnt. She spit it back into the cup and shuddered, then dialed Charles's number.

"Morning, Shelby." His voice was particularly warm today.

"Morning, Charles."

"You sound tired." Concern edged his voice.

"Elk," she said simply.

"Oh, no. Is it bad?"

"Not too bad. At least, I don't think it's too bad. They're still out there. I'll get out later and check it out."

"What do you think brought them in?"

"Who knows."

"Do you need a landscaper?"

"No, I've got it, thanks." Shelby would love to use a professional, but there was no way she could afford that right now. Besides, she was a one-woman show: business manager, HR director, landscaper, and maintenance woman. "On the bright side, the septic designer can get out to the property this afternoon. Everything okay with that?"

"Of course. When?" he asked.

"Three."

"Are you coming? I might be able to run by if you wanted to talk business, vent, or grab drinks."

It was tempting. "Let me think about it. I've got a lot to do this morning."

"Anything I can do to help?" She couldn't imagine Charles leveling the ruts in her lawn in his clean leather boots, but she smiled at the thought.

"Nah, I'm being a workaholic. I think I can make it. I can finish things up on Monday."

She had the morning to get some work done, and then she'd attempt to take Sunday off for herself. She could go kayaking or schedule girl time with Willa and Nell. She'd still need to plan for next week, but at least, she wouldn't be tied to her desk.

"I know what that's like." Charles chuckled. "You're speaking my language, but even we need to slow down and take an evening off once in a while."

An evening? See, Charles didn't get where he was by sitting around every day. Shelby rethought taking time off on Sunday.

"That sounds like good advice," she admitted.

Maybe she'd limit her work to a couple of hours in the afternoon.

By the time Shelby arrived at the land, Tim, the septic designer, was already on-site. He was backing an old Caterpillar excavator off his trailer. Charles hadn't made it yet.

The afternoon was warm, and she didn't want her jacket to get dirty, so she left it in the car. She'd also changed from her suede Chelsea boots to her work boots early in the day to work outside. They would be perfect to do a little exploration. Maybe Charles would walk the land with her.

"Hey, Tim." She waved a hand up at the man.

He lifted his hand in response, maneuvered the tracked machine to an open spot, then climbed down and came over to review her site plan.

They had about finished flagging the area by the time Charles' black Audi pulled in next to her SUV.

"Afternoon." Charles shielded his face from the sun and picked his way over the grass to meet them.

"Hi," Shelby said.

The two men shook hands.

"This looks like good spacing." Charles nodded while scanning the parcel.

"There's more back through the woods." Shelby pointed. "I have a guy lined up to do some clearing after we close. Not too much. I want to leave a lot of the trees."

"But with a good view of the mountains and the water, right?" Charles squinted through the branches. "People come out here for the views."

"For sure," Shelby agreed. "I think both are achievable."

"You can sell some of the bigger trees."

The old-growth maples and cedars had been here for hundreds of years. She wasn't going to cut them down unless she absolutely had to.

"Probably. I don't want to lose too many."

"It would help with the development costs."

"True." He was right, but she hoped it wouldn't come to that.

"I'm gonna get started over there." Tim pointed. "You don't know where the water lines are, do you?"

"Um." Charles frowned and pointed to the east. "I think it's over there."

"No, it's just by our cars," Shelby said. She'd felt the clean line near the road when she pulled in. It was totally different from the pleasant waters of the cove. It was kind of soft and almost weak, probably because it wasn't saltwater, but still very much there.

Charles' attention snapped to her with surprise.

"I saw it when I was walking around near my car," she lied, excusing her preternatural ability.

"Out of my way, then." Tim pivoted to return to his equipment.

Shelby nodded and watched him get started. To Charles, she said, "I'd like to walk the property a bit. Want to join?"

"Sure." He fell in step beside her. "Tell me about the elk."

"Ugh." Shelby sighed loudly. "It took most of the morning, but the ruts are smoothed over and the trash picked up."

She'd lucked out. Other than some chairs and the lawn, there was only a busted trash can and a couple of flowerbeds that would need replanting.

They were under a fire ban at the moment. Only small recreational ones were permitted. It was normal during the dry summer. She'd cut apart the larger pieces of broken furniture to be used in small, contained campfires. She'd also texted Nick, who said he could replace the chairs she'd lost. It would dig into her funds, but she couldn't afford not having the luxuries the campers wanted during her busiest season.

"Shelby, I told you I'd help." Charles stopped her with a hand on her arm. "My landscaper could have gotten over there within an hour."

"I know." She turned to face him. It sounded so simple to let someone land a hand, but it was work she could do, so why wouldn't she? "I'm just used to doing things by myself."

"You're so independent. I like that about you." He squeezed her arm. "But wouldn't it be nice to have a little help now and then?"

He wasn't exactly the kind of guy who would get his boots dirty and work alongside her. She might have actually taken that kind of help. A hired hand was the last resort.

"Sometimes," she admitted. "I'll think about it."

"Please do." He gave her a charming smile.

The fact that he wore nice clothes and didn't do labor himself wasn't a detraction. He was obviously intelligent and had made a lot of good business decisions. He was different from the men she typically dated, but that wasn't necessarily a bad thing.

"So where is the second row of buildings going?" He peered between the tree lines. Several game trails ran through the area they were walking. "I hope the elk herd doesn't come through here."

She'd steered them toward the ragged pulsing she was feeling. The buzzing had increased, but she hadn't seen any water or signs of wetlands yet. Interesting.

She hoped her powers weren't going wonky on her. Could they be temporary? She'd have to ask Willa if she noticed anything different.

"Over there." She pointed. "And I hope not. After we excavate, I'll keep an eye out for tracks and add fencing if I have to."

She mentally added a line item to her investment spreadsheet.

"Depending on what Tim says, I might go farther back on the lot," she went on. "There's a lot of space yet to take advantage of. And I want the units to have some privacy."

He frowned. "Every foot from the highway and the electrical box will add to the cost, though. Plus, the water. That's a long distance to bring both."

It was true.

Shelby chewed on her bottom lip. This had been a dream of hers for so long that she was having trouble letting go of the perfect secluded spot studded with yurts in the woods. It would be like romantic tree houses. Especially if she could build decks between them like she wanted. And if there were some decent-sized trees nearby, she could include them in the space. She'd have to leave room for extra growth, but it would be so dreamy.

Her logical mind was at war with her heart. She knew some of the vacationers coming to the area were here simply for a place to sleep between outdoor activities, but for the other ones, she wanted to offer a getaway that would let them forget their jobs and obligations to simply rest.

It sounded wonderful.

"With the repairs at the cabins, it's a good idea to be smart with your money." Charles jolted her out of her dream. "Are they worth saving? Would it be better to start fresh there too?"

The idea sunk to the pit of her stomach with a sourness that reminded her of the day after an all-out ice-cream binge.

"I need the income from the cabins to pay for the yurts." She shook her head. "They only need minor repairs. They will be fine."

They had to be. She could size down her initial plans. She'd done that with the cabins, and it had worked out fine.

"Shelby." Charles shook her from her planning. "Do you need some help?"

"Help?"

He ran a hand down her shoulder and took her hand. "A loan?"

"I don't want to have debt for this."

"An investor, then."

"Charles." She shifted on her feet, uncomfortable with the offer. "I want to do this on my own."

"It's a great property, and it would be a good deal for me, too."

She knew the businessman didn't need another investment. It would be peanuts for him.

"We could get started right away," he continued, smiling warmly. "You could be accepting bookings for Christmas."

"I'm not sure it's a good idea."

"Why's that?"

"Because of this." She shifted her hand between them. "I don't think business and romance should mix. I'm buying the land from you, sure, but that's only a sale. Real business is another thing altogether."

It would be fine until things didn't work out. And that always happened.

He nodded, watching her closely.

"I understand. I'm sure we could make it work, but I understand. Besides." He winked. "If I had to choose, I'd rather have a chance at this."

It was nice to hear, especially after the day she'd had.

"How about drinks at the café?" he went on.

"Sounds good to me."

She'd make time soon to return and investigate further.

CHAPTER 15

Keane stretched his arms over his head. He'd been painting all morning and most of the afternoon. He needed to get out of the house. Shaking his head clear of the wet canvas in front of him, he laced on his Vans and headed out through the back deck.

His new painting held all the chestnuts and multitudes of greens he'd been painting recently, but he'd included more of the cove in the center of his art. Staring out over the railing to the water, he watched it with new interest.

There was magic out there. Real magic.

Somewhere, deep in his gut, he'd always known it was true. It was impossible to sit on a board in the middle of all that power and not feel it. The sea was alive and teeming with life. It was one of the most powerful forces he'd ever encountered.

That and Shelby. The corners of his mouth lifted uncontrollably as his thoughts drifted to her. She'd been kind to him the night before. She *was* a kind person; that didn't surprise him. What did was that she'd been able to move beyond her anger toward him to actually tease him.

It wasn't a huge step, but it was something.

It still didn't mean she would reopen her heart to him. And it still didn't mean she was free to. He hadn't heard any mention of this other guy from her last night. Wasn't that a good sign?

He would focus on being a good friend to her and let her decide what she wanted from their relationship.

Keane took the stairs to the pebble beach and walked to the coastline. The loud rush of the water competed with the squawking birds overhead. A large bald eagle perched high up in a tall cedar off to his right, surveying the scene. He'd missed the hell out of the lush forests and open water during his years in the concrete jungle of New York.

Bull kelp and bladderwrack were washed onshore. He picked his way over them, closer to the marina. Willa had said she would call that scientist about the algae. It looked normal to him, but he wasn't an expert.

Four orcas slid through the water near the jetty to the west. He watched the pod come together and then move as one. It was hard to believe the beautiful creatures were able to shift into human form. Nature was an awe-inspiring, incredible thing, never ceasing to amaze him.

There was a fish carcass on the beach farther out, but that was fairly normal with the seals and otters in the cove. It didn't look any different than he'd expect. He hoped they didn't have a problem.

By this time of day, the fisherfolk had already sold their catch and were gone from the marina. Several families wandered about the docks, while one couple was helping their little girl drop a hook for sunfish or perch. She had dark-brown hair pulled into pigtails and reminded him of Shelby when she was young. He'd had a crush on her at the time, even though they weren't friends until much later.

While Gary and Nell had been together for as long as he could remember, Shelby had lots of friends and interests. She'd organized a student body in middle school and didn't give him the time of day. Probably because he and Duke were getting into trouble together. When Duke's home life got worse, Gary's dad took him in. The three boys got close. Gary had been a stabilizing presence for them.

Keane's parents loved Gary, and as much as they liked Duke, they hadn't loved the influence he had on Keane. Some of that wasn't Duke's fault. Keane had been just as wild and carefree. He was more interested in daredevil stunts on the water than some of the more questionable things Duke wanted to try.

The little girl caught a fish, and he watched her parents cheer at the accomplishment and help her pull it up. The dad showed her how to unhook it and throw it back. She patted it on its head before gently releasing it into the water.

He grinned like a fool and wondered, if Shelby ever had a kid, if he or she would look like her.

He hoped so. He hadn't much thought about kids, but at this moment, he ached to teach a little one how to be kind to fish and how to be in the water amongst them. They might even want to surf.

But that was too much dreaming when the woman had barely begun to speak to him again.

He'd made a living for himself, but for the first time, he was starting to wonder if it had been the right decision. All these years, he'd been convinced it was. It had been his driving force.

But if he'd have stayed, that might have been him and Shelby on the dock with their little girl.

Heart aching, he veered into town.

Wandering the streets, his hands tucked deep into his front pockets, he came across Mary Johnson pulling weeds along her walkway.

"Good afternoon." He raised a hand in greeting. He wasn't sure if she'd remember him.

The older woman raised her head to see who it was, then narrowed her eyes and grumbled something under her breath.

She remembered him. One thing he'd discovered after coming back to Orca Cove was that people seemed to think he was the same as when he left, as though he hadn't grown or matured. The woman they used to tease because she was so prickly didn't seem to think any different about him, either.

He made a right at the corner to see Willa and Duke standing outside her yoga studio back down a block. He headed in that direction to ask if she had news about the algae.

"Hey, Willa."

"Hi, Keane." She beamed.

"Terrorizing Mary again?" Duke teased him.

"Apparently, she thinks so."

Duke nudged him in the shoulder. "Give her time."

"Is she friendly now?"

"Not so much, but she doesn't scream at me anymore."

"That's because you're not toilet papering her house or playing football with her pumpkins," Willa said. "She's actually quite nice sometimes."

"When?" Duke raised an eyebrow.

"When I drop off the algae salve for her knee or the dried sea lettuce for her eyes."

Keane leaned in and lowered his voice. "The magical stuff?"

Willa nodded. "I think she was cranky because she was in pain. She even said thank you this last time...before she ordered me to leave."

"That sounds like Mary." Keane chuckled.

"She's not so bad," Duke said. "She just doesn't like being around people much. Sometimes, I understand that feeling."

Keane did too. He needed time to zone out while painting or surfing. People complicated that.

"Speaking of algae, did you call that scientist?"

"She said she's a marine biologist, but yes." Willa nodded. "She's going to drive down in the morning and test a few areas. See if she can figure out what's going on."

"I'm worried about the Clam Festival coming up." Duke pointed to the flyer taped to the door of Willa's studio. "If the water is bad, everyone in town could get sick."

"Definitely. Everyone eats seafood that weekend," Keane agreed. It would be a bad time for sure.

"Did Tracy hit you up yet?" Willa asked Keane.

"Tracy?"

"Tracy Ellis," Duke told him. "She's the new postmaster."

Keane remembered her from high school. He turned to Duke. "Did she ever forgive you for putting those frogs in her backpack?"

"They were all supposed to be freed." Willa frowned.

"It was only a few," Duke reassured her. "And I watched them. No frogs were harmed in the scaring of Tracy Ellis."

"Good." Willa firmly crossed her arms.

"That was, like, ages ago." Duke shrugged. "Tracy's over i t."

Apparently, they got over it much quicker when you didn't leave home.

"What does Tracy want?" Keane got back on topic.

"She's asking for donations for the raffle."

"At the festival?" Keane remembered the event. It always brought in good money for the town. "What are they using it for this year?"

"The school needs new technology," Willa answered. "I thought you might want to donate a painting or something."

Keane nodded. "Sure. I can come up with something."

"I'll let her know if I see her before you do," Willa said. "You guys have a good day. I've got to get ready for my next class.

"Thanks," Keane said.

"See ya, Flower Child." Duke shifted to let her pass, then asked Keane, "Where are you headed?"

"Just clearing my head, no goal."

"Sometimes that is the goal, man."

"True."

"Wanna walk?"

"Sure." Keane fell in step beside his friend as they headed back to the marina. "What's up?"

"How much do you know about Charles?"

"Who's Charles?" Keane asked.

Duke's face fell in a distressed expression.

"Oh," Keane said quietly. It had to be the guy Shelby was seen with. "So, it's true. She is seeing someone."

"I'm not sure it's that serious. Sorry, I shouldn't have brought it up."

"No, it's okay. I knew it was possible she'd found someone." Keane's shoulders slumped. Then he realized his friend wouldn't have brought it up for nothing. And he wouldn't be gossiping about Shelby's love life. He was too private for that. "Wait, what's wrong with him?"

"Nothing that I know of, but he threw a red flag for Maggie."

"Wouldn't Shelby have seen it too?" Shelby knew people.

"Maggie's got a keen eye for that sort of thing." Duke ran a hand through his hair. "Shelby would hate for me to be talking about this behind her, but I wanted to ask around. Lightly, you know. I was hoping you knew his last name."

"Sorry, I don't know anything about him." Keane studied the concrete sidewalk that stretched before him. "I've been avoiding news about her life, hoping to hear it directly from her."

"Sorry, man."

"We're good. I was bound to find out eventually."

"You guys were getting along yesterday."

"You mean she wasn't ripping me apart?"

"That *is* something." Duke chuckled.

"Yeah, she has reason to be pissed."

"Agreed, but you told her why you left, right?"

"That I felt like a loser, mooching off my girlfriend?" Keane shook his head. "I don't want a pity forgiveness. That's not the type of relationship I want with her. It feels manipulative, like I'd be guilting her into it."

"What did you tell her, then? You did tell her something, didn't you?"

"I explained that I needed to be in New York to make it as an artist. And I apologized."

Duke was quiet for a few moments. "How'd it end?"

"She stormed off. Said I was too late."

"Hmm."

Keane didn't ask what that meant. He didn't want to hear Duke's opinion on his future. It was better to hear his chances, slim as they were, from the woman herself.

"Wanna get in the water?" Duke said suddenly.

"The water?" Keane perked up.

"I have a couple of paddleboards. You could borrow one. We could do a little reconnaissance and investigate for evidence of issues with the marine life."

Joy sprung up on Keane's face. "Sounds great. I'm borrowing Loris' old one at the moment. It's a decent one. I can use it until I get one of my own."

"Check the shop at the west edge of town. They have nice ones."

"Will do." Keane was already itching to get moving. "I'll go change."

"Meet you at the coastline." Duke held his hand out to fist bump Keane's.

Then both men jogged off.

"What's that on the coastline?" Duke pointed from Keane's left, where he stood on a paddleboard.

Keane scanned the shore to see what he was referring to. A small square item caught his eye. Nothing in nature was perfectly square or round. He squinted, recognizing it. "It's a cooler. Probably left by someone, or it washed up onshore."

He made a mental note to walk back and pick it up later in the day.

"Let's try around that next bend." Duke pointed farther ahead.

Keane nodded, paddling in longer strokes to catch up.

When they rounded the curve, Keane saw a couple of orcas near the tip of the cove where it opened out to the rest of the Hood Canal. From this distance, he could see them more clearly. One of them had a deep white scar running from its eye down its face and side.

"Is that Percy?" he asked, coming alongside Duke.

"Yeah, he stays in orca form most of the time."

"Because he wants to or because he has to?"

"No clue. He's not a big sharer."

The water was still calm, even with the day growing late. They slid over the surface easily.

"You guys good friends?" Keane asked. He wasn't exactly jealous, but he was interested in the man.

"I wouldn't say good friends, but he seems friendly. Keeps to himself most of the time." Duke leaned as he paddled back and forth. "I think he's pretty protective of his crew. But he's come around. I don't get that he thinks we're much of a threat anymore."

"He was worried about it?"

"We weren't supposed to get powers. It was an accident. He was worried we would misuse them."

It made sense. He imagined Randall and Mick getting magical abilities. Even at their age, they would be impossible. He shuddered to think what they would do with that kind of gift.

"So, you can make the water move, huh? Is that why I'm struggling to keep up with you?"

"Nah, it's because you're out of practice and out of shape," Duke tossed behind him.

A water spray from a nearby ripple launched upward and splashed Keane's shorts.

"Dude!" Keane flicked his paddle up, spraying Duke's shirt. "Can't stop that, huh?"

"Too small. It has to be part of the main body of water."

"Really? Like, you don't have as much control over the smaller pieces?"

"Kind of. Maggie can pull water together, but I can't touch the droplets or molecules, whatever it is. It's different for me.""What does it feel like?"

"Honestly? Like the sea is an entity, and I'm asking for a favor. I give it a little nudge. Plus, it gets tingly in my chest, arms, and fingertips."

A thought popped into Keane's head. "Is that why it's so calm?"

Duke smirked. "Partly. It was already calm, but I did even it out a bit."

"That's way cool."

"It kinda is. I don't get to talk about it a lot."

They stood quietly, scanning the shoreline. Everything looked fine on this end as well.

"How do you normally use your power?" Keane asked.

"Just like this." Duke's hand floated over the water. "Calming it when I'm on a transport. Or if I'm in a rush, I might give myself a boost."

"That's handy."

"In my line of work, it's been pretty handy."

"You seem to be doing well for yourself."

"Business has been good," Duke agreed. "I have some good regulars. I help the Gil's on special orders too."

"I heard from Nell that you move specialty items as well." They would pay the most.

"There's always business for exotic items." Duke winked.

"You've got the connections for it."

"I got around a lot when I was younger."

A couple of Pacific white-sided dolphins that were playing farther out headed their way. One of them flipped up into the air. A sheet of droplets sparkled in the sunlight. It disappeared below the surface, then popped up and chirped at them.

They had drifted into deeper water.

"Maybe we're in their area," Keane wondered aloud.

"Nah, these two are just troublemakers." Duke grinned.

The two dolphins chattered at them before disappearing below the surface and reappearing farther out. The scarred orca glided through the water, coming in their direction.

The two men stilled. Even though Keane didn't believe Percy to mean them harm, he didn't know the orca shifter, and anything thirty feet long and weighing six tons was a potential threat when you were a mere human floating on a thin board on the surface of deep water.

The orca's blunt nose rose in the air to bump his paddleboard. Keane's knees flexed, and his core tightened to keep his balance even though the waves washed over his feet. He'd barely been able to stay onboard.

"He's messing with you," Duke said.

"You can't talk to him, right? Not like Solomon?"

"No." Duke shook his head. "I don't think he can speak to us in this form."

That made sense. The orca would have the wrong vocal cords for human speech.

"Hi." Keane raised his hand. "I'm curious about you too. I'm out here because I love the water. Surfing and paddleboarding are two of my favorite things to do."

The orca blinked at him. He dipped his rounded nose back under the water and spun toward Duke.

"Yes, I told him," Duke said to the orca. "He's part of my pod. Always has been. He's just been away for a while."

The other orca that had been swimming with Percy stayed farther out.

"Is that the one Willa calls Cora?" Keane asked Duke, remembering what she had said during dinner.

"I don't think so." Duke squinted. "I think that's Cora's calf."

The orca disappeared under the water, moving underneath Keane's board. If he surfaced right now, he would tip him over. Keane dropped to his knees.

Percy came up a few feet to his right, then spun his large body to face him. Keane could clearly see the long, deep scar that ran along his side.

"Just so you know, I'm no kind of threat to anything in the water. I like your kind, the marine kind, more than some people."

The orca's nose moved closer to his board again but didn't bump it this time. From Keane's vantage point, he could easily reach out and touch the black-and-white creature. Percy considered him for another minute and then moved away.

"Good to see you." Duke lifted a hand in farewell and said to Keane, "He doesn't say much more than that in human form, either."

Keane chuckled at that and watched the majestic, magical being move away. It seemed as though he had passed his test.

CHAPTER 16

"I almost forgot to tell you." Charles brightened. "The wetlands test came back."

"It did?" Shelby sipped her glass of local Mt. Olympus Cellars Barbara. Her friend had partnered with the wine owner, generating quite a nice bump in her business. "Did they find some farther back?"

She'd been curious ever since feeling the buzzing on the property. It was at a greater distance than she'd explored so far.

He frowned. "No, no wetlands were found."

"Oh."

"Were you expecting there to be some?"

"Not exactly." She fished for an explanation of her assumption. "It's the only area I haven't explored."

It seemed to satisfy Charles.

They were lingering on the back patio at Wild's Café, viewing the lapping waves. The sun was dipping low on the horizon. The bacon-wrapped figs with blue cheese and the mini salmon cakes with sriracha-lemon aioli they'd ordered as appetizers were nearly polished off.

They'd stayed longer than she'd expected, bypassing dinner altogether. Charles had shared how he chose his many investments, and she'd shared her grand starts as a youth and meager-in-comparison adult success.

"You'll have time to explore when you're building on the property." He picked at a salmon bite.

"That's true." Her curiosity wanted it to be sooner, but her priorities were delaying her desires. She had too many high-priority items on her plate. "How do you have time to do it all?"

Charles smiled softly at her. "I let people help me."

"Oh, so *that's* the secret." She laughed. "I need to take notes."

"Not a bad idea." He chuckled, lifting his glass. "And I never forget my end goal."

She knew that one. It was her mainstay. "It's impressive you've gotten as far as you have at your age."

"Don't sell yourself short, Shelby. You've built quite an empire here in little Orca Cove. You need to think bigger." He winked. "You'll get there."

She didn't want an empire, but she understood his implication. Go big or go home.

"Can I get you another round?" Maggie appeared at the table. "Or another appetizer? Those blue-cheese figs are to die for, aren't they?"

"They are spectacular," Shelby said with a flourish. "Tell Nell for me?"

"She'll love that." Maggie scrunched her nose in a way only she could do and still be adorable.

"But I think I'm good," Shelby said, lifting her almost empty second glass. She'd driven, and that was her limit, considering the hours they'd spent talking.

"Me too," Charles said. "Can we get the check?"

"Sure thing." Maggie magically furnished it from her apron and set it between the two of them. Charles produced his card, and she promptly disappeared with it to process it.

Shelby had spent two nights in a row on this back deck, having dinner and drinks. Each night had been vastly different from the other.

If she was being honest with herself, and she tried to be, it was nice having Keane back in the fold. He was funny and open, and had spent most of the evening listening. He was good at that. Patience was definitely on his good-qualities list.

Too bad he couldn't be trusted to stick around.

A tiny, minuscule part of her had thought it would be so easy to let it happen. To forget the past and let bygones be bygones. She missed the attention of a man. But she'd put everything she had into him. She knew no other way. And he'd been a bad business deal, cutting and running when it mattered, leaving her to hold on to a beach condo and no one to share it with.

At least Charles didn't seem like that type. He'd never leave a good business deal.

Maggie came by, setting the bill book on the table. "I hope you enjoyed everything."

"It was wonderful." Charles scribbled on the paper slip and shut the cover. He held out his hand to Shelby. "Want to take a walk on the beach? It's a beautiful night."

"That sounds nice." Shelby accepted his hand and stood, exiting through the back deck.

It was overcast, so even though it wasn't fully dark, it felt like dusk.

They walked quietly along the coastline for a few minutes.

"I'm not a small-town guy," Charles said. "But I see the appeal of Orca Cove."

Shelby appraised the cove and the sliver of moon hanging over the water. "She's a beauty, alright. I love simply being near her."

"Is that why you wanted land so close?"

She nodded.

"Do you enjoy boating?"

"I like to kayak. Although I admit I don't get around to it often enough." She inclined her head. "You know what that's like."

"Don't I ever. But it's fun to earn those afternoons when you can squeeze them in, don't you agree?"

"Absolutely."

"Don't let me forget to give you that wetlands report when we get back to the cars."

"Do you have the inspector's certification for my records?"

"Of course."

"Thanks. I'm interested in reading it. And anxious to hear back on the soils for the perc test."

"It's been tested before. I don't think you'll get any surprises," he said reassuringly. "When do you hear back?"

"Hopefully, on Monday."

"That's good." Charles brightened. "That's the last thing, then, isn't it?"

"It's the last test I need to do, yes." Shelby bit her lip.

"Then we can move up the closing date to the end of the week, and you can break ground next week. You'll be in good shape by winter. It'll be important to have them tight before the rainy season."

Winter was very wet, and no one wanted to be in the middle of a construction project without a roof when that happened.

"I'd need to call about the permits, but I think they should be in by next week." Shelby's mind was racing. It was fourteen days earlier than she'd expected. Could she do it? *Should* she do it?

She still had a few rough estimates on her investment spreadsheet for which she'd prefer to have quotes.

"Even better," Charles said enthusiastically.

"I haven't decided who to use for the land clearing yet. I was hoping to get one more estimate."

"There's no time to waste," Charles barreled forward. "The more time you spend figuring it out, the more dollars revenue you'll lose for the holidays, not to mention risking moisture where you don't want it. You can't afford that."

It was true. Summer was the busiest season, but this close to Seattle, the holidays were a perfect bow on the year. She was always booked solid. Couples loved to spend their time off curled up in one of the cute cabins with a fireplace. She even decorated each unit. It was the perfect getaway.

And she'd gotten mold in her shed before learning how to seal it in properly. It was not a lesson she wanted to learn twice.

But launching into it without finalizing the investment costs made her feel unsteady. Shelby stopped walking and stared at the waves lapping at the shore.

"I'm so sorry." Charles spun to her and took her hands. "I didn't mean to push you. I just am so excited for you, and I want to help."

"You've already helped." Shelby attempted a small smile, but her stress level had already spiked, and her stomach churned.

"It doesn't feel like it." Charles' eyes dropped to the ground between them. "I know you don't want to mix business with pleasure, but...what can I do?"

Shelby tried to ground herself to the space between them. He was trying to be there for her. "You've done so much already. You helped with the wetlands."

"That was nothing." He scoffed. "Are you sure you won't take the offer for a loan?"

"Honestly, I'm fine." Shelby took a fortifying breath. There was nothing to be worried about here, but a nice, successful man trying to help her out. "I need to get my head wrapped around it. Let me take tomorrow to do another round of obsessing over my numbers. I'll let you know Monday, after I hear back on the perc test, to decide on our closing date."

"Okay." He raised her hands higher and kissed her knuckles. "I'm so sorry I was rushing you. I never meant for that."

"I'm okay. Honest." She was already feeling more steady.

"Forgive me?" He smiled thinly at her, his eyes taking on a plea.

"Of course." She wasn't going to make any rash decisions. This was her future. But she felt better setting a plan and letting him know where they were.

Charles lifted his hand to cup her face, and his thumb brushed her cheek. "I only wish I could help you more."

It filled her with warmth. It had been a long time since anyone had gone out of their way to try to help her this much, and the knowledge felt nice.

"You found the land I wanted. It's close to the cove and my cabins. It's perfect."

"You deserve perfect." His gaze focused on her mouth.

Shelby knew she could back away now if she wanted to cool the mood. With everything going on in her life, it would be a smart move. But it was so tempting to be swept away in something more than her spreadsheets and maintenance lists.

She leaned into him, letting her worries fall away. Charles' hand moved behind her neck as his lips met hers.

The wind picked up, and a warm breeze lifted her hair. Scents of sea salt and driftwood made her think of Keane and *his* hand behind her neck.

Instead of fireworks, all Shelby felt was disappointment.

It wasn't an awful kiss. It was warm and comforting. And Charles was a handsome man. But the spark of something more, the excitement and passion of real chemistry wasn't there.

Shelby pulled away. "I should get home."

"Give me a call next week?" He squeezed her hand.

"Sure."

They walked hand in hand to their cars, and she gave him a quick hug before waving goodbye.

She watched the taillights of his Audi leave the cove. Maybe she was too busy or too stressed to feel anything deeper than friendship. Maybe after they closed on the land, things would be different.

Deep in her gut, she knew it was a lie.

Guilt settled in place of disappointment. No, she'd let Charles know things wouldn't go further between them when they talked next. It was the right thing to do.

Shelby walked into town with her sunglasses firmly in place under the bright summer sun to meet Willa and

Meredith at the marina. She hadn't seen the interesting woman since they met up at Point Peril on Solomon's fishing boat with Percy. He had helped her take photographic evidence of a nearly extinct trout species. The evidence had led to improved boating and fishing rules around the Snake River to protect the endangered fish.

She'd spent most of the previous evening reviewing her almost-relationship with Charles. It was disappointing that they didn't have any chemistry, a fact she was privately blaming on Keane.

Ice cream had helped her work through the worst of that. If he hadn't come into town, she wouldn't have the reminder of everything they'd had together. It was natural that she'd think about their old childhood relationship. First loves were like that.

Charles was a nice guy who also happened to be attractive and financially secure, with a strong business mind. She'd enjoyed having someone to toss ideas around with. He understood her drive, and she could have an intellectual conversation about financial planning. It wasn't a conversation she could have with many people. Not anymore.

If Keane's face hadn't appeared in her head, she might have been able to gather some kind of spark. Later on, after getting over the shock of his return or when he got tired of the small-town life and returned to big-city New York, she'd consider trying again.

But for now, she'd keep the relationship with Charles Timms limited to a business one.

Which meant she could take him up on his offer of investment in Siren's Song Yurts. She didn't like the idea of sharing her business with anyone, but if she was going to, he'd be a solid bet.

At least it was an option, one she also felt bad about if he already had serious feelings about her. She didn't think the logical man would take it personally, but still, the conversation needed to be had.

That morning, after reseeding the yard, she'd made a few more calls for quotes on an excavation. Shelby made a mental list for when she returned from the meeting with her friends. She needed to switch out a few more sink pipes. Several of her weekend renters were checking out today, and it was the perfect time to do it.

"Morning, Shelby." Willa handed her a travel mug of liquid.

Shelby lifted it to her nose and gave it a sniff. It smelled suspiciously like coffee. "What's this?"

"Herbal coffee."

"Decaf tea, then." Shelby raised an eyebrow.

"Not entirely decaf, but lower than coffee."

"If it's herbal, it's not coffee." Shelby took a tentative sip of the hot concoction. Even with Willa's abilities, it would have to be mighty powerful for her not to care about how it tasted.

A bitter flavor, not unlike coffee, trailed over her tongue. It tasted a little burnt, but also a bit like tree bark. She worked it over her mouth, then took another sip.

Willa brightened.

"It's not awful," Shelby said.

"It's good for your gut and helps with inflammation and high blood pressure."

"Is my blood pressure high?"

"You seem to be stressed." Willa stepped onto the docks.

"I'm gearing up for a big investment, and things keep going wrong at the cabins."

"Is it a bad deal?"

"That's not it." Shelby took another sip, enjoying the bite of the tea. "The land is the perfect place."

"What's wrong with it, then?" Willa tilted her head, studying her like she was reading a book.

Shelby frowned. She didn't like the feeling. "It's not the land. It's the water on the land."

"There's water on the land?"

"Only, there's not."

"You're confusing me."

"I'm confusing me." Shelby sighed loudly. "It has to be groundwater. The wetlands certification came back clean, and I have the inspector's certification. It's legit."

"What're you feeling?"

"The water is pinging."

"Pinging?"

"It feels jagged. Unsettled."

Willa nodded thoughtfully. "Have you felt that before? The pinging?"

"No." Shelby shook her head. "I was wondering if my powers were acting up. Have you seen anything different in yours?"

"Nothing that I've noticed."

"Could it be that it's wearing off? Maybe the infusion of magic isn't permanent."

"Percy would have said something if he didn't think they would last."

"Maybe he doesn't know."

"We should ask Duke and Maggie."

"Or Solomon." Shelby spotted the fisherman on the docks ahead of them, talking to Meredith. "Good morning."

"Hello, ladies." Solomon dipped his head. "How are you this fine morning?"

"Good, thanks." Willa hugged the lanky fisherman, then she turned to their new friend. "It's good to see you, Meredith. How are things at Point Peril?"

"Less than perilous." Meredith chuckled. "I'm sticking around a little while, until the Rutgers Trout hover is more established."

"It gives you time to see how things pan out with that Nathan guy, too." Shelby wagged her eyebrows playfully at the scientist.

Meredith blushed. "That's definitely a perk. I'll have to travel again eventually, but Nathan said he's always wanted to see more of the U.S."

At least some people's love lives were working out for them.

"Did you find anything out there?" Willa asked.

"Unfortunately, no." Meredith frowned. "I checked in all the areas Solomon suggested."

Willa and Shelby looked at him with a curious expression on their faces.

"Roy told me where not to fish. I figured it might have to do with the water." Solomon wiped his hands on a handkerchief and stuck it in his back pocket. "Sometimes, he says to throw a catch back but can't explain why."

"Are you having any trouble communicating with him?" Shelby jumped on the minute detail in his wording.

"No, I meant Roy's not sure why the fish is unwell. He just says not to eat it."

Bummer. She had been hoping something was going on with all of them, not just her.

"What about the clams?" Willa asked. "Has he said anything about the clams?"

"Not that I can think of." Solomon scratched his chin. "I've dug for clams a few times this season, and Roy's been happy to help me stick to my limit. He loves them. He's only mentioned the fish and typically deeper in the cove."

"That's good. At least, we don't have to worry as much about the clam festival," Willa said to Shelby.

"What did you test?" Shelby asked Meredith.

"I tested the water's cleanliness at several points in the cove and the Hood Canal. Mainly where Solomon mentioned he remembered Roy stopping him from bringing in catch," Meredith said. "But everything was well within acceptable limits."

"Strange," Willa said.

"I can come back in a few weeks and try again if nothing has changed," she offered.

"We'd appreciate that," Willa said.

"Sure thing. Let me know if you hear anything new."

Shelby nodded, then said to Solomon, "And let us know if Roy says anything about the clams. With the festival coming up, we don't want a town full of sick people. Willa will get overwhelmed. She'll need tea for *her* blood pressure."

Willa rolled her eyes at Shelby. "Somehow, I'll manage, but thanks."

"Wanna grab a late breakfast?" Shelby asked her friend. "I'm starving."

"You're always starving," Willa said, but she pivoted in the direction of the café with her friend.

CHAPTER 17

K eane stared out over the cove. He was sitting in a pile of blankets on his bed, his elbows on his knees. The waves rolled in and out in a rhythmic pattern that should have been comforting. Any other day, it would have made him itch to get on the water.

His mind drifted back to the night before, walking numbly, blindly placing one foot in front of the other up the beach. He'd gone to look for the cooler he'd noticed on the shore when he was out paddleboarding with Duke. And when he returned to the beach, he'd seen Shelby and a man in a sports jacket kiss near the marina.

The plastic, scratched-up thing dangled forgotten from his fingertips. He barely remembered dumping it on his back deck before coming inside to curl up in bed. But there it was, a damaged, dirty thing. It felt a lot like him.

He'd been holding out hope that whatever relationship Shelby had with this guy was platonic or so early that it might fizzle out, but obviously, it had grown into something more than that.

"That's it, then," he said out loud to the universe, wondering if that would make it more real for his heart and easier for his head to understand.

Lacing up his shoes, Keane grabbed a tote bag and headed out for groceries. He'd stayed indoors for a few days, trying to get used to the idea that Shelby and he may never be a thing again. It was hard on his heart, harder than the years in New York, where he'd still held out hope even if it was only a shred buried deep down.

Creating helped. He'd painted so much, that he had to put in another order for paints. Canvases too. Nearly all his canvases were covered in landscapes of the water and trees. He'd focused on another thing he loved. He'd concentrated on the waves, churning with emotion, and the wild colors in the sky. It was beauty and turmoil. At least he thought so.

His phone rang before he made it inside Gil's Market and Marina.

"Hello?"

"Hello, yourself," Gina said with a sassy tone.

"What's up?" It was good to hear his friend's voice.

"I could ask you the same thing." She waited a beat, and when Keane didn't answer, she sighed. "You're painting like mad."

The orders. As his assistant, she helped with his finances. She'd seen the orders come through.

"Yeah, I've had some time on my hands."

"All okay?"

"Yes."

"Liar."

He shrugged, even though he knew she couldn't see it.

"You know, Jerry's never seen the Pacific Northwest." She went on since he hadn't spoken. "He's been interested in seeing your cove of orcas after the first time you talked about home. What was that, five years ago?"

Her husband was a funny guy who was always easy to be around. They were a cute couple.

"Give or take." It had been a sacrifice to hire her, losing some of his scraped-together savings, but it ended up being one of his best decisions. She'd made up for it with her ability to handle his calendar of flights and gallery shows. She'd created her own connections with the teams at the galleries as well and had, somehow, managed to get him invitations from other high-value painters. Everybody liked Gina.

She was the reason these last few years had been so successful, and he finally got to a point where he didn't have to be in New York anymore.

"You always said summer was a beautiful season. I can grab a flight for the two of us. Need me to bring anything with us?"

"You don't need to come. I'm fine. Honest."

"And the painting?""It's very inspiring, being back home after so long."

"It's hard to return home."

He debated brushing her off again. "It is. But it's not all that bad. A lot has changed, but not everything."

"Your parents are good?"

"Yes, and Duke and I are getting back into the swing of things."

"That's good. And Willa? Still wild?"

"She's good too. A little more grounded, but still as openhearted as ever. She has a new guy, Nick. And Nell has a new guy, Emiliano."

"Really? Good for her."

"Yeah, he's younger, but it seems to be working for them both."

"Then, *really* good for her. Well done, Nell."

Keane chuckled. Gina'd never met them, but she and Jerry had heard about them enough over the years. "The guys all get along well. Duke's pretty tight with them."

He left out the part where they had all been gifted magical abilities. Well, the original crew plus Maggie.

"And Maggie," he added. "The waitress Mom and Dad told me about. She's part of the new crew, too."

"You like her?"

"She's hard not to like. Probably the sweetest person I've ever met. Literally."

"Sweeter than Willa?"

"Willa is kind and fair; Maggie is sunshine defined."

"Wow, that's something. But seriously, I do want to meet these people. Jerry and I both do."

"I'd love to see you guys, but give me a little time, okay?" He knew she was leaving one person out on purpose, and he appreciated it. He also knew Gina, being Gina, understood why he didn't want to talk about it.

"With what you've already painted, we can include you in an exhibit in Italy next month."

"Next month?" He'd just gotten home.

"Unless that's too early for you." She left it up to him. "I wasn't going to suggest it, with the move being so new. But you have enough new pieces. Or you will by then."

He thought about it. He wanted to at least get the next few canvases done. It would complete a series he'd been working on.

It might be good to get out for a while, might give him some perspective.

"Okay, as long as it doesn't coincide with the Clam Festival. I don't want to miss that."

They reviewed the schedule. It was shortly after the festival, so he should be able to do both.

"Francesca is going to be so happy. You turned down a few other galleries this past year, and people are getting anxious to see your new work. This move might have been good for you. You're in demand."

"Hopefully, they like my new stuff."

"I can't imagine they won't. A Keane Lennox painting? No way they won't."

The validation settled warmly in his chest. "Thanks, Gina."

"You earned it, buddy. Now, get to finishing up what you need for the show, and I'll get our tickets and hotel rooms. Let me know the details, and I'll organize shipping."

"Will do."

Gina clicked off, probably already booking the flights.

He was heading back to Italy. Francesca's gallery was an old one in Florence. It was smaller but very charming and highly in demand. He wouldn't have to paint too many more pieces for a showing of that size.

But did he want to take the Shelby pieces? He'd never had trouble parting with paintings before. The new stuff, sure, but he'd have to think about the other ones. The ones filled with her colors.

Keane pushed through the glass doors of the market. Bright lights sparkled over the older wooden shelves. It wasn't a large grocery store, but there was generally more than one option for whatever you'd want. And somehow, they always seemed to have what you needed.

He perused the fresh produce. Berries were in season, so he bought a couple of containers of wild marionberries. The tiny, local blackberries were his favorite and hard to find in New York. He wasn't much of a baker like Nell, but he could throw them into some pancakes or yogurt.

Bulk items lined one wall in large five-gallon buckets. Granola sounded good.

As he filled a small paper bag with the cereal, the doorbell chimed.

Raising his head, he saw Shelby enter the market, and his pulse kicked up. His first trip back into town, and he'd run into her. Just his luck.

She had probably felt that same way when he first returned home.

He had to figure out how to be in her life even if they were never going to be romantically involved again.

"Morning, Greene." He raised a hand to catch her attention.

Her green eyes found him, and she tensed before easing into a relaxed posture. She nodded. "Morning, New York."

The dig only made him grin. The thinly veiled insult also meant she was teasing him. He liked that.

"Did they rope you in to a donation for the festival?" he asked.

She nodded. "I'm donating a weekend stay in one of the cabins. You too? Don't tell me Tracy got a hold of you so fast."

"You'd better believe it." He chuckled. "I'm donating a painting. It's not as useful as a vacation, though."

Shelby frowned. "There's nothing useful about a painting. It's art. I'm sure it'll be popular at the silent auction. Might not get what you're used to in value, though."

"I'm not worried about that," he said, then asked as though it wasn't breaking his heart, "Are you going to bring your boyfriend to the festival?"

She stiffened at his words. "News travels fast in a small town."

But she nodded and ran a hand over her richly hued chestnut hair. It reminded him of the deep, luxurious shades of chocolate. "I don't know yet."

He went for it. "Greene, I don't want it to be weird between us." It was better to be honest, right? "I'm glad you've found someone. I hope he makes you happy."

Shelby was quiet.

"I know you're still pissed at me and for good reason," he continued. "I know I said I'm sorry, but I want you to know it is true. I never meant to hurt you."

"What did you think would happen?" she asked curiously.

"I knew you wouldn't like it, but I thought we'd figure it out after I made it big." He tucked an escaped hair behind an ear. He tried to maintain eye contact with her, but it was difficult. So he chuckled nervously and cleared his throat. "Dumb kid."

"You weren't a dumb kid. But it *was* a dumb thing to do."

"Pretty ignorant," he agreed.

"A year." She exhaled loudly and rolled her eyes. "To make it famous."

"I know, right?" The corner of his mouth kicked up. "But seriously, I don't want it to get weird for you with the crew. If I need to, I'll step out."

"It's fine." She brushed it off as though it was nothing. But he knew how much she internalized behind her perfectly poised shell. "Dinner went fine the other night. You weren't completely awful."

Hope soared within him, but he played it cool. "Thanks for that. And thanks for bringing me into the conversation with the new people."

"You looked pathetic out there by yourself," she said, but her eyes had a glimmer to them. "I couldn't just leave you on the outside like that."

"Even so, I appreciated it."

She dipped her head.

"I want us to be friends if you can stomach it." He pushed her, knowing she'd take the challenge.

She pressed her lips together and raised her eyebrows in a smirk. "I'll do my best. I might need some ginger to calm my stomach, though."

"I'll keep stocked up in it," he said sagely. "Or have Willa mix up something."

"That's cheating. She'd make it way too easy."

"Can't have that." He frowned, but his heart felt as though he'd caught a big wave. It swelled and began to race. "It has to suck at least a little."

"Agreed."

"Normal ginger chews, then."

"And nothing from Nell, either."

"I wouldn't dream of it. And if you bring your new guy around, *when* you bring your new guy around, I promise not to tell him about that time you cut all your hair by yourself or how uneven it was."

He held out a hand diagonally in front of him, his face twisted in a grimace.

"Hey! I was doing my best." She jutted a hip out and propped one fist on it. "And I was twelve."

"Or about that time when you made all those buttons to be Middle School Body President and the principal had to tell you they didn't have a student body in middle school."

"They let me hold a vote after school anyway." She preened.

"And you won."

"There was no one else running, so of course."

"But the next year, Principal Sweeney let you start a student body."

"I pestered him for months." Her eyes twinkled. "And that time, I had running mates, *and* I won."

"I hope this new guy knows how competitive you are." Keane shook his head as though pretending to be concerned. He didn't like talking about him, but he wanted her to know it was okay for her to.

He could handle it. He would have to be able to handle it.

Not being in her life wasn't an option anymore.

"He's pretty competitive himself." Her voice wasn't playful now.

"Businessman?" he guessed, having seen the sports coat. Also, Heath and Tommy had said he drove a fancy-schmancy car, their words.

"Yes, he's in property."

"The property you're buying?"

"It's from him, yes. That's how we met. He got it in another larger deal. Charles couldn't use this piece of land."

Charles. His stomach clenched.

"Well, I hope to meet him at the festival."

"Yeah." She drew the word out. "If he can make it."

"I won't keep you." Keane stepped into an aisle. Every part of him wanted to stay and banter with her more. "I've been holed up painting for days and am dying for food."

"We have delivery now, you know."

"From the café?"

"Heath brings it."

"Of course he does." That kid got around. "I like him."

"Me too." Her nose scrunched with her smile. "He's got a keen business sense. How do you know him?"

"He helped me bring the furniture home from Liberty."

"That wardrobe is something." The glow in her eyes said she liked it. That made him happy.

"It is. I love the carvings on it."

"I expected you to bring your New York furniture. Figured it'd be expensive."

"Only a couple of things from my travels. I'm still me, Shelby. I don't want anything too fancy."

"Your art is fancy."

"It sells for a decent amount." The fact still humbled him. "Not the same thing."

"I guess." She moved away as well. They stood in the center of the aisle, and the silence stretched between them. "Enjoy your breakfast."

"You, too."

"I'm starving. It's been a busy morning."

He took another step away from where he wanted to be. "See you around, Greene."

"New York."

Keane checked out, forcing his gaze from returning to where his one true love still shopped.

CHAPTER 18

Shelby watched her childhood boyfriend and the former love of her life walk away. It was tempting to press him for details on the painting he was donating. Was it one of the beautiful ones in greens, golds, and browns that she'd seen in his studio? She had a desire to see the one left unfinished on the easel. Light was streaming through the trees, highlighting the pine-needle walkway below.

Pictures of his paintings were all over online, but she'd never seen one in person. It had texture. Thick brush strokes, layers of paint, and lighter, dreamy strokes danced across the canvas. She'd wanted to touch them.

Being polite at their dinner last week had been an effort, but today, it was easy to converse with him. Too easy. She'd nearly launched into her plans about the property, eager to share more.

What did that mean?

They had always been friends. It made sense they'd still get along. At least, he wasn't pushing the *"is it too late"* card again. Today, she hadn't felt the pressure of anything deep or emotional. That was nice. He'd even asked about Charles as though it wasn't a big deal.

Maybe it wasn't.

She and Charles weren't going to be a thing, but Keane didn't know that.

Maybe he had grown.

Maybe he'd moved on.

She could too. Like, truly move on and let go of the anger she'd been holding onto for so long.

She'd been holding it for so long that she wasn't sure how to let go.

Shaking off the swirling thoughts, she grabbed a mason jar of yogurt parfait stocked from the café and headed to the checkout. Up ahead, Keane paid and headed out.

She raised a hand. He responded in kind.

Weird.

It was still weird.

"Maggie?" Duke said, noticing her and breaking from his conversation with Keane on the docks.

She only had five minutes, ten minutes tops, before the breakfast crowd shifted into the lunch crowd. The last few lingering tables would be good for a little while.

"I don't know which one of you needs this, but here it is." She shoved a piece of paper between the two of them.

Duke was finally back. She'd tried to find him after Shelby and Charles stopped by, but he was out with his ship.

The courier immediately took it and unfolded the small piece of paper from her order pad. The name Charles Timms was written on it.

"What's this?" Duke frowned.

Keane watched her with quiet interest.

"There's something not right there," Maggie said. She'd gotten it from the man's credit card when he paid for their order. She knew she was risking her job by sharing customer information, but she hoped Nell would understand.

She believed in finding the good in things, especially in people. Positivity had gotten her through many hard times in life.

But some people had little to no brightness to them.

"What do you mean, exactly?" Duke asked.

"It's hard to explain." She pursed her lips. "But I'm getting bad vibes. I assume you want that."

She pointed to the paper, her eyebrows high on her forehead in question.

He considered the paper, then her, nodding slowly. "Shelby won't be happy."

"I know." Maggie raised her chin in unusual defiance. "But she's going into business with him. I think looking out for her right now is more important than to be her friend. That sounds awful, but it's true."

Duke nodded.

"It's that bad?" Keane asked, his eyebrows drawing together in concern.

"She wouldn't be here if she didn't have a good reason." Duke folded the paper and tucked it into his back pocket. "Maggie's a sweetheart, but she knows people."

The man's statement shocked her. She knew Duke regarded her as one of theirs, and he kept watch over her. But she hadn't realized he respected her like that. It rocked her to her core.

"Thanks," was all she could muster.

"We'll take it seriously," Duke said.

"Do what you need to do." With that, Maggie spun on her heel and headed back to the café.

Shelby rolled over in bed. It was raining outside, and she didn't want to get up. Groaning, she threw her arm over her face to shield it from the gloomy light coming through the rain.

If she didn't get up, she would set a bad example in the office. Besides, she was expecting an answer from the final excavation company. It would be the last numbers she needed before signing with someone to clear the land.

With effort, she lunged up, swinging her legs out from the warm flannel sheets and planting them directly into her waiting slippers. Wiggling her toes in, she pushed to her feet and found her robe at the foot of her bed.

By the time she'd brushed her teeth and splashed water on her face, the day didn't seem as dreary. The sun was peeking out from between the clouds, and the rain had died down to a light drizzle.

She could even fit in a short run if she hurried.

Her phone rang. It was Cleo from the office.

Shelby checked the time. She wasn't late. Dread settled into the pit of her stomach. That was a bad sign. Either she was sick, or there was a problem.

"Hello?" she answered.

"Shelby." Cleo sounded stressed. "The Thomases in cabin three called. Their son, Jonas, said it's raining in his room."

"Raining?" The bottom of Shelby's world fell out. "I'll be right there."

She threw clothes on, not even paying attention to what she'd grabbed, shoved her feet into boots, and headed out to cabin three.

"Hello?" The Thomases answered her knock almost immediately.

Mrs. Thomas was still wearing a bathrobe. She didn't appear too stressed. That was a plus. Mr. Thomas, however, was frowning.

"I came right away. I heard you have a leak?" Shelby kept her expression helpful, not showing the panic behind it.

"Jonas knocked on our door this morning, saying it's raining." Mr. Thomas pointed into the living room. His tween son was on the fold-out couch.

The globe lamp on the ceiling-fan fixture had filled with water and was spraying it around the room. Shelby flipped the fan switch off. She'd need a bucket to catch the drips.

"Looks like we got a leak from the rain last night." She faced the Thomases. "I'm so sorry this happened. We have another cabin open where we can move you while we repair the roof here. I know it's an inconvenience to switch rooms on vacation."

"It's no problem." Mrs. Thomas said brightly. "Things happen."

She could have hugged the woman. "I'll get you a free night's stay coupon for your next visit out here. We'll make this right."

Mr. Thomas nodded. "That would be nice."

Renters's vacation fixed, Shelby hurried into the main office.

"Write up a free night's stay for the Thomases," she told Cleo, who nodded.

"Already on it, boss. Should I call Simon?"

Shelby wrinkled her nose. "Not yet. Let me check out the roof. See if I can fix it first."

"Are you sure?"

"Yes. We'll call him if we have to."

"You're the boss."

She made a beeline for the shed, found the ladder, and carried it to cabin three before setting it carefully against the gutter. Climbing up, she examined the roof. She'd recently cleaned them, knocking off the mold growth from the winter due to the wet climate. She hadn't noticed the broken shingles she saw now. The wind must have been rough last night, allowing rain to get under them and spread into the living room.

Luckily, it was the dry season, and they weren't expecting rain for another few days. She pried up a damaged shingle. Gouges marked the edge, as if a branch had lodged itself under the flap. Whatever broke it had also cut the felt underneath it. She'd need to replace a handful of them and coat them in Black Jack to prevent further leaks.

Defeated, she lay her forehead on the roof in front of her. What was she doing out here? Charles wasn't doing this sort of panicked repair work. Hell, *she'd* never dealt with this much maintenance in the nearly fifteen years she'd been in business. Why now? Particularly when she was trying to get her expansion off and running.

Was she moving too quickly?

"Morning!" A voice from the ground got her attention.

Schooling her face for her renters, she peered over the roofline. It was Keane.

"What're you doing here?" She scowled.

"I brought coffee." Keane smiled, holding up a small travel mug. It dropped into a frown at the expression on her face. "All okay?"

"Yeah." Shelby sighed. The damage wasn't his fault; she shouldn't take it out on him. She hadn't had any coffee yet. It was probably part of the reason her mood was so crappy. She hopped back to the ground, took the offered drink, and breathed in a long sip of the life-affirming brew. This. This was magic. "Good Lord, that's amazing."

"Nessie made it."

"Nessie? Like the Loch Ness Monster?" Her eyebrow ticked up.

He nodded sagely. "But more like espresso. She's my espresso machine. Gina sent it with my painting supplies."

Who was Gina? Shelby let the pause hang between them, hoping he'd elaborate but not wanting to ask. Unfortunately, the painter was eyeballing her ladder.

"What's going on?" He indicated the roof.

"Leak." She pressed her lips together.

Cleo took that moment to come out to the lawn, the *bare* lawn that was covered in grass seed. And last night's rain. Correction, she stepped out onto mud. And her foot slid.

Shelby had already reseeded that patch, and the gouge, combined with the roof damage did her in.

"Shelby?" Cleo grimaced. "I'm sorry."

"It's okay, Cleo. Not your fault. It was the elk."

"Any idea when cabin four will be waterproof? We got a few more bookings. I booked the rest of the open spots, but a couple wants to come tomorrow, and this cabin is the only one left. Will it be ready by then?"

Not if she had to do it all by herself. She'd have to run to town for Black Jack, but she had some extra shingles in the back of her shed from when they'd built the last of the cabins. It would take a while to get the old shingles down the ladder plus the new ones up.

No, if she set her mind to it, she could do it. If Heath or Tommy were off today, they might be able to help with the cleanup. But who knew what kind of mess she'd have to deal with once she tramped across the lawn over and over?

And she had a list of things she'd wanted to do today.

Everything felt overwhelming. Swallowing hard, she held back her tears and nodded. Right now, she couldn't lose the rent.

Cleo disappeared back inside the office.

"Do you have extra shingles?" Keane said from above.

Turning, Shelby found him on top of the roof, assessing the damage.

"Yes."

"I'm happy to help if you need an extra hand." He descended the ladder like a billy goat. He'd always had good balance.

"That would be"—annoying but really helpful—"nice of you."

"An elk herd did all this?" He scanned the lawn.

She nodded. "Yeah, but they've never come through here before. I don't have any fruit trees, and all my plants are deer-and-elk resistant. I don't know why they picked now to visit the cabins."

"Cool place, though." Keane's eyes took in the rest of the area.

In them, she could see appreciation. It felt good to have him see the fruits of all her hard work. Even though a firepit was missing a couple of chairs, a few of the grills could use a layer of paint, and the lawn had patches of mud, he still looked impressed.

"Thanks. What're you doing here anyway?"

His eyes shifted to the ground for a moment before meeting hers.

"Just making coffee and thought I'd take a walk. I haven't been by to see Siren's Song Cabins." He shrugged. "If I was coming by this early, I figured I'd better come bearing coffee."

She laughed at that. "Smart move," she said, raising her coffee in salute.

"Now, what do we need to do first?" He let her take the lead.

It's where she liked to be.

"I need to get the shingles from the shed, but it's best to take off the damaged ones first, so we know how many we need. And set up a fan inside. If it dries quickly enough, I should be able to throw a coat of anti-mildew paint up later today." She thought quickly. "If you can drive into town and get the Black Jack, I'll get started on the shingles."

"If that's what you want, but I'm happy to start up there." He pointed to the roof. "I can pry them off pretty fast."

She didn't say it out loud, but he was right. She was strong, but it would be easier for him. Faster too.

She considered arguing. "Okay, thank you."

"No sweat." He shrugged off the flannel he'd been wearing and tied it around his waist. "Do you have a pry bar in the shed?""Be careful not to damage the other shingles or the roof decking," she warned, watching him head in the direction of her shed.

"Aye, aye, Captain." He saluted her, then spun around and jogged the rest of the way, his Vans squishing through the mud as though he didn't even care.

There was no way Charles would have helped her out. He might have sent a worker, but she couldn't imagine seeing him get muddy or crawl up on her roof to help out.

Unsettled by the thought, she hurried to follow him to point out the pry bar. She grabbed a couple of extra box fans and placed them in the cabin, pointing upwards.

Then she jumped into her little, red Trailblazer and headed into town.

By the time she got back, Keane had pulled his hair back into a small bun and was bringing a load of shingles down the ladder with him. A frown was on his face.

"Everything okay?" Shelby asked, carrying the bucket. She'd also swung by the Wild Café and picked up two breakfast burritos that she'd called ahead to have ready.

"Yeah." He wiped the sweat from his brow onto his flannel and retied it around his waist, then took the burrito she handed over. "Thanks, this is perfect. I was getting hungry."

"Figured. You didn't plan to work when you left the house." Neither of them had. It was the least she could d

o.

"How does it look up there?"

"Good. I think that's the last of the shingles." He took a big bite of the burrito and moaned. "Man, that's good."

"Nell."

"Weird that only one cabin had wind damage."

"There were some big branches on the roof I tossed off." She pointed behind the building, but they were gone.

"I moved them to the firewood stack over there. I figured you'd want to cut them up and use them. I hope that's okay."

"It is. Thanks." He'd been able to accomplish what would have taken her hours to do.

"Still." He glanced up at the roof again. "I wouldn't have thought it would have caused that much damage."

"Nature's a beast sometimes."

"That's true." He widened his eyes with appreciation. "A wild, wondrous beast."

Shelby dug into her burrito as he wolfed down the last few bites of his. Then he bent down and hoisted a pile of shingles.

"Want these in the dumpster?"

"Yes, please." She pointed behind the office. "I'll open it for you."

"No sweat. Enjoy your breakfast. I can get them." He carried the pile, adjusting its weight to one shoulder so he could throw open the lid, and levered it into the dumpster.

Shelby watched his back muscles move. Keane certainly hadn't lost his youthful strength. If anything, he'd filled out quite nicely. As he jogged back, she blinked to focus before he caught her ogling him.

She might have completely misread him the first few days. It sounded like he might have a girlfriend. Gina.

They were history. Just friends now, remember? she chided herself.

Anything more was a bad idea. Right?

CHAPTER 19

Keane almost stumbled on the way back over to Shelby. Not from the mud, but from the expression he thought he had caught on her face.

There was no way she was checking him out. Was there?

Nah, she had a boyfriend.

Even though the guy had raised red flags with Maggie, Shelby was with him. She'd picked him. That had to mean something. Besides, she wasn't a bad judge of character. It would take a smooth guy to pull the wool over Shelby Greene's eyes.

He wondered what made Charles so special. He was a businessman. Was that what she was looking for in a man these days?

Keane was careful not to brush by Shelby with the rest of the shingles. She was dressed casually, but she still looked exceptional. He couldn't remember a time when she hadn't.

"I think nine shingles should do it." He returned to her.

"If you don't mind taking them up there, I need to check the ceiling."

"No sweat." After making his way back across the mud, he wiped his feet again on the patch of grass outside the shed so he wouldn't track mud in. He found an opened box of shingles in the back. It was almost a full bundle. Counting out what he needed, he loaded them onto his shoulder and headed back out.

As he stepped into the sun, he noticed something in the half-trampled bushes behind the shed. He peered down and toed it. It was pink and opaque white in areas, like raw rose quartz. Dropping the shingles onto a clean patch of grass, he kneeled to inspect it. He lifted a chunk and sniffed it. Salt block. Why were salt-block chunks behind the bushes?

Maybe a hunter had been baiting deer or elk to a spot and broke up the remainder of the salt block before he left, scattering it behind the shed as a means of disposal.

It sounded fishy. Poking around behind some other broken bushes, he found a few more chunks and some sandy pieces that were crushed.

Interesting.

Could this Charles character be sabotaging her cabins by luring the elk here? The roof damage seemed heavy for the branches they'd found too. Things happened, sure, but that much?

He chewed his bottom lip. If he brought it up to Shelby, she'd think he was accusing her new boyfriend of nefarious deeds out of jealousy. It might even make her lean harder into the man. It was best to do some research into Mr. Timms first.

If he was wrong, it would be even worse and might ruin what little friendship they'd been able to rekindle.

Hoisting the bundle back onto his shoulder, he carried it to the cabin. Shelby reappeared in the doorway.

"It's nearly dry in there," she said brightly. "I'll be able to get a coat on later today."

Keane dropped the weight he was carrying again. He could only take half up the stairs at a time anyway. "That's great. You'll have this fixed up by the end of the day."

"With your help." She didn't seem pleased with her admission.

"I honestly don't mind."

"I know," she mumbled. "But you shouldn't have to. It's my business."

"Lots of people help me in my business." He shrugged it off. "It's part of the process."

"I guess." Shelby threw a glance back through the door she'd left ajar.

Keane tilted his head to peer inside. It was furnished with buffalo plaid and live-edge furniture, playing up the cabin motif. "It's cute."

"You can check it out if you want." She edged farther inside. "I barged my way into your space."

"Not today. I'd track in mud." He lifted a foot covered in brown sludge up to his ankles. He must have slid more than he'd thought. "And I guess it's only natural that we're curious about what each other built."

"After you left."

"Yes." He swallowed.

Shelby raised her chin an inch. "I built all this. And I'm expanding. The new land will have yurts for larger families. Ten. That's the plan anyway."

"That's a lot to build by yourself. It's impressive."

"Mostly by myself. I got a loan for this first set of cabins."

"A lot of people do. I've had to get loans to make ends meet. You're still the one paying it off."

"These repairs are dipping into my investment fund." She peered up at the roofline with her hands on her hips.

Charles wouldn't want to sabotage this if he expected her to invest in his land. That wouldn't make sense.

"I might have to consider accepting help if I want to keep all ten yurts." She jerked her head back his way as though she'd just realized he was still standing there. "Sorry, I'm boring you with all this."

"Not at all. I like hearing your plans. Ten yurts. That's going to be very cool. I've always liked them. They're charming."

"I agree. They'll bring people in from Seattle, I think."

"I would think so. It's unusual and adventurous." He hated that she was considering downgrading her dream. Would she be offended if he offered to help? They were friends now. "You know, if you want a loan, I'd be happy to help."

It was why he'd done what he had. So he had something to offer her. To help out when she couldn't do it on her own.

"First Charles, now you." She rolled her eyes. "I am perfectly capable of getting one from the bank. My credit is excellent, I'll have you know."

"I wouldn't think any different, Miss Greene. But I could give you a better rate." Free, he could give her a zero-percent interest rate. But she'd never accept that.

Wait, Charles had offered to help her? That might have given him the motive to damage the cabins. Maybe he wanted to force her hand to let him invest in the yurts.

"It's not a good idea." She pivoted away from him, shutting down the conversation.

Did that mean she wouldn't accept help from Charles either?

"It's there if you need it. I'm more than happy to help." Keane selected five shingles from the pack and carried them to the roof, leaving her with the offer. He knew better than to push her on the topic.

By the time he came back down the ladder, shingles in place and Black Jacked to seal them from additional leaks, he found her inside the cabin. She was stretching a tarp over the furniture and setting out paint supplies.

He stood in the doorway and admired all the little touches in the room. "It's a nice cabin. Does yours look the same?"

Shelby peered up from stirring the paint can. "Yes, I wanted it as nice as the others so I could rent it out if needed."

"You ever need to?"

"In the beginning." She tapped the lid back in place. "But I still had a space in the office. I didn't have a receptionist back then. It was a one-woman show."

"For how long?" He was genuinely interested. He'd missed so much of her life.

"A couple of years. Then I got Cleo. She's been with me the longest. She's great. I had a guy a few years ago and hired Terri when he moved to Aberdeen."

Had he been a boyfriend? He bristled, even though he didn't have the right to.

"You going to move to the yurts when they're built?" he asked instead.

"I think so. I'll be able to rent them for more, so it would be a reduction of income." She smiled shyly in a way that made his heart ache. "But it would be nice to have a little more room. These cabins are small, with a very small closet."

Right then, all Keane wanted to do was buy her a big house, with a huge closet, on the side of the mountain overlooking the water. If it made her smile like that, he'd give her anything.

"You've earned nice things, Greene. You should enjoy it."

Back in high school, she'd always needed a gentle push to rest. Working too hard put the focused woman deep in a zone. It was hard for her to lift herself out of it. It wasn't currently his place to pull her out, but hell, she should reap the rewards of her hard work.

"Thanks." Shelby reddened in her cheeks, and she cleared her throat before moving away from the paint. The wall was back up between them. "You're right. I have. And I've done a damn good job at it."

"No one could convince me otherwise." He should leave before she asked him to. "Roof's done."

"All of it?" She glanced up at the ceiling as though she could see through it.

He nodded. "I'll let you be the judge, but I think it looks good. I used the Black Jack, and with the sun coming down right now, it should be sealed up by the end of the day."

"Thank you for doing that." Her eyes softened.

"My pleasure.""Not how you expected to spend your day, I guess."

"It was good to get out of the house. I needed a breather from painting. Besides, I need more canvases."

"You went through all of those in the spare room?" Her eyes widened.

"Yeah, it's been a quiet week, and I've been inspired. It's nice being back home." He'd needed to paint to keep sane from his thoughts of Shelby and Charles. It was one thing when he thought the businessman had swept her off her feet. It was even worse now that there was a chance the man might be bad news. "Can I do anything else?"

"You've done enough." She wiped her hands on her jeans. "While this unit is free, I have a little plumbing to d o."

"Plumbing?"

"A few of the sink drains had wear in the P traps. I'm swapping them out preventatively to PVC. Better to plan ahead."

She'd had leaks in her sinks as well? That was too coincidental.

"I could lend a hand," he offered, wanting to stay and help even though he knew better.

"Nah, I've got it. I have some other work to do anyway. How's Kalani?" she said suddenly.

He'd been preparing to leave, but his foot paused, hovering off the landing. "She's doing great. Her birthday is next month. She wants to go to the beach."

"The beach." Shelby's mouth widened, and her deep-green eyes drifted off. "Kalani is such a sweetheart. I haven't seen her in a while."

"She asked about you."

Shelby's eyes snapped back to him. "Tell her I said hi."

"I will." It was time to go. "See you around, Greene."

"See you, New York."

Keane finally stepped off the porch. His heart ached to take Shelby back to the beach with his parents for his mom's birthday. He wanted to sit on low chairs on the pebble shore and watch his mom and the woman who held his heart share a laugh like they so often had. His Dad's eyes would sparkle when he watched his mom giggling over being the center of attention. He'd race out into the water to catch a wave, then sat on the board, waiting for another one while watching the people he loved relax on the shoreline.

When it was his birthday, he'd get to invite the rest of the crew. He and Duke would sit out and catch waves for a couple of hours before joining the rest of them.

Memory after memory washed over him like a big swell.

It would make his freaking year.

Keane answered his phone. "Hey, Gina."

"Hey, yourself. Sorry I couldn't pick up when you called earlier. I was sorting out the details for the Florence show. Tickets are all booked. You should have gotten the info in your email box."

"Thanks." He hadn't checked yet, but he was sure they were there.

"What can I do for you?"

"I have an odd request." He sat down in one of the chairs looking out over the cove. It was particularly rough with the tide going out. The set waves were cresting beautifully.

"Oh?"

"I'd like you to check into someone for me. Use those amazing skills and connections you have."

"You're buttering me up. This must be important to you." He could hear Gina's wheels spinning. "Is this about her?"

"Her?"

"Don't play dumb."

He sighed loudly. "Yes."

"New boyfriend?"

"Not because of that. There are red flags."

"Okay. What's the name?"

He hadn't expected it to be that easy. "Charles Timms."

"Approximate age?"

"My age?"

"Currently living in Orca Cove?"

"Not sure, but somewhat close by. Maybe on this side of the Seattle area. Wealthy."

"Anything else you know about him?"

"Not really." He had painfully little. Duke didn't know any more, either. And after Maggie dropped this bomb on them, they'd both decided to do some careful searching, then meet up with what they found.

He'd have to tell Duke about the salt blocks and the gouges in the roof shingles.

They could take turns keeping an eye out on the cabins for a few days. Wasn't Nick a retired cop? He barely knew the guy, but he somehow felt like he could call him.

"Family? Vehicles?" Gina rocked him from his thoughts.

"He has a black Audi." Heath knew cars.

"That helps." He could hear her clicking on a computer. "This might take me some time. When do you need it?"

"No serious rush. A few days if possible." He didn't know when she was closing on the land, but it couldn't be too far away.

"Easy. I'll work on it. I might need to reach out to some people. That will take longer."

"That's okay. Whatever you can find." He rubbed his forehead, worried about Shelby. "Thank you so much, Gina."

"No sweat. This is what you pay me for."

"I don't pay you for background checks." He chuckled.

"No, but you pay me for my mad office skills."

"Very true. You're the best."

"I know." He could hear her chuckle as she hung up.

CHAPTER 20

S helby sat slumped at her desk. One foot swiveled her absently from right to left on her office chair. Terri had long since left for the day.

The roof was fixed, thanks to Keane, and the ceiling had a fresh coat of paint on it. She'd put another coat on first thing in the morning and open the windows to air it out before the new renters came in.

That was the good part.

Her eyes reviewed the completed spreadsheet in front of her over and over. Nick had looked over her quotes and estimates with her earlier that week and had helped her decide on which company to use. She had gotten a better deal with one excavation company and would hire the construction team for the yurts separately. Nick would help oversee things to make sure everyone was pulling their weight, while building decks and the gazebo.

Eight. She was down to eight yurts. And even at that, it was going to be a stretch. Had she not been booked for the entire summer, she would have had to cut further. Keane's assistance with the roof was the only reason she was able to get the cabin ready for the two-week rental, helping her funds immensely.

The thought made her stomach clench. Shelby never ran this close on her finances. It wasn't a comfortable place to be.

Picking up her pencil, she spun it between her fingers. If she called Charles, he would still be open to investing. She was sure of it. And now that she knew there wasn't any real chemistry between them, she could consider it.

But would he feel the same way?

And just because she could, did that mean she *should*?

Either way, she needed to talk to the man. She owed him a call.

Dialing his number, she stood and paced her office.

"Hello, beautiful!" Charles's voice was smooth through her tiny speaker.

She winced. "Hey, Charles. How're you?"

"Good. I've been expecting your call, but I must admit I didn't think it'd take you all week."

"Sorry about that. I've been busy."

"I know what that's like. Everything okay?"

"Of course," she lied, not wanting to talk about the cabins and her misadventures. "I have all my bids in now. And the permits were signed off this week, too. Things are ready to go."

"Excellent!" His voice pitched up a notch. "We can close on Saturday if you'd like. You can cut ground next week."

Her stomach dropped, and she felt the pull from the cove even more than usual. She knew it was a good idea to start as quickly as possible, but what difference would two more weeks make? It wasn't as though they would make or break a Christmas deadline.

Her gut told her to wait.

Still, the excavation crew said they were ready to start any time. What harm could there be to start two weeks earlier? She'd pulled the money. It was sitting in her account. Why did she hesitate?

She'd assigned a meager incidentals fund for her cabins in case of any additional repairs, but not a lot. Was that what was causing her fear? If so, two weeks wouldn't help that situation any. Charles was right in that regard. The faster she started, the quicker she'd be pulling income.

Biting her lip, she answered, "No, let's leave it as it is."

She heard his pause filled with disagreement over the line. "You know, the earlier you can get the rentals going, the quicker you can gain revenue."

See? she thought to herself. It was only fear. But when she opened her mouth to say what she knew he wanted to hear, her stomach clenched again and the pull of saltwater grew even stronger.

That was weird.

She'd been making decisions for herself from an early age. Her parents weren't around much. If she wanted stability growing up, she had to create it for herself. She'd learned to take advice from successful people and put it to good use. And here she was, getting advice from Charles, a markedly successful guy, but every time she thought about agreeing with him, her gut told her no.

Once again, she frowned. Standing, she cracked her window open and let in the cool evening air.

"No, Charles. I'm leaving the date as is." Her stomach eased, and the draw from the ocean calmed back to normal.

"Is this because of the cabins?" he pushed. "I told you I'd be willing to help financially. I know they have been a burden."

Shelby's head whipped back as though he had smacked her. "My cabins aren't a burden. They're doing very well, thank you very much."

"I didn't mean it like that. I only meant that you've had a lot of repairs recently," he said in a rush. "I'm sorry, Shelby. I didn't mean to offend."

She narrowed her eyes in the dark room and considered his words. She had been complaining a lot about repairs. "It's not because of the finances. It's because, once everything starts, I'll be knee-deep in project work. I'd like to take these next two weeks to get ahead on some things."

"I understand," he said slowly. "Still, the offer stands. If you change your mind, I'm happy to help."

"Thank you."

"You know this just means I get to see you more often."

She needed to get to the land and figure out what was going on with her powers. Other things kept getting in the way. But most importantly, she needed to be honest with him. He deserved that. "I'd love to see you and talk business. I value your insight, but I'm not sure a relationship is in the stars for us."

"Oh? I thought we had something between us." His voice sounded confused.

"I know. I thought so too, but I think we might be better as friends."

"Did I push too fast?""Not at all. It just isn't clicking like it should be for me. I'm sorry."

"Don't be. I'm glad you're honest with me. Not everyone can be that forthright. I admire you, Shelby."

"Thanks," she said, surprised. She'd expected him to be a little hurt. The guy had class. She'd underestimated him.

They exchanged pleasantries and hung up.

She locked up and headed home, anxious to pull out a tub of ice cream and create a countdown list of everything to accomplish before being head down and knee-deep in another all-consuming project.

Time on her kayak and with her friends were at the top of that list. She had work things to get ahead of, but time off was important right now. She would be limited for that soon.

For the next two weeks, she was going to let her hair down.

Saturday came quickly. Her days had been full of list making and finishing tiny projects around the cabins. As of yet, Shelby hadn't taken much time for any fun, but this evening would be different.

She busted through the back door of the Wild Café and into Nell's kitchen.

"It's Clam Festival Day!" she sang loudly. It was one of the best days of the year in Orca Cove. Better than Christmas...almost.

Nell blinked up from a big stock pot with wide, harried eyes. "I'm well aware."

Shelby sat down quietly at the table in her kitchen. "Everything okay?"

Emiliano hurried through the kitchen door and over to Nell, pressing a kiss into her hair. "I got everyone out of the market and closed up. How are you doing here? What can I do?"

Then, finally seeing Shelby, he said, "Hey, Shelby."

"Hey, yourself. Are you stressed, Nell? Has something happened?"

"No." Nell used a kitchen towel to wipe her brow and then threw it in a bin in the corner. It left a streak of flour across her forehead. "I was worried about the clams even though Meredith said they were clean, so I only used those from fisherfolk I know. I could make sure where they were coming from on the cove. You know, from where she tested."

"She tested several locations along the tidelands," Shelby said. "Meredith thought the clams would be safe to eat."

"I know." Nell turned from her pot to give Shelby her full attention. "But after worrying that my magic was making the townspeople sick, the last thing I needed was bad clams."

"And you did everything in your power to keep them safe," Emiliano reassured her before turning to Shelby. "We even tested some this morning."

"Not all of them!"

"We did what we could." Emiliano ran a hand over her back. "Is it good enough?" Nell peered up into her boyfriend's eyes.

He smiled warmly down at her. "I think it is. We have no reason to believe otherwise."

"Okay." She nodded, her gaze unfocused. "It'll have to be. Thanks."

Emiliano patted her on her back reassuringly, then pointed at the big basket of sourdough baguettes on the table. "Want me to take these down to the tent?"

"Yes, please. This is almost ready." Nell's focus was back on her chowder. She took a deep breath.

"You're not going to make everyone stressed out tonight, are you?" Shelby teased her.

"No!" Nell's hands went to her hips. I'm not touching it until I have my nerves under control. "Emiliano, can you switch on the music again?"

"Sure thing." He flipped the switch on the radio on the table and set his hands on her waist, pulling her close. Calming jazz music drifted over the kitchen. "Does this help?"

"We don't need the entire town turned on," Shelby said dryly. "Unless you want to increase the population in Orca Cove."

Nell ignored her, closed her eyes, and leaned back into Emiliano's arms. Then, cracking an eye, she straightened. "You're hilarious."

"I like to think so."

"Good, babe?" Emiliano asked Nell.

"Yeah, I think I am." Nell's drawn features looked visibly relaxed. Shelby was jealous and wished she had someone to help her focus when she was stressed.

"I'll take the bread down." Emiliano hefted the overflowing basket up. "Wait for me, and I'll carry that down, too. You can bring the electric hot plate."

"Thanks, honey." Nell's eyes softened as she watched Emiliano leave with the wicker basket. "He's the best."

"He's pretty great," Shelby agreed. He wasn't Gary, but he was good for Nell, and everyone, including Shelby, liked the young man. "What can I do? I'm headed for wine, so put me to work while you can."

"That stack needs to go to the tent." Nell pointed to a few boxes.

"Is that it?"

"Yes, that and the hot plate."

"Do you want me to turn it on to preheat?"

"No, this pot is still simmering. It won't drop in temperature that fast." Nell considered the full stock pot in front of her. "I have another one already done in the fridge, too. I hope that's enough."

"I'm sure it will be." Shelby balanced two of the three boxes. "There will be other food, and lots of people are going to go out at low tide and dig for clams later anyway."

"True." Nell frowned, already worried.

"Let me drop these off, and I'll be back." Shelby backed through the door and into Keane's strong arms.

"Hey. Sorry." He caught the tipping boxes.

"I can get these." She inclined her head, taking them from him. "But there is another one in there that needs to come out, plus the electric burner."

"On it." Keane disappeared into the kitchen.

Shelby found the café's table and plunked the boxes under the counter. Keane was right behind her. Plugging the hot plate into the long extension cord, she set it on a back table, next to where Emiliano had left the bread and gone back for the chowder.

The sounds of the festival were already kicking up. Carnival games pinged in the center of the parking lot between the Wild Café and Gil's Market and Marina. It was the heart of downtown Orca Cove.

Tents for food and drinks lined one end, and the stage was set up like always near the other. Parking was limited to the street or at the post office during this time.

"It's just like I remember it," Keane said, wistfully taking in the festivities around him.

"Did you turn in your painting for the silent auction?" Shelby asked, peering over the other tables to catch a glimpse.

"Yes, this morning. You?"

"Cleo dropped it off. I was finishing some things at the office."

"The roof holding up fine?"

"Yes, thanks again for saving me the other day." Shelby straightened the tablecloth Nell had laid out. "That rental was for two weeks. I would have hated to lose it."

"It seriously was nothing. I was glad to help."

"I need wine," Shelby said suddenly, scanning the vendors.

"Long day?" Keane chuckled.

"Long month." Shelby buzzed past him and made a beeline for the Mt. Olympus Winery table across the walkway. Frank, the owner and winemaker had been partnering with Nell. Today, she had a suggested pairing to match the chef's clam chowder. "Do you want one?"

It was the least she could do. She owed him.

"Sure, but is there beer?" He looked around at the tents. "Beer goes better with clam chowder."

"True, but Fran's Sauvignon Blanc is pretty incredible." Shelby ordered the recommended pairing, then stopped at the tent next to it. Talking over the growing crowd, she asked Keane, "You like West Coast IPA?"

He nodded. She paid and brought it back to him.

"Thanks." Keane sipped it, and his eyebrows raised appreciatively. "It's good. Is Charles coming?"

The open expression he gave her had no agenda, no judgment.

"No, we're only business partners." It didn't feel right to keep up the pretense. He'd figure it out before long anyway, living in a small town.

"But I thought—" He let the word hang.

"It wasn't going to go anywhere." She shrugged.

"I'm sorry to hear that." He actually sounded like he meant it.

"Thanks. It's all good."

Nell had arrived and was organizing her table the way she wanted it. Emiliano and Maggie were setting up stations, getting ready to open.

"Need help?" Shelby asked her chef friend.

"No, all good here. Get out there and have a little fun." Nell waved her away.

Scanning the festival, Shelby searched for Willa or Duke. Neither had shown up yet.

She wanted to see Keane's painting. Was it the one he hadn't finished? "I'm going to check out the silent auction."

"If you find something cool, let me know," Nell said.

Shelby wandered around the items and bid on a few things. She spied a large painting near the end and made her way to it. Growing closer, a small thrill thrummed up within her to find it was the one she had seen unfinished.

Greens and golds with hues of browns and ivory graced the canvas. The picture was of the forest. Dew sparkled on its branches, lit by a beam of light through the center of the piece to veer to the bottom left. It held so many mysteries that she took two steps closer until she realized her hand was hovering over the textured paint.

Catching herself, she dropped her arm and found the auction form below. Several bids had already been made, and they were growing in value, but they were still way under what she'd read online his paintings were going f or.

Making a rash decision, she scribbled her bidding number under the last one and added twenty bucks. She could check on it later, before the auction closed.

On her way back out to the main part of the festival, she found Keane standing in front of the dart tent. She worked her way over to him and leaned in. "You think you still have it?"

Startled, he glanced over at her. Catching onto her meaning, he gave her a lazy smile.

"I do." His gaze traveled over the prizes in front of him and landed on a small plushie. He tilted his head to her. "Do you still have your stuffed orca?"

Shelby's heart skipped a beat. No way would she admit she still had the one from high school, shoved into a shelf in her closet. "I doubt it. Who knows where it went."

"Want one?"

She shrugged blandly. "It would look cute on the reception desk."

He nodded and paid the man, then moved back and focused, eyeing the target. He held his breath and let a dart loose. It popped a yellow balloon outside of the target. Keane glanced at her, twisting his face to the side. He tucked one end of his hair behind an ear and lined up his next shot. Eyeballing it, he let it loose. It hit right on the line between the target and the first ring, but didn't pop anything.

She could feel the frustration in his jerky movements. "You've got this, New York."

Keane glanced at her briefly and took a fast, focused final shot. It hit the red balloon in the center of the target, and the bells went off in the stand.

Collecting the orca, he passed it over to her. "For the desk."

"Thanks." She studied it, her fingers sinking deep into the white-and-black toy. It was so like her original one, but fluffier, with softer fibers. What was she going to do with two of them? Her heart clenched at the reminder of a similar scene many years ago.

The soft expression Keane gave her made her uncomfortable, so she moved into the walkway.

"The band is starting up," Tommy said as he and Heath ran up to them. The two young men were vibrating with excitement. "Come on!"

The live music was one of the highlights of the annual Clam Festival. That and digging for clams.

"Are they any good?" Keane asked.

"That's JD from The Uprising of the Dung Beetle. You bet your ass they're good," Heath said.

"They play at the café on Saturdays," Shelby filled him in.

"Sounds like a grunge band," Keane said.

"They play a lot of Nirvana and Pearl Jam," Shelby said as the two boys ran forward, waving for them to follow. "Lots of nineties alternative and grunge."

"My kind of music." Keane slowly followed behind.

The band's speakers turned on, and feedback blared. People in the crowd covered their ears at the noise. One of the band members adjusted the speakers, and the sound softened to the guitar and drums testing. They pounded out a few lines that hit Shelby to her core. Suddenly, she was back in high school.

Grinning, she followed Keane and found a spot near the front.

"Need another round?" Keane eyed her empty glass.

"Sure, but then I need food."

"I can get both," he offered. At her nod, he was off.

Before long, he had a bowl of clam chowder and drinks for each of them balanced on a tray. She'd found a small round table to stand at the edge of the crowd.

"Man, this is better than I remember." Keane wiped his mouth on a napkin. "Nell keeps getting better and better."

"You're telling me." Shelby dipped a sourdough point into her bowl. "There's no reason to try to be a good cook with her around. It's a waste of time."

Keane laughed.

"They're good, huh?" Shelby tilted her head to the band on stage. "They might even make a name for themselves if they write some of their own stuff. They've got potential."

"Yeah." He gave her a wink. "And at least, he doesn't have long hair."

Shelby laughed at the old game.

"Yeah, definitely. He's got something." She nodded sagely. Her parents had said exactly the opposite about Keane a long time ago. The two of them used to tease each other anytime they saw someone her parents would have approved of. "Yeah, and *he* doesn't wear ripped jeans."

"Right." Keane lifted a hunk of bread to accentuate his remark. "He has *direction*. He's going somewhere."

Shelby chuckled at the line she'd heard a dozen times, but for the first time, she caught a tiny pinch at the corner of Keane's eyes. "Wait. You didn't believe that, did you?"

He shrugged, taking a long pull from his beer, his eyes focused on the band.

Heath and Tommy appeared at their table. Their heads were bobbing along with the music. "What'd you think?"

"They're pretty good," Keane said, smiling at the two.

The young men both had flannels tied around their waists, looking an awful lot like Keane and Duke around that age.

Had he felt like that the whole time they were together? She hadn't thought he took her parents' feelings seriously. She certainly hadn't.

Was that why he had left?

It didn't sit well with the clam chowder in her stomach.

"You guys going down to dig?" Tommy asked, pointing to the beach.

Several people had already moved out. Shelby saw Keane's eyes follow a couple heading for the tidelands with shovels and a clam gun.

Something in her gut urged her. "You probably lost the skill."

Keane's eyes snapped to hers, and he frowned. "What?""Identifying clams in the mud." She picked a piece of imaginary lint from her cardigan. "It's only natural. You've been living in New York too long."

"I can still do it." Keane's eyes narrowed with the challenge. "Are you game? I bought shovels earlier this week. Of course, if you aren't worried about getting muddy, Greene."

"Have you met me?" Shelby shoveled the last bite of chowder and bread into her mouth and wadded up her paper bowl and napkin.

CHAPTER 21

The two of them made their way east, to the tide-lands. Keane's Vans slid on the pebbles. Boots would have been smarter. When his beach condo came into view, he said to Shelby, "Let me put your orca on the deck, so it doesn't get muddy."

Keane didn't know if it mattered to her, but the fluffy orca was a significant moment to him. It was an important memory, one that she'd let him repeat. It had to mean something.

Shelby handed it over. Their hands brushed in the transfer.

She was free now. Charles was out of the picture.

Did he stand a chance?

Keane propped the soft stuffed toy on top of the battered cooler he'd found discarded on the beach. It felt like a representation of him: older and scarred, but with a bright beacon of acceptance that somehow made it okay.

He smiled wryly when he brought the shovels and nets back to her.

"What's the smile for? Feeling cocky?" she asked.

It only made him grin harder. "Maybe."

"We'll see about that, New York." A look of pure determination settled over her fine features. It was one he knew well.

Keane stood back and watched her stride confidently to the muddy strip of coastline. A few other people had already started further out. Realizing she was getting a head start while he was admiring her, he hurried to follow. She wouldn't go easy on him.

Without a clamming gun, they'd have to dig quickly. It would be hard work. They were used to that; unless Duke had "procured" one, they'd dug in their youth.

"Got you, sucker!" Shelby rammed her narrow shovel into the mud, sliding it out and diving again for another, deeper slice of wet, squishy earth. She ran her hand over the mixture of rocks and sodden black dirt to find the clam she was searching for already working its way back into the beach. Digging her fingers in, she plucked it out. "Nope, you're mine."

"Still as tenacious as ever, I see." Keane handed her one of the two nets to tie around her waist.

"You'd better believe it." Shelby proudly dropped the clam into her net and scanned the ground for another. "Catch up, New York. Unless you've forgotten how."

Few people could spot the telltale wiggle of the clam ripple on the surface better than Shelby. Fortunately, Keane was one of those people. His eyes zeroed in on the tide pulling out. It was easier to catch the break in the surface in the glistening sand-and-mud mixture.

Spotting his target, Keane eased in his shovel quickly and surely. He got a shiny clam on the first try. As he was dropping it into his net, he saw another one right away.

After working in silence for a while, he raised his head to notice she had tied her short hair into a mini ponytail that stuck straight out in the back. It was endearing as hell. Mud caked her hands to her elbows, and a smear brandished across her chest.

"Going well?"

She glanced up, and her eyes caught his, then moved on to the larger catch tied to his waist. "Beginner's luck."

"Oh, Greene. There's no beginner here." He shot her a smug smirk and then, spying another ripple to her left, dove after it with the shovel. His foot slid into hers in the mud, nearly knocking her down. He righted her and launched back after the mollusk. After a minute of digging and scraping through the mud, he hoisted his prize up in the air. "Ha! See? Some things, you don't f orget."

The tenacious zeal that had graced Shelby's fine features was gone. Instead of targeting another clam to beat him to his catch limit, her gaze was locked onto him with such intensity it lurched deep desire to his core. He noticed twin muddy handprints on her arms from where he'd righted her.

"Oh, I'm sorry. I didn't mean to make you dirty." He moved closer to see what was wrong. Was she mad about the mud? That didn't make sense. He was covered up to his knees, as was she. He smiled a one-sided grin at her, hoping it would diffuse her odd mood. "I think we might have gone a little overboard, Greene. We're going to need a hose to clean off."

A strange expression of desire shimmered over Shelby's face, stirring emotions deep inside, and suddenly her mouth found his surprised one. She crushed herself against him. Blind lust thundered through Keane, feeling her against his body. He dropped the clam he'd been holding and wrapped his arms around her, finally touching her as he'd wanted to, accepting everything and anything. Her hands wove into his hair, removed the tie he'd wound around it earlier, and pulled his head down even harder to me et hers.

Keane tilted his neck to give her better access and drew her even closer. Their mouths parried in a frenzied ballet of want and desire left unrequited for years. Her chest rose and fell against him. It had been so long since he'd touched her, kissed her like that. He felt as though she was slipping through his fingers, and he had to keep her from disappearing again into memory.

Shelby tugged at his shirt, her nails digging into his exposed skin. Keane's hands roamed down over her back, then farther to cup her butt. The beautiful, round one he'd remembered was firmer now. She lifted the leg he was caressing as though she wanted him to continue the exploration of her older, more adult form. Brain cloudy,

he took an unsteady step forward, hauling her up against hi
m.

His foot slipped in the mud. He tried to stop it, but the smooth soles of his shoes couldn't catch ground. Keane braced, trying to take most of the fall. Shelby's arms wrapped back up around his neck, holding on for dear life, and they went down in a pile of limbs.

Lifting his head from hers, Keane searched her face. Would she regret kissing him now that the moment was broken?

Forest-green eyes flicked to a couple several yards away who were pretending not to watch them. Her chest started shaking, and laughter bubbled from her perfect throat.

So relieved she wasn't shoving him away, Keane closed his eyes. Her arms were still wrapped around his neck and shoulders. He didn't have the strength to move until she wanted him to. He let out the laugh that was aching to escape and noticed the tears trailing down Shelby's face.

Finally, wiping away a tear, her gaze found him again. It was full of desire. It hit him hard, igniting long-buried feelings.

"Take me home." The words were spoken clearly. There was no misunderstanding in her intent.

He gulped, then brought one knee up and helped her to her feet. They were covered in mud from head to toe, quite literally.

"To?" He indicated the beach house a few hundred yards away.

She nodded, never breaking her gaze from him.

Taking her hand, he left the shovels in the sand and led her home.

The pair stumbled up the back deck before they let go of each other. Shelby dropped down on the top step and toed off her boots and socks. Keane dumped their netted clam bags in the bucket of water he'd set out on the back deck and followed suit. She stood, went to the door, slid it open, and swiveled to him. The slow, coy smile she gave him was one of pure female power. It was like lightning in his veins.

She stepped inside, pulling him with her.

After tugging his muddy shirt off, then her own, she dropped them in a pile on the floor. Then, digging her fingers into his waistband, she drew him to her.

Keane couldn't keep his hands off her any longer. Sure palms slid up her velvet skin, illuminated by the moonlight coming in through the windows and glass door. He reveled in the feel of her. Walking them backward and out of the eyes of anyone on the beach, he lifted his hands to her face, tracing her features like a memory.

Shelby closed the space between them, pressing against his chest. Even through the thin fabric of her bra, the pressure of her breasts spreading against his skin sent any thought he had from his brain. Keane lifted her, and she wrapped her legs around his waist. He backed the last few feet to the bed, and they dropped into it.

A sheet of chestnut hair spread around Keane's face as he kissed the woman he loved with everything he had. Shelby's hands pressed against his chest, fingertips biting in. She slid down him, her hands finding his waistband yet again. This time, breathing ragged, Keane didn't stop her. Shelby flicked the button of his jeans open and pushed them down his legs. When she reached for her jeans, Keane sat up and took over. She flipped over and wiggled out of them, tossing them over her shoulder to meet the growing pile of muddy clothes on the floor.

Before she could resume her position, he pulled her underneath him and stole her breath in a heated kiss. She dug her fingers into his hair, tugging him closer. He worried she might regret their impulsive act, but when Shelby lifted her legs to pull him against her and ground against him, he didn't have the strength to deny his soul the one thing it had dreamed of for the past fifteen years.

He kissed down her throat, making her throw her head back and moan. His lips sketched down her cleavage, along her bra line, smelling the citrusy scent of her heated skin over the saltwater that covered them both. She arched from the mattress and reached behind her to unclasp her b ra.

Keane greedily watched her slip her arms out, then palmed one perfectly round, pearly breast into his hand and took its rosy nipple into his mouth. His tongue swirled around it and flicked the tip, causing her to moan again. Shelby pressed him back and over onto the mattress, moving back on top of him. She kissed him hard, then crawled down, pulling his underwear off before biting his inner thigh playfully.

"Are you sure about this?" Keane's voice sounded as ragged as his shattering strength. When he'd decided to let her take the lead, he didn't expect her to run with it.

She nodded.

Swinging his legs over the side of the bed, he rummaged around in a box for a condom that Gina had sent. He'd laughed when he found it, but now, he was considering giving her a raise. Or a car.

When he returned with it, she took it from him and beckoned him back onto the bed. She ripped it open and took charge, spreading it over his length. Keane's eyes closed in concentration against the sensations traveling up and through him. Then, crawling up, Shelby's mouth found his again and she centered herself over him.

He wrapped his hands around her waist, stopping her. He had to ask again. He didn't want her to regret what they were doing. He wanted to hear it from her.

"Are you really sure, Shelby?"

"I need you, Keane." She rocked against him, asking for entry.

Hearing his name on her lips after all this time broke whatever resolve he had left. He pulled her hips to join the two of them. Pleasure surged through him, and he bucked to meet her. She threw her head back, riding him, her hands braced on his abs.

Needing to be deeper, he flipped her back over and kissed her passionately. Her heels dug into his butt, squeezed him tighter to her. Nails scraped down his back as she threw her head into the pillows again.

He kissed down her neck, keeping his motions painfully slow.

"Keane." She panted into his ear. "Keane, please."

In so many ways, she was different. She looked and felt more mature than she had when they were young, but his body remembered hers. He found her nipple while rocking against her, grinding harder.

Shelby's hands dug into his back, and she cried out. His mouth met hers, and they drank in each other as he plunged deeply and heavily as his own release matched hers.

Gasping, he dropped his head to the pillow next to her.

They lay wrapped up in each other until their breathing evened out. It was pure, unadulterated heaven. He heard her breath slow even further. Realizing she had fallen asleep, he eased out of the bed to clean off.

When he returned, she was curled up on one side. Her face was soft and peaceful. Russet hair spread across his sage sheets. His fingers itched for his paints. But instead, he drank every inch of her, every hue of her skin, committing it to memory.

Needing to be closer to her, he edged back into the bed, careful not to wake her, and he pulled a corner of his sheet up. They were still covered with mud and saltwater, but he didn't care. The sheets could be washed. Nothing was more important than holding onto Shelby with every breath he had.

She curled into him, throwing a leg over his, and dropped back into sleep.

Keane kissed the top of her head and breathed in her hair, knowing he had everything he wanted; Shelby was in his arms, and the water lapped against the shore before him.

CHAPTER 22

Shelby woke feeling a little sore but completely relaxed. A comforting hum from the water buzzed through her body. It felt wonderful. Except for the crunchy feeling on her arms. *What was that?*

Keane's scent was all around her, and her memory flitted back into place.

She'd seen the old Keane last night. She'd missed him badly. And she finally understood why he'd left.

He was still a dumbass for leaving, but at least, it made sense to her now. She'd needed that. And they'd fallen back into the same rhythm over the past weeks. It felt so good to be with him again.

Then on the beach, digging for clams, he was so much like his old self. When he'd flashed that cocky, sure grin at her, she'd been a goner.

She'd thrown herself at him.

Wincing at the memory, she stretched her leg out. Not finding a body, she cracked her eyes open.

The waves crashed against the shoreline in front of her. Glorious mountains lit by the rising dawn crested over their cove. Her eyes traveled the scene, calming her rising concern about what she'd done.

One leg was left exposed, but otherwise, her nude form was covered. Scanning the room around her, she slid the leg under the sheet.

Keane lounged, fully dressed, against the kitchen bar. He'd been watching either her or the surf.

"Coffee?" he asked, his expression neutral, but concern marked his brow.

"That'd be great, thanks." Shelby knotted the sheet tighter to her chest. She'd overslept. Thank goodness it was Sunday. She didn't need to work, but she would have at least checked in to see how things were going. Cleo would be wondering where she was.

Keane. She focused back on the man. He definitely was a man now. Technically, they were both adults when they'd been childhood sweethearts, but she'd seen and touched how he had changed. He was heartachingly the same and yet thrillingly mature.

Adulthood looked good on him.

Calmly, he turned and pressed a button on the grinder. It whirred to life.

"I'm going to use the shower, okay?" She stood, wrapping the sheet around her as she did.

"Of course." He tossed the words over his shoulder but didn't turn.

She was grateful for the privacy.

Waddling in a sheet wasn't easy. She eyed the lock on the bathroom door. He wouldn't come in without knocking, but she flipped the tiny latch anyway.

On the sink counter lay a clean black T-shirt and board shorts folded on top of a towel. A brand-new toothbrush rested on top. He must have gotten up much earlier than she had.

The kind gesture made her feel squishy inside. She wasn't sure she liked it. She quickly showered and found toothpaste in the nearly empty cabinet to brush with. Not sure where to put her used toothbrush, she left it on the counter. Dressed in the clothes he'd left out for her, she exited, carrying the wadded-up sheet.

What should she say? What should she think about what happened? The fact that they'd slept together was still a bit of a shock to her. She didn't do unprepared.

"It feels nice to be clean again. Dried saltwater itches." Shelby fluffed out her wet hair and dropped the tangled mess of a sheet back on the bed.

Keane had resumed his position against the kitchen island. He was sipping on a cup of coffee. A second cup sat steaming on the counter next to him.

He smiled crookedly. "Yeah, it's rough on the skin if you don't rinse it off."

His calmness was unnerving. Was he not thrown off-kilter by what had happened?

"Thanks for the clothes." She met his gaze and dropped it, then ran a self-conscious hand up her arm.

"No problem." He picked up the second coffee and handed it across the distance between them, not coming too close.

"Thanks." Shelby stayed where she was, sniffing the hot brew. It had a thick layer of crema on top. She nodded to the fancy stainless-steel espresso machine on the counter. "So, this is Nessie?"

He nodded again. "You still take it black?"

"Of course. Why anyone would want to cover up the perfection that is a good cup of coffee is beyond me." She took a sip. It was life affirming, this stuff. She'd had the one he brought her the day he helped with her cabin roof, but fresh like this, with the espresso foam, it was like a spiritual event. "Holy crap, that's good."

He grinned. "It's my one big splurge item."

"Worth every penny." She was still standing in between the bed and the kitchen island. The chairs at the island were intimately close to him. Too close for as exposed as she was feeling in his clothes, bare feet, and wet hair. There was no lady blazer of professionalism to hide behind here. "You brought it with you?"

"Gina sent it to me. With a few clothes and things I left in New York."

Shelby bit back her frown. Gina again. If she was sending his clothes to him, it sure sounded like an old girlfriend. Had to have ended well if she was shipping his stuff, though.

If it had ended. Last night could have been a one-time thing. She *had* thrown herself at him.

Reluctant to leave it, Shelby set down her half-finished cup of coffee and edged over to her dirty clothes. They were still in a rumpled heap in front of the sliding glass door. "Well, I should get out of your hair."

She could figure out what to do with the whole sleeping with Keane thing after she had more time to think about it.

"You're going to leave it at that?" His voice was firmer this time. Not angry, but not with the casual tone he'd been using.

Shelby froze mid bend, then straightened. It seemed they were going to address the elephant in the room. "I had hoped to."

He simply raised his eyebrows.

"I don't know." She turned her hands up.

"You don't know what?"

"What to think about what happened last night."

He said nothing.

"You just came back," she explained. "I think I understand why you left, but you still left. I don't know if I'm ready to forgive you. Are you even free to start something like this?"

She had to know.

"I wouldn't have come back if I wasn't."

She'd like to know more about the Gina thing, but didn't want to sound jealous. "What if you're different? What if *I'm* different? What if we don't work anymore? Did we ever really work?"

"You said you were sure."

What was he talking about? A flashback from the night before and her tugging at his clothes flashed through her mind. She gulped. "Things were heated last night. A lot of memories stirred up."

"You regret it?" His words were rough.

"I don't know!" She threw her hands up in the air sharply. "I told you that."

"You think it's better to leave than talk about it? Together?" "Together? Gee, I don't know Keane." Her mouth twisted bitterly. "Do you think it's better to talk about things together rather than take off and make decisions for the both of us?"

She felt a little bad, throwing that one at him, now that she knew everything her parents had said hurt him all those years ago. But her pain was still raw.

"You made decisions for the both of us all the time," he volleyed back.

And he was right. She hadn't asked him when she bought the condo they now stood in, but she'd thought he was okay with all that. In reality, she could have talked to him too.

"Not those that separated us for fifteen years." Shelby pointed her finger into his chest. She could feel emotions rising within her, but she'd be damned if she cried in front of him now. "I made decisions for us as a couple, not to separate us."

"I did too. It just took longer than I expected. I was trying to be responsible."

"It was a dumb thing to do. You ruined us, Keane. You ruined me." She bit her lip from quivering. "That's not true. You didn't ruin me. That would mean I was gone for good, but I built myself back up, piece by piece, after you left. By myself."

"And you did a damn good job of it."

"You're damn right I did." She shoved the words back at him. Wait, weren't they fighting? Anger was easier than feeling the pain. She wasn't ready for the way his words diffused some of her fury.

Keane stood in front of her, anger and pain both visible on his tense face. But his eyes were open, and she knew all she'd have to do was lean in and he'd accept her.

God, it was tempting.

"You don't know what it was like when you left," she said quietly.

"Tell me, then," he pushed back.

"It was awful," she said accusingly, her ire rising again. "I found out from your mom. I kept calling, and she told me I had a letter. So, of course I ran over there and read it in front of her."

Shelby blinked back tears. Yes, anger helped.

"That was a stupid move." He agreed angrily, as though he was fighting himself for her. "You never should have been treated like that."

"*So* stupid. I deserve better." Her hand landed on his chest as though she was going to shove him away from her, but she couldn't bring herself to hit him like that.

"So much better," he repeated, agreeing with her. She saw the pain in his eyes again. It was a flash of the same she'd seen at the festival the night before.

Suddenly, she was in his arms again. His mouth slanted down to meet hers in a hungry, hot kiss. She fisted angry hands into his T-shirt and pulled him closer. He was what she wanted.

Was he?

Gaining some semblance of control, Shelby tore herself away from him, leaving shreds of herself on the floor.

"I can't do this." She took a tattered breath.

Keane stepped closer to her, then stopped. "Can't do what? Us?"

"Run into this." Her hand gestured between them. "It's too easy."

"Couldn't that be a good thing?"

"I don't know yet."

"We could figure it out together." His eyes pleaded.

"Not if it's not a together kinda thing." She pressed her lips tightly. "I need to figure this one out by myself first. Jumping you again isn't going to help that."

"Darn." He gave her a sloppy smile that made her laugh out loud.

He was adorable with the goofy expression on his face, but it wasn't fair to jerk him around while she was figuring her shit out.

"Look, we obviously still have chemistry and get along well. But those things were never a problem for us."

"Nope."

"I need to make sure we're not acting on feelings from the past and that our adult versions are still compatible. We don't even know if we want the same things in life."

"I want to be with you, Greene." He said it as though it was the simplest thing in the world, and it made her heart ache. But it didn't change her resolve.

"I need to make sure I can forgive you." That was the truth of it. She'd been angry for a very long time. If she let him back in, it would kill her to have him stomp on her heart again.

"I understand." He nodded slowly. "Take all the time you need."

"Thank you." Feeling emotionally wrung out, Shelby went back to her discarded clothes. What she needed was some morning ice cream.

Sliding the door open, she shoved her feet into the muddy boots. She hoped no one would see her walking in board shorts and Chelsea boots, but it's what she was dealing with.

Keane followed her onto the deck, sticking his hands into his jeans pockets. "Can I get you a bag?"

"Nah, I'm good."

"I can drop your clams off tomorrow after I change the water out a couple of times to clean them."

It would be better if she took a few days to herself. She needed distance to think clearly around her childhood sweetheart.

"Just give them to Nell. She'll do them better justice than I would anyway."

He nodded silently.

"Would it be awful to ask for a coffee to-go?" she said suddenly, longing for another fresh cup. She'd only had two, and she was already addicted to the fancy espresso machine's brew. Could she find a place in her budget for one in the registration office?

Keane let out a bark of a laugh. "Not at all. I'll go make you one."

Shelby waited outside, enjoying the contenting buzz from the ocean and the breeze on her damp hair.

He brought out a travel mug a couple of minutes later and handed it over. "Here you go. It's hot."

"Thanks." She took a sip and sighed at the delicious, velvety bitter breath of life it gave her. "Nessie may be my new best friend."

"Anytime."

"We will talk," she told him, walking down to the pebble beach. "I promise."

"I'll be here."

CHAPTER 23

The ache in Keane's heart grew as Shelby walked away. It had been the perfect night. Holding her in his arms felt like he was finally breathing pure oxygen again. He left the door open to get his coffee and brought it to sit on the bench. The morning sun hovered over the cove, highlighting the gently lapping waves. Dorsal fins were clustered near the jetty.

He'd tried to give her space when he woke, worried she'd need time to think things through. Then he'd ended up pushing her on it. Had it been a mistake? The pushing, not the sex. That definitely wasn't a mistake. He'd never regret sharing anything with the woman.

His phone pinged.

It was a message from Gina. The shipping company was coming later that day to pick up his paintings for the show. He'd forgotten it was so soon.

The timing was good. At least it would give Shelby days without him around to think. If he was distracting her from thinking clearly, the last thing she needed was to see him around town to muddle up things.

If she chose to try with him again, he'd rather she be completely certain about it. No regrets.

Standing, he saw the clam bucket. He took them to the outside hose, dumped out the old water, and added fresh one. As he headed back to his condo, he saw the plush, stuffed orca on the cooler. She'd forgotten it.

He took it inside. If she didn't want him to drop off the clams, she wouldn't want him to drop the orca off at the registration desk. He set it in the crook of the chair facing outside. The little dude could keep him company while Shelby contemplated their future.

Gina had sent packing supplies the week before for his paintings, but he was finishing up a few last-minute pieces for the show. Keane settled into his studio, carefully wrapping and boxing up each of the new Orca Cove-inspired paintings. He was keeping the Shelby-inspired ones for himself for a while.

Doing it on his own, without Gina, took him much longer than expected. An hour later, he put the final piece of tape on the last box.

It felt strange leaving home now that he'd finally made it back. He was reluctant to step away from the place he'd been working to return to.

Keane thought through anything else he needed to take care of before he left. He didn't want to call Shelby; he would respect her wishes, but he could let Duke know. And Nick. Keane and Duke had taken turns walking by Siren's Song Cabins in the evenings, but he hadn't made it out to talk to the ex-cop.

Hopefully, the two of them would keep an eye on her in case something was going on.

It was a long walk out to Nick and Willa's house. The land was familiar, but Hostettler's old cabin had been replaced by a cozy log one with large windows.

Keane knocked on the door in the hazy morning fog. Hopefully, it wasn't too early.

Nick opened the door with a confused expression on his face. "Keane?"

"Hope I didn't wake you," Keane said.

"Not at all. I just didn't hear a car."

"Don't have one." Keane shrugged.

"You walked all this way?" Nick peered onto the driveway as though he didn't believe him.

"I like a walk. I haven't had a vehicle in years."

"I guess you wouldn't need one in New York."

"Not so much."

"Come on in." Nick opened the door wide.

"Thanks." Keane took in the cottage core decor. It was obvious his free-spirited friend had had a hand in decorating it. But it was the exposed beams and large rock fireplace that grabbed his attention. "This place is amazing. Did you build it yourself?"

"Thanks." Nick scanned the room, rocking back on his heels. "Mostly. Duke helped with the heavy lifting. Willa's at her studio, teaching yoga this morning, but I started breakfast. Want some?"

"No, that's okay." He didn't want to trouble the woodworker.

"Come on." Nick headed into the kitchen. "No one says no to breakfast."

Nick flicked on a burner at his stove. A carton of eggs and a pound of sausage sat on a large wooden cutting board to his right.

The man's instant acceptance warmed him. "Thanks, man."

"No sweat." He selected a coffee mug from an exposed cupboard, filled it with coffee, and slid it across the bar counter to Keane. "I make a pot of it when Willa goes into town. Her herbal coffee is good, but I still miss the real stuff now and again."

"Herbal coffee? I haven't tried it yet. Like with mushrooms?"

"It's better than that. It does have some mushrooms in it, but it's mostly chicory root and pau d'arco. Definitely not things I would have known about before meeting Willa." Nick grinned like a besotted man. "It's actually pretty good. You'll have to try it sometime. Shelby doesn't like it, but she doesn't like a lot of Willa's concoctions."

That made Keane smile. "Sounds like Greene. She's why I wanted to stop by."

"Everything okay?" Nick set sausage patties into the hot cast-iron pan. The pork sizzled happily.

"I hope so." Keane sat down on one of the barstools. "I think someone may be messing around with the cabins."

"Have you talked to Shelby about it?" Nick cast him a curious expression.

"No, not yet." Keane cupped his coffee in his hands. "I know this sounds bad, but you know how headstrong Shelby is. She thinks she can handle everything on her own. And I'm worried about this Charles guy she's buying the land from. I don't know what's going on, but something isn't adding up."

"Tell me what you know." Nick leaned against his countertop and faced Keane.

Keane told him about the damage to the cabins and what he'd seen. He also told him about Maggie's red flag.

"What did Duke say?" Nick asked.

"He was going to check into the guy. I've asked my assistant to as well. She's a whiz at research, but she hasn't found anything yet. I'm expecting to hear something soon."

"You should have come by right away." Nick slid the cooked sausage onto a clean plate and cracked four eggs into the skillet. "How do you take yours?"

"Over easy."

"Good man. I still have some contacts on the force. Although you know she'll be pissed if she hears we're poking around her business behind her back."

"I know." Keane dropped his head. "But I'd rather have her mad and safe."

"Oh, I get it."

"She's so detail oriented. She won't believe she missed anything in the man's nature. I can't figure out what his motive is, but if he is at fault, he must be good."

"Agreed."

"And I'm leaving tomorrow for a short trip to Italy, so I won't be around to help keep an eye on things. Greene mentioned you were going to be helping out with things on the property when they cut ground."

"I am. What are you doing in Italy?"

"A gallery exhibit. I have some new paintings to sell. I'll be back in a few days."

Nick frowned and stared off in thought. "I'll talk to Duke. See if he found anything. He's got contacts in

Seattle who might know something. I can also call some friends."

"I appreciate it."

"No sweat, man." Nick slid a plate with eggs, sausage, and buttered toast in front of him. "I take care of my friends. Eat up."

The unease in Keane's stomach lessened at knowing that not only was he being brought into the new fold, but his girl would be safe. Maybe not his girl, but in his heart, she would always be.

The flight to Italy was a long one, but Keane had gotten used to sleeping on the plane. A good neck pillow and flying at night was the trick. He'd be exhausted by tomorrow night, but it was better than tossing and turning, unable to sleep. Besides, the exhibit would keep his attention.

The hotel Gina had put him up in was a nice one not far from the gallery. He'd freshened up, gotten food, and changed before the show. Luckily, Gina had saved a couple of his suits and sent them ahead, so he hadn't needed to go shopping that afternoon and was able to check in with Duke and Nick back home.

Nick had called his contact and was waiting to hear back. They weren't starting on the land for another week, so he was going to stop by and go over the plans with her. He could see what he thought about the cabins while he was there.

Duke hadn't found anything at all about Charles Timms yet either, but had put out a few feelers.

Keane's cab pulled out in front of the gallery. Gina and Francesca met him at the front door, dressed in gowns for the evening. Gina's dark-plum shift accented her graying hair beautifully, and Francesca had on a scarlet-red dress that clung to her curves.

"It's good to see you." Francesca gave him a hug and kissed him on both cheeks. "It's been too long."

"Good to see you too, Francesca." Keane kissed her cheeks and then hugged Gina. "You too, Shorty."

Gina swatted his shoulder playfully. "You're just too tall, Keane. That's all."

"Where's Jerry?" Keane peered around her shoulder for her other half. The jovial man was retired and liked to travel with his wife when they had shows.

"He stayed home this time. Fishing trip with the guys."

"Ah, the only thing that would keep him from you. Fishing." Keane chucked her on the shoulder. "It's good to see you."

"You too." Gina cocked her head. "You've gotten a little sun."

"Surprising in Washington, I know. I've been on the water."

"You look good." Gina took his arm, and they entered. "Your paintings came in this morning. It appears you've been inspired. I set them up in this room here."

"I have an entire room to myself?" Keane stepped into the small area filled with his work. He'd packed them himself, and he hadn't realized there were so many until he saw them on the walls. The colors flowed from one piece to the next in an almost hypnotic pattern. The scenes were there, but the textures swirled and danced. He was proud of this series.

"They're exquisite, Mr. Lennox." Francesca moved around the space. "I had to give you a full room to appreciate the experience."

"The move has been good for you," Gina said.

"I told you it'd be fine," Keane chided his assistant in a friendly way. She'd been worried he'd quit painting when he moved home.

"Now that you're here, I'm grabbing a bite to eat." Gina tapped him on the shoulder. "I'll be back before it starts."

The show would be open through Friday, and Gina would handle the sales for him. He wasn't expected to be in attendance for more than two nights, though, especially now that he'd made a name for himself. Hopefully, the paintings would be sold by then. If not, Francesca told Gina they could move them into the galleries' main inventory until they sold.

"I was worried as well," Francesca said in her Italian accent, turning to him. "We all were when we heard you'd left New York. It caused quite a stir."

"No need. I don't think I could quit painting at this point." It was as much a part of him now as surfing was. And loving Shelby.

"I was relieved when you agreed to come. I think the art world was waiting to hear if you'd attend. We have collectors from all over Europe coming. All are anxious to see what you've been doing."

"Thank you for having me." It still floored him that people knew his name.

"Would you like a drink?" She walked over to a table already set up with champagne. At his nod, she took two glasses, bringing one over for him.

It would be a long evening of talking to people he didn't know. Not his favorite thing to do.

"I'd be surprised if there are any left after tonight," Francesca said.

"That would be amazing."

"But then you'll go home early, and I won't see you again for another year or two." The woman pouted her perfectly red lips. "I would like more time with you, not less. We could meet after the show."

Keane was shocked. She had never come on to him before.

"I'm sorry, Francesca. I'm in a, um," he stuttered. He wasn't in a relationship exactly. What was it?

"You don't sound certain." She laid a hand on his suit jacket, stroking it down to his stomach.

"I'm not free." Keane took a step back. She was a beautiful, confident woman. Definitely his type, but not the one his heart called home. "I'm in love with someone else."

"In Washington?"

He nodded.

"Too bad." She sighed. "We would have had fun."

"Not if I'm thinking about someone else the whole time."

"True. I want a man's full attention." Francesca strode out of the room. "I must meet with others. I will see you later."

At least the gallery owner wasn't holding it against him. It would have been an awkward early ending to the show.

CHAPTER 24

Shelby sat down in her chair and leaned back. The last couple of days had passed like a blur. She was supposed to be thinking about herself and Keane, but instead, she'd been making plans and meeting with people for her upcoming building project.

Not that she hadn't thought about him, just not in the way she needed to be.

Green-and-yellow brush strokes caught her eye from the corner of her office. She had won Keane's painting from the auction. Tracy had brought it over to her the day before. Her meager amount majorly undervalued the artwork. It was almost embarrassing what little she paid for it.

The townspeople probably had no idea what it was worth. Had word gotten out that a Keane Lennox painting was on sale, she'd never have been able to afford it. Now that he lived here, she imagined they'd get fans poking around and someone would find out. Next year might be different. The colors enthralled her, and it reminded her of the forest behind her cabins.

It reminded her of a lot of things: the fluid nature that was Keane and the way they'd each taken the lead when they were together, moving back and forth in an ageless dance on his large bed.

She breathed in sharply to clear her mind.

Should she keep it in her office? Was that a good idea?

She was supposed to be reevaluating what she wanted in life, not staring at a painting from her first love. It wasn't as though she wasn't open to dating. She knew that if they got back together, that would be it.

It all came down to the subject of trust. Not that Keane would cheat on her, but it was more about him acting on rash decisions. Then again, it had been many years, and who knew what kind of relationships he'd been in since they broke up. Like with this Gina w oman.

There was a lot they didn't know about each other yet. Did she even want to know all about the women?

She wasn't a sharing kind of person.

And she held a grudge. A major one. It kept her safe. Was she ready to let go of it and risk getting hurt again?

"Are you sure?" Shelby asked Mike, the contractor she'd selected to work with. He wasn't the lowest bid, but it was on the lower end. Besides, she knew a lot of people who had worked with him previously. There was less of a chance of him adding costs or cutting corners. Right now, he was telling her the yurt walls would need additional support within the frame. Extra building material and extra labor meant extra expense.

"Yeah, right here." He pointed to the engineering plans. "If we put up the wall here and here to get the bedroom size you want, even if we mount this wall at this point, the other mounting point will land here."

"Can we move the other wall? Adjust where it connects?"

"It would leave the other room much smaller. And I don't think we can adjust both of them, or you'll lose too much room in the kitchen. It's not that much additional cost."

It wasn't, but it was eating into her contingency fund.

Shelby glanced over the hood of Mike's truck at Nick. He had agreed to meet at the land to review the plans. Charles had asked to join too, so they could catch up. He'd even brought her coffee. It was a latte with way too much milk, but it was better than nothing.

"What do you think?" she asked Nick.

"It'll look better to have the walls symmetrical anyway," Nick shrugged. "But it's your call."

"I agree. Let's do it." Shelby ran a hand over her freshly cleaned and straightened hair. The yurts were nice, but they still needed a lot of adjustments to be comfortable.

"Are you sure I can't talk you into letting me stick build your rentals?" Mike laughed. "We could adjust everything a bit larger to save on wood."

"Then it wouldn't be a yurt, would it?" Shelby replied.

"But I could add more insulation to the walls."

"They have insulation."

"Not on the windows. You'll spend more to heat them in winter."

"True, but most windows aren't as insulated as they should be. Besides, this is what the job is for. I appreciate your feedback, but the yurts are staying." The novelty of the stretched-fabric, canvas tent and the luxury of a fully furnished kitchen was what would draw people to Orca Cove and her rentals. She was sure of it.

"You're the boss."

Mike folded up the plans, and took some pictures of the land where the first couple of yurts were going up. Charles was listening quietly.

"For what it's worth, I think the yurts are pretty cool." Nick moved to stand next to her. "And I know you've done your research, but you're right on the insulation. The rating on the yurts isn't bad. It will be the same as the original cabin I bought and lived in."

"Thanks." It was nice getting his opinion. Shelby flexed her hand from the odd buzzing radiating up her arm. It felt particularly jangled, like clanging bells, today. "Are you sure that gives you enough time to build the decking for the yurts?"

"Eight platform decks, definitely." Nick surveyed the land. "If I was doing the full wraparound with railings, it would add more time."

"It's better if that's done after the fact anyway." Shelby reviewed her mental checklist of the best order for things. "It'll give Mike and his crew more space to set up the yurts."

"I agree."

Mike jotted down some numbers in a spiral-bound notebook he carried. "Did you hear back from the excavators? Are they still ready to start on time?"

"Yes, they're ready to begin anytime."

"Perfect. And the yurts will be delivered when?"

"They're putting together the order this week. They can deliver them the week after closing." She had put money down for the order. It was a scary moment but also thrilling. She couldn't wait to see them go up.

"If everyone's ready to go, we could move up the closing a week," Charles offered.

Mike checked with her. "It's okay by me. My crew just finished a job. I didn't want to start them on anything else before this one. They could use the extra work."

The buzzing moved into Shelby's gut, feeling like she'd eaten something bad.

"It's your call, Shelby," Nick said from where he stood at her elbow. "If you've got everyone scheduled to start the following week, it might be best to leave it as is."

It would only be two more calls, to the excavator and the yurt manufacturer. Everyone else was right here. Charles was right. With the rising costs, the quicker she started, the faster she could get revenue coming in. And it wasn't like she was going to let herself spend time relaxing on the beach. There was work to be done.

"Can you start decks next week?" she asked Nick.

"I can."

"Hell, then, let's do it." The work would keep her distracted for a while and give her time to think about Keane and her ability to forgive. Besides, Charles knew what he was doing. There was a reason he'd gotten where he had in life. It wasn't by sitting idly by.

"Great. All set, then." Charles beamed. "I'll reschedule closing to this Friday."

"I'll call the excavators and have them come out on Monday," Shelby said. Her gut wasn't feeling any better, but her brain told her this was the right thing to do.

"I'll let the guys know," Mike said. "Give me a call next Friday to confirm that the clearing went well and the delivery was completed. We'll start the following Monday."

"Sounds good." Shelby shook Mike's hand and watched him walk to his truck.

She took a sip from the cup of coffee she was holding to calm her stomach. Too much milk. It wasn't as good as Nessie. Instead of steadying her, it made her feel even worse.

"I'll see you Monday too, then?" she asked Nick.

He nodded, eyeing Charles curiously. "Want me to stick around and check out anything?"

She'd love to check things out. She'd put it off for too long, wrapped up in emotions. She would come out before closing, she promised herself.

"No. All good here. Charles and I are grabbing lunch at the café."

"Ah, see you later, then." Nick slowly exited to his truck.

"I know costs are rising." Charles fell in step beside her. "And I heard you reduced your scope to eight yurts. That offer is still on the table. And now that we're just friends,

we could be business partners. There'd be no complicati-
ons."

It was tempting. Should she take him up on the offer?

"Do you mean like a loan? I don't think I'd want an
investor. I'd rather make my decisions myself." She could
get money from the bank, but didn't want to have to pay
the construction-loan rates.

"Sort of. How about instead of paying interest, you
pay me a portion of the revenue? And you retain all the
decision making. I'd be like a minor silent partner."

That didn't sound so bad. "I'd want to buy my share
back from you later."

"Of course." He smiled warmly. "It can be temporary.
It's good to have extra cash around. Projects like these
always require more funds than you expect."

She knew that to be true. She'd added a decent cushion,
but she already expected a few things to hit the high end
of her estimates. It was going to be a big job.

"Let's talk numbers over lunch." Charles gestured to
their cars.

She'd struck a deal with Charles at the Wild Café. His terms were reasonable, considering the percentage of cash outlay he was prepared to invest. It wasn't a huge amount of money for him, or a big percentage of her revenue for her. A win for them both. He'd be sending her a contract later that day to review.

She shook his hand as he left the restaurant. She wanted to stay a little longer and say hi to Nell, who hadn't made an appearance during the busy lunch hour.

Even being on the back deck of the restaurant, her stomach hadn't lost the odd, jarring sensation. Maybe it was just nerves. She'd never made a jump as big as this one before.

As Charles said, it takes money to make money. She'd sure found that to be true. It sucked, but it was true.

If things went as planned, within a year or two, she'd pay Charles back and be the sole owner of Siren's Song Yurts. And she could afford to push a little faster on things. Holiday reservations weren't sounding that difficult to believe.

"Hey." Shelby walked through the swinging kitchen doors.

Nell looked up from her cooktop, where she was tasting a sauce. She made an approving sound and dropped the spoon in the dirty utensil bin. "Hey, yourself. Good lunch?"

"Yep." She fell into a chair at the table the chef kept in her kitchen. "Stellar, as always. But I need something else. My yurt project is a go; the date was moved up to Friday. Any chance you have any of that Relaxed Rockfish around? I could use a stress reliever."

"Unfortunately, no, sorry. I think I have a little Giggle Geoduck, though."

"It's just as well. What I really want is chocolate." Shelby perked up. "Do you have any of that chocolate cake leftover from last weekend?"

It was twelve shades of delicious. Shelby dreamed of eating it piled high with chocolate-brownie ice cream. The very definition of perfection.

"Probably."

Shelby was already rummaging around through her refrigerator. "It's upstairs, isn't it?"

"It is. It's too old to sell here. But it's still good. I promise."

Shelby frowned. Normally, she wouldn't think twice about barging into Nell's personal kitchen, but Emiliano lived there now. And he'd been expanding their little apartment above the café. They'd had construction workers milling about for the past few weeks.

"What's wrong? You don't want it anymore?"

"Emiliano might be up there. Naked."

"Shelby." Nell spun, propping a hand holding a spatula up on her hips. "He does not walk around naked all the time. Besides, he's over at the market, working, this afternoon."

"There's always a risk." Shelby feinted disgust.

"And you'd be lucky to get a peak of that." Nell wagged her eyebrows. "He's in perfect shape."

She couldn't argue that. The younger man was pretty fit. But he was taken. So taken it wasn't even funny.

"Speaking of shape, you look pretty amazing yourself." Shelby took another assessment of her friend. Gone was the loose T-shirt she normally wore. The top tied at the waist and soft knit fabric fitted to her curves. "Dang, girl."

"Emiliano said I looked amazing in it." Nell blushed. "I'm feeling more comfortable with my body lately."

"You should. And he's right. Amazing." Shelby spontaneously hugged her friend. It was good to see her so happy after being depressed for so long. "As long as you're sure he's not naked, I'm gonna go steal all that you have."

"Of course you are. Enjoy." Nell waved at her with the spatula.

Cake and pilfered fork in hand, Shelby hopped out the back deck and dug into the corner of it while gazing out over the coast. Chocolate to celebrate. And calm her nerves.

What she honestly wanted to do was see Keane. She wanted to tell him all about her news and her plans. He didn't have to understand all the details; she just wanted to share them with him.

In the distance, a pair of orcas glided gracefully through the water. Willa and Nell found good guys. Even the orcas were pairing up.

Truthfully, she had paired up, but she had walked out on him.

Maybe if they spent a little more time together, she could get past the bitterness. It hadn't come up at all at the festival.

She had to remind herself to keep her lips to herself. As hard as that was, no kissing would be allowed. It only clouded her judgment.

"I see you found the cake." Nell came out on the back deck with napkins to fold while enjoying the sunny day.

"It's delicious." She popped another large chunk into her mouth. It was a huge slice. "I'm thinking about sharing the rest of this with Keane, though. It's too much for one person."

She could wait on the brownie-ice-cream topping for the next time Nell made it.

"Have you seen your sweet tooth?" Nell raised her eyebrows. "Anyway, Keane's not here."

"What do you mean he's not here?"

"He's in Italy."

"Italy? But he can't be. He's waiting—" The words "for me" died on her lips.

Of course he wasn't waiting for her. He hadn't before. *She'd* waited. Until she hadn't.

Nell said something, but she didn't hear anything. She thundered down the back steps of the deck, her fingers dialing Keane's number. It had only been three days.

"Keane Lennox's phone. This is Gina speaking," a feminine voice answered the call.

"Um," Shelby stuttered. It didn't even make sense. He hadn't just left. He'd left with *her. Gina.* "Where's Keane?"

"He's getting dressed. Can I have him call you back?"

Dressed?

"Absolutely not."

Shelby hung up and stormed out to the parking lot. She needed to get home. She spotted her Trailblazer. No, she couldn't drive like this. It would be better to walk home and burn off some of her frustration. She could pick her car up tomorrow or whenever she was ready to leave her house.

CHAPTER 25

"Can you help me with these cuff links?" Keane asked Gina as he walked out of the bedroom of the suite she'd rented for him. The hotel was gorgeous and way bigger than he needed. She probably wanted it for the view of the Arno River.

The distressed expression on her face stopped him in his tracks. Gina's eyes were wide, and her mouth was open in terror.

"What's wrong?" He hurried over to her.

"I have bad news and worse news," she said, twisting his phone between her hands.

"Tell me."

"First, I haven't found much on Charles Timms, only that he owns some kind of a production plant. So, I checked into his other real estate holdings. This is where it gets weird. He owns a house in Shelton, but it's pretty small, with a low value. On the satellite photos, it does not look like the house of a tycoon or businessman. I found the land sale on the outskirts of Orca Cove, the one you said Shelby is purchasing from him. It was underpriced as well for the area. Very strange. He bought it from the same owner as the production plant. That's the weird part."

"That's the weird part?" Keane asked. "She said he owned a lot of properties."

"Nothing other than the plant, the land, and his house."

"How does he have an Audi? How does he dress that way?"

"The vehicle registered to him is an old Toyota Camry. A person can rent an Audi."

"What's the worse news?" he asked reluctantly. "Don't tell me the man has a warrant out on him?"

"Not that I've found." Gina winced. "Shelby called. I answered it because it's international and the caller ID didn't show me who it was. I thought it might be Francesca."

"That's okay." She'd answered his phone before. "Why is that worse?"

"I might have told her you were getting dressed. She sounded pissed and hung up."

"You said what?"

"I mean, you were." She held up her hands, palms up. "I tried calling her back right away to clarify things, but she didn't answer."

"Did you tell her your name?" Keane's mind was racing to find a way to make this right. If she thought he had run off with someone else, he'd never get her back. That would be it.

"I did, but she didn't sound happy about it."

"She knows who you are, though." Doesn't she? He went over their conversations. He was certain he'd mentioned Gina before. But had he said she was his assistant? He couldn't be sure. "Crap. Crap, crappity, crap."

"That's not what I said." Gina shook her head. "It was much worse."

It was so much worse. He and Shelby were tentative at best. She wanted him. He was sure of that, but that was all he was confident about.

"I need to go."

"Go? But the second gallery show starts in less than an hour. A lot of people came to see you."

"I don't care. None of it matters if I lose her." Keane headed to his room to pack up. "Book me the next flight out."

Things couldn't get any worse. He'd been able to get to Rome without much delay, but the flight Gina had found from there to SeaTac wasn't until after midnight. Keane had talked to Nick and Duke while waiting at the airport.

He filled them in on what Gina had found. Nick had uncovered similar information, but also that Charles had been involved in shady business deals. He'd been taken to court a few times for falsifying a contract. Duke said he had a gambling debt as well.

This guy was trouble waiting to happen.

Speeding in the rental car he'd picked up in Seattle, he pulled into Siren's Song Cabins and knocked on Shelby's door.

When she didn't answer there, he went to the registration office.

The clerk at the desk blinked in surprise but didn't stop him. He found Shelby's office and headed directly in.

Shelby shot to her feet. "What are you doing here?""You didn't answer my calls or my texts." He stood across from her desk, only then realizing he still had his suit jacket on from the night before, the day before in Washington time. The navy suit was wrinkled from the airplane ride and over twenty-four hours of wear.

"No, I blocked you," she said calmly. "I didn't need to hear anything else your girlfriend had to say."

"She's not my girlfriend. She's my assistant."

He saw a flicker of something cross Shelby's rigid features. Hadn't he explained who Gina was?

"I'm not an idiot. Please don't treat me as one." She tugged at her suit jacket and ran a hand over the arm to smooth an invisible wrinkle. "She said you were getting dressed."

"For the exhibit." He indicated his suit. "And it was a suite. She was doing some bookkeeping in the living room. She wasn't staying there."

"I'm sure."

"She's married."

"And her husband was present?" She raised a perfect-ly manicured eyebrow.

"He went on a fishing trip instead, but they're good together. Trust me. Nothing has ever happened be-tween Gina and I."

"Trust you? I think that ship has sailed. You burnt that bridge."

"Greene. You know me better than that. I've never cheated. I would never do that to you."

"I don't know that, do I? I knew you only half your life. What about the other half? Who knows what you've done or didn't do? Certainly not me."

"But why would I run off with someone when we had connected like that?" He begged her to see reason.

"I have absolutely no clue. As long as it takes, you said. I guess three days was too much."

"It was a show. Booked a while back. I should have told you, but you asked me to give you space. I thought if I called you, it would look like I was trying to push y ou."

Her stony expression softened the briefest amount. Maybe he was getting through to her.

"You could have at least texted."

Damn, why hadn't he done that? "You're right. I could have. I wasn't thinking. All I was focused on was boxing up my paintings. I figured I'd be back within a few days, well before you'd want to talk again."

"Well, you were wrong."

"I'm so sorry I gave you a reason to doubt me again." He stepped closer to her desk. "I left right away to make things right."

He closed his eyes in silent prayer.

"I can tell." Shelby blinked and dropped her gaze to her desk. "Look, I'm pretty busy right now. Can we talk another time?"

"Sure." He meant to go, but his feet wouldn't move. He could see a contract sitting on her desk. Nick said she had moved the closing up to Friday. Nick, Duke, and he were supposed to meet up and decide how to tell Shelby what they'd found, but what if she was too busy and they didn't get to her before she signed? "Is that the land contract?"

She pursed her lips. "It's a contract between me and my business partner, Charles."

"You're going into business with him?" Oh, no. How did it keep getting worse?

"He's helping with extra capital. It's a good deal."

"Greene, he's not who you think he is. He doesn't even have land."

"What are you talking about? Of course he does. I've seen the deed in the paperwork."

"Not that land. Any other land. It's the only land he owns."

"You're just jealous."

"I won't deny that, but it's still true. He didn't get it in a deal with other undeveloped land, but with a manufacturing plant. He doesn't even own an Audi."

Shelby blinked. Her face drained to white, then turned red. "How do you know this?"

"I asked around. I had to. I wanted to make sure you were okay. I care about you."

"And you just assumed I didn't know what I was doing?" Shelby leaned forward slowly and carefully. "I'll have you know I've done fine while you were gone. I built all this by myself. Guess who helped me? No one."

"I didn't assume anything. Maggie had a red flag, and we had to look into it. Duke said she's a good judge of character."

"And I'm not?" Shelby blinked hard.

He could see the blind rage building within her. Nothing he was saying was doing any good.

"He must be really slick, because you are. You know you are. You don't need his money. I'd happily loan it to you. Hell, I'd give it to you."

He'd earned it for her anyway.

"Maggie, Duke, and you. That means Nick was in on it too."

"Yes, and he said Charles has been taken to court for questionable deals. He has a gambling debt. This guy is bad news."

Shelby's fist came down hard on her desk, sending papers fluttering. "Enough. I've heard enough of your bullshit. I don't know why you're doing this, but you're messing with my business now. I want the land. Even if he's had some issues in the past, it's a good price. I've seen the contract. I'm buying it, and Charles is going to be a five-percent silent partner. It's done."

"At least let me have my people look at the contract." Keane tried one final time. "I have an agent that's great at legal stuff. To make sure you're not missing any-thing."

"Remember when I said I did fine while you were gone?" Her eyes narrowed into tiny slits. "I did better than fine. It's possible you held me back."

"I—" His breath caught in his throat. It had been his biggest fear. "That's why I wanted to be more, have something to offer you."

"Charles *is* more," she said slowly and clearly. "And he doesn't have long hair."

Icy shards from her words hit him like a rogue wave in January, biting into any exposed skin it could find.

It burned and froze at the same time.

He took a halting step back. She agreed with what her dad had said about him.

"You're right. I didn't deserve you. I don't even do now." His heart lay bare for her.

"That's not going to work this time." She rolled her eyes.

"I'm not trying for it to." Keane ran shaky hands through his hair. Shit, should he have cut it? "But please don't sign that contract with Charles Timms. Please have someone review it first."

"You used up all your cards, New York. Maybe it's time you go back where you belong."

"Shelby."

He saw her bite her lip. "You messed up. You ran off, then you insulted me and tried to bring Charles down with it."

"I'm honestly not. Talk to Nick and Duke. Please, Shelby."

"I know what I'm doing. Please leave. I'm not going to ask again."

He thought he'd grown. He thought he'd become someone Shelby Greene could be proud of. He'd been lying to himself. Nothing he'd done did anything but hurt her.

Catching her doorframe, he dragged himself out of her office and drove the rental car to the place he'd hoped would be home.

Duke and Nick were waiting for him when he got out of the shower. He was clean, but he still felt run over.

"That's not how you do it." Duke took the espresso tamper away from Nick. "You press and twist it like this."

The two were standing in front of Nessie.

"How'd you guys get in?"

"Ex-cop." Duke pointed at Nick. Then he pointed to himself. "Ex-delinquent."

He winked at Keane, but Keane couldn't muster a smile in return.

"I'm not really up for company."

"I know." Nick glanced at Duke. "That's why we're here."

"You know already?" Keane said.

"Duh, man. Have you been out of the cove that long?" Duke slung an arm over his shoulder. "You know how fast word travels. Cleo called Terri, who called Maggie, who told Nell and I."

"And Shelby called Nick and I, too." Nick elbowed Duke. "Way to make it sound like everyone was talking."

"They have anyway." Duke shrugged. "Shelby's pretty pissed."

"That's an understatement." Nick hooked his foot onto a bar stool to pull it closer and sat.

"But did either of you convince her Charles is bad? She's going to sign that contract with him tomorrow."

"I'm not sure we can stop her," Nick said. "If that's what she wants to do."

"What do you think?" Keane asked Duke.

"I'm not sure yet." Duke pulled the lever of his espresso machine, and it whirred to life, filling the kitchen with the exquisite scent of coffee. "I've considered a few things, but they all have bad ramifications."

"You can't hurt him." Nick looked pointedly at Duke.

"I don't know if it would change anything anyway."

"Except you getting in trouble, too."

"Wouldn't be the first time." Duke shrugged.

"What do we do?" Keane slumped onto a barstool next to Nick, glad to have the two of them help figure things out. Things had been feeling pretty dire.

"We keep an eye on her." Duke slid an espresso in front of Keane. "Drink up."

"Why? It's getting late, and I haven't slept in over twenty-four hours." Keane sipped the luscious liquid anyway.

"That's why." Duke slapped him on the shoulder. "Can't have you falling asleep out there."

"Out where?" Keane watched the two men head to the back deck. Emiliano was coming up, carrying paddleboards.

"Night paddleboarding." Duke winked and unbuttoned his flannel. He had a wetsuit under it. Nick followed suit. Duke shoved a bag on the floor with his foot. "I think this one will fit you."

Even though it wasn't going to make everything better, being on the water was one of the only things that could have helped at that moment. That and this crew of men who had come to pull him out of his own undertow.

CHAPTER 26

Shelby adjusted her suit one final time before exiting her vehicle. This was a good decision. She had money invested in it—down payment, architectural diagrams, permits, all paid. She would go through with it. She hadn't even given herself a chance to rethink it.

She'd retreated to her cabin the night before, locked the door, and shoveled Chunky Monkey ice cream into her mouth until the sugar coma prevented her from seeing straight. She'd woken up in a pool of melted ice cream, in her pajamas.

It wasn't a proud moment.

Neither was what she'd said to Keane. Her words were aimed to kill, and she'd struck bone.

But this was going to be different. Closing on the land would be the beginning of a brand-new chapter.

Not that she was ready to forgive Keane and the other guys for going behind her back. She was going to give them hell for that. But she had been harsh. She'd never thought she'd throw something like that in his face in a million years.

She'd started to let her guard down with Keane. Hope had blossomed like a sunny orange California poppy.

What a mistake.

It hadn't taken much for Keane to run off and leave without warning again. Regardless of who Gina was to him, she couldn't trust him. She'd known better and still started to let that hope unfurl.

Not anymore.

Sliding her sunglasses in place, she carried her portfolio like she was in control of everything in her world. Even though that was far from the truth.

With every carefully placed step, she pulled the mantle of her walls back up over her and settled it protectively on her shoulders.

"Ms. Greene." Charles met her inside the lobby. "Good to see you this morning."

"Good to see you as well." She took his hand in a firm shake.

"Ready to do some business?"

She gave a short nod. "I am. Ready to expand my business."

"Me as well." Charles displayed a comforting smile. "I couldn't imagine a better business partner. I am surprised I'm saying this, but I'm glad we decided to leave it at that. I'd hate to have missed out on this."

She selected a peppermint candy from the jar at the receptionist's desk. Popping it into her mouth, she hoped the minty sweetness would calm her roiling stomach.

"Me too." Shelby let him lead her to an office where a notary reviewed the contract with them. They signed paper after paper until it was done. The land was hers.

Saying goodbye, she took her copies and went on a drive. She'd done it. She'd put in motion the final stage of her retirement plan. It would take her many years yet, but it would put her on a stable financial path to her goals.

Once the yurts were up and running, she would be able to sit back and enjoy it a little more. Until she got bored, that is. Who knows what she'd do then.

Feeling steadier than she had in days, she decided to fulfill a promise she'd made to herself weeks ago. She drove out to her new land.

The windows were down on her Trailblazer, and she let her hand ride in the saltwater-rich air. Wispy clouds danced around the mountain in the distance, and the sky appeared as though it could go on and on.

She kept an old pair of boots in her trunk and pulled them on when she parked on her new property. Planting her feet on the earth, she reveled in the fact that it was finally hers. And it would never look like this again.

The buzzing pulled at her hands again. She flexed them to release the feeling, but it didn't stop.

"What the hell is that?" She frowned, scanning the land. There were no wetlands. The Hood Canal was visible across the street, but it wasn't coming from that direction. It was coming from farther out.

Maybe the wetlands evaluator had missed a lake or a small pond at the back of the lot. Or even in the Department of Nature Reserve lands behind it. Maybe that's what she was feeling.

It was her land now, and she didn't have to notify anyone of her presence. Shelby tramped through the ferns, around the orange poppies, and slid through the thorny wild blackberry bushes, all while following the distressing buzzing in her hands.

The ground dipped, and she balanced on a large cedar to climb onto a rotting nurse log before finding the forest floor again. The foliage opened into a small glade where Pacific bleeding hearts covered the floor. Their purply pink buds were in full bloom dotting the landscape.

The buzzing was stronger here. Shelby shook her hands again, pursuing the feeling.

This far into the woods, it should appear untouched, unvisited by anyone. She was far from any Olympic National Trails she knew of, but at the heart of the glade was a rough path. One that didn't look like it was made by animals.

Old-growth cedars and giant redwood sequoias surrounded her. She stopped to peer up to their barely visible tops high above. A few steps farther, and the buzzing grew to a stabbing throb.

There was no sign of water. Nothing seemed out of place. She continued to pick her way through, and the stabbing eased. She stopped and swiveled on the ball of her foot.

What was back there?

Returning, she scanned the ground. She walked a circle around the area, and the throbbing picked up around a wide tree where the ground swelled into a small hill. Around the back side of it, she saw an overhang of moss over the rocks at the highest point of the land.

Squinting, she squeezed between some thick ferns and brushed away the brush and vines in front of the hill. Her hand went through, revealing a crack in the ground where it had buckled and opened to a cave below.

Shelby took out her phone and turned on the flashlight. Boot treads in the mud were visible farther below, as were dark-blue barrels. Frowning, Shelby half slid down to the muddy earth below. A trickle of water ran through the center of the small space.

It felt different down here, like a cacophony of vibrations. More than one strand was echoing into her hands and up her arms.

Now that she was standing in it, she could see it wasn't a cave. It was a wide spot in the curve of a tunnel. Her light slid over the ground to find several barrels scattered around. A few of them were on their side. A dark-brown sludge trickled from one near her. It smelled sharp, like mashed-up old tires mixed with damp soil. It was close to the center, where a thin stream of water ran. Dappled sunlight filtered through the ferns at the mouth of the cave. Shelby turned off her flash and pocketed her phone to study the liquid.

"What the hell?" she murmured aloud.

"It took you long enough." A voice sounded above her.

Whirling, Shelby found Charles crouched at the opening. One hand braced on the rock border overhead, and the other held a gun.

"What's going on?" she stuttered.

He sighed loudly. "Isn't it obvious? I'm taking your business for myself."

"You can't do that." Her heart raced at the threat. Could he?

"You signed it over to me."

"I did not." She'd read the details. He only got a portion of it. Unless...

"Unless you die." He grinned widely, showing teeth like a wolf.

"But I have a beneficiary for Siren's Song." She said the words, but she knew he was right. As her business partner, he would take ownership of the property. There was normal language in the contract around things like that. Her stomach sank at the realization.

Keane had been right. They'd all been right. And she'd been too stubborn to listen.

"I was disappointed that you got a second LLC for the yurts to split them from the cabins." He sneered at her.

She may have missed the signs with Charles, but she'd read the contract. She wasn't completely stupid.

"You were only getting the five percent of the revenue. Why should that automatically apply to the entire business?"

"I hoped you'd miss that. But that's irrelevant. I have someone playing with the wording as we speak. It might not get challenged."

She knew her friends. They would challenge it. Every last one of them.

That was if she didn't make it out of this alive. And she had to. She had a crew of people who cared about her enough to investigate Charles at the expense of her fury.

"So, what's with the barrels?" She kept him talking. Wasn't that how they did it in the movies?

"Petroleum byproduct." He sniffed. "Stinks like the devil and toxic as hell. They were left in a warehouse I bought. No wonder it was so cheap. Thought it'd be an easy flip and I'd make a killing, but I discovered I was the proud owner of waste that had to be properly disposed of. I wasn't going to do that. I considered demolishing the place, burying it in the ground, and selling the land, but manufacturing facilities get more scrutiny by the EPA than land out here in the woods. When I investigated the property that came with the deal, I realized why. They'd obviously not dumped in a while, but it's the perfect spot. This place was the answer."

He gestured into the hole and took an easier way down than she had. The gun bounced around but stayed trained on her. Maybe keeping him talking wasn't the best idea.

"It has a natural aquifer running through it. This cave has perfect access to it. All I had to do was dump the remaining waste and sell it separately before anyone investigated too much," he went on. Seeing Shelby glance behind her, he tsked. "Don't even think about it. You'll get lost in the maze and die of starvation. What a terrible way to go."

"How did you afford it in the first place?" Shelby asked to change the topic. Keane said Charles didn't have much.

"I'm pretty good at cards." The leer he gave her soured her stomach. How had she ever found that charming? "And I'm good at sleight of hand. A little money for the wetlands certification, and it was set. I just had to convince you to use my contact. It was easy."

How had she not seen it in him before? The man was a slimy prick. The cocky attitude was evident in every single thing about him. Had she been that desperate to find a business partner?

"You must be good." She kept up the charade. "You certainly fooled me."

"You were a tough bitch." He snarled. "Always paying attention to everything. I thought I'd lost you after that cold-ass kiss you gave me, but you still came around. I can be persuasive. Still, it would have been nice to get a little play time out of the deal too."

Shelby baby-puked in her mouth. She had kissed the conniving asshat. She shivered, the feeling traveling down her back and arms. The buzzing separated, then snapped back together.

Interesting.

Focusing, she concentrated on the sensations in her hands. There. She could feel the thick, jagged current she associated with this portion of the land. A light, gentle, almost nonexistent one she felt around fresh water was there, too. A strong pull of saltwater that felt like the Hood Canal tingled heavily. And finally, the warm, comforting hug of the water from Orca Cove. It was the same one as the fjord, but as distinctive to her as home.

"Don't you think they'll find me?" Shelby said suddenly. She'd been quiet for too long.

"Not if you're stuffed into one of those barrels." He scratched his chin. "Of course, I might have to pound you up enough to fit."

She went white at the thought. She had to get out of there.

If she could feel the water, she could follow it through the tunnels. He'd said it was an aquifer, but that didn't mean there was an opening. It could be groundwater. But the tunnel had likely been created by running water. Or by pirates during the prohibition. Either way, it was a better fate than the one Charles Timms had in store for her.

"What would you have done if I'd found this place sooner?" She'd been planning on coming for weeks.

"I have cameras at the front of the property, hidden in the ferns. But you were such a good girl, calling before you stopped by." He said the words with a sickening sweetness. "You made it so easy. And if you had, I'd have stuffed you in here and forged your signature. Not as clean, of course, but it would have worked."

"But why Siren's Song?"

"It's easy to sell and has a bigger cash prize. You have quite a large asset there."

Shelby resisted the urge to inwardly pat herself on the back. His approval wasn't the one she wanted.

That was Keane's.

Crap. Why'd she have to be so mean to the man who meant so much to her? She hadn't even told him how much she loved his accomplishments. Tears pricked in her eyes. The painting in her office was almost too beautiful. And he'd created it with his bare hands. It was nothing like what she did. She had help to build something tangible that brought joy, but he created it practically out of thin air

.

"Besides, I owe a little money," he said.

"I thought you said you won that money."

He shrugged. "I won some. I had to take out a small loan for the rest of it. I'll pay off the original one and what I owe with some to spare. I'll come out on top, as I should."

"Why should you? I worked hard for all this, not you."

"This isn't easy, you know. You're a difficult person to keep interested." His mouth twisted down. "That dinner at Tusks was expensive as shit. And you ask too many questions. I should have picked someone easier."

"Maybe you're just not that smart." The words left her lips before she was able to stop them.

Charles' eyes hardened. "You think I'm not that smart, huh? Bet you didn't figure out what was causing all the problems at your cabins."

"My cabins?"

"The wires, the pipes, the roof, the elk." He ticked them off his fingers.

"You didn't." Her teeth ground. The sniveling weasel had set her back a lot in time and money.

"I did," he said proudly. "It was hell, crawling up on that roof in the middle of the night to pry up the shingles and carry up branches. A little acid, and the pipes under the sink started to eat away. I didn't do too much, either. I made sure I left it so they would naturally fail. I had to start months ago."

It clicked. Keane had known. He'd asked questions about the roof and the sink. She should have noticed only the pipes under the sink had thin areas.

"But I found mouse droppings near the wires."

"I got them from the pet store." He laughed.

"And how did you get the elk to come to the cabins?" It wasn't like he could redirect an entire herd.

"Salt blocks. I broke them up and hid them in the bushes to cause the most damage, then scattered them out to the woods where I've seen them. It took ages, but it was worth it. Those daft animals ignored it for the longest time."

"But why? Why sabotage Siren's Song?" It still didn't make sense.

"So you'd be desperate to expand your business. You'd need to start over if your current place was falling apart."

It'd nearly had the opposite effect. She'd nearly doubled down on her existing business, but then, he didn't know her. She'd never abandon something she'd put so much blood, sweat, and tears into.

Keane's face popped back up into her mind. They had always worked when they were together.

But he wasn't reliable. Things got tough and he retreated. He'd leave at the drop of a hat.

"See?" He gestured with the gun. "I worked hard for this. I deserve it. Maybe more than you do. Life wasn't handed to me on a silver platter by Mommy and Daddy."

"It wasn't handed to me, either," she shot back. Her parents had done well for themselves, but they certainly hadn't helped her. "You could have put that ambition to good use instead of criminal acts. You could have something of your own by now."

"I do," he snarled, waving the gun again. "Now, come here. Let's get this over with, so I can put the rest of my plan into action."

She held up a hand to stall him. "If you wait until the rentals are up, you'll make even more money."

"I considered that. But there was too much risk of you getting income and paying me off early. Besides, I get the funds in the accounts saved for the teepees. It's part of the LLC. That's even better."

"It'll be worth more once it's built."

"I can't wait that long." He rubbed his shoulder and rolled it back. Maybe whoever he owed money to had roughed him up. "Quit stalling. Come on."

Shelby had to make her move. Stretching her fingers out, she focused on the vibrations. They were singular again. The Hood Canal water was behind her. She knew right where to go. At least she didn't have to get around the madman.

He came at her in the dark tunnel. Luckily, he didn't have a flashlight. Moving fast, Shelby shoved a barrel at him and took off running. She heard him slip in the sludge.

His gun went off.

The sound was sharp and terrifying in the narrow tunnel. She crouched down and dipped to the left, jumping over the trail of water, but she kept moving.

Another shot went off, but it was farther away now. The tunnel curved and split. They had to be prohibition passageways. Feeling the saltwater, she took the path to the left and ran as fast as her feet would take her.

She settled into the jog as though it was any morning, except for her feet splashing in the water. Panic wouldn't help her. She heard the gun go off again and Charles curse her name.

Remembering her phone, she pulled it out to try calling for help. She didn't have any bars.

Damn it!

The jagged, unclean pulsing had lessened here, but she could still feel it. The sludge must be what was causing the water problems in the Hood Canal. Charles had been the cause all along.

The tunnel split again. She headed to the right, following that trickle of power, but her stomach churned. It felt like it had when she was with Charles, the feeling she'd written off as nerves.

Reaching for the left tunnel, she felt the tug of the cove. Should she go that way?

No, it'd be longer. The fjord was closer.

She took a few steps into the other tunnel, and her stomach felt like it flipped upside down. Just like it had when she'd agreed to being business partners with Charles.

Not a good choice.

"I'm listening," she said under her voice and backtracked down the other tunnel and toward the cove. Hopefully, whatever guided her had a better sense of direction than she did.

The water got deeper here. Shelby lifted her legs high to march through it. Soon, she was wading in it. There still wasn't visible light ahead, though.

Another hundred feet, and the water was nearly waist high. As she considered going back, she heard splashing far behind her. But before jumping in, she tried her phone once more.

Yes! She had bars.

She dialed Keane's number. It was the first thing she thought of. Probably because she was still so angry at him.

"Shelby?" His voice was pitched high and excited. "I'm—"

"I can't talk. Charles is coming after me. I'm in a tunnel, heading into the cove. I think. I need help."

"Where?"

"I don't know, just get to the water."

She disconnected and jumped in, taking sure strokes away from the yelling behind her.

Up ahead, the top of the tunnel dipped down until she reached the end of it. Feeling with her hands, she could tell it went farther. The tide had come in.

Shit.

She'd have to either go back, wait and see if he'd leave, or hold her breath and continue. How far was it? Could she make it?

Focusing on the call of the cove, she considered it. It felt strong. She had to be close.

"Shelby, damn it!" Charles called. "You're never going to make it. Let's talk about it. We can come to an agreement."

He was full of shit. She focused on breathing steadily and thinking about diving under the water. Her stomach didn't flip. That was weird.

She was terrified. That alone should have caused her some discomfort. She could feel the fear, but it was further down. In front of it was the knowledge that this was the right way to go.

Her gut told her so.

She could do this. Taking a deep breath, Shelby dove under the water and kicked with everything she had. She stretched her arms and moved through the current as she had many times before.

She swam until her lungs got tight, but there was still no sign of light. She kept close to the roof of the tunnel, her back bumping into it every few strokes. Without a wetsuit or the sun, the water was cold, and her fingers were growing numb.

Lungs burning, she thought about her friends. She should have spent more time with them. She shouldn't have been so dead set on keeping her walls up. She shouldn't have said what she had to Keane.

There!

There was a glow ahead. Exhaustion was creeping into her, and she badly wanted to take a breath. As close as it seemed, she still hadn't reached it.

Her arms swept out in front of her in a stroke, and she paused for a moment to gather her strength. She might not make it.

She took another one and kicked her legs out. She had to do this. She kicked again, wondering if she could reach the other side.

A flash of shimmer appeared before her. Was her vision going from the lack of oxygen?

There it was again!

Iridescent green-and-blue scales glistened in the water. It came closer. Long, bleached hair floated in a pool around an odd face, so pale it was tinged in blue. Purply blue, feminine eyes stared back at her from a face that was as foreign as it was human. A hand reached out to beckon her.

It had to be Willa's mermaid.

She took the smooth and firm fingers and resumed kicking with everything she had. The mermaid pulled her through to the surface.

Shelby gasped for air, taking in large gulps into her burning lungs. She felt safe for the first time since Charles had brandished the gun at her, knowing it took a strong swimmer to make it through. Even she'd needed help.

The water creature bobbed to the surface next to her, studying her curiously. They were out near the edge of the cove. She'd never noticed caves here. With the distance they'd swam to the surface, even at low tide, they probably weren't accessible without diving.

It was a perfect spot for smugglers.

"Thank you," Shelby said, her chest still burning for air.

The mermaid blinked at her. If that's what she was. She exhaled out of twin, angled slits more similar to a blowhole than a nostril. The smooth, shallow bridge of a nose graced a slim face with high cheekbones. Smoother skin stretched over softer features than a human's. Water shed from her like it would from a whale, sheeting off it and leaving it to appear dry.

She had a full tail, that part looked like the descriptions from fairy tales, but at her waist, the large scales transitioned to thicker pearly ice blue skin that reminded her of a dolphin, but thinner and bonier. And a slim fin ran along her forearm and pinky.

Gauzy fabric was draped around her like layers of scarves. Pearls and pieces of thin rope were braided into strands of her long, flaxen hair. Peering closer, Shelby could see the rope was made from a fine mesh netting.

As foreign as she appeared, her striking amethyst eyes and flowing hair made her strangely beautiful.

The silent mermaid suddenly jerked to look behind herself, then back at Shelby before disappearing below the surface.

Following her gaze, she saw Keane on his paddleboat, making a beeline for her.

CHAPTER 27

K eane's panicked heart flooded with relief the moment he saw her.

"Shelby," he hollered, using his arms to paddle out to her while lying on the board. He didn't have the patience to use the oar.

Jumping into the water, he pulled her to him and pressed her to his chest. She was safe.

"I'm okay. I'm okay," she said, but her arms wrapped firmly around him in response.

He smoothed back the wet hair from her face. "What happened?"

"Charles; that's what happened," she ground out, breathing heavily. "He wanted my property and thought he'd use the clause about reverting ownership in the contract."

"He was going to kill you?" He gripped her arms tightly. Anger and protectiveness like he'd never felt before overtook his relief. "Where is he?"

"I left him in the tunnels. I don't think he followed me." She clung to him, and he could see exhaustion in the hint of gray in her green eyes.

"Come on. Let's get you out of here." He pulled the paddleboard attached to his ankle closer and hauled her to the side.

Helping her get her legs up on it, he pushed her, kicking their way through the water.

A boat veered towards them.

"Who's that?" she asked.

"Probably the guys. I called them before I jumped in."

"You didn't even change." She eyed his jeans and T-shirt.

"Hell no. You needed me."

He'd ran straight for the water with his board after hanging up his phone with Duke, knowing the courier would find a way to get a smaller boat than his Aurelia. One they could get into easily.

As his friend came closer, he made out Duke, Nick, and Emiliano on board.

"Nice day for a swim," Duke said casually, but he caught the tightness in his eyes.

"What happened?" Nick leaned over the railing and reached out a hand to pull Shelby off the board and into the johnboat.

"Charles Timms." She gathered her knees close to her chest, and her teeth chattered. Wet hair clung to her fine face.

Emiliano shrugged out of his flannel and wrapped it around her. Keane pulled himself onto the paddleboard and sat with his legs straddling it. He'd rather have joined her so he could hold her close, but the board wouldn't fit in the small boat.

"Where is he?" Nick scanned the coastline.

"Probably back on the property by now." Shelby pulled the shirt tighter around her. "He wanted my business."

"He was going to kill her." Keane snarled, his hands gripping the side of the aluminum hull.

Nick dialed a number on his phone. "We need to get to shore."

Duke nodded to Keane, who pushed off so they could move faster. He quickly paddled to follow.

When he reached the docks, Keane lifted himself out of the water, pulling the board's tether and unhooking himself from it. When he reached Shelby, though, she had already launched into the story with Duke and Emiliano. Nell, Maggie, and Willa had joined them on the marina.

He wanted to hold her close again, to reassure himself that she was alright, but she was surrounded by her people and wasn't reaching for him as she had out on the water.

"Here." Nell handed him a towel.

"Thanks." He dried his hair and flung it back, listening to her story.

Anger rose in him, and he moved closer to her side to be near her, his hands aching to touch her, to reassure her somehow.

"Warner is headed out there now," Nick said, checking his phone. "I'm going to meet him and his team."

"I'm coming too," Duke said.

"I'm staying with Shelby." Keane's jaw clenched. He would stay with her until she asked him to leave or he knew she was safe.

The rest of them went back to the café, now closed for the afternoon. Nell made sandwiches for everyone gathered in the back dining room with the doors locked.

"You could have died," Maggie said, her eyes wide. "I can't believe you went in that water not knowing if you could make it out alive."

"I didn't really have a choice." Shelby's hands wrapped around the hot coffee Nell had brought her. A blanket was still around her shoulders, but she seemed more like herself. Color had returned to her cheeks.

"I can't believe the mermaid came to save you." Willa's voice was barely above a whisper and full of awe. "I wonder how she knew you needed help."

"No idea, and I'm not sure she's a mermaid. She could be some sort of shifter that had half transitioned. There's a lot we don't know about her," Shelby said, ever the logical one.

"We know she's magical," Maggie said. "Percy said our powers came from her."

"Did she do anything magical?" Willa asked.

"Not that I could see, but we did make it through the water pretty quickly. That might have been hard if she was only pulling me." Shelby frowned. "Maybe she can move water like Duke."

"Percy said something about our powers transferring from her. Maybe we all have some of what she can do," Maggie said.

"That makes a lot of sense," Shelby said. "But if lightning caused the transfer, she'd have to have gotten hit."

Willa's eyes rounded. "Did she look injured?"

Shelby shook her head. "Not that I could tell."

Keane's phone pinged. It was Duke. He read it out loud. "Chief Warner has Charles in custody. They're taking him to the station right now. Shelby, they'll need you to stop by sometime to give your statement."

"That's fine." She stared out the window. "Should I go now?"

"You don't have to until you're feeling better," Keane said, a little more forcefully than he should have. "I'm sure tomorrow would be fine. I can take you."

Her eyes met his, then dropped away. "Tomorrow would be good. I'd like to get home and clean up."

"At least he's behind bars." Maggie's eyes narrowed. "There's no more threat to you."

"Probably not," Keane said. "But he may have people working with him, like whoever he owed money to. They may be waiting for this deal to go through for their payday. I'll see if the chief can get a car to sit outside overnight."

Shelby nodded and stood slowly, lost in thought.

"I can walk you home." Keane gathered the towel that was lining his seat and handed it to Nell.

Shelby wordlessly walked to the door.

"Do you want me to stay with you?" Willa asked.

"I'm fine, but thanks," Shelby said.

Out in the fresh afternoon air, Keane's hand touched her shoulder.

"Would you rather stay with me?" He'd prefer to have her where he could keep an eye on her all the time.

"No, I want to be home." She pulled the blanket tighter around her.

They walked side by side to Siren's Song Cabins and up the narrow driveway to hers at the end. Everything looked normal. He had texted Nick to ask Warner to assign someone to keep an eye on the place.

"I don't have my keys." Shelby scanned around her like she didn't know what to do. It was completely out of character.

"Does the lobby have a spare?" Keane asked.

She nodded. Cleo jumped up from her desk when they entered, still half soaked.

"Omigod. Are you alright?" she asked.

"I'm okay." Shelby managed a thin smile. "I need the extra key. The other one is in my car at the new property."

Cleo hovered where she was. "Of course."

Then she disappeared into a small closet and came back out with the spare.

"I'll fill you in tomorrow," Shelby said, taking it from her. "And thanks."

"Of course," Cleo said.

They went back to the cabin, Shelby unlocked it, and he followed her inside. It was identical to the other cabin he'd seen, cute and practical, but it had a little more life in it than the rest of them. Personal items sat neatly on the coffee table and in the kitchen. It was homey.

In the corner of the couch, he noticed a small stuffed orca. The one he'd just won for her was still at his place. It had to be the one from high school.

She had kept it? She'd said she didn't know where it was.

"Can I stay?" The thought of leaving her there frightened him.

"I'm sure I'll be okay." She took off the blanket and set it on her kitchen table. Spinning to face him, she took a deep breath. "You need to get cleaned up too."

"I'm fine. I'd rather be with you. Make sure you're safe."

"You said they're sending a cop car."

"Still." He took her elbows. "I don't want to leave you. But I will if you want me to. It's your choice."

"I need to process everything." She shook her head, then rubbed her forehead. "I have to figure out what to do about the property and our contract. Can I buy him out if he's in jail?""I can't see why you couldn't. If it's in the terms."

"It says I can pay it off at any time. I need a loan to do that."

"I'll give it to you."

She frowned. "I don't know if that's a good idea."

"I can take his place in the agreement. We can do the same deal." He'd do whatever made her feel better about the situation.

"I need to think through it all." She stared down between them. "You were right about him."

"He must have been a helluva conman to convince Shelby Greene." He gave her a lopsided smile.

"Thanks, but I think I might have been too eager to find a partner to talk business with. After Gary died..." Her voice broke off.

"I'm so sorry I wasn't there for you."

"Me too." She stepped back and away from him. "Thanks for walking me home, Keane."

It was nice to hear his name on her lips, but it would have been nicer if it wasn't while asking him to go.

"I'm going to wait outside until the car comes." He went to the door and looked back at her one last time.

"I'll be okay," she said, but he wasn't sure if she was telling him or herself.

Keane toweled off from his shower and pulled on clean jeans and a T-shirt in case Shelby called. He knew she was safe and Ronnie, the cop who was parked outside her cabin, would stay there all night to ensure it. But it still ate at him. He wanted to keep her within sight.

It was selfish, really. She'd asked for space. And he understood how it must have appeared. Not only had he left town, but a woman answered his phone when she'd called. Gina still felt awful about the whole thing. Luckily, he'd already sold most of his paintings, and the remaining ones were snapped up due to his absence. He'd become a hard-to-get audience by nothing less than making choices for his happiness.

Sleep clawed at him, but it was early. If he didn't stay up another hour or so, jet lag would continue another day. Padding to his kitchen, Keane went through the ritual of making espresso.

He walked out onto the back deck with it and leaned over the edge, surveying the water. The full moon hung low, its reflection cascading out in an echo with each recurring wave. Mysteries lay beneath. He'd always known it; most people did. It wasn't surprising that Percy and the mermaid existed. If anything, it made more sense than not.

And he was okay with not understanding it all. He didn't need to. Knowing that magic existed and thrived beneath the surface was enough for him.

His phone rang and cut through his pensive mood.

"Hey, Dad. What's up?" Keane stood from the deck railing.

"Son." His father's voice was filled with alarm. "I'm so glad you're back."

"What's wrong?" He was already in his house, searching for his shoes.

"It's your mom. She came out of the bathroom and wasn't making sense. I thought she was being funny, but then she got mad." The words came out rushed. "Anyway, we're at the hospital. We don't know a lot yet."

"I'm on my way." Keane hung up, shoved his feet into boots, and headed out the door. His first instinct was to call Shelby, but he'd promised her space. She'd been through a lot. If he reached out to her now, it would appear as though he was looking for sympathy. He wasn't about to manipulate her with his mom's health.

He stopped suddenly on his front porch, finally realizing he didn't have a car. He'd returned the rental the day before, and Duke had driven him home.

Peeling to the right and toward the marina, he dialed his friend's number. By the time he made it to the parking lot, his friend's figure was visible, jogging up the docks. He grabbed him by the shoulder in a tight squeeze.

"Let's go." They got into his old, gray truck and took off.

They found his dad pacing in the waiting room of the E.R. His eyes reflected the panic he felt.

"Dad." He met him in a hug. His father's arms wrapped around him, and he sagged against him in the shared burden of fear. After a few long moments, he pulled back and sniffed. "Thanks for coming."

"Of course, I came." Keane kept a hand on his shoulder. "Have you heard anything?"

"Not much yet. The doctor said it might be a stroke. They're still testing." He glanced at the secured medical door. "They said it was a good thing we came as quickly as we did."

"That's good." He gave a reassuring squeeze. "You did good, Dad."

"I wish I could do more." Keane found Duke standing nearby but also giving the men space. "Do you think Willa would come?"

"In a heartbeat. I can call her," Duke offered.

"I don't know that herbs can help." His dad frowned.

"She might have some ideas to make her more comfortable or strengthen her immune system." He tried to think of a reason for Willa to help with a serious medical condition without telling him she had the ability to magically boost the efficacy of herbs. "Only if you're okay with it. I don't think it will hurt. It feels like *something* we can do."

His dad nodded. "Yeah. Maybe she has some teas to calm her. We'll have to ask the doctors first."

"Absolutely." He nodded to Duke, who stepped aside to call their herbalist friend.

Then they settled in to wait.

Duke stayed until Willa arrived, and then left to be close in case Shelby needed anything. Keane appreciated it. It let him be present for his dad.

CHAPTER 28

S leep eluded Shelby. In the haze of the cold, numbing knowledge that she could have died hovered the fact that she had missed the signs in Charles, signs the others had seen. She fought the urge to call Keane.

But she wasn't going to lean on him like that if she couldn't let him in. That wasn't fair to him.

So, she gave up on trying to get sleep and met Chief Warner at the police station as soon as he arrived the next morning. Ronnie was glad to leave her with another cop and go home. He probably didn't have trouble sleeping.

"How are you feeling?" The chief led her into a side room. He dropped the notepad he was carrying on the table, but his focus stayed on her.

"I'm fine." She waved off his concern. "Feeling pretty dumb about the whole thing, but otherwise, fine."

"I'm mighty glad you made it out the way you did. You must be one strong swimmer." He leaned back in the chair across from her.

"I used to be. Must be muscle memory."

"I'll say."

And an underwater mermaid creature.

"It's a good thing Keane showed up as quickly as he did."

"Wish he'd have called us, too."

"I don't think he took any time to do anything but jump in the water. It was the only way he got there that fast."

"I can't say I'm glad neither of you called us, because it might not have played out like it had, but I hope you keep it in mind in the future."

"Will do, sir."

"Now." He tapped the notepad. "You feeling good enough to do this?""I am."

He slid the pad across to her and held the pen aloft. "I have to tell you that you have the right not to testify, although I hope you do."

"Oh, I have no trouble testifying." She'd bust down doors if that's what it took to expose the creep and get him off the streets.

He nodded sharply and handed her the pen. "Just write your statement, what happened to you, in detail. Make sure you don't elaborate."

"I'll stick to the facts, sir."

"Alright then."

"Is he denying what he did?"

"He is," the chief said plainly. "But when we got there, he was in a rage, half soaked, and waving a gun around. With his history, I don't think any jury will believe him."

"I hope not."

"Once we get your full statement, we'll try again. Hopefully, we can get more information out of him."

"Thanks, Chief."

Chief Warner left her in the room to put her words down. It took her a few tries; she wanted it as clear as possible. It was cathartic to review everything in detail. He had manipulated her so well. If she wasn't so upset about it, she'd be impressed with his knowledge of people and psychology.

She emerged with the final version and found him chatting with Duke at the front desk.

"All done?" The chief asked.

"It's as good as I can get it." She handed the notepad over to him.

The older man slowly reviewed her notes, then nodded. "This will do nicely, Miss Greene. Lots of good facts we can check up on. Hard to argue with these points."

"I certainly hope not." She tucked one edge of her hair behind her ear. With the purging activity over, she felt she could take a nap. "Am I free to go?"

"You are. I'll keep you posted. And, Shelby?" He waited until she stopped. "I'm going to post a car at night while we dig into this thing, but stay around people you trust and keep your eyes peeled until I let you know otherwise."

"Sure thing, Chief."

Duke followed her out onto the sidewalk. The morning air brought her the scent of saltwater, and her hands gently buzzed, pleased with the proximity of the cove.

"Did Keane call you?" He fell in step beside her.

"No. Why?" Something in Duke's expression worried her. "What is it?"

"It's Kalani."

"Keane!" Shelby saw him standing near a window with a forlorn expression on his face. His head snapped up at the sound of her voice.

She'd barreled to the hospital as soon as Duke told her the news, nearly running a red light in the process.

"Shelby." His voice came out gruff. He'd pulled his hair back in a tie, and she could see dark circles under his eyes and redness around the edges.

She raced to him and right into his arms. "I came as soon as I heard. Is she okay?"

Keane gripped her tightly to him, his head falling to her shoulder. "I don't know. I just don't know yet."

"Kalani is strong." She consoled him. "I'm so sorry, Keane."

"I can't lose her." The words came out weak and ragged. It tugged at her heart.

"I know. I'm here." She ran a hand over his back.

Keane sniffed and lifted his head. "Willa came last night. She and Dad had a long conversation, but she's brought some things for her."

"That's good." Shelby brushed a strand of hair that had escaped the tie behind his ear. "She knows her stuff."

Only now did she notice Keane's dad sitting nearby and realized how intimate their stance was. She released her hold on him but stayed close. He needed her support right then, and she'd be there for him.

"Do the doctors know what happened?" she asked.

"They're thinking she had a stroke."

"A stroke? How? Kalani has always been healthy and active."

"It can be hereditary." He shrugged.

"It's possible that it's just a TIA, a transient ischemic attack," Elias added, standing to come over to them. He looked as rough as Keane did. They must have had a hard night. He put a hand on Shelby's shoulder and gave it a squeeze. "It was nice of you to come."

"Of course." Shelby smiled.

"They said her chances of recovery are good because Dad brought her in so soon," Keane informed her.

"That's great news," Shelby said. "How long until you know more?"

"Should be soon." Elias shook his head. "It's been a long night."

"Can I get you something? Coffee? Food?"

"Nah, I'm good. Duke brought coffee early this morning, and I'm not hungry."

"Me either, but I'll take coffee," Keane said. "I'll walk to the cafeteria with you. I've been standing around too long."

The two of them made their way down the long hallway to the elevator.

"How's he holding up?" she asked of Elias.

"He's doing better. Last night was rough."

"Probably on both of you." She touched his arm.

"It was worse on Dad." He shrugged. "Mom too."

"I bet. Have you gotten to see her yet?" They left the elevator and walked down the hall to the cafeteria. He shook his head. "Not yet. Doctor said she's stable and they are letting her rest. They didn't want her to try talking too much and get frustrated. We should get to go in before too long."

"That's good. If I know Kalani, she'll be back to her cheerful self in no time."

"I sure hope so." Keane stared off into the distance to the stands of coffee pots and creamer.

Shelby grabbed two cups, filled them, and paid the clerk. "Do you want to sit?"

"Nah, too much sitting." He took his cup from her and gave her the only smile she'd seen on him since she arrived. It was a weak one at that. "Thanks."

They walked side by side back down the hallway.

"How're you doing now?" He bumped her on the shoulder. "Quiet night?"

"Yeah, uneventful. No wild parties for me."

That got him to crack another smile.

"I wish you would have let me stay."

"Then you wouldn't have come here. And you needed to be here for Elias."

"Maybe."

"It was a rough night for me as well; I didn't sleep well. Mortality threatened and all." They reached the elevator and got in. Shelby took a sip of her coffee and grimaced. "This is truly awful. I would have stopped by the café on the way, but I was in a hurry."

"Thanks for that."

"Of course." He'd have done the same for her. Hell, he'd *done* the same.

Keane took a sip. "You're right. This isn't good.""You should feel bad. I'm pretty much ruined on coffee now. I've actually been checking my budget for when I can swing a Nessie of my own. Only, I'll come up with a better name for it."

"Oh?" He watched her with interest.

"Yeah, I was thinking Marlon the Magnificent."

"Marlon?"

"It's a nice, strong name."

"I can see that."

"Probably just Magnificent One for short."

"That's short?"

"It's an espresso machine." She cast him a serious expression. "It deserves pomp and circumstance."

"Both? Wow. I missed the boat."

"Entirely."

They got off the elevator.

"Do you still need to go make a statement at the station?"

"No, I already did that this morning. I wanted it over and done with."

"How'd it go?"

"Fine. I didn't like reliving it in detail, but it was cathartic." She waved an arm in the air. "I wanted to give enough information to help the cops. Apparently, he's saying he's innocent."

"What?" Keane stopped and faced her. "He's denying everything when he was caught with a gun?"

"I know. Chief Warner said my testimony should help."

"That greedy bastard," Keane ground out.

"Hey." She grabbed his arm. "It'll all work out. I'm safe, and he's behind bars."

They resumed their stroll down the corridor.

It was now or never. She had to talk about the other thing that had kept her up all night.

"I'm so sorry about what I said, Keane." Shelby shuffled her feet. "I can't believe I said that. I was hurting, and well, there's no excuse for that."

He nodded slowly. "I know."

"It was awful of me."

"The whole situation was awful." He faced her. "I'm sorry I left you. I should have texted. That would still have been giving you space. It must have felt like I just took off again."

"It did," she admitted, kicking at the ground. "I'm struggling with holding a grudge against you."

"I know."

"But what I said wasn't okay."

"I never should have left you, in the first place, all those years ago." His eyes bore into hers, and the whole world stood still. He hadn't said it was a bad decision before, only that he should have handled it differently. Had he changed his view on it? "That's where this all began. We were good before."

"*I* thought we were." Her voice was soft. "But not if you felt you weren't good enough."

Keane shifted on his feet. "I was young. I didn't know how to talk to you. I also didn't know who I was. It seemed better to figure it out now than later, after we were married and you realized you had a wishy-washy husband."

"You weren't wishy-washy. You were easygoing and fluid. You still are. You just…"

"Know who I am."

"Yeah."

"Where I was fluid, you were rock steady. You had everything under control. You knew who you wanted to be and what you wanted to do. Hell, you've already built what you said you were going to, but you've accomplished it in half the time."

"I'm a workaholic." She tried for a wink.

"But you don't have to be. You shouldn't have to be. You were always taking care of everything for us. I knew I could provide for you, too. I wanted that."

"You always helped me slow down. And you supported me in everything I did. That was all I needed."

"For a time. It wouldn't have lasted, the way it was. I needed direction. You deserve someone who has his shit together. Someone who can provide for you, so you don't have to work so hard all the time."

"Idiot. Don't you know I love what I do? I love creating something out of nothing, building something that can help the town. Increase tourism, create memories, all of t hat."

"I feel the same way, creating something out of nothing, creating emotion."

"It's similar, but different. I'm glad you found something you love. I am. But you'd have found it, eventually."

Her heart ached for the younger Shelby. "Why couldn't you do that *with* me? Together?"

"I didn't want to hold you back. Or put another thing on your list of to dos." Keane took her hand in his. "You were already holding the world."

"Hardly."

"It felt like it at that age. It was the world to me."

"But fifteen years, Keane?" Her eyes widened to drive the point home.

"Yeah." He hung his head, then peered up at her through his lashes. "It took way longer than I planned. I guess I'm not as efficient as you are."

She scoffed. "I had the help of the town. You would have too."

"What, selling to farmers' markets and bazaars?"

"Yes."

"That would have taken even longer."

"You have been way more successful than I have." She leveled her gaze at him.

He shrugged. "When it finally came, it came quickly. I had to keep up steam long enough to make sure it would stick."

"Well, it did. The world knows you."

"That was never important to me. It still isn't." He was silent for a long moment, then he gave her hand a squeeze where it still lay in his. "Do we have a chance, Greene?"

Her heart squeezed tight, skipping a beat, then began again. "I honestly don't know. Maybe we're star crossed. Maybe we weren't ever meant to make it."

He dropped his gaze.

"It seems like every time things are going good, it falls apart around us," she said.

"You mean I leave."

She shifted her gaze away. He dropped her hand. The loss of it stung more than she'd expected. And that jagged, nagging feeling in her gut started up again.

CHAPTER 29

When they got back to the waiting room, the doctor was talking to his dad. Keane jogged over to hear the news, and Shelby stayed at his side.

It was an odd feeling. He knew she'd always be there for him, but she couldn't open her heart back to him. He'd ruined that.

"So, she can come home?" his dad asked excitedly.

"I think she's stable," the doctor said. "But I'd like to keep her a few more hours. She's making an amazing recovery. It was good that you brought her in as quickly as you did. She must be very strong. I've never seen anyone recover as quickly as this."

Willa. It had to have been Willa's medicines.

"But it's still going to take some time for her speech to come easily again. It'll take her a little longer to form words, and her memory will be slow," he went on.

"That's okay. She can take all the time she needs," Elias said. "I'm just glad she's okay."

"That's one tough wife you've got there, Mr. Lennox."

"Oh, don't I know it?" He beamed.

"Why don't you get some rest, Dad," Keane offered.

"I'm not leaving my girl. You rest." His dad pulled him in and hugged him. "You need it."

"Thanks," he said sarcastically, knowing they both looked ragged. He sincerely needed fuel and rest. He found Shelby watching the two men. "Maybe I will. Want to get breakfast?"

She shrugged. "Sure."

"I'll eat, get some rest, and come to check in on you and Mom later, okay, Dad?" Keane made sure his dad would be okay without him there. When his father nodded, he added, "Promise to call if anything changes?""Of course." His dad pulled him into a tight hug that lasted a lot longer than normal.

They each needed the other to get through this. Keane was keenly aware of how it could have been much different for both of them had he not come home when he did. His choices gnawed at him once again. How much else had he missed while he was gone? He'd already missed being there for his friends when Gary passed. What other life changes had they gone through and needed support for?

He sure as hell had needed theirs.

Shelby drove him to the café. It was a quiet ride. Each of them had a lot to think about. It wasn't just about their relationship, but their own issues swirled above them, taking up space in her SUV.

As soon as they sat down in a booth, Maggie and Nell appeared side by side at their table.

"How is Kalani?" Nell asked first.

"Doing well, thanks to Willa," Keane said. "She's going home later today."

"How're you?" Maggie asked Shelby.

"I'm great. That bastard is behind bars, and I armed Chief Warner with a solid testimony." Shelby raised her head confidently, but Keane knew it was her way of convincing herself too.

"You're still going to be careful, right?" Keane asked her. "We don't know if he was working alone or not."

"I promised the chief I would stay around people during the day. He's going to keep a car posted at night," she told him. It settled his fear a little.

"Thanks."

"Did the doctors figure out what happened?" Maggie asked.

"They're thinking it was a TIA, a small stroke," he said. "It was caught so quickly; she should recover well."

"What a relief," Nell said.

"Good for Elias," Maggie said.

"He wasted no time." Shelby bobbed her head.

Keane nodded. His dad always made his mom a priority. He'd not done as good of a job at that with the woman he cared about in his life. The thought hit home hard.

Sure, he'd been a kid when he left, but somewhere along the line, he should have course corrected earlier. Fear had held him back. He wasn't going to let it control his actions anymore.

"Now that things are settling down, we should get everyone together," Nell suggested.

"I was thinking the same thing." Shelby propped her arms on the table in front of her. "I have some thoughts about my powers I want to share with the group."

"And we need to see what we can do about the waste that was dumped in the water," Maggie said.

"Dinner tonight? I could probably close early." Nell scanned the room only half full of breakfast guests.

"I want to be with Mom and Dad tonight, but you all don't have to wait for me." Keane shrugged.

"You're a part of us. We can adjust to make it work for you." Shelby shot him a look that made his emotions bubble back to the surface. Maybe it was because of the lack of sleep or the emotional couple of days, but it struck deep. "Besides, Solomon is a part of us too, and he prefers afternoons. He gets up early."

"Right." Maggie nodded.

"Tomorrow at two?" Nell offered.

"I can make that work," Shelby said.

"I think I can, too," Keane said. As long as things kept going well with his mom. He couldn't think like that. Of course they would.

"Perfect. That's settled. And I'll send some food over to the Lennox house later," Nell said. "Now, what can I get you two?"

"Eggs and bacon," Shelby said, her eyes widening. "And some sourdough if you have it."

"Of course, I do." Nell scoffed, then asked Keane, "You?"

"Sounds good to me. Scrambled eggs, please," he said.

"Done." Nell disappeared.

"Black coffees, right?" Maggie asked. At their nod, she followed Nell into the kitchen.

"I'm exhausted, but I'm even hungrier than exhausted." Shelby dropped her head in her hands.

"Same." He grinned at her.

After they got food into their bellies, they both looked better. He felt a bit better too, even though everything still hung between them.

"I'm going home to nap," he finally said. He hated to leave her, but he needed to rest. "I can take the couch if you want to rest at my place."

Shelby toyed with her napkin as she considered his offer, then she shook her head sharply. "No, but thanks. I need to check in with Cleo. I left her last night without any explanation. There's still a cot in the back of the office. I can take a nap there while she's at the desk. She'll call the chief at the first sign of trouble. Besides, I have people lined up to start on Monday. I've got to do a few things so I'm r eady."

"Let me know if you need anything. I'm happy to help."

"Nick's going to be there, but thanks. I'll let you know." She studied the remaining few tablespoons of coffee in her mug. "Are you sure about that loan offer?"

He perked up. "Of course. Whatever you need."

"I need to take one out anyway. If you're really interested, you can benefit from the interest."

"I could." He wouldn't charge her any if it were up to him.

"Or you could take Charles's deal and be a silent partner and reap five percent of the revenue until I pay you back. But it would have to be a silent partner. I make the rules." She said the words firmly, then wrinkled her nose. "That's not to say I wouldn't ask your opinion on things. We are friends, right?"

He grinned at her cute expression, no longer the businesswoman but the friend. He'd missed that.

"You can count on it." He thought about the best way to help her financially without her feeling like it was a gift, one he would gladly give. "I won't take Charles's deal, because he's an asshole and outright crook. But if you want to come up with a new plan for us, I like the idea of being a silent partner. I'd make the bet on Shelby Greene any day."

Besides, she would only have to pay him back when it was prosperous, not a set percentage. It seemed like a better deal for her.

"You got it. I'll review his contract and come up with one to show you. Get your feedback on it." She waved a hand in the air.

"Whatever you think is fair. Just let me know how much you need. I'll need a few days, but it shouldn't be a problem." For the first time in weeks, he was feeling better about the time he'd spent away. It might not have been the best decision for them, but at least he could do this for her.

"Must be nice, Mr. Lennox," she teased him, but he knew she was normally the one with the financial security. She was just in the midst of a huge outlay.

"At least my mistakes were good for something," he teased back, hoping it wasn't too soon.

"I might as well get some benefit from it." She smirked at him.

Things between them were starting to feel more like themselves than they had in a while, but in a new and interesting way.

Keane took the back steps up to the Wild Café's deck later that evening. He'd had a decent rest, then spent the afternoon with his parents. His mom was doing well, the band around his chest had lessened, and his dad had reluctantly taken a couple of hours to nap on the couch while he was there.

Nell had sent chowder and sandwiches over to his parents' house. It had been enough for him to accept the offer to join them for dinner. He was still a little tired, but if he had any chance of sleeping tonight, he needed to get out and about.

It was late, and the sun was beginning to set over the cove. Mind still full of everything from the past few weeks, he headed to the outside bar.

"What can I get you?" Barnaby, the bartender, asked.

"I'll take a lager, please."

"Make that two." Duke appeared at his side and slapped him on the back. "How's it going, man?"

"Better." Keane turned to face him. "Mom's doing well. She's resting now. Willa brought some more teas for her and a tonic for tomorrow. The doc gave her some exercises, and she has physical therapy scheduled next week. I think she's going to be okay."

"That's great, but I was asking about you." Duke raised his eyebrows. "You've had a rough time of it."

The breath left him, and he plunked down on the barstool beside his friend. He hadn't stopped to think of himself in a while. "It's kinda sucked, to be honest."

Duke nodded slowly. "I'm glad you're back."

"Me too, man." He couldn't imagine dealing with all this without the help of his friends.

Duke thanked Barnaby for their beer and peered into his glass. "Things have been changing between you and Shelby. I heard about what happened on the tidelands."

"You did?"

"The whole town did." The corner of Duke's mouth crept up. "Don't you remember what it's like, living in the cove? Whether you do something great or something dumb, everybody knows."

He should have realized. "You didn't mention anything when I left for Florence."

"You were worried about Shelby. It didn't seem like the right time."

Duke had a point; Keane had been pretty raw about it. He'd had a taste of everything he wanted, and it was painful to think she might never forgive him. It still was. "Thanks for that."

Duke lifted a shoulder to brush off the gratitude. "Do you want to talk about it?"

"Not really." Keane took a long gulp of his beer. The cool liquid tingled on his tongue, quenching his thirst. "Shelby is exceptionally good at a lot of things; holding a grudge is one of them."

"She's hurting," he said it gently. It came across as more of an explanation than a chide.

"I know. And I'll give her whatever time she needs. I'm not going anywhere." He rethought his words. "Particularly without telling her first."

Duke burst into laughter at that. "Might be a good idea."

"We'll figure it out. We're friends at least."

"That's good. Shelby is a fair person."

"Painfully fair." Keane gazed off into the water, where Duke's ship sat tall. The sun set behind it like a waking dream. He made a mental note to paint it for his friend. "How's business going?"

"Being a courier?" Duke's lips curled into a knowing smile. He never gave a lot of detail about what he did exactly. "It's probably not the life most people would want, but it suits me. I'm happy."

"You're your own boss."

"I am. And I get to set my hours and the work I take. It took me a while to be able to do that."

"I get that." Boy, did he get that. "I used to have to take every single show I could get accepted to."

"Everyone says your twenties are your prime, but I sure am enjoying my thirties." Duke lifted his beer in salute.

J.D. and his friends were moving around behind them, bringing in their gear for their Saturday-night gig. People flocked to the back bar and tables to settle in for the music.

"The Wild Café's doing great, isn't it?" Keane admired the number of faces he knew, but also the ones he didn't.

"She is now," Duke agreed. He downed the rest of his beer in a long gulp. "How about we get out of here? It's a great atmosphere, but it's hard to talk with the music. I've got bourbon on the boat."

Bourbon sounded good right then. He hadn't indulged in a while, and the week had taken its toll on him.

He nodded, stood, and paid Barnaby. Their seats were instantly claimed by a couple.

"Did Nell tell you about the meeting tomorrow at two?" Keane asked.

"Yep. Everyone's able to make it, even Solomon."

"I haven't seen him in years. How's he doing?"

"About the same, but older."

"Profound."

Duke smirked. "He's still a bit of a loner."

"That's calling the kettle black."

"Even more than me."

"Yikes."

"Yeah, the crew's been good for him. The ladies fuss over him." Duke stuck his hands deep into his pockets as they strolled down the marina and onto the thick, wooden planks of the dock. "Willa's always bringing him teas and tonics."

"Sounds like Willa."

"Our little Flower Child. I'm glad she never changed."

The sharp smell of pine tar drifted up through the briny breeze as Keane followed Duke down onto his deck.

"Want to come down or sit up here?" Duke asked, surveying the sky. "Night's clear."

"I'm good sitting outside. It's nice out." Thankfully, he'd grabbed a flannel before heading to his parents. Even in the summer, the nights still had a chill.

Duke dipped his head and disappeared into his cabin. Keane dropped onto the bench that sat against it, staring off into the distance. The waves lapped peacefully against the metal hull.

"You haven't gone to sleep on me, have you?" Duke handed a tumbler to him.

Keane blinked. "Nah, just relaxing." It wasn't the first time he'd been on his ship, but it was the first time he'd viewed it through the lens of his younger self. "You really did it, didn't you?"

Duke rocked back on his heels and scanned the deck, a slow smile spreading across his face. His eyes were half closed as though remembering everything it took to get here. "Yeah, I guess I did."

"Gary would have been proud of you," Keane said suddenly.

Duke sat down hard next to him. "Thanks, man." He studied his bourbon, then lifted his head. "He was proud of you, too."

Keane looked away. "I left."

"Somehow, I think he knew why."

"You think?"

"I think that's why he read your interviews out loud in front of Shelby. Like he wanted to make her see."

"I still can't imagine she took that well."

"About as good as you'd expect." Duke looked away. "I didn't take it well at the time, either, I'll admit."

"How I wish I would have taken those few steps. I had convinced myself you all wouldn't want me." Keane shook his head.

"What steps?"

"At the funeral." It weighed heavily on him.

"Wait." Duke turned to face him on the bench. "What are you talking about?"

Keane let out a long, heavy, emotion-filled breath. He was embarrassed to talk about it, but he needed to.

"I had just gotten back from a six-month-long exhibit tour in Europe, ending in Spain. Going through my mail, I found Nell's letter. I'd been so busy; I had avoided my mail and phone the entire trip. I'd barely slept." He swallowed. "I took my still-packed bags straight to the airport and flew out on the next flight to SeaTac, but I was too late."

"You came?" Duke whispered the words.

Keane nodded. He'd watched them from a distance, standing at the tree line several yards away. He hadn't seen Shelby's face, couldn't smell her spicy citrus scent, couldn't feel the toned muscles glide under the soft skin of her arms. And she hadn't seen him. No one had.

"I didn't have the courage to approach the group I abandoned fifteen years ago. I didn't think I deserved to be a part of it with you." Keane's voice cracked. "Didn't deserve to grieve with you."

Duke glanced away and worked his jaw. "I wish you had. I could have used another friend to lean on at that moment. The women were great, but they didn't really get what we had together, you, Gary, and I."

"Yeah." He remembered all too well. The three of them, running around, getting into trouble half the time. It was immature, but also the best times of his life. "Shit, I miss h im."

"Me too." A tear ran down Duke's cheek. "You are always allowed to grieve with us."

His friend wrapped an arm around his shoulder and gave him a side-squeeze.

Keane nodded, sniffing up tears of his own. "Thanks."

"There, at the end, he used to say"—Duke blinked up at the night sky and the shining stars—"'Keane's the best painter that ever lived. You know, he could probably even give Van Gogh a run for his money.'"

Keane laughed out a sob, swirled his drink, and took a long sip. Van Gogh was one of his inspirations. "That's amazing."

"He always found a way to keep our spirits up, even when his body was failing," Duke went on. "He had trouble with the stairs up to the apartment over the café after a while, but he refused to sleep anywhere Nell wasn't. So, when he had appointments, I carried him down."

"I'm so sorry you had to do that all on your own."

"It was my privilege." Duke laid a hand over his heart. "But it didn't break him, being carried by his friend. He would smile at me like he knew it was a gift to me, to do something like this for him. And it was. I was proud to be that for him."

"I would have been too." "You inspired him. He made a map of your travels and would talk about what kind of food you probably were eating. Talk about the exchange value of Budapest and Prague."

"Really?"

"You were never that far away from his mind, especially at the end." Duke put a hand on his leg, his eyes growing wide. "Hey, you've gotta tell Shelby."

"About what? Being there?"

"Yes, she needs to know."

Keane shifted in his seat. "I don't know, Duke. I don't want to make her feel bad about it."

"She thinks you weren't there for her, but you tried to be. You just got in your own head about it all."

"I can't imagine that's the only thing keeping her from wanting to be with me. What could that change?"

"I don't know, man, but I feel like she should know."

"I'll take it into consideration, I promise."

Duke nodded.

They sat in silence for several minutes, enjoying the rocking of the ship and their respective bourbons.

"Do you think you could tell me more?" Keane finally asked.

"About Gary's last days?"

"Yeah, it makes me feel like I didn't miss everything. Is that selfish of me to want to know even though I wasn't here for it? For him?""Not at all. He'd have wanted you to be a part of it. He always said you were a part of the crew. Always. And he knew you'd come back."

The knowledge was a balm to his heart. It was painful, but it was also healing.

Duke launched into stories that made them laugh and made them cry. And sitting out there, on a weathered wooden bench, both men healed a little.

CHAPTER 30

Shelby's strokes were long and sure in her paddle out to the jetty the next morning. The early light shimmered off the water. Her sea kayak cut through the waves quickly due to its extended hull. She'd promised to stay near someone trusted, but she'd been with Cleo all day, and the water was well populated already by fisherfolk, so the calculated risk was minor. Still, she had her whistle with her.

The natural, long, narrow strip of land was one of the reasons the cove was so protected from the rest of the Hood Canal. One side was sheltered with the natural curve of the cove, the other, the jetty.

It also happened to be the place where Willa and Duke had seen the iridescent flash of a tail when they were investigating what had happened to them early on. Having finally seen the possible mermaid, she was anxious to know more.

Rocks made the last hundred feet of the journey difficult for her fiberglass hull, but she had learned where they were and carefully avoided them. Bobbing in the clear, deep water at the end of the jetty, she peered over the edge.

Nothing but teal, watery patterns of the waves traced through the sun-drenched water on the boulders below. Scanning the cove, she saw the river otters farther out and one lone orca dorsal fin. It had moved closer to her but hadn't yet intruded into her territory.

Sound traveled better underwater than through air, but was that true if it originated above the surface? She had no idea.

"Hello?" she called out and waited, peering through the depths. Light played on the large rocks, but she didn't see anything. Paddling farther along the jetty, she pulled alongside a large boulder that protruded from the water. One hand braced on the rock to prevent it from scraping her hull, she called again. "Hello? Hello?"

Her eyes fixed on the images she could see long enough that they felt hypnotic. Shaking her head to clear it, she noticed a long shadow had come alongside her. One of the orcas. The scar identified it as Percy.

"Hi." She raised a hand in welcome, not knowing if he understood her or not. She had hoped to avoid him in orca form. It still freaked her out when she was in the water. The animals had never bothered her before, but at thirty feet in length, it could upend her in a heartbeat.

She also didn't know how much human brain he had in this form. Not very reassuring.

A black nose rose from the water, which cascaded off it in sheets. A black eye stared at her curiously.

"She helped me," she tried to explain.

Percy blinked at her.

"We found the origin of the waste dump, what is killing the fish." She glanced back over the edge, but there was still nothing. "Or maybe *she* did, I'm not sure. Either way, the guy behind it came after me with a gun. I took off but almost died in an underwater tunnel. She saved me."

The rest of the orca's head rose above the surface, showing the white bottom jaw and wide stripe on the side of his head. She had no idea if he understood her, but he appeared interested.

"The authorities are going to dispose of the barrels, but I'm not sure how to clean the toxins off the land. We're going to meet later today to discuss everything that's happened." She had an idea. "If you want to join us, you can. It's at two o'clock at the café."

Still nothing but a blinking eye. Percy tilted his head under the water, then back up to her. She didn't know what it meant. Was he indicating the sea creature?

"I wanted to come and say thanks. Could you pass it along for me?" It was eating at her that she had neglected to thank the woman, er, mermaid.

She also wanted to ask her about her powers. She had a nagging suspicion it wasn't simply knowing where water was. That alone was pretty cool for the directionally challenged businesswoman, but there was more to it. The sensation in her gut felt too similar to what she sensed in her hands. It had tugged at her in a negative way when she decided on the deal with Charles, and it was silent when Keane had asked if they still had a chance.

Percy dipped his head in what she thought looked like acceptance. The exchange was getting a little strange for her, so she said thanks and pushed off the rock to paddle to shore.

Keane wasn't a bad decision. That, she knew. Any woman would be lucky to have a man like him. But if she couldn't let her walls down around him, how was it supposed to work?

Packing up her kayak, she drove back to the office. She'd stay close to Cleo until they met up with the others that afternoon. She was very curious if Percy would show up.

Shelby rubbed her eyes after the third time reviewing the contract. She'd rewritten it with similar terms. One small item she'd neglected to notice was the payback fee was nearly a quarter of what he'd loaned her. It would take even longer to repay that amount. Thankfully, they'd caught it early, and she wouldn't have to give the con man any more than absolutely necessary.

Keane said he'd loan her whatever she needed, so she could include it in the final total, but it still grated on her. Still, it was a good, fair partnership, and he was an honest man. She'd be grateful to put the whole thing with Charles behind her.

Sighing, Shelby reached her arms up high over her head and stretched her neck out. She'd been sitting too long, and it was nearly time to meet the crew at the café. She'd skipped lunch, and she was starving.

"How could you?" Cleo's voice came from her doorway. Her eyes were rimmed red, and she was scowling.

"Excuse me?" Shelby frowned.

Cleo barged into her office, her hands in fists at her side. "How could you lie about Charles like that?"

"What are you talking about?" Shelby stood.

"Sit back down. You're going to listen to me," Cleo ordered. "Charles was just trying to make a good deal to finally get ahead in life. He's made some bad decisions, but he's trying to fix all of that. You telling that lie about him threatening you so you can get the land and he doesn't get anything is awful. I can't imagine you ever doing that, Shelby. And making him kiss you? You should be ashamed of yourself!"

"You'd better take a step back and think before you say anything else, Cleo." Shelby remained where she stood. Anger clawed its way up the back of her neck and into her hairline. "I did no such thing; he tried to kill m e."

"Charlie would never do anything like that." Cleo burst into tears. "I know him better than you."

Shelby blinked through the fury, realization starting to dawn on her. The weasel had played both of them. "He's a con man, Cleo. Can't you see that? I'm paying him off. He's getting a hefty profit for the contract he got me to sign, but he was going to kill me and take my business as his own. They caught him with a gun."

"Only because he was afraid for his life." Her voice squeaked. "He told me so."

He must have used one of his phone calls to contact the receptionist and feed her the story.

"He told both of us a lot of lies. He's very good at it." Too good.

"I don't believe you," Cleo pushed on. "You're going to tell the chief the truth and that you lied in your statement, or, or I'm going to tell them about you paying people under the table."

"What?"

"That's tax evasion," she stammered. "It's a criminal offense."

"I don't do that."

"I've seen you pay in cash!" She raised a finger.

"Yes, but there's a paper trail behind it." She could tell the younger woman wasn't going to believe her. "Whatever, tell them whatever you want to. I've got receipts and billing to prove it."

Cleo searched the room with panicked eyes and launched herself over the table at Shelby, her fingers wrapping around her throat.

"Cleo," she gasped, getting her hands between her and the girl. "It's a lie."

They both went down. Cleo's hands slipped. The two tumbled around in the small area behind her desk until Cleo sat on top of her. She slapped Shelby hard on the face. Hard enough to leave a sting.

"No," Cleo wailed. Shelby could tell the receptionist was getting desperate. That was dangerous. She could do anything. "Tell the truth."

"I am telling the truth," Shelby snarled. She shoved Cleo off her, and they crouched in front of each other like they were in a showdown. "If you leave now, I won't press charges. You're fired either way, but I believed his load of shit too. I'll let you go."

"I thought you were a good person, Shelby." Cleo started crying.

Shelby hauled herself to her feet and left Cleo sobbing in the corner. Taking the other way around her desk, she pulled the door shut behind her and propped a lobby chair under the knob. Sitting in it, she dialed Chief Warner.

A collective gasp precluded Shelby's welcome at the café. Maggie ran to her, her eyes wide. Nell's mouth hung open. She had seen herself in the bathroom after the chief left and knew the red mark gracing her cheek looked angry. Makeup would only hurt more.

"What happened to you?" Nell demanded.

Keane was sitting, talking to Emiliano, but seeing her, he was off his seat and in front of her.

"Cleo." Shelby gingerly touched her cheekbone. "Apparently, I wasn't the only one Charles conned."

"Where is she now?" Keane's eyes scanned the parking lot as though Cleo was following her.

"At the station," Shelby answered. "She believed his story and tried some lame blackmail attempt. Since I'm not doing anything shady, it fell through, and she came at me."

"Looks like you came out on top," Duke said, arriving.

"Don't I always?" Shelby winked, but then winced at the pull of her bruised cheek.

"I'm so sorry." Keane's hand cupped her face with the whisper of a touch. She closed her eyes for a second. Her heart wanted her to lean into it.

The walls she'd so carefully built up before she arrived loosened. Cleo had been with her the longest and was her best receptionist. Replacing her would be difficult.

She'd also been a friend. It hurt. And Cleo represented yet another person she'd misread. When had she gotten so bad at that?

"At least we know how he got into the cabins," Shelby said. "I was worried he'd gotten a key somehow."

Maggie, who she hadn't seen leave, reappeared with a bag of ice and a towel. "Here."

Keane led her to a chair and sat down beside her. "I shouldn't have left you."

"I'm okay." She gave him a sideways smile.

"Is this where the cool kids are meeting?" Solomon's bald head appeared at the railing.

"You bet." Nell ushered him in. "You left Roy in the parking lot, right?"

"He's fishing." Solomon grinned. "He'll leave us alone, as promised."

Nell liked Solomon's pelican friend, but didn't want the ever-hungry bird hopping all over her deck. It tended to scare away customers.

Emiliano came out of the café; Willa and Nick followed close behind. The newcomers stopped short, seeing her.

"I'm fine," Shelby said again. "Once everyone finds a seat, I'll fill you all in."

The crew settled into chairs. Nell set lemon-basil-infused waters down for everyone.

As one, they gave her their full attention.

"I guess I'm up, then." Shelby took an icy cold glass of water and gulped half of it. By now, she would have normally raided Nell's kitchen, but her appetite had disappeared with her current sense of control.

"The land I bought from Charles Timms"—she started at the beginning so Solomon could get caught up—"had petrochemical waste barrels in an underground tunnel system. He acquired them in a manufacturing-plant deal and was using my land to dispose of them."

Everyone's gaze lifted to a figure behind her. Percy had joined them. That must mean he was able to understand her in orca form. She waved for him to sit, and Nell got up to get another glass from the bar counter.

The large orca-shifter took up a space, leaning against the railing instead of sitting. His biceps bulged when he crossed his arms, and the thick scar stood out, appearing silvery against his dark skin.

"A natural aquifer runs through those tunnels, directing the toxic water into Orca Cove. I think the initial dump was what killed the fish, but there's residual sludge underground. Chief Warner's contacted someone from the state to remove the barrels and dispose of them properly. They said they would clean the cave to prevent further contamination, but I'm worried there will still be runoff."

"Is there anything we can do?" Willa asked.

"I'm not sure," Shelby answered.

"Some of it's bound to get into the water when they're clearing the land." Duke frowned.

"What if I made it rain?" Maggie asked quietly.

"That might create more runoff," Percy's voice rumbled.

"Not if I pull the water out," Duke offered. "But what would I do with it? And how would I know which water is bad?"

"I can tell." Shelby raised a finger. "That's the other thing. Not only can I locate water, but I can tell if it's salt or fresh, healthy or impure."

"That's a nifty skill to have." Keane bumped her knee with his. "Is that how you knew where to go in the tunnels?"

"Yes," she answered. "It's interesting. I could feel multiple water sources down there. When I concentrated on them, I could separate them out."

"That's new," Nell said.

"It's more than that." She glanced at Keane. "That same feeling of wrongness hits my gut when I'm thinking of making a bad decision. Kinda like super-intuition. But it seems to be stronger the closer I am to water, so it took me a while to figure it out. I ignored it several times now."

Keane watched her curiously but said nothing.

"Now, that's a cool power." Duke whistled. "Wanna trade?"

Shelby eyed Percy, who hadn't said anything yet on the topic. "I don't think it works that way."

Inwardly, she was glad her gift wasn't as lame as she'd initially thought, comparatively. It seemed their powers helped them personally, and she'd chalked it up to her ability to get turned around, even in tiny Orca Cove, but aiding in decision making was even better. She couldn't wait to put it to further use.

"When are they coming to clean the land?" Percy asked.

"The EPA is expected Tuesday," Shelby said.

"Are we still scheduled to start tomorrow?" Nick asked.

"Yes. They said they could work around us as long as they have access to the tunnel's opening." Shelby was relieved at that. She'd had too many setbacks already.

"Duke," Percy said. "If you can move water, can you pull it out of the area? They'd have a better chance of clearing it without any present."

"I've never done it anywhere but in bodies of water, but I should be able to," Duke said. "And with the dry summer we've had, they won't be surprised to see how low the water level is."

"It might be summer, but it's still scheduled to rain tonight," Nell said.

"I can keep the precipitation away from Shelby's land," Maggie offered.

"Maggie to the rescue with the coolest gift," Shelby said, but she smirked at the cute bundle of a young woman who blushed. "And I'll recheck the water after they've left to see if there's anymore bad signals. We can decide what to do then if there are."

"Good plan," Duke said.

"I'll pass the news along to the underwater community." Percy pushed away from the railing. He stopped at the table and let his gaze rest on each of them before continuing. "She was right about you all. You're honoring the gifts you were given, even if it was accidental. We thank you."

It was more than he'd ever shared before.

"The mermaid that Shelby met?" Willa's eyes were lit with excitement.

Amusement curled Percy's mouth. He tilted his head in acknowledgment.

Willa squealed.

"Thank you for trusting us," Duke said solemnly.

"I didn't." Percy raised his eyebrows. "But I'm glad you proved me wrong."

The mysterious man nodded at them and clambered down the steps.

"Well, that was interesting," Shelby said.

"There's a community?" Maggie whispered.

"Sounds like it." Duke stood from his chair and wandered over to the water jug to refill his glass. "I'm glad we can prevent further illness."

"For the fish and for our residents," Emiliano added.

"And we have confirmation on the mermaid." Willa's fingers dug into Nick's hand where they were laced.

"That doesn't mean she's a mermaid." Shelby rolled her eyes, knowing it would frustrate the herbalist.

"But you said she has a tail, and Percy nodded," Willa stammered.

"She does, but she sure doesn't look like the cartoon version we've all grown up on. And Percy hardly agreed. Did you see the smirk?" She intentionally riled her friend.

"Of course she doesn't look like an animated character." Willa humphed. "That doesn't mean she's not a mermaid. It could have been based on those like her."

"If you say so." Shelby shrugged.

"Sure sounds like a mermaid to me." Nick kissed Willa's knuckles.

"She's magical either way," Duke said, eyeing Shelby.

Shelby pressed her lips together to keep from smiling, but she winked at Keane, who was watching the interaction with a wistful expression on his face.

"What can I do?" Solomon propped his hands on his knees as he asked the group.

"Roy can pass along the news to the non-magical animals," Duke suggested.

"He and I both will," Solomon promised.

"Right, I forgot you can talk to animals," Keane said. "What's that like?"

"I don't know." Solomon scratched his head. "I still talk like normal, but I can hear what they're saying clear as day. Only the ones in and around the water, though."

"That's so awesome," Keane said.

"Most of the time. Roy is right funny." Solomon made a clicking noise with his mouth. "But those harbor porpoises, they're chatty."

"The porpoises?" Keane's eyes went as round as saucers.

"Yeah, dramatic too," Solomon said. "It's handy. I can hear the orcas now, in orca form, I mean. I'm glad you didn't mind me inviting Percy. I figured he needed to know what was going on with the water."

Shoot, so maybe he hadn't understood her. And he'd left before she could pass along the message to the mermaid. She'd been so sure he had.

"Can they understand you, in orca-form, I mean?" Shelby asked the fisherman.

"Of course." Solomon stood and pulled a beanie from his back pocket. His thin hands passed it back and forth. "Well, I'm off. Rounds to make."

Ha! She'd been right. Shelby sat back in her chair comfortably. Maybe someday she'd get to thank the mermaid creature in person.

"How about dinner tomorrow?" Nell suggested to the crew after the wizened fisherman left. "I can make pizzas on my day off."

"Yes." Emiliano fist-pumped.

"I can save Solomon some for when he stops by with Roy the next morning," Nell said. The chef always set out leftover seafood that couldn't be served in the café for the bird. It was as thanks for notifying Percy when Willa was kidnapped a while back. And also, because she was a generous woman.

"I'd love to, but it has to be after the crews leave. I'm not missing out on the first full day," Shelby said.

"Me either, I have work to do," Nick said excitedly.

She was glad she'd been able to give the cop-turned-woodworker additional work, even though he didn't seem to need it. He was making a name for himself on the peninsula.

"Meet at dusk, then?" Nell asked. "We can celebrate Shelby's new business venture."

That felt better than her failures with people.

Everyone nodded and split away. Everyone but Keane. Shelby stood and he followed suit.

"Are you really okay?" he asked.

"Mostly," she admitted.

"We still don't know if Charles has any accomplices."

"Other than Cleo." Shelby's mouth pressed into a thin line.

"That must have been hard."

"It was, but I've got you all."

"Yes, you do. Anytime." His eyes followed their friends on the emptying deck. "I don't suppose you would consider company this afternoon? It doesn't have to be me."

She hadn't even thought about it. "I have that contract for you to review. You could stop by and take a look at it."

"I would be happy to. I can sign it and get the money in transit. Do you have much to do for tomorrow?"

"Just rerunning numbers yet again."

"Do you need to?" He raised an eyebrow.

"Well." She was pretty set for the following day, except for the nerves in her stomach. "Not really."

"It's beautiful out. I picked up an extra paddleboard. Unless you're too rusty."

Shelby narrowed her eyes at the surfer boy she grew up with. He was goading her. "I guess we'll have to see, then."

CHAPTER 31

Keane stepped back from his newest painting and swiveled his head to inspect it from different angles. It was shaping up nicely. He'd spent the morning at his parent's house. To his relief, his mom was doing better each day. He swirled the paintbrush in water before washing it out in the bathroom.

It was nearly time to meet the crew for dinner, and he was starving. He'd been too focused on his work to grab lunch. Checking his reflection, he tugged the tie from his hair. It fell nearly to his shoulders.

Was it too long?

As an artist, he got away with being a little eccentric, but he'd always loved his hair. Shelby's words, even while spoken in anger, might have had some truth at their source.

Was it time to grow up?

They'd had a blast on the waves the day before. His mouth widened at the memory of them both falling into the water. Not because they weren't experienced, but simply because they'd been showing off.

It was a good moment.

She'd reluctantly agreed to stay at Willa's house, since Nick was driving out to the land with her the next morning anyway, and Keane was anxious to hear how the first day of excavation had gone.

Pulling on a clean flannel, he laced his Vans and took the route along the beach to the café. The rocks shifted and crunched underfoot, and he peered up at the fading sun. Regardless of what happened between him and Shelby, he was grateful they'd found friendship again.

Music drifted on the saltwater breeze. It lifted his spirits, and he took the back steps two at a time to see if Shelby had made it yet.

He'd stayed quiet during their meeting the day before, not yet feeling like he had much to add without any powers of his own. But he had done what he could for Shelby. He'd helped her take a much-needed break. One that he'd needed as well.

"Good evening!" Maggie waved from the two tables pushed together she'd been setting out on the back deck. "Can I get you a drink?"

He wondered if anyone could ever get angry with the perpetually sunny woman. Even her eyes sparkled when she spoke. "Hey, Maggie. Sure, that sounds good."

"Beer or wine?"

"We always drink wine at group dinners," Duke said, arriving at the deck stairs, holding two unmarked bottles in his hands.

"Or kombucha." Willa's voice was bright with laughter as she and Nick followed him up.

Keane peered behind the couple and found Shelby bringing up the rear. The sight of her still warmed him inside. All the way down.

"Kombucha today, Willa?" Maggie asked her. At her nod, she disappeared behind the bar.

Duke busied himself with a bottle opener he'd snagged from the bar top.

"No sparkling today?" Shelby raised both hands, palms up in question.

Maggie turned and produced two bottles of French Champagne and set them on the counter.

Shelby laughed. "I was only kidding."

"Keane brought them by earlier, so they'd be chilled." Maggie gave him an approving look, her small fists on her hips.

Shelby turned to him, her mouth parting in surprise.

Heat crept up Keane's neck, and he rubbed behind his head. "We have a lot to celebrate today, don't we?"

She pursed her lips in a knowing smile. "That, we do."

"How did today go?" He'd been dying to hear.

"It was amazing! They still have a couple of days left of excavation, then they're hauling off the brush, but it's actually starting to look like what I had in my head."

"Of course it does. No one plans like you, Greene."

"I expected you to stop by." She tilted her head, finding a seat at the table. "I was hoping for a cup of the good stuff."

"That's it; you're addicted," he teased, then leaned in to sit next to her. "That's okay. I am too."

"Seriously, though, it is your new business venture too."

He'd been trying to give her space. "Not until you get that check. It should be in my account on Thursday."

Had she missed him?

"Awesome, I'll be out of the contract with the weasel by the weekend."

"Who's hungry?" Nell burst through the back door, arms loaded with pizza peels. Emiliano followed her, balancing several more. The chef took her place at the brick oven in the corner and gently fed additional wood into its mouth. When she was satisfied, the first of them disappeared into the opening to be licked by the flames inside. The smell of yeasted bread baking wafted over the deck.

Keane's mouth watered.

Duke and Maggie passed out champagne flutes to everyone. Willa's was filled with her sparkling fermented tea.

"Should we toast Shelby?" Willa lifted her glass, and the rest of them followed suit. "May your new business venture be smooth sailing from here on out."

"Hear, hear." Keane lifted his drink.

They all cheered and took a sip, solidifying Willa's wish.

Shelby's cheeks were flush with joy. She caught his eyes and mouthed, "Thank you."

He dipped his head in welcome.

"Oh, and I have an update from the chief," Shelby said suddenly. "Cleo spilled everything Charles told her. She even admitted to letting him into the cabins, although he told her he was going to make it right in the business investment, reducing his partnership percentage. She believed he was only trying to increase his chances of going into business with me and that he needed the leverage."

"That man must have some sort of a silver tongue." Nell shook her head from where she stood at the pizza oven. Reaching in, she rotated one and then pulled it expertly out and slid another in.

"You don't think he has some sort of power, do you?" Keane asked. He wasn't sure how often that sort of thing happened.

"I don't think so." Maggie shook her head. "I saw through him."

"I wish you would have told me." Shelby dropped her head a notch.

"Would you have listened?" Maggie asked gently.

Shelby scrunched her nose. "Probably not. I'm pretty hardheaded."

"It all worked out in the end." Keane set a hand over her knee and gave it a light squeeze of encouragement. "Did Charles cave?"

"Like a house of cards." Shelby beamed. "He tried to play the hand that he was only evening the playing field. That if he'd had wealthy parents helping his businesses get off the ground, he'd be as successful as me. Chief Warner informed him that I am a self-made woman. My parents didn't invest a penny into my business."

"That's right," Keane said.

"Except he was wrong." Shelby lifted her head. "Nobody invested in me, and I might have put in the actual work, but you all helped me in one way or another throughout the years. And I appreciate it." Her eyes lingered on his before she continued. "Oh, and I guess he was trying to pay back some loan sharks in Seattle for some gambling debts, but they don't know about me. He didn't want them to go around him to try to steal his target."

The tug on his heart that had been nagging at him ever since he hauled her out of the water loosened, and he closed his eyes. She was safe.

Nell rocked a knife through the steaming pizzas and brought the first couple to the table. "Eat up."

"Marco's pizza is my favorite." Emiliano snagged a slice with green sauce.

"What's that?" Keane asked.

"Pesto. Loaded with nuts." Shelby grabbed one too. "Quick, get one before it's gone. It's amazing."

Not one to argue with Shelby's taste buds or Nell's abilities, Keane reached for one of the last two slices. He folded it in half and nipped the tail off. Melted Feta and Parmesan filled his mouth, along with bits of toasted walnuts. Then he flipped it and bit into the chewy, charred crust. It was perfect.

"New York," Shelby said sarcastically.

"I've had some pretty good pizza over the years." He shrugged.

"I took the idea from a pizzeria in Chicago, young guy named Marco." Nell slid two more bubbling ones onto the table. "Making a name for himself with green pizza."

"Marco's?" Keane squinted. "I think I've heard of him. His dad's some sort of mafia guy, right?"

"Something like that, but I don't think he's in the business," Nick said mid bite. "I did some research on him."

"How's Kalani doing?" Shelby asked Keane.

"Amazing, thanks to Willa." He beamed. The herbalist blushed at the praise. "She's got speech therapy, but she doesn't really need it. Mostly, she has trouble coming up with the words she wants to use. It's more recall than anything. And physical therapy too. Her left arm is a little slow to respond, but I've already seen improvements."

"The spirulina is helping with circulation," Willa said. "And I steeped some gotu kola in distilled cove water. Those two babies are responsible for it."

"Whatever it is, I'm grateful." Keane laid a hand over his heart.

"It's my pleasure."

They fell into a comfortable silence. The sounds of plates scraping and the smell of garlic, Parmesan, and basil paired with the hearty scent of yeasted bread.

"Have you made any wedding plans yet?" Maggie asked Willa.

Their curly-haired friend shook her head, sending the mass of strawberry-blond locks in a wave around her. "Not yet, but I'm thinking about it."

"Do you need help with that?" Shelby asked.

"Maybe." Willa placed a finger on her chin.

"You need a dress," Nell said decisively.

"We should take her shopping," Shelby suggested to the girls. "It's been a while since we got away from these guys and did girl things."

"I'd like that," Willa said.

"What kind do you want?" Nell asked.

"Something flowy, I think." Willa considered. "Maybe vintage."

"What about bell sleeves?"

"That would be romantic. Oh, and an eyelet. I like that."

The two women dove into a deep conversation about the merits of linen versus lace.

"Did I tell you I won your painting?" Shelby said in aside to Keane so as not to disrupt the other conversation at the table.

"You did? I didn't realize you bid on it." He'd been sad to lose the piece, having painted it for her, but he'd never expected to be able to give it to her. It felt like fate.

"The colors are so peaceful."

"You know green is my favorite color." He grinned at her. A quizzical expression flitted over her face, and he could tell she was putting the pieces together.

"How long have you been working on that one?" She watched him carefully, reading his features.

"Oh, fifteen years, give or take," he said honestly.

It was true, although his first attempts now lay under other layers of paint all over the world, he'd been practicing with the colors of Shelby almost as soon as he put media to canvas.

Her eyes softened, but she remained silent.

"Who wants dessert?" Nell announced. Somewhere during their conversation, she'd disappeared into the kitchen to bring out a plate of rich, fudgy brownies. They were dotted with walnuts, flake salt, and something bright green.

"Is that green salt?" Keane asked.

"No, it's dried wakame," Nell answered. "Just a little briny bite on top."

Keane loved seaweed. He gladly accepted a square. It was wildly rich with decadent chocolate and irresistibly soft and fudgy inside. The bright salt and wakame added a balancing bite that lingered at the edges of his taste buds. He covered his mouth with his hands, unable to contain his reaction. "Holy cow, these are delicious. Is that espresso?"

Nell beamed. "Yes, and a little tahini."

"These are easily the best brownies I've ever had in my life."

"Okay, you can have two." Nell laughed. She plated brownies onto everyone else's dessert plates. Then she straightened and reached over the bar to get something from the back. "I almost forgot. I promised to get you a copy of this."

She handed Keane a photo. It was one of the five of them in high school at the beach. Gary stood between him and Duke. Their arms were thrown around each other's shoulders. Nell and Shelby sat in front of the bonfire they'd lit back when you could have wood fires on the beach. They looked so young and happy.

Memories flooded through Keane. He glanced at Shelby, whose attention was still zoned in on him.

"Thank you so much." His words were thick with emotion.

It was Shelby's turn to give him an encouraging squeeze to the knee. He was grateful for the contact.

Duke's eyes tracked the two of them from across the table.

"I'm glad to have you back in town again, Keane," Duke said.

"Thanks, man," Keane said. "I'm glad to be back."

"Man, it was a long hiatus, huh?"

"Too long." What was his friend getting at? Was he trying to rub his face in it? That didn't seem like Duke.

"How long has it been since you were here anyway?" Duke squinted.

"Fifteen years." Shelby snorted, emphasizing the length of time.

Keane adjusted in his seat, getting Duke's meaning. He'd told the courier he would consider telling Shelby. He hadn't promised.

Duke gave him a pointed expression that he knew meant she had a right to know.

"A little over a year," he breathed the words out.

"What?" Nell said.

Shelby turned as though she were moving through sand to look at him. Pain pinched her eyes.

"I, uh." Keane ran a hand through his hair. He stood up, his chair scraping against the wooden planks of the deck. He couldn't sit through the uncomfortable topic. "I came as soon as I got back from a long trip through Europe. I hadn't heard in time. I was too late."

"You were too late for what?" Nell asked.

Shelby's eyes had shifted from pain to anger.

"Too late to say goodbye." The words caught in his throat.

"And you didn't visit anyone?" Shelby accused.

"I was a coward," Keane admitted. "I saw you all gathered there, leaning on each other."

"Where?" Shelby's voice was hard. "Where were you?"

Keane swallowed. He refused to lie to her. "At the gravesite."

"And you just left?"

"I hadn't been there for you all when it mattered. I was too late. I didn't think I deserved to join you."

Nell covered her mouth with her hands, and tears filled her eyes. "Keane."

Shelby glanced away but not before he saw understanding click in her brilliant, green eyes.

"We could have been there for each other," Nell whispered.

"I didn't think it was right."

"I'm glad you're here now. Gary would be too," Nell said, walking over to lay a hand on his shoulder.

"Seems to me Keane needed the gut-feeling, decision-making thing more than you, Shelby," Maggie piped up, breaking the tension.

Shelby blinked over at her. "No way. That one's mine, Lennox. Get your own power."

"I'd love to." Keane chuckled nervously. "Where's a lightning storm when I need one?"

The conversation flowed more easily after that, but Keane could see the wheels spinning in Shelby's mind. He could practically hear it; she was thinking so hard.

And here, he had hoped not to cause her any more stress.

CHAPTER 32

"Don't work too hard tonight, team." Shelby waved goodbye to the crew still at work clearing her land.

"Don't tell them that," Nick teased her.

He had already become one of them. They respected him and listened to his direction. They'd be fine without her there. Which was great for her; she had to interview two more people tomorrow. Fingers crossed that one of them would work.

"Is Keane going to bring one of those fancy coffees for everyone today?" one of the workers asked her before she got too far away.

Even with the tension from last night and all the thoughts she was still reviewing, it had been good seeing her old flame for the few minutes he stopped by with hot drinks.

The coffee? That had been glorious.

She'd reviewed her plans with him. He was interested, asking intelligent questions about the space and how she planned to set everything up. The man had an artist's eye.

And he never called them tents. Not once.

They'd make good business partners.

"Probably not, Frank." Another, taller man cuffed him on the shoulder.

"Why not?" Frank frowned.

"Because you're not as pretty as the boss lady." The first man shot her a worried expression. "No offense, boss lady."

"None taken." Shelby saluted them.

She slid into her Trailblazer and drove the five-minute trek into town. She loved that she could stay so close to town, not caring that it wasn't walkable. Things were shaping up well. It felt great to see her vision come to life, even if it was only wide spaces of empty dirt. As soon as it started taking shape, she had thought to share it with Keane. It wasn't just the coffee she'd been looking for.

Parking in the lot between the café and the market, she contemplated saying hello to Nell and Maggie, but she didn't want to talk about last night's dinner yet. Keane's news had thrown her. Instead, she turned into the market to grab a quick sandwich before bed. It would give her time to review the resumes while she ate.

Win-win.

Strolling through the busy dinner crowd, she snagged a sandwich and got in line. Tourists were great for Orca Cove's businesses, including her own, but the waiting in line during summertime was the price to be paid.

A teenage girl on her cellphone ran into her elbow. The phone hitting her funny bone. Shelby rubbed it. Why did they call it that anyway? There was nothing funny about it. Glancing up, she saw Randall and Mick standing shoulder to shoulder, pestering someone.

Rolling her eyes, she almost disregarded them until she picked their familiar voices out of the crowd.

"See?" Randall said. "I told you Keane couldn't get her back."

The hair on the back of her neck lifted.

"Even with that fancy dude turning out to be a criminal, she still doesn't want him." Mick snickered.

Those bastards were talking about her! She caught sight of Keane's face between the two men. The sad silence in his eyes broke her heart.

"He couldn't even tempt her, could he?" Randall was talking about Keane as though he wasn't even there. Somehow, that made it worse, being completely judged like that. "That's just sad."

Half the town had heard about them making out in the tidelands while digging for clams. How had the two bullies not heard? She had wanted him, at least for the night. But Keane didn't say a word.

It made the strained expression on his face even more difficult to watch.

Shelby wanted to grab their collars and put them in their places, but that would make it even worse for Keane, like he needed her to fight his battles. They'd only tease him harder when they saw him alone again.

Keane tried to move past Randall, and he wouldn't let him by.

"I mean, look at him," Mick said.

Keane closed his eyes, searching for patience. Either that or in too much torment to do anything about it.

The two men finally left him. They strolled over to the fish case and leaned against it, continuing their tirade more quietly, all the while pointing and whispering. Every part of Shelby wanted to do major damage to their irritating rat faces.

Keane caught her gaze and shook his head, as though saying it wasn't worth it. He shrugged and gave her a small smile.

Breaking from her line, Shelby strode right over to him, standing close. He met her eyes with a look of curiosity. She took his hand, and his gaze turned hopeful. She wished so badly to be able to give him what he wanted. It was still scary to think about after all this time.

Impulsively, Shelby leaned forward and pressed her lips against his, pulling him into a passionate embrace. Keane dropped the tote he was carrying. Absently, she heard cans clatter to the ground. Something rolled into her shoe, and she poured all the feelings she'd been having into him until the gasps around her subsided and Keane's arms came around her as he fell into the act as w ell.

Damn, could the man kiss. Tingles curled down from her center to her toes.

It was more than she had intended, but unable to break away, she wobbled and set a foot behind her to balance herself.

A throat cleared behind her, and she jolted, having forgotten for a moment they still stood in the check-out line at Gil's Market and Marina.

Emiliano had an eyebrow raised at them and a smirk playing on his lips. Shelby cleared her throat and bent to help Keane collect the oranges, apples, and bell peppers that had rolled away. He wasn't in much of a hurry to gather his items. His eyes bored into hers, searching for the meaning behind the kiss.

"Come on." Shelby moved forward in the line to the space that had cleared in front of them. She handed her sandwich to Tommy, who was on the register. He was grinning like a fool.

Keane was still unloading his bag onto the conveyor belt when she finished paying. She waited for him nearby, trying to decide how she would answer his questions. She had some of her own too.

"Can we talk?" he asked.

She nodded and brushed past Randall and Mick. They were stunned. Randall's mouth was hanging open.

"Excuse me," Keane said with attitude, edging past them to walk at her side.

It made her smile inside.

"Are you hungry?" he said when they hit the parking lot. "I'm making your favorite."

"You are?"

He grinned sheepishly. "Well, if you still like Kung Pao chicken."

"I do." Her mouth watered at the thought. "Did you get peanuts? I love nuts."

"I know." He tossed her a coy smile. "I already have peanuts. I was picking up bell peppers plus a few other things to have on hand."

They walked along the beach to his condo.

When they got inside, she toed off her boots. The sauce was already bubbling on the stove.

"Good Lord, that smells delicious." She sighed.

"It's not as good as Nell would make," he said, unloading his groceries and storing them on the shelves.

"Nell doesn't make Asian food."

He shrugged. "If she did, it would be better."

"Nonsense." She elbowed past him and took a big sniff of the sauce. Then, turned to him, eyes wide with anticipation. "Can I taste it?"

"Of course you can, but it's not finished." He had his hands on his hips, watching her.

"Fine, I'll wait." She hopped up to sit on the bar top near him to watch.

He chuckled under his breath and cut up the bell pepper, adding it to the sauce. A rice cooker sat steaming on the counter beside him.

"It needs to simmer a while." He gave her his full attention.

She took the initiative. "Why didn't you tell them?"

He cocked his head. "About what?"

"About the night." She waved her hand toward the tidelands down the beach. "We did kiss."

He shook his head sharply, crossing his arms. "That's private. I'm not sharing that."

"Half the town knows."

"So?"

"So, they were being awful to you. You could have told them they were wrong."

"Are they wrong, Shelby?" The use of her name hit her to the core.

"Of course they're wrong." She slid off the counter. "I'd be with you today if you hadn't left."

And that was the truth of it. That was why it stung so much. He'd stolen a large chunk of their lives, her life.

"I'm here now." He took a step closer.

"But." She searched the room for answers. Her chest rose and fell with the emotion that ratcheted up. She did not want to talk about that right now.

"But what?"

"But you did leave." She pleaded with him to understand what she was saying without her having to explain. He knew what that had done to her.

"I did. It was the biggest mistake of my life."

"Was it?" she questioned. "You wouldn't have everything you do. You said when you got back that you regretted how you left, not that you left." She'd noted the distinction.

"You're right." He glanced down at the distance between them. "It wasn't worth it. Not missing all those years with you. Not risking the chance to make a life with you, a family. I was doing it for you. For us. I should have trusted us more. I should have trusted you more."

It was what she'd wanted to hear. Her throat grew thick, and she cleared it. "You're right."

"Why'd you kiss me?"

"Which time?" She let out a huff of air.

He raised an eyebrow.

"Because they were teasing you." She wrinkled her nose. "I hate bullies. And because they were wrong. I wanted you. We came back here and made love."

"Is that what we did?"

"Maybe not." She bit her lip and dropped her eyes. She'd thrown herself at him and had her way with him. She'd been half angry and half mad with desire, but it hadn't been making love.

"You didn't have to kiss me to prove that point." He wouldn't let it go.

"It was what I thought of at the time." She frowned briefly, thinking through her actions.

"You came over and took my hand," he reminded her. He took hers again, and her pulse sped up. "Why'd you kiss me?"

"Because I wanted to," she said honestly, searching his eyes for understanding.

"I want to kiss you now," Keane whispered, lifting his other hand to brush her hair behind her ear.

"Go ahead," she whispered back. "I threw myself at you twice now."

"What do you want, Shelby?" He took her other hand in his, holding both now between them.

"I don't know." She was having trouble keeping the tremor from her voice.

"Don't you?"

She pursed her lips together. Should she let him in? *Could* she?

She tried for a little crack of opening. "I'm afraid."

Tears welled up in her eyes, and she blinked them back.

"What are you afraid of, Shelby?"

"We're good at being friends," she deflected. "And we're good at being business partners."

They were. For the first time, she felt like she had a partner. It was different than the mentor Gary had been for her. And different from the simple acceptance of Keane when they were younger. He listened and gave good ideas. It was a relief to have him to lean on.

She hadn't realized she needed that.

"We are."

"And we're still good in bed."

That earned her a lopsided smile. "I would agree."

"But that's not all that makes a relationship."

"What else is left?"

"All the relationship stuff," she mumbled.

"Like what?"

She broke eye contact with him and found a spot on the ceiling to study. "I don't know."

"What are you afraid of?" he repeated.

Her heart pounded at her walls, begging her to let him in. It was painful and terrifying. She felt the crack in the mortar widen. The tears that had threatened to escape earlier were now harder and harder to keep at bay.

She let out a choked sob as chunks of her walls fell away like broken concrete. "I'm afraid of you leaving again."

"Oh, Shelby." He pulled her to him in a crushing hug as sobs wracked her body. He held her close, running a hand over her back. "I'm here. I'm right here."

"I couldn't find anyone like you." Now that her wall had broken, it came pouring out. "I compared them all to you, but they weren't you. I couldn't make it work."

"I'm so sorry."

"I was alone. So alone. And lonely."

"Oh, Shelby," he murmured again, holding her close. "I won't leave again. I promise you that."

"But you did already." She hiccupped, hot tears flooding down her face.

He pulled away and held her face in his hands. "It was a gallery exhibit. How I sell my paintings. Is that a deal breaker for you?"

She didn't want him to lose business because of her. She closed her eyes and shook her head. "No, I just want to know about it ahead of time. No more leaving without warning. Ever."

"Done." He kissed her cheeks, still wet with tears. "You can come with me if you'd like."

"To Italy?" She opened her eyes.

"Or Greece or Prague." He shrugged. "Wherever I go."

"How often will you have to leave?"

"I set my schedule now. How often could you get away?"

"Not for a while now that I just cut ground on an expansion."

"We could hire a contractor."

They could. They were in business together. She considered it. "Maybe. But how often would you have to go without it impacting your business as a painter and sales?"

"A few times a year would be good. Five or six would be better."

"Every couple of months?" Her voice rose to a squeak.

"Not without you." He took her hands again. "Okay?"

"Okay." She nodded.

He smiled. "Okay, okay?"

She laughed, coughing at the tears still in her throat. "Okay, okay."

Keane's eyes softened. They were full of hope and longing. He traced her cheek again. The redness had faded drastically from where Cleo had hit her, she knew.

"I want to kiss you now, Miss Greene."

"I want you to kiss me too."

"Just for tonight?" He was ultra focused on her.

"No." She shook her head, and the last rock fell to the ground. Another tear slipped down her cheek. "For always."

Tears filled Keane's eyes as well, and he pulled her to him. Warm, soft lips touched hers in a slow, easy dance. It wasn't rushed or hurried. She opened to him, letting him set the pace.

He held her nape gently in one hand and left her lips to kiss along her neck. He slowly tasted his way down to the crook of her shoulder and bent to kiss between her collarbones. Her pulse beat harder, and her breath came quicker.

His other hand traced the front of her throat and down her front, caressing her stomach.

"My god, I missed you. Every bit of you."

"I missed you too." She ached to pull him back to her. Her fingers tightened on his hips. "I want you, Keane."

He pulled back and touched her cheek. Then he switched the stovetop off and led her into the living room he was using as a bedroom, and over to the edge of the bed. She sat down, peering up at him through dark eyelashes.

"The last time, you took what you wanted. This time, I want to savor you. Are you okay with that?"

"Yes." She could barely nod; her desire was so high.

Keane sat down beside her and kissed her again. Slowly, agonizingly so. Then he trailed along her neck, unbuttoning her blouse. Shelby leaned back on one arm as he kissed down the center of her chest to her stomach. He leaned up and traced a finger over her rib cage.

She reached behind her and unclasped her bra. He helped her slide her straps down her shoulders and cupped her breasts. His thumbs scraped across her nipples, sending sparks down to her core. She arched in response.

He took her mouth with his again, deepening the kiss.

Shelby's hands fumbled between them and tugged at his T-shirt. He separated long enough to pull it over his head. It landed on the floor, next to hers.

Moving to her jeans's button, he unsnapped it. She slid back farther onto his bed to let him unzip her and slide the denim down her legs. He stood and divested himself from his. Not waiting for him, she wiggled out of her underwear, and he followed suit.

Keane came back to her and lay down next to her, crossways on the bed. He propped himself up on one hand and ran the other searchingly over every inch of her skin. His fingertips left tingles on her flesh in their wake. His eyes traveled over her as though he was memorizing her.

Sure hands traveled down her back, and she rolled onto her stomach so he could repeat the pleasureful exploration. She heard his breath hitch with desire, and she arched, knowing she'd caused that level of desire in the m an.

Keane's mouth lowered to her back, and he trailed down to the valley in the middle. Hands moved to caress her butt and down her legs. His mouth followed their path, kissing and gently nibbling the sensitive skin where her butt met her thigh. It was enough to make her moan.

He turned her over so she lay flat on her back, and continued his path, starting on her shoulders and down her arms. Then, fingertips barely touching her, they floated over her breast and stomach to continue down her legs.

Shelby panted at his touch. "Keane."

"I don't want to rush it," he said almost in a trance.

"I know, but I need you," she begged.

His eyes found hers, and a slow smile spread across his mouth. "I guess we do have the rest of our lives."

Her breath caught in her throat.

He got off the bed and found a small silver square. Tearing it open, he brought it to her, laying down beside her. Their legs tangled, and he pulled her to him. He kissed her more heavily this time, his breath now matching hers.

One hand found her nipple and gently rolled it between his fingers. She whimpered. "Keane."

He turned onto his back and slid the condom in place. She got on top of him and straddled him. Sitting up, he took her arms in his hands and kissed her again, rolling her back underneath him.

She smiled back up at him, happy to have him where she wanted him. But he didn't move. He stopped and stared down at her.

"What's wrong?"

"I love you, Shelby Greene." His eyes were as raw and naked as she'd ever seen them. Tears sprung to hers. "I always have, and I always will."

Without waiting for her to reply, he entered her, and tears rolled down her cheeks as her heart splayed open for the man. She leaned up, catching his mouth with hers, drinking it in as he moved within her.

Her fingers grabbed his back, digging in as the pressure built inside. She pushed him over, settling back on top of him and rode him. His hands gripped her hips as he urged her forward. Her breathing grew ragged, and she rose to brace herself on his chest.

Keane pulled her close, his forearm behind her back, and propped himself into a sitting position. They rocked together, fingers intertwined and mouths locked.

"My turn." He took the opportunity to flip her back over. She pulled him tight, fingers raking down his back. He bent to her breasts, suckling one and then the other. The sensation was more than she could handle.

"I'm close," she whimpered.

Slowing, he changed position and ground on her, sending shock waves to her core. Over and over, they rocked together as fireworks traveled down her arms and legs and out her fingertips and feet. She curled her toes at the racking pulse that took over her body and clutched him to her

.

"I love you too, Keane Lennox."

He crushed his mouth onto hers, and she felt tears where her cheeks met his.

CHAPTER 33

K eane watched Shelby's eyes flutter open. She had woken him during the night, tugging at him in need. He'd been more than happy to oblige.

Stretching like a cat, she wrapped her legs around him and wiggled in closer, her hand slipping into his. The act was deeply intimate and comforting. He stroked lazy trails down her back with his other hand.

"The sun's not up yet," she whispered.

"Not quite." Colors were beginning to illuminate the skyline. Tall evergreens stood in silhouette around the cove.

"I don't have to go to work until it's all the way up." She nuzzled his chest.

"You want to go again? I'm not sure I'm there yet," he said sadly. "But I'd be happy to—"

"No." She cut him off. "I meant I can be lazy with you a while. To enjoy this."

"I could get used to this." Keane pulled her tightly to him and kissed the top of her head. She smelled like citrus and spice.

Shelby laid her head on his chest; her hand caressed his skin.

"Can I ask you something?" he asked her.

She propped her head up on her elbow, peering dark-green intelligent eyes speckled with gold up at him through long, dark lashes. The freckle near her eyebrow accented their grace. "Hmm?"

"Did you change your mind about me because of the funeral?" He had to know.

She sat up and crossed her legs.

"Please don't pull away." He reached out to her as he sat up and propped a pillow behind him against his headboard. Slowly, she unfolded her legs and let him lead her back to him. She curled into his side.

"Not because of the funeral," she said softly into his chest, clinging to him. "But it did have to do with it. I feel awful that you didn't think you could grieve with u s."

He lifted her head from his shoulder and studied her bright eyes. "Please tell me you didn't change your mind out of guilt."

"Of course not." She shook her head. "I respect myself better than that."

"Good," he said. "What, then?"

She searched the ceiling for the right words. "Because I knew Nell had written you. Had you simply ignored it, ignored Gary and the rest of us, it would have been much worse than leaving. It would have been turning your back on that, on what we all had together."

He hadn't thought about it like that. "I'm sorry you thought that. That I gave you the impression I didn't value any of it."

She nodded. "It makes more sense now."

He loved having her open to him again. His heart had missed this side of her, when her walls were down. This is how they were best. It meant the world to him that he could help her feel safe and shake off the weight of all her responsibilities. Maybe he had contributed more to their relationship than he'd ever given himself credit for.

"I'm glad." He hugged her. "I meant what I said. I still love you."

She leaned back to look up at him. "Me too. I meant it too."

He was hoping she would say it again. He needed to hear it in the light of day.

"I tried not to. So many times. I pushed it down and thought I had gotten you out of my system for a long time. Until you came home. Then it all came flooding back. I tried to protect myself from getting hurt again with the wall."

"I'm glad you trusted me enough to lower it. I tried not to, as well." At her surprised expression, he added, "I thought you had moved on. I thought you would be better off without me."

"I really wasn't. I turned into a workaholic."

"We're going to have to change that."

"I love working," she warned.

"I know. And I'd never ask you to stop, but maybe you don't have to do everything by yourself."

"Maybe I don't."

"And maybe you can play a little more. When you want to."

Her eyebrows tilted away in a wistful expression. "That sounds nice. And kayak more."

"Lots of time on the water more." He smiled warmly at her. "I should get a kayak too. Try a little rock gardening."

"Adrenaline junkie." She rolled her eyes playfully.

His fingertips found her side and gave her a tickle that sent her squealing, her legs kicking at the bed to get away. He let her go when she grabbed his hands to make it stop.

"You're awful." She stuck out her tongue at him.

"Want coffee?" He offered.

"I love you," she said.

He laughed out loud, sliding from under the covers. His heart felt so full it throbbed. He circled around the bed and kissed the top of her head again, trailing his fingers down her arm. She lifted her hand to stay connected with him until their fingertips parted.

Shelby was a natural leader, and he'd always been happy to let her take the lead. But he'd found more of himself in his time away, whether it was because he had been on his own or by growing up. Either way, he knew who he was now and what he wanted.

He wanted Shelby. He wanted to make her feel good, he wanted to support her, and he wanted a life with her. Because she made him happy. Making her happy made him happy. He wanted his art and his surfing too, but Shelby was the perfect woman for him, not because they'd always been together, but because they fit.

Keane exhaled a breath of pure happiness. He turned to Nessie and pressed the button on the grinder. The room filled with the smell of coffee beans. He leaned against the counter and found her turned to watch him, kneeling in the bed. Her arms were propped against the wrought-iron headboard. Shoulder-length, chestnut hair was ruffled around her face. The cove rolled with waves in the distance behind her.

He committed the picture to memory so he could paint it one day.

After he brought their coffees back into bed, she settled back in at his side and they stared at the waves. His arm was wrapped around hers, and she found his left hand with hers, their fingers playing and dancing with each other.

She tilted her head up to look at him. "We ended up back where we started."

"Where's that?"

"In this beach condo." She indicated the room with her head.

"So, when are you moving back in?"

She laughed; the sound tinkled in his ears. She let go of his fingers and trailed them along his chest and up his neck. She touched his hair, moving it away from his face, and played with the long strands. "Soon."

"I don't want to rush you."

"You're not. It's my place, remember?"

He smiled at that, then stilled her hand on his hair. "I was thinking about cutting it. It's probably time."

She gasped, her mouth dropping. "You wouldn't!"

"Why not?"

Wrapping her fingers into his hair, she pulled his mouth down to hers. "I love your hair. Don't you dare cut it."

"Are you sure?" He watched her expression. She seemed truly horrified by the idea.

"Absolutely. Don't you dare."

"Okay." He relented. He hadn't wanted to, but he wondered if she'd meant what she said about it. She meant more to him than his hair. "It stays."

"I'm glad that's settled." She poked him in the chest and laid her head back down.

"I'd like to ask you one more thing." His mom had bugged him again yesterday when he checked on her.

"Of course." She sat sideways and threw her legs over his, giving him her full attention.

"My mom's birthday is coming up. She wants us all to go to the beach in Port Noble, like we used to on my birthday. She misses it."

"That's sweet."

"She'd like you to come too."

Shelby's eyes lit up. "I'd love to come."

"She may not be up for much talking, but she wants to see everyone. She asked if I could invite the whole crew. She wants it to be like the old days and listen in on all our conversations."

"It's probably not as dramatic as it used to be. But everyone loves Kalani; I'm sure they'll all be happy to join. And you can go surfing."

"You gonna join me?"

"Don't bet on it. I'll leave that to you and Duke."

"Maybe we can get Emiliano in the water. Nick was pretty good on the paddleboard the other night, but Emiliano had trouble standing. He said he never really learned."

"When did you guys go paddleboarding at night?"

"Last week. The guys kidnapped me."

"Duke," she said with certainty.

"Yeah, I was having a rough day."

"I'm glad they were there for you."

"They were. I like adult Emiliano. Not that I disliked the younger version."

"Right? He's pretty awesome."

"Nick too. They're both good guys."

"I agree." She laid her head back on his chest. "Tell me about it."

And he did. He replayed the evening on the water, their mistakes in the dark, and even how he got scared by an otter. He kept some of the more private moments between the men but shared a few of the less-personal jokes.

It was the perfect way to start the day. He hoped it was the start of many years of mornings like this.

The waves rose and crested, falling over themselves a hundred feet out. They were almost ideal. Keane unfolded his mom's beach chair, and his dad helped her sit, his hands hovering over her like she was going to break.

"I'm okay, Elias," she said.

"I know." He dropped a kiss on her head. "Want your water?"

"Yes, please." She smiled up at him.

It warmed Keane's heart to see how much his parents still loved each other. He'd learned to love from them. He hoped to give Shelby as much of that as he could. She was setting up her chair next to Kalani's, angling it so his mom could hear her better.

"I brought sandwiches." Nell set a large cooler down on the pebble beach beside Kalani. Emiliano was behind her, bringing their chairs.

Nick and Willa set up on the other side of Elias. Cross conversations would put Kalani smack dab in the middle of it all. He looked at the two couples with a thankful expression. Willa only smiled in reply and shook out a large blanket on the ground in front of them. Maggie put a tray on it filled with plastic plates, bamboo silverware, and napkins, then she sat down on the other side of Willa. Duke pulled up the rear with lemonade and flavored water.

"Dessert first." Nell lifted a large strawberry cake out of her cooler and set it down on the tray.

"Oh!" Kalani gasped. His mother loved strawberries. She repeated the chef's words in surprise. "Dessert first?"

"On your birthday? Most definitely." Nell lit the single, pink candle in the center.

They gathered around and sang happy birthday to his mom. Keane's heart swelled so much it physically hurt.

He had the best friends in the world.

Nell cut the pink-and-white-decorated cake. Thin slices of strawberries overlapped around the side like fish scales. She set a piece on a plate. The fluffy pink interior had a thick layer of what looked like homemade strawberry jam.

"You get the first piece." She handed it over to his mom.

Kalani's hand shook a little, and his dad took the plate for her. She grabbed it with her other hand instead and set it on her lap. She took a bite and smiled. "So good!"

Nell smiled in reply and cut slices for the rest of them.

After they finished their portions, Nell brought out sandwiches wrapped in parchment paper. Their contents were scrawled in marker on the paper.

Keane got up from his chair and dug a gift box from one of the bags he'd carried to the beach. He took it to his mom. "Happy birthday, Mom."

She peeled the lightly taped paper away to reveal the little Romanian box she loved so much. The deep recesses of the carvings had darkened over time, but they appeared particularly feminine in her lap. Her hand went to her mouth. "Oh, son."

"Open it," he urged her.

She lifted the lid to see a golden bracelet of plumeria flowers. She'd always loved the delicate flower, saying they reminded her of her youth in Hawaii. She'd often told him of one like it her mom used to wear. "I hope it's similar enough."

"Thank you." She wrapped her arms around his neck and kissed his cheek. His dad laid a hand on his shoulder. "It's perfect."

Happiness settled around Keane like an old cloak. It felt like pieces of him had finally come back together, making him whole.

"So, who's ready to brave the waves?" Duke pulled his wetsuit up over his shorts and let it hang down at his waist. "You coming, woodworker?"

"I'm going to try," Nick stood, rummaging around in a bag at his feet. Willa pulled her camera out to take pictures.

"How about you, computer dude?" Duke teased Emiliano.

"You guys are crazy." Emiliano laughed, snagging a sandwich off the tray. "Maybe after I can actually stay upright on the paddleboard."

"Are you going to go?" Shelby asked him.

"I'll come out in a few minutes," Keane told Duke and sat back down next to Shelby. He brought her hand to his lips for a quick kiss. "How's the new guy working out?"

"Lawrence is picking things up fast!" Shelby said, leaning forward. "I think he's going to work out great."

"You going to hire the other kid?"

"Ruby?" she asked. He nodded. "I've considered it. It wouldn't be bad to have an extra person. I'd have three, then."

"You'll need it when you open."

"True. It doesn't hurt to get them trained up now."

"And give you a little more time. Maybe one of them can help manage one of the properties."

"We'll see." She pursed her lips. "I'll consider it."

"Speaking of new guys," Nell said, setting out a couple more sandwiches and a few containers of fruit. "Did you hear that Meredith's brother moved into town?"

"Yeah," Shelby said. "Frank, one of the construction crew, told me he took the arborist job for the Mt Olympus National Park. Ben is his name. There's some sort of pest in some of the trees. He's an expert in it."

"Well, that's good," Willa said, snapping pictures of her fiancé squeezing into his wetsuit. "Where's he staying?"

Maggie spoke up. "Across the street from me."

"When did that happen?" Shelby asked.

"Last week." Maggie took a bite of her sandwich. A dot of pesto smeared on her nose, and she wiped it off with a napkin.

"This is juicy news." Shelby leaned forward. "What's he like?"

Kalani's eyes lit up at the fun conversation unfolding in front of her.

Maggie lifted a shoulder and let it drop. "He's a big guy." She raised her hand up over her head. "Huge."

"Ooh, is he cute?" Shelby teased her and shot Keane a wink.

"Uh, I guess." Maggie pursed her rosebud-shaped lips. "The other women on the street have made a big fuss about it."

"How so?" Shelby asked.

"Like, when he's out, washing his truck. They must not have anything better to do."

"Really? Does he take a long time washing it or something?" Shelby pushed.

"Not really. I think it's only because his shirt gets soaked." Maggie stopped, realizing what she'd said. Pink bloomed on her soft, round, cherubic cheeks. "I mean, that's what they said."

"Sure." Shelby drew out the word.

Kalani giggled.

"I'll have to stop by to meet him," Willa said, saving Maggie from Shelby's teasing. "I haven't seen him in the café."

"He doesn't come in often," Nell said since Maggie had tucked into her sandwich and ignored the rest of the conversation.

Keane snagged Shelby's waist when she got up to get a cup of fruit. He pulled her down to his lap and whispered into her ear, "Poor Maggie."

"She's fine." Shelby squirmed in his seat to peer back at him. "I'm just shaking her out of her comfort zone. Besides, Kalani enjoyed the drama. She probably isn't getting a lot of girl time."

"Not lately, she hasn't." Keane thought about it. "She has friends in Olympia. I should talk to Dad about that. Maybe she'd want to have them over."

"That's a great idea. I don't know what I'd do without you all." Shelby planted a light kiss on his lips.

"Me either." He now had everything he could have ever wanted in life, after almost messing up every bit of it. His mind drifted back to the marina weeks ago when he'd first thought that he'd lost her forever and the eyes of that little girl with her dad.

He wrapped his arms tighter around Shelby and brushed her ear with his lips. "So, what do you think about kids?"

Shelby shivered, but he wasn't sure whether it was from the tickle of his lips or what he'd said. She turned slowly in his lap; her eyes had grown wide. "You want kids?"

"I was thinking about it a while ago when I thought we'd never find a way back to each other. We might have had one by now, had I stayed. We are both in a good financial position to have a child, not that a person has to have a lot of money for it."

"But it does make it easier."

"It does."

"I'm pretty busy all the time."

"You are, but do you want to be?" he asked her honestly.

"Not as busy as I have been." She caught her bottom lip between her teeth.

"Anyway, I felt a loss about that kid we might have had." He touched her chin. "What do you think?"

"It's scary as hell." Shelby widened her eyes. "But the idea is growing on me. I wouldn't have considered it with anyone but you."

It warmed his heart. He buried his face in her soft hair, breathing in her citrus scent.

Around them, Willa, Nell, and Maggie were discussing Willa's developing wedding plans. His mom was enjoying every bit of the conversation.

And everything was finally right for him. His heart felt full.

The scarred cooler he'd found washed onshore sat near his feet. He'd cleaned it up. It turned out to still work. The slide opened easily with age, was still latched securely, and the inside appeared brand new.

It was a lot like their relationship: it looked a little different, a little more beat up than it had been when they were younger, but it still worked as good as it ever had.

Maybe even better.

CHAPTER 34

"Here?" Nell pointed to the wide, hand-carved wardrobe that stood against the wall of the living room.

"Yes," Shelby said. "He said there would be plenty of room, but I haven't checked yet."

It had taken Shelby all of three weeks before she was ready to move back into the condo on the beach she'd purchased fifteen years ago for the two of them. She hadn't even consulted her gut on it; she simply knew it was right.

Financially, she could rent out an additional unit. Personally, she had plenty of rooms she could move back into if she wanted to, but something told her that she wouldn't need that option. She and Keane hadn't left each other's sides much in the past month.

She flexed her hand, feeling the comforting tug of the cove. It felt so right. It felt like home. Back where she had started, she was finally fulfilling her dream of living in the beach condo with Keane. It had just taken a little longer than she had expected.

The girls had decided to shoo the boys off to paddle-board while they took care of the move. Shelby didn't have many personal items at the cabin she'd been living in. A small closet of clothes, a handful of dishes, and a couple of boxes of personal items. Most of the things she used on a daily basis were for the cabins and housed in the shed.

"My goodness, this thing is huge." Willa pulled the door of the wardrobe open. It was twice the width of the one in the cabin.

Over half the space was empty. Nell hung the clothes she'd carried, and Shelby brought another stack, adding them to the right of them. She could have her coat and lady blazers all in one closet. This was awesome!

She'd need a shelf for shoes at the bottom—she had quite a few of those—but Willa already said she'd ask Nick to build one for her.

It was a good day. They'd spent the morning at a wedding-dress shop in Olympia. It was the first real girls' day they'd had since the cabins had started needing major repairs. It felt good to step away from work to hang out with her friends.

Shelby had initially been concerned when everything Willa came out wearing was either tiers of lace or simple, shapeless linen shifts. She loved her friend and would support whatever she decided to wear, but it was difficult to muster a positive face when it was so completely opposite from anything she herself would wear.

Then Willa came out in what she said was her favorite pick. It was perfect. It had lace overlay over the entire gown with full-lace, bell sleeves. The bodice was a V-neck that dipped low on her firm yoga-instructor stomach with a peekaboo button under her breasts. It was modest, but still sexy. A fitted waist and lace train completed the look. She could already see Willa's hair filled with braids and flowers.

It was unanimous. Everyone loved it, and Willa had agreed to it on the spot.

"What about these boxes?" Maggie carted one into the living room.

"Kitchen." Shelby pointed. "Those are plates and glasses."

Keane didn't have many, but it was okay with her if they scrapped them all and bought new. They could shop on their trip to Estonia the following month.

She'd met Gina and Jerry the weekend before and instantly liked the friendly woman. Her husband was just as sweet and funny too. They'd spent most of that trip fishing, but they were both going on this one, and Shelby would get to know them better. She was practically buzzing with the excitement of traveling to Europe with Keane and seeing him in his other natural habitat.

The one without the sea or their crew of friends around him.

Shelby carried a box of odds and ends into the extra bedroom that served as a sitting room for guests. Keane had already mounted the television in there for her to catch up on Virgin River episodes when she had the time.

He'd installed a few shelves in the closet there for storage. Shelby opened the box and stored the few items in one of them. She had a small jewelry box from high school filled with a few odds and ends. Maybe it would be better at the top of her side of the closet.

The final object in the box was her old stuffed orca from high school. Holding it close to her chest, she brought it back into the main room. Nell was reorganizing their kitchen tools.

Walking to the bed, she tucked the little plush whale next to the new one that sat on top of their bed. It still felt unorthodox, having the bed in the living room, but she was getting used to the idea of being a bit extravagant every once in a while.

"I think this is the last one." Maggie brought in one final box of shoes. Willa took it from her and started lining them up at the bottom of the wardrobe.

"Nick said he'd have that shelf done by tomorrow, depending on the gazebo," Willa said.

"No rush."

"I'm so glad Charles got jail time." Nell pulled Keane's wok from a drawer and moved it to the same one as his skillets.

"Me too," Shelby said. She wouldn't have to worry about seeing him around for a long time.

"They got him for falsifying information, too, didn't they?" Willa asked.

"Yes, the wetlands evaluator wasn't even certified. The certification was phony too. And they found copies of our closing documents, edited, on his laptop. That, combined with the attempted murder and Cleo's testimony, sealed the deal."

"It was nice of you to drop the charges on Cleo," Willa said.

"She just got caught up in it." The poor woman had cried when she apologized and asked for her job back. "I think the community service was fair, but I can't have her working for me again. It's not worth the risk."

"It's okay to set boundaries," Willa said.

She was trying not to hold a grudge, but that didn't mean she had to hire the woman back. She'd find something else. She was a great employee, except for the attacking-your-boss part.

"There, that's better." Nell closed the last cabinet.

Shelby reached into the fridge and pulled out a bottle of champagne and one of kombucha. "Now, we celebrate."

She poured each of them a glass, and they toasted her moving in with her childhood sweetheart.

"Now that you've got a dress, you need to set that date," Nell said, nudging Willa.

"I wanted to talk to you about that," Willa said to Shelby. "We'd like to get married on the winter solstice. Nick said things were coming along quickly with the yurts. We'd really like to stay in one for our honeymoon. Hole up for the winter and begin our life as a married couple in the new year. Do you think there's a chance it will be ready?"

Things had been coming along well. She and Keane had decided to hire a couple of extra men with the goal of being open by Christmas. The solstice would only be a few days early. "We can do it."

Willa threw her arms around Shelby's neck. "This is going to be so perfect!"

"Did you talk to Mary yet?" Nell asked the bubbling bride.

"Mary?" Shelby couldn't imagine what she'd be wanting from the eternally grumpy woman.

"I want her to come to our wedding," Willa said. "She's a part of this town and one of the first few people who let me treat her with my salves. Besides, she was Gary's great-aunt."

"It might have been Gary's mom's cousin, I'm not exactly sure how they're related," Nell said.

"Either way, I'd like to have her there," Willa said decisively. "If she'll agree. I'm not sure she will."

"She doesn't like people," Shelby said. She never had.

"I think she's just reclusive and set in her ways," Maggie said.

"Either way, she's part of my family here," Willa said. The herbalist kept the cranky woman supplied in salves and tonics for her hips and eyesight. Kalani was on that list as well, now.

"It's going to be a beautiful wedding," Maggie smiled. "What are your colors?"

"Sage green and lavender." Willa's eyes were wistful.

"And you'll have flowers in your hair," Shelby filled in.

"Yes!" Willa spun in a circle.

"Now, it's your turn." Shelby tilted her glass to Maggie, who turned scarlet. She wagged her eyebrows up and down.

"Heh." Maggie took a too-big swig of her wine. "Not me."

The other three had found their matches.

"Maybe Duke's next," Maggie deflected.

"He's a loner." Shelby shook her head.

"You thought you were too." Willa nudged her.

It was true. Maybe their rebel-turned-ringleader friend would find a match at some point.

"Either way, I'm predicting it's you." Shelby raised her glass. "Maybe this Ben fellow."

She'd caught sight of the dude. Maggie wasn't kidding; the guy was built. He was easily a head taller than Emiliano and a good bit taller than Duke and Keane, but he was twice Keane's slim surfer's build.

The two of them would be an unlikely couple. Him tall and wide, Maggie short and adorable. It would be like a lumberjack and pure sunshine.

Maggie let out a squeak at the suggestion.

"Whoever it turns out to be"—Shelby put an arm around her—"remember that you deserve love too. I almost didn't open my heart to it. I'm glad I did."

Tears sprung to Maggie's eyes, and she nodded.

"I think the guys are back," Willa said, peering through the back window. Love radiated from her face.

Excited to tell Keane about their day, Shelby took off out the back door and ran right into his arms. He dropped his paddleboard and caught her, still sopping wet in his wetsuit.

Laughing, he tossed back his wet hair to look at her. "You keep throwing yourself at me. I could get used to i t."

"Then, get used to it. I don't intend to stop." And she kissed him with everything she had.

FROM THE AUTHOR

Thank you so much for your support. I hope you enjoyed Willa and Nick's story as much as I did. I've had Willa's story in my heart for a long time and am thrilled to finally being able to give life to it.

If you liked it, the nicest thing you can do is leave me a good review on Amazon, Bookbub, Goodreads, or wherever you review books.

Connect with me online:

Website: **jenflanaganbooks.com**

Follow me on Amazon

Facebook: **@jenflanaganbooks**

Instagram: **@jenflanagan_author**

Bookbub: **@jen_flanagan**

Join my reader group on Facebook: **Flanagan's Fanatics**

Please visit my website and subscribe to my newsletter at **jenflanaganbooks.com** for upcoming books, events, and free content.

ABOUT THE AUTHOR

Jen Flanagan is a #1 Amazon best-selling author of enchanting magical romance and cozy mysteries, set in the mystical Olympic Peninsula. Her stories weave adventure, intriguing locations, and a touch of magic into tales of love and mystery, featuring richly drawn characters. A lover of travel, history, and culture, Jen offers readers a delightful escape into worlds where magic feels real.

Author of the Orca Cove and Detective Malone series, she also writes non-fiction as Willa Daniels. When not writing, she enjoys culinary magic, surrounded by good food, friends, coffee, and her beloved pups.

Connect with her at her website, Facebook group, or newsletter:

jenflanaganbooks.com

WHAT'S NEXT?

Looking for more Orca Cove? Can't wait to find out what happens next? Stay tuned for Maggie & Ben's story in 2026!

If I've piqued your interest in herbalism, look up ***An Introduction to Herbalism,*** by none other than Willa Daniels, my non-fiction penname. I've got several more non-fiction books in the works as part of The Natural Path series.

If mystery is more your thing, check out ***The Detective Malone Series***, a non-paranormal, cozy detective mystery series. To read the first chapter of *Bad Company*, turn the page.

Bad Company

Chapter 1

The stapler sailed through the air to hit the brick wall across the room with a loud, satisfying crunch, pairing well with the guttural scream echoing from my chest. I rarely resorted to throwing things, but I'd been working on the Mennon case for a full week with absolutely, positively, no successful lead. It was the most frustrating seven days I'd ever had. I had been so sure this last lead would go somewhere.

Collapsing in my chair, I shoved away from my desk and further office-supply destruction. I sat, defeated, slouching deep as it rolled to the wall behind me, reddish-brown hair floating around my twisted face.

After all that time, I had found only two people who had seen Suzanne Mennon the afternoon after she walked out for her lunch break. The gas station clerk and a contact the clerk said she spoke with. When I finally got ahold of the contact, Jeremy Jones, he gave me no further leads to follow.

All Jeremy had shared was that he bumped into her at the gas station near her work. After further cajoling, followed by some light harassing, he explained he had swung by on his way home from an all-nighter at the betting parlor for some Mickey's. I pressed him for more information, but he said he didn't remember what she was buying. No memory of anything strange about her mood or appearance. He didn't give me anything to go on. He said he only remembered Suzy because she had a big rack...Cue the eye-roll.

Over the past week, I had canvassed the neighborhood around Suzy's home and workplace, trying to find anyone who might have seen her or anything that might give me a lead to go on. I felt like I was circling the drain.

Trying to focus my thoughts, I took several deep breaths. I most certainly wasn't going to get anywhere by sitting in here, sulking, no matter how appealing it seemed. I had to figure out my next move. I shoved up from my seat, snatching up my keys and my leather jacket to head out for a walk. Maybe it would clear my head.

Stepping out of the old brick building where my PI office was located and into the warm spring morning, I slipped my jacket on. It was a beautiful day, and the sun was out. My boots crunched on the left-over road salt from winter, and the typical Chicago wind tossed my shoulder-length auburn hair around my head. I couldn't keep it straight to save my life, the constant gusts adding to its natural wave. I had long-since stopped trying and tucked a particularly pervasive chunk behind an ear. Crossing the street, I turned into Grounds, my favorite coffee shop. Earning that title because it was ten steps from my office and I really liked Maurice, the fifty-something shop owner.

Maurice looked up when I walked in and waved hi. "Good morning, Mal!"

"Morning, Mo," I answered, sliding to the counter. The fresh air—correction: the coffee-scented air improved my mood considerably.

"Working on a case?" Maurice asked thoughtfully. I noticed the slight gray on his temples was getting more pronounced.

I often talked out issues with Maurice for input, leaving out details to protect confidentiality. It helped me put perspective on things. He was a good listener, or so I'd discovered after many a late night at the café, notes and coffee in front of me.

"Yeah, but no good leads right now." I blew a straggler from my face and toyed with a coffee stirrer in front of me. "No leads at all, in fact. My last one just fizzled up."

"That sucks, Mal. But I know you'll work it out," Maurice said with a wink as he slid my usual to me.

I tipped a cinnamon shaker over the foam of the cappuccino to add a light dusting. "I guess," I murmured, taking a sip of the little slice of heaven. "I just need to get a different angle on it. I'm missing something."

I wasn't much of a girly girl, but I did like fancy coffee when I could get it. Caffeine being a main staple in my diet, I believed variety was good.

After paying Maurice, I pushed away from the counter and headed back into the sun. I stretched my long legs and turned down the street in a nice stroll. Breathing in, I took a long sip and surveyed the streets. It was still early, and there were a lot of people wandering in and out of the shops in downtown Roscoe Village.

I loved my little suburb of Chicago. It wasn't as crazy as downtown Chi-Town, and it had more charm, too. It was located in North Center and was just the right mix of cheap enough for me to afford, yet relatively safe enough to walk through the streets at dusk. I let the atmosphere roll over me, people watching and smelling the local pizza place across the street.

Sam Mennon had come into my office a week ago, eyes drawn, hair on end, and clothes crumpled. It was obvious he hadn't had much sleep. His wife, Suzy, had gone missing from work three days prior.

Suzanne, 35, goes by Suzy. The facts rolled through my head amid the distractions. Sweet face, long straight brown hair, worked as a teller at Heward Bank. She was seen on camera leaving the building around lunchtime and again by the clerk at the gas station down the street. The gas station clerk remembered Suzy checking out at the same time as a regular, Jeremy Jones. The same Jeremy Jones who had just told me he didn't remember anything pertinent about Suzy.

The cops had the case, but with no leads and others piling up, it was no longer being actively worked. According to them, Suzy's absence could be a simple matter of an unhappy wife leaving her husband. It happened all the time. There wasn't any sign of foul play, so the cops moved on to bigger fish. She had passed the critical forty-eight-hour mark. The likelihood of finding her had drastically decreased.

Sam was entirely distraught. I honestly couldn't see how a man so completely lost without his wife wouldn't have known if his wife was having an affair. I mean, it was always a possibility; people could be clueless. But I was leaning toward kidnapping or murder, and my gut didn't typically fail me.

Besides, Sam was the client and he didn't believe Suzy had left him. He was paying me to find her, not necessarily to spend my time pursuing a route that involved her voluntarily leaving him. Something had happened to Suzy, and I planned on finding out what.

I really hoped it wasn't murder, though. Murder cases sucked.

I took another sip of my coffee, enjoying the warmth before I noticed unusual movement down the street. It wasn't until I saw the smoke, that I smelled it in the air.

A couple of blocks down, two people came running out of a brick building, dark clouds puffing around their heads. Flames leapt out the upper-story windows.

I ran forward to help a blonde woman who was stumbling out. Helping her down to the curb to catch her breath, I pulled my phone out of my pocket and dialed dispatch to report the fire.

"Are you okay?" I asked her, searching for signs of a burn.

The blonde coughed and looked back, trying to see through the smoke. "Yes, I'm fine, but my coworkers are still inside!"

I relayed the situation to the dispatcher and put her on speakerphone.

"There's a fire in the kitchen. I don't know what happened. We tried to grab the fire extinguisher, but the fire spread too fast!"

The dispatcher sent trucks and asked me to keep the woman close till the ambulance got there.

Only a few more people came out, so I worried there were still others upstairs. Moving toward the doorway, I peered inside. All I could see was smoke pouring out in big, rolling plumes. I had to move back to the fresh air, biting my lip in indecision. I hated leaving anyone in there, but I didn't think I could make it inside. I wasn't trained for that sort of thing.

The siren announced the fire truck only moments later. It wheeled to the curb, men jumping off and grabbing axes before heading inside the building. Another two trucks and an official-looking SUV came around the corner immediately after. One hooked up to the hydrant across the street, and its crew went to join the others inside.

I went back to check on the willowy blonde. Her coughing had died down, but she was shaking from the adrenaline rush. I helped her up and walked her over to meet the arriving paramedics.□

"I'll be all right," the blonde said, smiling. "Thanks for your help."

The paramedics got busy, checking over everyone who had escaped the building. Their work looked choreographed as they moved around the scene. I was impressed by how quickly and efficiently everyone responded. A firefighter in charge stood outside with his radio, shouting orders and keeping a keen eye on everything.

The sheer amount of black smoke coming from the building was startling, like diseased air crawling to the sky. I always figured fire would be bright and yellow, but everything about this building was dark, and black smoke billowed out of the doorway and windows. I was surprised at how difficult it was to simply look inside. How could they even see in there?

Suddenly, a loud explosion followed by a crash erupted from the building. Smoke flared out of the windows in an initial rush, then died back a bit to where it was before. The firemen and police officers ushered everyone, myself included, farther away. A few more headed in, and everyone stood in tense silence until they finally came back out again

Two firefighters had someone slung over their shoulders, a woman and a man, while another looked to be hurt and was leaning heavily on his teammate as they made their way out of the building. I heard someone yell into his radio, but it seemed like the tension had somewhat abated.

The fireman helped the injured one to the side of the truck where I was standing. After stripping off his Air-Pak and helmet, he leaned over to help his buddy do the same. Checking the other fireman's eyes, he laughed jovially and slapped the other guy on the back in a brotherly way. The back of his bunker coat read "RHODES."

He was a big, well-built man with broad shoulders, average height, and a commanding presence. He was obviously in charge of one of the crews, and his incredibly intense gaze scanned the scene to take in every detail. It seemed he wasn't just a good-looking man; there was more to him than what was on the surface.

Rhodes seemed to be satisfied the other fireman wasn't too badly injured, because it sounded like he was teasing him for getting under falling debris. Still, when he sent him over to the paramedics anyway to get checked out, I could see a little worry crease his eyebrows as he ran a hand over his shaved head.

The air was still filled with smoke, and while it was spreading, it seemed like everything was under control. Not that there was much I could do to help.

As I turned around to go, I noticed someone skirting around the back of the onlookers. It looked like a kid, maybe sixteen years old, wearing a gray hoodie. He was edging towards the paramedic's vehicle. The skin under his eyes was dark, and he looked sick. I couldn't tell what he was up to, but my gut said it wasn't good. Deciding to follow, I edged forward.

The kid was watching the paramedics closely, but they were busy with the fire victims, and he slipped into the back of the ambulance. I moved over to a female police officer nearby, nudged her, and nodded slightly toward the van.

Turning, she took in the situation immediately and moved into action. Catching up with the kid, she yanked him out. In the scuffle, the kid pushed and shoved the officer into the crowd, where she tripped on the curb and fell to the ground.

I jumped forward to catch the kid just as a large body came up behind me. Looking up, I saw it was the firefighter Rhodes. The two of us surrounded the young man each grabbing an arm.

My eyes met his over the kid's head: his intense, mine quizzical. I was surprised he had been paying attention to this part of the scene. I twisted the kid's arm lightly but firmly to secure him as the officer made her way over to us, dusting off her uniform slacks.

"Thanks," she said to Rhodes and me.

I knew quite a few of the officers from the local precinct, but she didn't look familiar. Her name tag said Mathews, and I nodded as she took the boy from me.

"Drugs," said Officer Mathews, pulling out a couple of vials from the boy's pockets. "Buses are stocked with drugs for emergencies."

"Buses?" I asked.

"The ambulance," Rhodes answered, still watching me intently.

"I'll take this one in," Officer Mathews said, walking the kid to her cruiser.

I looked back at the fireman. "What kind of drugs?"

"Morphine, typically. It's worth quite a bit on the street," Rhodes said, crossing his arms, assessing me.

"You jumped in there pretty fast," he added finally.

I turned back to him, one side of my mouth tilted up. "So did you." I hadn't even seen him come up behind me.

Rhodes stood eye level with me and a little close, so I stepped back to put some distance between us. Chemistry was sizzling unspoken in the air, but I had an afternoon meeting with a new client and had to get back to the office. Turning to head back, I noticed the fireman made a move to say something. I paused, but he looked back at his crew and turned to join them instead.

I got halfway back to my office before I remembered my coffee on the sidewalk, by the blonde. "Crap." I sighed. "Probably cold by now anyway," I muttered to myself as I trudged on, still without a new lead and no idea where to look next.

<u>**Jen Flanagan Fiction Books**</u>

Orca Cove Series:

Saltwater Cures

Uncharted Waters

Star Crossed

Red Skies (coming 2026)

Rogue Wave (coming 2026)

Books in the Detective Malone Series:

Bad Company

Here I Go Again

Under Pressure

<u>**Willa Daniels Non-Fiction Books**</u>

Stand-alone books:

The Art of Living Seasonally

The Natural Path Series:

An Introduction to Herbalism

An Introduction to Soap Making

An Introduction to Sourdough (coming 2025)

Home and Cleaning Solutions (coming 2026)

Body and Skincare Solutions (coming 2027)